Lesbian
FICTION

an anthology

ELLY BULKIN (*b.* 1944), co-editor of *Lesbian Poetry: An Anthology* (Persephone Press), is a founding editor of *Conditions*, a magazine of writing by women with an emphasis on writing by lesbians. She has written about teaching lesbian poetry in *College English, Radical Teacher,* and *Women's Studies Newsletter*; about racism and writing in *Sinister Wisdom*; and about heterosexism and women's studies in *Radical Teacher*. Co-editor of *Amazon Poetry: An Anthology of Lesbian Poetry* (1975), she is a member of the Editorial Board of the Lesbian-Feminist Study Clearinghouse. She has reviewed women's poetry in a number of feminist periodicals. An intermittent college teacher of English and Women's Studies, she worked for five years at the Women's Center of Brooklyn College. A Jewish lesbian whose father and maternal grandparents emigrated from Eastern Europe, she grew up in the Bronx and has lived nearly all of her life in New York City. She now lives in Brooklyn with her lover and their eleven-year-old daughter Anna.

Lesbian FICTION

an anthology

edited by: Elly Bulkin

PERSEPHONE PRESS
Watertown, Massachusetts

Cover design by Maria von Brincken.
Text design by Pat McGloin.
Typeset by Eileen Brady.

First Edition. Second Printing.

Library of Congress Cataloging in Publication Data

Main entry under title:

Lesbian fiction.

   Bibliography: p.
   1. Short stories, American—Women Authors. 2. Lesbianism—Fiction. I. Bulkin, Elly, 1944-
PS648.L47L4   813'.01'089287   81-12194
ISBN 0-930436-11-3   AACR2

Lesbian Fiction: An Anthology is free to women in prison and elderly women in nursing homes.

Contents

Elly Bulkin

Introduction: A Look at Lesbian Short Fiction

I have burned many a book of lesbian fiction. Not outside on grass or pavement, book upon book, but individually, secretly, each paperback novel tossed down the incinerator of my Bronx building. I was fourteen—or seventeen. It was the late fifties, then the early sixties. The books left my house as they had arrived, stealthily. I bought them at the corner drugstore, hoping the man wouldn't look as I pushed my money over the counter, hoping he saw only the price, not the women touching or staring intently at each other, certainly not the words on the covers: "the tragedy of forbidden love," "a shocking love," "I am a woman in love with a woman—must society reject me?" I smuggled them into the house stuck in my pocket or under a package until I could get past my parents to my own room, where I could read, door closed, working my way through a quarter pound of chocolate filbert patties, hoping that no one would knock, no one force me to slide my book under my pillow. I always read my books in the evening, always finished them in a single sitting, always burned them before going to sleep.

So I discovered lesbian fiction. And knowing no other lesbians, learned from it what was possible, what were the options—renunciation of the loved one, loneliness, alcoholism, suicide, or a return to heterosexuality (or at least the facade of heterosexuality), possibilities that contributed to my postponing coming out as a lesbian—to myself or others—for over a decade.

Not till I had come out did I begin to find other types of lesbian fiction. As I read more and more lesbian-feminist magazines, I found an increasing number of short stories. While I continued to read newly published lesbian novels, I began to find that the short story—in terms of the range of its characters, its situations, its perspectives—had become the best contemporary fictional representation of the lives of lesbians. I found that I began to appreciate the accomplishment more fully as I learned more about the history out of which it had emerged. It was, after all, partly the history of my own thirty-six years. And partly the history of what had been hidden from me for most of them.

The American lesbian short story has a history that falls into three broad, sometimes overlapping periods: 1) the first from the late nineteenth century through the early fifties, a time of some openness about love between women, especially initially, as well as much masking of lesbian subject matter and predominant negativity in the images of those characters who were explicitly depicted; 2) the second from 1955 to the very early seventies, a time that spans the life of the pioneering lesbian magazine, *The Ladder*, whose fiction for many years offered some of the few positive representations of lesbians then available, both before and after the onset of the women's movement; 3) the third from the demise of *The Ladder* and the appearance of *Amazon Quarterly*, both in 1972, through the present, a time filled with a growing and diverse literature catalyzed by the lesbian-feminist movement and facilitated by the emergence of a lesbian-feminist writing and publishing community.

Historically, lesbian short fiction can best be understood within the context of other lesbian literature, especially the novel, the most generally recognized form of "lesbian fiction." In the last decade, the development of the lesbian short story has been closely connected as well with the flowering of lesbian poetry that has taken place since the late sixties. Consistently, this literature has been created within a newly-developed network of feminist periodicals, presses, and bookstores. As a result, many lesbian writers have been able for the first time to make assumptions about the woman-identification of their audience which have had significant implications for the openness and directness of their writing.

As in the past, some lesbian writers today feel unable to acknowledge publicly their lesbianism. The reasons are many: the threat of loss of one's job, one's children, one's political and/or literary credibility in non-lesbian circles. While I see contemporary lesbian literature as written by women who identify themselves as lesbians, I am also aware that any collection or discussion of lesbian writing must omit work by contemporaries who have not made their lesbian identification public. In fifty years, women will probably be reading between the lines of their published work, poring over their unpublished stories and letters, looking at different facets of their lives—whom they lived with, what they wrote about, where they put their energies. They will be doing the type of work that, with few exceptions, we do now: looking for our literary history in earlier writers whose lives often remain shrouded in silence and deeply affected by economic, social, and literary pressures which shaped each woman's decision about how openly to live and what to write.

Through much of this century and the end of the last one, lesbian literature has been almost exclusively the province of white lesbians—or of white women of indeterminate or unknown sexual/affectional preference—who are either middle- or upper-class. Only fairly recently has this situation even begun to change: white working-class characters are depicted in some of the fiction of *The Ladder* and of the pulp novels of that period, and a growing number of lesbians of color and poor and working-class lesbians of all races have written much poetry since the late sixties and are, along with other lesbians, producing a growing body of powerful fiction.

I.

If I were looking at the period from the late nineteenth century to the early fifites as anything but a backdrop to contemporary lesbian short fiction, I would look at the differences between popular magazine fiction and that appearing in literary magazines and individual fiction collections; at the differences between a woman's short fiction and her other writing; at the issues of class and race in those stories that did get published; at whatever publications did exist edited by people of color, political radicals, and others outside the American mainstream, literary and otherwise. I would look also at the first two decades of this century, in terms of its role both as a reflector of earlier positive attitudes toward love between women and as a precursor of those negative ones that have been passed down to us. Then I would move on through the twenties to the Depression, and to World War II and its aftermath, the beginning of the Cold War.

Since those lesbians who did write short stories did not, of course, always deal with woman-identification, any detailed look at lesbian short fiction would certainly need to examine the whole of each writer's work. Rather than considering this range, however, or short stories by non-lesbian women (and by men) that have explicitly lesbian subject matter, I want to focus briefly on some of the short fiction about women-loving women written by women who were or might have been lesbians, and to examine how they described—or evaded—the lesbianism of their characters.[1]

When the whole subject of pre-women's movement lesbian fiction is raised, certain English-language novels almost always get discussed: Gertrude Stein's *Q.E.D.* (written in 1903; published posthumously in 1950) and *Fernhurst* (1904); Radclyffe Hall's *The Unlit Lamp* (1924) and *The Well of Loneliness* (1927); Virginia Woolf's *Orlando* (1928); Djuna Barnes' *Ladies Almanack* (1928) and *Nightwood* (1937). Other lesbian novels have received considerably less attention, including, for example, Gale Wilhelm's *We Too Are Drifting* (1935) and *Torchlight to Valhalla* (1938), precursors of the popular lesbian novels that women like me read in the fifties and sixties; and Jo Sinclair's *Wasteland* (1946), with its focus on Jewish identity, its working-class characters, its radical politics, and its unequivocally positive view of lesbianism.[2]

The obstacles which have helped define who has even been able to contribute to this literary past can be illustrated by Black lesbian Angelina Weld Grimké, a literary figure of the Harlem Renaissance. The relatively privileged class position and formal education that made her atypical were crucial in allowing her to publish what work she did. While she is known primarily as a poet and dramatist, not as a fiction writer, Grimké's history has implications for other lesbians who might have written fiction. Gloria T. Hull's outlining of her situation as a Black lesbian writer in America at the beginning of this century pulls together the strands of an oppression that—in the case of Grimké and untold other lesbians—proved a crushing burden:

> First, it meant that you wrote (or half wrote)—in isolation—a lot which you did not show and knew you could not publish. It meant that when you did write to be printed, you did so in shackles—chained between the real experience you wanted to say and the conventions that would not give you voice .... It meant, finally, that you stopped writing altogether, dying, no doubt, with your real gifts stifled within—and leaving behind (in a precious few cases) the little that manages to survive of your true self in fugitive pieces.[3]

When Grimké did manage to get a short story published, the details of publication demonstrate nothing so much as the thwarted avenues for creativity. Writing about her, Hull has said:

> In 1919, she published a short story in Margaret Sanger's *Birth Control Review* called "The Closing Door." This is a terrible saga of a pregnant Black woman who hears that her brother has been lynched in Mississippi. Then, she begins crying out against having children "for the sport—the lust—of ... mobs." When her son is born, she painfully refuses to have anything to do with him and one night steals into his room and smothers him, afterwards going mad and dying herself. It seems somehow wrong that this tale should appear in such a journal and even more peculiar that the killing societal reasons for the heroine's misfortunes would be used as an argument for birth control among Black people. Grimké also wrote other unpublished drama, fiction, and some expository prose. In this work, lynching and racial/sexual prejudice are thematic targets and women predominate as characters and subjects.[4]

Published and unpublished, Grimké's work reflects the complex intersection of lesbian with class and racial identities which, in whatever form they take and however they are affected by the prevailing attitudes of a given era, are pivotal in the life of each potential lesbian writer.

In 1880, Octave Thanet published one of the earliest American short stories focusing on a romantic friendship between two women, "My Lorelei: A Heidelberg Romance." For thirty years, Thanet, whose real name was Alice French, was one of the best paid writers in the country. Reaching maturity during the late nineteenth century, when financially independent women could live together in "Boston marriages" that were assumed—accurately or not—to be nonsexual, Thanet lived for nearly fifty years with her Iowa childhood friend Jane Crawford, primarily on an opulent Arkansas plantation where they entertained people like Theodore Roosevelt and Calvin Coolidge. Unlike Sarah Orne Jewett, whose writing career partly overlaps hers, Thanet chose not to make woman-to-woman relationships a central part of her writing. The most woman-identified of her stories combines love between women with an ending guaranteed to satisfy the most staunchly heterosexual reader. Published in *The Western*, "My Lorelei" is a record of Constance's diary entries about her strong attraction to Undine, a wealthy woman whom she meets while on vacation in Germany. Soon after the married Constance declares her love for her, Undine is stabbed repeatedly by a "cretin" and dies. In addition to ending their relationship, her death allows Constance to write five years later in her diary: "Undine's legacy has prospered with us. I am more in love with my husband than ever."[5]

In her short stories, Jewett wrote openly and positively about love between women, with no man needed to provide a satisfactory conclusion. Jewett's stories were set in her native New England, where she lived for thirty years with Annie Adams Fields in a supportive community of similarly unmarried and coupled women. In *Deephaven* (1877)—whose stories originally appeared in magazines and were only later collected—the two female protagonists end by wishing to "copy the Ladies of Llangollen and remove ourselves from society and its distractions," an explicit reference to the Welsh retreat of the well-known pair Lady Eleanor Butler and Miss Sarah Ponsonby.[6] Twenty years later, Jewett's "Martha's Lady" describes the inspiration that Martha finds in her love for her employer's cousin, Helena (enough to make her a model servant, not enough to make her question her subordinate status). Helena had visited their village home only briefly before returning to Boston and marriage, but is reunited with Martha after forty years at the story's end: " 'Oh, my dear Martha,' she cried, 'won't you kiss me goodnight? Oh, Martha, have you remembered like this, all these long years!' "[7]

Prior to the 1920's, as Lillian Faderman has demonstrated, stories describing love between women were acceptable to white popular magazines.[8] So Jeanette Lee could publish in a 1919 *Ladies' Home Journal* "The Cat and the King," which has its own place within a whole genre of upper- and middle-class lesbian literature: the boarding school or college story. Nothing emphasizes the story's assumptions as clearly as the fact that it is an

authority figure, the school doctor, who helps the smitten Flora. Understanding Flora's love for the senior captain of the school ballteam, the
doctor first arranges for her to work each week in her laboratory with the
senior, and then sends Flora out to substitute for an injured player with
the words: " 'You are to report to the captain—in her room'."[9] The un-
selfconsciousness of the ending, the sense that sending one young woman
to another's dormitory room did not set the scene for a torrid sexual
liaison, reflects the pre-Freudian attitude that was fast losing currency in
the United States.

While, as Faderman writes, "love between women, openly treated, was
dead as a popular literary theme in America by the 1920's,"[10] for some
white lesbian fiction writers, its treatment had been stillborn. Gertrude
Stein, for example, consistently disguises her subject in the short fiction
published during her lifetime. In "Miss Furr and Miss Skene" (1922) Stein
masks the two women's relationship through the repeated use of the word
"gay" at a time when it was not yet generally known to mean homosexual.[11] Her reticence about lesbian subject matter, however, is a much
earlier development, one probably influenced by her early medical studies
and her general awareness of European culture, which defined homosexuality as "abnormal" well before that idea had been planted firmly in
American thinking.[12]

In "Melanctha," a reworking of Q.E.D., her autobiographical novel
written in 1903 but not published until after her death in 1946, Stein does
deal directly with a lesbian relationship. But in this story, which she published in 1909, she effectively distances the lesbian content from her own
experience by transforming the three white women in Q.E.D., one into a
Black man and the other two into Black women. The presentation of part
of the subsequent triangle as heterosexual clearly masks the consistent
lesbian theme in Q.E.D. At least as striking as the introduction of a heterosexual couple in this masking process is Stein's appropriation of Black
characters to disguise the closeness of the story's plot to her own life. Her
references in its opening pages to "the warm broad glow of negro sunshine"
and "the simple, promiscuous unmorality of the black people" immediately reduce her Black characters to a level of sexual irresponsibility—and
general racist stereotype—that would have led her readers to place the lesbian relationship in a world totally separate from Stein's own.[13]

Masking of lesbian subject matter seems hardly to be expected of Willa
Cather, given the openness of her comments in a Nebraska classmate's
album: "The greatest wonder according to my estimation is: a good looking woman"; and, perhaps youthfully underestimating the threat of writing as an open lesbian, "The fault for which I have the least toleration in
another person: lack of nerve."[14] Though she lived intermittently with
Isabelle McClung and then for forty years with Edith Lewis, Cather studi-

ously avoided any focus on woman-to-woman relationships in her fiction. Her use of male personae in "On the Gull's Road" (1908) prompted the following reply from her mentor Sarah Orne Jewett, a member of an earlier generation with very different attitudes toward writing about love between women:

> The lover is as well done as he could be when a woman writes in the man's character,—it must always, I believe, be something of a masquerade. I think it is safer to write about him as you did about the others, and not try to be he! And you could almost have done it as yourself—a woman could love her in that same protecting way—a woman could even care enough to wish to take her away from such a life, by some means or other.[15]

While Cather slips onto the title page of *Youth and the Bright Medusa* (1908) a quote from Christina Rosetti's strongly woman-identified "Goblin Market," a narrative poem "drenched," as Adrienne Rich has written, in "oral eroticism,"[16] the stories in the collection are definitely non-lesbian in subject matter.

For generations of white lesbians to follow, the choices made by Stein and Cather—not by Jewett and Lee—remained pre-eminent. And the alternate options hardly presented more positive directions for lesbian short fiction writers. English writer Radclyffe Hall, for instance, presented the congenital inversion theme in "Miss Ogilvy Finds Herself" (1926), the story of a woman who is really a man trapped in the wrong body, who finds her only satisfaction in life working at a man's job, as a World War I ambulance driver.[17]

With its Scandinavian immigrant characters and Midwest farm setting reminiscent of Cather's novel *My Ántonia*, Os-Anders' *Little Review* story "Karen: A Novel" capsulizes the attitude toward love between women—and "acceptable endings—that characterizes so much of the short fiction about lesbians in the following decades. Os-Anders tells of a Norwegian immigrant farm woman Karen, who loves her Norwegian neighbor Dorothea, and feels "full of wonder that . . . [Dorothea's daughters] and Dorothea and she were all women."[18] After Dorothea's death, Karen marries her husband as a means of remaining close to her. "Never wife" during thirteen years of marriage and under threat by one of Dorothea's daughters to " 'go to the church and tell them why you were my father's wife',"[19] Karen is finally disabled in an accident. She is thereby prevented from "going in the night, as she had done in all the years since Dorothea died, with bucket and soap to wash Dorothea's tombstone: to keep it white."[20] Here we have much of our fictional legacy: the hopelessness of lesbian relationships, the need to settle for whatever crumbs are offered, the absence of sexuality or its perverse sublimation into other activities (scrubbing tombstones, for example), the final punishment—death, or even better, a lingering illness or serious disability.

Publishing options for lesbian short fiction during the twenties were slim. Even in a magazine like *The Little Review* that was edited by lesbians Margaret Anderson and Jane Heap, only two explicitly lesbian stories appeared: Os-Anders' "Karen" and Bryher's "Chance Encounter," which was too abstract and elliptical to have been likely to have offended anyone.[21] Of the Black magazines of the Harlem Renaissance, none published a lesbian story, though a very explicit gay male one did appear.[22]

The political climate of the thirties, that contributed to the general acceptance by many editors of Freudianism or Marxism, eliminated the possibility of publishing such fiction. It was further discouraged at the end of the decade by the Dies Committee, a Congressional Un-American Activities Committee that charged that the government was filled with "Communists, homosexuals, and traitors."[23] In the magazines of the thirties and early forties, lesbian writers could, however, publish work concerned with themes that were not explicitly lesbian. In *Wasteland* (1946), for example, Jo Sinclair depicts a Jewish lesbian with cropped hair who works for the federal Works Progress Administration Writers Project and publishes stories about Black people and about the Spanish Civil War in *The New Masses*, a radical political magazine.

As in earlier years, occasional stories with explicitly lesbian subject matter appeared: Anna Kavan's "Asylum Piece VIII" (1940) about the relationship between a predatory middle-aged woman and a younger female patient abandoned by her husband in a French asylum; Isabel Bolton's "Ruth and Irma" (1947) about the unstable relationship between two "lost girls" vacationing in St. Tropez just before the Wall Street crash; Jane Bowles' "Camp Cataract" (1949) about the unhappily intense connection between two sisters, one of whom drowns at the story's end.[24] These stories all reflect the prevalent negative view of lesbianism and lesbian relationships.

Twenty years later, however, writing under the name Isabel Miller instead of Isabel Bolton (retaining in "Isabel" an anagram for "Lesbia"), Alma Routsong wrote the unabashedly positive lesbian romance *Patience and Sarah* (1967) and found a ready audience for it.[25] The time frame made all the difference. Except for those few who had found support from the Bloomsbury crowd or the Paris Circle, isolation had been the consistently dominant mood for lesbian writers as a group during the first half of the century, not only in their writing but in how their work was received. Not till a political understanding of lesbian existence began to emerge could there exist groups of lesbians who struggled toward their own affirmation and toward changes in the literary representations of lesbian lives.

II.

Since the mid-fifties the development of the contemporary lesbian short story has been especially dependent on the existence of lesbian periodicals. One of the key features of *The Ladder*, originally the publication of the important pre-feminist lesbian organization Daughters of Bilitis, was the fiction appearing regularly in its pages.[26] Within this fiction we can trace changes within white lesbian consciousness during the nearly two decades in which *The Ladder* was published (1956-1972): early stories focused almost entirely on sexual relationships, most often carried on within a framework of butch-fem relationships; as lesbian-feminism emerged as a powerful force in many lesbian communities, the fiction in *The Ladder* changed too.

While the stories that appeared during the first decade of *The Ladder's* existence do not repay careful rereading, they do have a definite place in the history of lesbian literature. They were written during a period when hundreds of lesbian novels were being published, primarily by paperback publishing companies which packaged them with suggestive cover photos and semi-pornographic plot summaries or excerpts from the book on the back cover. Many were written by men using female pseudonyms (one man wrote over 500)—a fact that never occurred to me when I read them as a teenager.[27] Often set in urban bars, the novels were built on lesbian relationships and sexuality. In this writing sexual tension had less to do with a concrete description of lovemaking than with a gradual build-up of erotic interaction and a final fade-out that left it to the reader to fill in the specific sexual details: a classic example is Beebo and Laura's dash through Greenwich Village streets in Ann Bannon's *I Am a Woman* (1959), barely reaching Beebo's apartment before they start making love, "wracked with passion, kissing each other ravenously, tearing at each other's clothes."[28]

Regardless of their setting, the pulp novels, like the stories in *The Ladder*, were almost invariably about white lesbians. Even when they were not, the exceptions were almost certainly by white lesbians, rather than by lesbians of color themselves: notable examples are Della Martin's *Twilight Girl* (1961), the story of a Black lesbian, a piano player, who becomes lover and maid to a rich white woman; and, in *The Ladder*, Emily Jones' 1958 story about the tense meeting in a Paris nightclub between a Black singer, the daughter of a sharecropper, and a wealthy white woman from Virginia and her husband.[29]

The *Ladder* stories fit into the general framework of popular lesbian fiction of the time. Their focus is clearly on questions of relationship: What are these feelings I have? Should I tell her? Will she reject me (either because she's not interested in me or because she's disgusted by the whole idea of Lesbianism)? Is she seeing someone else? Will we stay together? Unlike most of the popular novels of the time, however, a great many of these stories have happy endings. While I can look back at the endings of some of these stories and complain of the superficiality of their romantic wind-up, they nonetheless offered validation in literature, where practically none else was available, that lesbians did *not* have to end in misery.

The appearance of these stories—as of *The Ladder* as a whole—involved a degree of risk not shared by many of the lesbian novelists of the twenties and thirties. Not only had those earlier writers a secure financial position that was unthreatened by what they wrote, but they had, for the most part, the label "Literature" appended to their work (T.S.Eliot, for example, wrote the preface to Barnes' *Nightwood*). *The Ladder*—and its readers—had no such support. While some earlier writers masked their subject matter and kept their most explicitly lesbian fiction in manuscript, some of the *Ladder* contributors used pseudonyms which allowed them to write what they wanted. Without feminist or gay bookstores, *The Ladder* attempted for several years to reach more lesbians through distributors. But, since no other distributors would handle a lesbian magazine, they could only work with distributors who placed the magazine in sleazy bookstores along with male-oriented sex magazines and books. So, from 1963-1967, the copies of *The Ladder* that appeared in bookstores had the words "For Adults Only" emblazoned on the cover. Ninety percent of *Ladder* readers subscribed to it, preferring getting it in the mail in a plain brown wrapper to buying it over the counter if they did live someplace where it was for sale.[30] Yet they bought—and wrote for—this magazine which gave "a voice to an 'obscene' population in a decade of McCarthy witch hunts."[31]

"*The Ladder*," as Joan Nestle has written, "brought off a unique balancing act for the 1950's. It gave nourishment to a secret and subversive life while it flew a flag of assimilation."[32] Its fictional characters were not involved in what activism was an issue in its non-fiction pages, complete with discussions of "appropriate" modes of dress for demonstrations (shirtwaists rather than pants). It is relatively easy in looking back on the early *Ladder*'s butch-fem fictional characters from a more recent and far different perspective to see "a radical, sexual, political statement of the 1950's . . . as a reactionary, non-feminist experience."[33] But it is more historically accurate, for those of us who came out since the late sixties, to acknowledge what was radical and courageous about *The Ladder* as a whole and the fiction it published.

By the early seventies, however, *The Ladder* had begun to print short stories reflecting the feminist concerns that Black playwright Lorraine Hansberry, for example, had expressed in its pages over a decade earlier. In a 1957 letter signed only with her initials, she had said:

> I think it is about time that equipped women began to take on some of the ethical questions which a male-dominated culture has produced and dissect and analyze them quite to pieces in a serious fashion. It is time that "half the human race" had something to say about the nature of its existence. Otherwise—without revised basic thinking—the woman intellectual is likely to find herself trying to draw conclusions—moral conclusions—based on acceptance of a social moral superstructure which has never admitted to the equality of women and is therefore immoral itself. As per marriage, as per sexual practices, as per the rearing of children, etc. In this line of work there may be women to emerge who will be able to formulate a new and possible concept that homosexual persecution and condemnation has at its roots not only social ignorance, but a philosophically active anti-feminist dogma. But that is but a kernel of a speculative embryonic idea improperly introduced here.[34]

Such analyses of sexism, and of the connections between "homosexual persecution" and "anti-feminist dogma" began to take root, most notably in the early seventies during Barbara Grier's tenure as editor (1968-1972).

The magazine's short stories began to change correspondingly. Whereas nearly all of the early ones had focused on sexual relationships between two white women and raised issues almost entirely about their relationship, the later ones began to place these questions within the framework of other issues of central importance to the characters—or at least to acknowledge the existence of such issues. For example, Lynn Michaels published two stories, one in which disability is central, the other in which it is simply an acknowledged fact: the first is about a fifteen-year-old's relationship with a gym teacher who, like her, had had polio as a child—an experience which catalyzes early memories, especially of her mother's lesbian relationship; the other is about a grown woman, also disabled, coping with the end of a relationship. The women in Beverly Lynch's "The Shade" are under-age prostitutes worrying about the response of their pimp. Susan Daily's protagonist mentions her seven-year-old son in the course of a story about two ex-lovers; the ten-year-old girl in Patricia Fullerton's "Lincoln Park" watches with fascination a lesbian in the park and is finally saved by her from being sexually molested; the girl in Jane Rule's "My Father's House" learns that if she wants to get recognized as being as important as the boys, she is going to have to fight for that recognition.[35] Rather than allowing Rule's story to stand by itself, the editors added a short note on it as "an excellent example of early knowledge of the necessity of the liberation of women, by themselves."[36] As much as Rule's story, the editorial comment was a measure of the changes *The Ladder* had undergone since it had begun publication.

III.

By the early seventies, when *The Ladder* had folded and *Amazon Quarterly* first appeared, the lesbian short story had begun to exist within a framework that encompassed both a resurgence of the lesbian novel and a flowering of lesbian poetry. The development of these forms overshadowed lesbian short fiction during the first half of the decade, although by the mid-seventies Sandy Boucher, Elana Dykewomon (Nachman), and Jane Rule had published short story collections.[37] As always, the lesbian novel continued to be considered *the* form of lesbian fiction, the fiction that had to be taken seriously, despite the comparatively few lesbians able to publish such work in the lesbian or male commercial presses. The preference of many lesbians for writing poetry helped make it the dominant short form. In turn, this writing contributed to the development of lesbian short fiction.

In many ways, *Amazon Quarterly* (1972-1975) illustrates the preeminence of the novel and poetry over short fiction during the early seventies. The most memorable fiction it published was, in fact, excerpts from three of Daughters, Inc.'s most popular novels by and about white lesbians: the brilliant, beautiful, totally self-confident Molly Bolt, moving meteorically up from a background of Southern poverty in Rita Mae Brown's *Rubyfruit Jungle* (1973); the collectively-living, politically active dykes of different ages in June Arnold's *The Cook and the Carpenter* (1973); the young Jewish lesbian coming out in a private school and making a financial killing in a counter-culture drug sale in Elana Dykewomon's *Riverfinger Women* (1974). *Amazon Quarterly* also published a dazzling array of poetry: Judy Grahn's "A Woman Is Talking to Death," Susan Griffin's "The Song of the Woman with Her Parts Coming Out," Audre Lorde's "The Same Death Over and Over or Lullabies Are for Children," Adrienne Rich's "From an Old House in America," and other poems which reflected the political concerns and poetic sensibility of poetry editor Lorde, "born in the middle of NYC of West Indian parents & raised to know that America was not [her] home."[38]

The short stories selected by editors Gina Covina and Laurel Galana were, on the other hand, far more representative of those lesbians who expected/hoped that their connection with other lesbians would transcend both difference and conflict. They represented, in part, as Barbara Macdonald has found, two necessary fictional stages on the way to today's "new realistic fiction": the "fantasy" in which "new lives are tried on . . . to see how things will fit and how they will feel before we take on the new life for real"; and the "romanticized love story" which "depends upon lesbian love, *per se*, to carry the tale, rather than on situation or development of character," and which protests that "this-woman-is-stronger-warmer-more-to-be-trusted-than-any-man."[39]

Typical of such writing is the striking lack of individuality in character and concreteness in setting. Seven of the fourteen *Amazon Quarterly* stories have protagonists who have no given names and instead are referred to as "the one" and "the other," "the woman," "the old woman," "The Woman Who Loved the Truth"; and one story (by co-editor Laurel) has three characters, only one with a given name. The action often occurs in a vaguely specified rural setting. Region and any concrete sense of place are clearly far less important than the sense, communicated by not naming the characters, that lesbians are very much alike, "our" situations and relationships almost interchangeable, our differences—age, class, ethnicity, physical ability, race, regional identification—muted to the point of disappearing entirely.

This implicit message is carried less by any one of the stories than by their cumulative impact. The atmosphere (like that, in many ways, of *The Ladder*) is insular. *Amazon Quarterly* appeared during years when the Vietnam War finally ended, the movements for equal rights and self-determination on the part of people of color in this country (and outside it) continued, the women's/lesbian movements went through a succession of intense struggles (internally as well as in the context of the larger society). Yet nearly all of the characters in its stories seem to live in a white, totally woman-identified world.

The fiction in *Amazon Quarterly* represents an early stage of the white lesbian-feminist movement during the seventies. As with other lesbian publishing of that period, the value lies not only in the work itself, but in the possibilities created by its very existence: although it ceased publication in 1975, *Amazon Quarterly* helped open the way for the subsequent creation of several journals that contained more stories, representing a far wider range of voices.

The lesbian novels published in the early seventies by Daughters, Inc., demonstrated, as nothing had done before, that such novels were not only possible, but could be published under the editorial control of a white lesbian publishing company. Made possible by the creation of feminist book-stores, the huge success of the early Daughters' novels seemed to presage the appearance of a large number of substantial lesbian-feminist novels which did not materialize.[40] While it printed Linda Marie's *I Must Not Rock* and M. F. Beal's *Angel Dance* in 1977, Daughters published with de-creasing frequency after the mid-seventies, putting out its last book in 1978. Naiad Press published its first lesbian novel in 1974 and gradually increased its yearly output of novels which in many ways seemed literary descendants of the popular fiction of the fifties and sixties. Persephone Press and Spinsters, Ink began publishing fiction at the very end of the decade. An occasional self-published novel appeared, most notably, I think, Red Arobateau's *The Bars Across Heaven* (1975), a book about a working-class Black lesbian.

Perhaps most striking during the second half of the seventies was the unprecedented willingness on the part of commercial publishers to print novels about lesbians (or heterosexual novels with "obligatory" lesbian scenes) by women who may or may not be lesbians. The trend was striking-ly reflected by the purchase by Bantam Books of *Rubyfruit Jungle* from Daughters, Inc. and the book's 1978 appearance in a mass paperback edi-tion suitable for supermarket display. Primarily, the novels published since the mid-seventies have offered the impression that lesbian lives are now be-ing well-represented in the commercial press. In their discussion of seven-teen commercial press books published from 1974 to 1979 (fifteen white authors, two Black ones), Maureen Brady and Judith McDaniel show that this is not at all true; instead, they find that the image of the lesbian pre-sented is predictably and overwhelmingly negative and/or unrealistic, even in the works of publicly identified lesbian writers Rita Mae Brown, Jane DeLynn, May Sarton, and Ann Allen Shockley. Brady and McDaniel show that themes such as consistent punishment, disempowering eroticism, iso-lation from any community, or little or no concern with basic economic survival mark these works of commercially published fiction.[41] In the world of conglomerate publishing, the work of someone like Jane Rule, author of four novels dating back to 1964, or Elizabeth A. Lynn, author of a recent fantasy trilogy, is very much an exception; hardly any lesbian writers have been able to get novels published that are about lesbian char-acters who are strong, struggling women with as much chance of finding a positive resolution to their problems as anyone else.[42]

Less reliant on commercial publishers than the novel, more easily read at lesbian conferences, celebrations and rallies than fiction, allowing for direct expressions of personal feeling, poetry had a particular attraction for many lesbian writers during the early- and mid-seventies. A conse-quence was a time lag between the publication of poetry and the publication of fiction by more than a relative handful of lesbian-feminists. The early issues of the lesbian literary magazines that began after the demise of *Amazon Quarterly—Azalea, Conditions, Feminary, Sinister Wisdom—* contained relatively few short stories, especially compared to the number of poems printed. The tremendous recent increase in the attention given by women to writing short fiction is reflected in the periodicals themselves: in the special fiction issue of *Azalea*, the six stories in *Conditions: Six* and the four in *Conditions: Seven,* the five stories in the latest *Feminary* (Spring, 1981 double-issue), the eight in *Sinister Wisdom 16* and the five in the following issue.[43] To some extent, this fiction reflects both the work of lesbians who have only recently started writing fiction and the work of those who have consistently been writing it, even though some have published their stories only recently. But, to a large extent, this fiction has rolled in on the wave of lesbian poetry which opened up so many aspects of lesbian lives as potential subjects and which involved a diverse group of women in its writing and publishing.

The impulse among lesbians to write poetry during the early seventies is perhaps best exemplified by the moratorium on poetry submission called by *Amazon Quarterly* in 1974, since Audre Lorde had been receiving 500 poems a month and had a backlog of accepted manuscripts for several forthcoming issues. First published in mimeographed form and sold for less than a dollar; later gathered together in offset books with glossy covers; self-published as well as published by such lesbian presses as Diana Press, Out & Out Books, Women's Press Collective, and Violet Press, lesbian poetry swept through the mid-seventies in full force, gaining further momentum from the growing number of feminist poets who came to define themselves as lesbians—Paula Gunn Allen, Susan Griffin, Marilyn Hacker, Adrienne Rich, and others. [44]

A number of reasons existed for the tremendous growth of lesbian poetry. As with so many aspects of lesbian writing and publishing as a whole, economic considerations were critical. As Lorde has written:

> . . . even the form our creativity takes is often a class issue. Of all the art forms, poetry is the most economical. It is the one which is the most secret, which requires the least actually physical labour, the least material, and the one which can most easily be done between shifts at the plant, in the hospital pantry, on the crowded subway, and on scraps of surplus paper. This past year, while writing a novel on very tight finances, I experienced the enormous differences between the material demands of prose and those of poetry. As we are reclaiming our literature, poetry has become the major voice of poor, working-class, and Third World women. A room of one's own may be a necessity for writing prose, but so are reams of paper, a working typewriter, and plenty of time.[45]

Another aspect of the attraction of poetry during the early- and mid-seventies was the impetus felt by individual women to express themselves in a form that allowed for a direct statement of *personal* experience. For women just gaining an awareness about how our lives had been falsified—lied about—by male writers (and women writers who wanted male approval), the freedom at last to tell the truth, and to hear it, overwhelmed all else; for many lesbians the words in the consciousness-raising group or at the public speakout seemed to have value far above what was "made up." So in her introduction to her 1975 story collection, *Assaults and Rituals,* Sandy Boucher has written about herself during the early seventies:

> I threw it out of my life—the idea of myself as writer, and with it the attempt to make what is known as "art." I no longer even *read* fiction. All I needed to read, all that served me, was the raw testimony women were making about their own lives. And for the next three years all I wrote (never thinking of myself as a writer while doing it) were journals on what was happening in the collective we had formed; political articles and poems for *Mother Lode,* the paper we put out; and, pardon me, love poems because I was in love and couldn't help it.[46]

As a result, for many lesbians poetry (and direct autobiographical narrative) seemed easier to write than fiction, more in keeping with the political times, more immediately accessible to the woman who was only just recovering from the traditional notion—drummed into her through reading "literature" in school—that writing at all was the appropriate preserve of the white, formally educated male (or, alternatively, of the white, formally educated heterosexual woman). The overwhelming majority of the lesbian poetry written during the seventies, particularly during the early seventies, has challenged this elitist notion of literature. Most often the poets have done so in ways that allow them to speak directly and in their own voice. While the "I" in any poem can be read as a persona for the poet, most often in contemporary lesbian poetry that voice seems to be so close to the poet's own as to be indistinguishable. The strength and impact of this poetry has rested on the sense of a woman—the poet—talking directly to another woman—the reader or listener.

The investigation of "fictional" possibilities has been a comparatively muted strain in contemporary lesbian poetry. Yet there is increasing evidence of an impulse to employ extended narrative form or clear persona. This impulse also finds expression in the prose narratives of a growing number of lesbians whose primary identification has been as poets but who have found in this form the freedom to explore characters and situations in ways that they could not in poetry: Julie Blackwomon, Jan Clausen, Judy Grahn, Irena Klepfisz, Audre Lorde, Aleida Rodríguez.

IV.

The short fiction in this anthology mingles the strengths of early lesbian poetry with the characteristic strengths of the lesbian novel of the same period: it combines writing that is personal, direct, attentive to the rhythms and sounds of language with writing that June Arnold has characterized as developing "away from plot-time via autobiography, confession, oral tradition . . . experience weaving in upon itself, commenting upon itself, *in*clusive, not ending in final victory/defeat but ending with the sense that the community continues."[47] The use of "autobiography, confession, oral tradition" has been, in fact, part of lesbian writing in an ongoing way: Stein's novel *Q.E.D.* is about a triangular relationship in which she herself was involved during her student days at Johns Hopkins, while she based "Miss Furr and Miss Skene" on a couple she knew in Paris; Kate Millett's *Sita*, which, she's said, "refuses and eludes any literary category," has been discussed by Julia Penelope (Stanley) both as "confessional" writing and as a novel.[48]

I see lesbian fiction as encompassing different kinds—and degrees—of prose fiction: a continuum that ranges from what is "made up" (though drawing on the author's experience) to what is based on the author's direct experience, though screened through her consciousness, worked on by her imagination, deviating as she wishes from an objective rendering. While accepting the concrete autobiographical base of much that has traditionally been described as fiction (made-up prose stories), I am also broadening the definition of what has traditionally been thought of as fiction. My definition also incorporates the blurring between genres— poetry and prose, fiction and non-fiction—that has been characteristic not only of lesbian/women's writing but of much other contemporary writing. The concept of genres itself has also functioned as one way for the white male literary establishment to grant or withhold prestige. Given this, the broadening of the definition of fiction (at least until we can come up with language that better reflects our realities and our work) emphasizes not the ultimately arbitrary category but the writer's active role as the *shaper* of the raw material of her stories—a mix of her imagination and her experience.

A result is the type of fictional truth that emerges from a writer's intimate connection with her subject. Maureen Brady, for instance, originally felt she was "making up" the characters in "Grinning Underneath," two women who work together in a factory and live in adjoining trailers, "but later came to realize she was unearthing very familiar characters from her past, the burial of which, in her conscious mind, was provoked and supported by the encouragement to upward mobility of our class system with its consequent alienation from rootedness."[49] Julie Blackwomon, a mother, and Jan Clausen, a co-parent, tell stories that are not about their *particular* children, though they are certainly grounded in the language, the perceptions, and the realities of girls/young women of a certain age, class, and race. Other stories too were built on a foundation of first-hand experience: Jo Carrillo grew up knowing of many Chicanas living in couples; Judith McDaniel hikes and camps frequently in the Adirondacks; Lynn Michaels had polio as a child, and spent part of her childhood as a Jew in the overwhelmingly Christian South.

For the fiction writer, the reader's personal connection with her story, her flash of recognition, her sense that "I know someone just like her," can be an extremely high form of praise. But for those writers who "make up" their characters and who see them clearly as separate from themselves, the assumption by some readers that a story is—or should be—factual can create problems. Clausen's "Daddy," for example, a story told from the point of view of the elementary school-age daughter of a lesbian, was rejected by one feminist periodical on the grounds that some members of the collective "did not like to read an adult writing from the perspective of a make-believe child." And Jane Rule has written about becoming enmeshed in the possible legal consequences stemming from assumptions about her fiction:

> I remember how surprised I was when my first novel was about to be published and I was informed that I could be sued for anything any one of my characters said. "But I often don't agree with what they say," I protested. The lawyer was not interested in the clear distinction I make between my own voice and the voices of my characters. Neither, I have found, are many of my readers.[50]

Other writers in this anthology appear as actual characters in their stories, at the same time as they control the depiction of events—screening everything through their perceptions, using their imaginations, departing from a literal rendering of fact. Audre Lorde has made up a word for the kind of semi-fictional writing she does—"biomythography"—which recognizes that the line between "fact" and "fiction" is not nearly so clear as we might believe, using, for example, composite characters and fantasies to move the telling further into the fictional realm.

As she has in such earlier seventies stories as "Mountain Radio" and "Retaining Walls," Sandy Boucher appears as a character in "Kansas in the Spring," in a story that, like Lorde's, is a "hybrid." Some years back

Boucher made the choice to be *inclusive* rather than exclusive, to include *herself* in her stories, even though that made the story seem less obviously fictional. As she writes: "It is the transformation of the material, rather than its correspondence to real events or characters, that distinguishes it; the interplay of memories, of formal quotes and informal gleanings, gives it a complexity beyond the actual events."[51] And Dorothy Allison describes her own view of this dynamic between "real-life experience" and "fiction" in this way:

> I think I am a storyteller. I tell the stories I have seen, experienced myself, heard or imagined. Before I became a storyteller I was a liar—because the story I told did not respect the reality of the other people who had something to do with it. "That's not how it was," I've been told, or, "You sure we were at the same place when that happened? None of that went on near me."
>
> The stories I've written about my family, about growing up poor in South Carolina embarrass or anger people who were there. They tell me about the stuff I've left out or how "he wasn't that bad," or "she never said that." Of course not. I write from my life but with a purpose in mind. I am conscious of the effect I want to create, the way I want the reader to think about things. If I write history or ethnography or political analysis, I have to be fair. When I write fiction I have only to present truth as I see it.[52]

The concept of storytelling that Allison mentions, which stresses her roots in an oral rather than a written tradition, is particularly closely connected to lesbian stories which have too often gone unpublished and unrecorded—those of elderly women, women with a rich ethnic or regional history, women of color, women for whom English is a second—and alien—language, poor women, women who worked in fields or factories, working-class women, women who came out before the women's movement, disabled women. For the most part, these lesbians are furthest from "literary history," the history of what gets written down by certain people—male, middle/upper class, and white.

The literary silences which have affected all lesbians have been greatest for those groups of lesbians without a written tradition in English, access to publications whose editors share their background, and/or the financial resources to begin their own publications, to self-publish their own books, or to risk their jobs by writing and publishing overtly lesbian material. For these women, the impetus has been to create modes of expression reflective of their own experiences and cultural traditions, often through song or storytelling, but also through reaching back into the past to reclaim a part of that history by making it into written fiction.

Though not herself a lesbian, the grandmother in Jo Carrillo's "María Littlebear," who, reminded by a single word, can go on and on with her narrative, exemplifies the storytelling gift of generations of Chicanas from northern New Mexico, as well as of other women whose history has been passed on by word-of-mouth, embroidered with each retelling, sliding definitively at some early point over the line between "history/fact" and "myth/fiction." And the generations of poor whites with their own stories to tell that stand behind the lesbian narrator's South Carolina relatives in Allison's "A River of Names" certainly were too caught in the crush of survival even to *think* about writing stories. Nor would *written* stories emerge from the Midwestern farm women in "Kansas in the Spring," the daughter of Jewish immigrants in "Celia," the lesbian in "The Attic of the House" who had lived for thirty years with a woman who was convinced that they'd "burn in hell" for their sexual feelings and who now tells snatches of her story only when drunk.

Because even the most cursory look at short stories is a look at what is written and, for the most part, published, it can only be done accurately within a context that acknowledges the existence of those stories that never made it onto paper or into print. The sense of *this* history, the need to uncover and share it, is in the biographical statement of one of the contributors to *Lesbian Fiction*, Flying Clouds:

> Stories are important to me. There is a great deal of freedom in telling stories and freedom in listening to them. This is a good freedom for me, like I imagine the birds flying. And if we were to have lots of stories, lots and lots of them from Indian women there would be not only that much freedom and beauty but also a *pride*, the feeling that comes from watching the stream of blackbirds travelling in the fall, unable to see the beginning or the ending, just many, many passing overhead, hearing their voices.

For these women, the initial task involves finding a historical tradition of *lesbians*, not lesbian *writers*. Lakota/Sioux, Lebanese/American Paula Gunn Allen, for instance, has begun the process of exploring the lives of lesbian women in ways consistent with tribal existence.[53] Japanese-American writer Barbara Noda has likewise suggested the need for uncovering history in ways that do not involve going to the library and rummaging through someone's collected letters and unpublished diaries: "Perhaps," Noda writes, "I could ask my 87-year-old grandmother who is one of the still remaining Issei women *if* she remembers any 'strange' women who did not marry and associated mainly with other women."[54] And Jo Carrillo addresses this problem from her own perspective when she says:

> I am a Chicana lesbian from Northern New Mexico. Part of
> my family settled the land in the early Seventeenth Century. I
> have learned from my background that lesbians have lived to-
> gether as recognized couples, or families, in my culture. The
> sexual aspect of their relationship, however, is often ignored;
> they are called "las tias, old maids, etc." so that the truth of
> their lives will not draw attention in the intensely religious
> atmosphere of their rural communities. There is much resis-
> tance to naming the "unspeakable."[55]

"Naming the unspeakable" has been neither a quick nor an easy process
for lesbians. For lesbians without an economic cushion and/or white skin
privilege, being able to commit to paper their stories has been an especially
recent development: as late as 1977, for example, Barbara Smith wrote
that "Black women are still in the position of having to 'imagine,' discover
and verify Black lesbian literature because so little has been written from
an avowedly [Black] lesbian perspective."[56] The changes that have been
wrought in short fiction in the past few years, the breaking of silences for
lesbian women, have depended, in large part, on a remarkable number of
lesbians who are among the first generation in their families not only to be
published writers, but to be comfortable enough with written English to
write down their stories.[57]

My work on this anthology has its roots in my adolescence, long before
I kept lesbian fiction on my bookshelves or in any way supported its continued existence. It has roots too in the functional amnesia that followed
that time of furtively read paperbacks: when I forgot the books, the
thoughts, the feelings, went through years of school—and six of marriage—
without coming across anything that I then identified as "lesbian literature." So my impulse to edit emerges too out of that gap in my life, when
lesbian life went on without me and, without my knowledge, lesbian literature continued to appear.

I began work on this anthology also because of my increasing awareness
of a tremendous growth in lesbian short fiction of the past half-dozen
years. In part, this has been reflected in lesbian literary magazines, where
individual issues go out of print with considerable rapidity. In part, it has
been reflected in the publication of short story collections by a number of
lesbian writers, among them Linda J. Brown's *The Rainbow River* (1980),
Jan Clausen's *Mother, Sister, Daughter, Lover* (1980), Andrea Dworkin's
The New Woman's Broken Heart (1980), Ruth Geller's *Pictures from the
Past* (1980), Elizabeth A. Lynn's *The Woman Who Loved the Moon*
(1981), Jane Rule's *Outlander* (1981), Barbara Sheen's *Shedevils* (1978),
and Ann Allen Shockley's *The Black and White of It* (1980), as well as

the contributions of many lesbian writers to Judy Grahn's multi-volume anthology *True to Life Adventure Stories* (1978; 1981).[58]

Because of this strong contemporary tradition of the lesbian short story, I resisted the impulse, in editing this anthology, to include selections from the lesbian novels of the last decade. While two anthology selections—Maureen Brady's "Grinning Underneath" and Audre Lorde's "The Beginning"—will eventually appear in full-length works, both were stories before their authors decided to write books.[59] None of the previously printed stories had been published prior to 1976, though a couple were begun before that date. All were published in periodicals based in the United States. All but two of the previously printed stories appeared first in lesbian periodicals or in feminist periodicals which are not specifically lesbian but have lesbians on their editorial collectives/boards: *Azalea, Chrysalis, Conditions, Heresies, Sinister Wisdom, Women: A Journal of Liberation*. The range of publishing options in itself offers support for writing about a far broader spectrum of lesbian experience than was possible during the days when *The Ladder* was the sole lesbian magazine or *Amazon Quarterly* was the only widely distributed one.

Many of these stories seem to assume the lesbianism (or at least the woman-identification) of their readers: as a result, lesbianism is a given and various sides of lesbian lives—sexual and otherwise—can be explored, not explained or justified. While some lesbian writers have spoken of a continuing pressure from periodical editors to write stories that present lesbians in a uniformly positive light, the stories in this volume seem to me to present us in ways that are fundamentally realistic, most often stubbornly refusing to ignore the complexities of our lives, and occasionally describing us in our less admirable moments.

In this fiction, the simple romanticism of much earlier lesbian writing is, for the most part, absent—as it has been, except fleetingly, from nearly all of our lives. Looking back at her 1967 novel *Patience and Sarah*, for example, Alma Routsong (Isabel Miller) has said, "I think the book's true, but it's also naive. I've been around quite a lot since I wrote it, and I know better how difficult most relationships are. I didn't make Patience and Sarah's relationship difficult enough—I hinted at the difficulty, but I didn't make it as difficult as most really are."[60]

The stories most often do not turn on the question of the relationship itself but on the day-to-day life in which the relationship plays a significant part, but only a part—the fictional counterpart to Judy Grahn's poetic question:

> Love came along and saved me
> saved me   saved
> me.

However, my life remains the same as before.
O What shall I do now that I have
what I've always been looking for.[61]

If the stories in *The Ladder* and *Amazon Quarterly* often incorporated only the first three lines of this poem, the stories that have been written
more recently tend to reflect the realism of the last three.

Even when very positive, most of the sexual relationships in the stories
in this anthology exist in a complex framework: Katherine Sturtevant's
Maline is looking for a sexual and emotional distraction, not "true love,"
after the breakup of a serious, long-term relationship; the lovers in "Another Place to Begin" and "A River of Names" experience great tension
over their class differences; Miss Katheryn and Miss Renita in "A Day's
Growth" are fenced in by the homophobia in their small town; Audre and
Ginger in "The Beginning" last only until Ginger starts spending time with
another woman and Audre returns to New York; Irena Klepfisz' Rachel
and Dia are working out the daily dynamics of a long-term relationship
which forms a piece, but not the central one, of the whole story; the triangle in "Oxblood Shawls" involves issues of disability, region, and religion. For the most part, the stories end at a place where more of the same
is promised—or with endings that are certainly not conclusive: tensions remain—around monogamy, class, race and age differences, the needs and
expectations of individual women.

Because so many lesbian writers have reached a stage at which we can
assume the commonality that stems from our lesbianism, many of the
stories are grounded in differences among us. The women in them are
Cubana or Chicana, Japanese-American or Chinese-American, American
Indian or Black, Northern urban Jewish or rural white Southern; parent-
ing children or without them; in Kansas farm towns or at rodeos; in elementary school or retired from fifty years of teaching; concerned only
with the present or tracing the lives of mothers and grandmothers; surviving somehow on drugs or alcohol; isolated geographically or near women's
communities; lesbian separatist or member of a Left sectarian group;
waitress, teacher, factory worker; filmmaker, maid, writer.

Other differences are reflected in form: the first sequence of Aleida
Rodríguez' "Sequences" is a prose poem; Barbara Noda sees "Thanksgiving
Day" as reminiscent of the vignettes that twentieth-century Japanese
writer Yasumari Kawabata called "tanagokoro no shosetsu" or palm-of-
the-hand stories[62]; Elizabeth A. Lynn's story is like a legend or folktale,
Kitty Tsui's has a dramatic structure, Flying Clouds' and Irena Klepfisz'
read like journals. While the stories are most often serious, where there is
humor, it depends largely on the lesbian's knowledge as an insider: the

male assumptions that the women in "Boys at the Rodeo" must be four-teen-year-old boys because only males would have self-reliance and strength; the sexual expectations placed by a small-town woman on someone she sees as "a real live Greenwich Village Bulldagger"; the happily incestuous sisters "passing" behind the facade of the perfect American family and parodying the view of lesbians as hopeless narcissists.

While these stories show considerable diversity, they in no way form a comprehensive collection of fiction that lesbians are writing today. No single book could encompass the breadth of that fiction. The very vitality of lesbian short fiction alone makes any published anthology less than totally up-to-date and comprehensive. My position as an editor of *Conditions* has allowed me to see in manuscript over the past five years short stories by many lesbian writers, as well as those appearing in a range of lesbian and non-lesbian feminist publications. My physical proximity to the Lesbian Herstory Archives enabled me to read through both un-published manuscripts and less widely distributed periodicals and books. Reading through these stories, I have been well aware that I was putting together a book that reflects my own literary tastes and personal/political priorities. I am aware too that the work I could consider was limited to that authored by women willing to be identified publicly as lesbians or to publish their work under a pseudonym.

In large part, the writers represented here are among the many lesbians who have not only written about our lives but have been actively involved in the creation of a feminist and lesbian writing community—founding presses, self-publishing, editing magazines and newspapers—as well as printing their work in lesbian (and non-lesbian) feminist publications. In these ways, unlike earlier lesbian writers, they have both helped create and been a part of a writing and publishing network that has allowed lesbian fiction writers to *assume* that their readers are other women, other lesbians, and thereby to ask questions and to speak about aspects of their lives in ways that before were far less imaginable. This fiction both draws from the lesbian-feminist movement and returns to it a literature firmly rooted in the strengths of our commonality *and* our differences, a literature which reflects in ways that once seemed hardly possible the varied realities of our lives.

Notes

1 The Lesbian Herstory Archives lists short stories in its collection in *Lesbian Herstory Archives News 5* (Spring 1979) and plans to update this listing (P.O. Box 1258, New York, NY 10001). For other works by and about lesbians, see Lillian Faderman, *Surpassing the Love of Men: Romantic Friendship and Love Between Women from the Renaissance to the Present* (New York: Morrow, 1981); Jeannette Foster, *Sex Variant Women in Literature* (Vantage Press, 1956; reprinted Baltimore: Diana Press, 1975); Barbara Grier, *The Lesbian in Literature*, 3rd ed. (Tallahassee: Naiad Press, 1981); Grier, *Lesbiana: Book Reviews from The Ladder* (Tallahassee: Naiad Press, 1976); J.R. Roberts, *Black Lesbians: An Annotated Bibliography* (Tallahassee: Naiad Press, 1981).

2 Wilhelm, *We Too Are Drifting* (New York: Random House, 1935); and *Torchlight to Valhalla* (New York: Random House, 1938), both reprinted by Arno Press (New York, 1975). Sinclair [Ruth Seid], *Wasteland* (New York: Harper, 1946).

3 Hull, " 'Under the Days': The Buried Life and Poetry of Angelina Weld Grimké," *Conditions: Five* (1979), p. 20; available from Lesbian-Feminist Study Clearinghouse.

4 Hull, p. 23.

5 Thanet, *The Western*, New Series, Vol. VI, No. 1 (January, 1880), 22. Thanet is discussed in Gene Damon [Barbara Grier], "Journey to Obscurity: Octave Thanet," *Lesbian Lives: Biographies from The Ladder*, eds. Grier and Coletta Reid (Oakland: Diana Press, 1976) and Faderman, pp. 215-216. Faderman characterizes "My Lorelei" as Thanet's "most extensive literary discussion of romantic friendship" (p. 449n).
See Faderman's chapter on Boston marriages (pp. 190-203). In "The Female World of Love and Ritual: Relations between Women in Nineteenth-Century America," Carroll Smith-Rosenberg writes: "The essential question is not whether these women had genital contact and can therefore be defined as heterosexual or homosexual. The twentieth-century tendency to view human love and sexuality within a dichotomized universe of deviance and normality, genitality and platonic love, is alien to the emotions and attitudes of the nineteenth century and fundamentally distorts the nature of these women's emotional interactions" (*Signs*, Vol. 1, No. 1, Autumn, 1975, p. 8). For a discussion of a "lesbian continuum" in woman-identified experience, see Adrienne Rich, "Compulsory Heterosexuality and Lesbian Existence," *Signs*, Vol. 5, No. 4 (Summer, 1980).

6 Josephine Donovan, *Sarah Orne Jewett* (New York: Frederick Ungar, 1980), p. 31.

7 Jewett, *Atlantic Monthly* (October, 1897); *The Country of the Pointed Firs*, Preface by Willa Cather (1925; reprinted Garden City: Doubleday, 1956), p. 261.

8 Faderman, pp. 297-308; and Faderman, "Lesbian Magazine Fiction in the Early Twentieth Century," *Journal of Popular Culture*, Vol. XI, No. 4 (Spring, 1978), 800-817.

9 Lee, *The Lesbians Home Journal: Stories from The Ladder*, eds. Grier and Reid (Oakland: Diana Press, 1976), p. 163. The story was printed in *The Ladder* in 1972.

10 Faderman, p. 308.

11 Faderman, p. 308. Stein's story was first published in *Vanity Fair*.

12 I am grateful to Joanna Russ for reminding me of these influences on Stein's view of homosexuality.

13 Stein, *Three Lives* (1909; reprinted New York: Random House, 1936), p. 86. Carolyn Faunce Copeland, in *Language & Time & Gertrude Stein* (Iowa City: University of Iowa Press, 1975) notes that such critics as Edmund Wilson saw "Melanctha" as "a perceptive story about Negroes" (*Axel's Castle*).

14 Quoted in Jane Rule, *Lesbian Images* (Garden City: Doubleday, 1975), p. 78.

15 Cited in Donovan, "The Unpublished Love Poems of Sarah Orne Jewett," *Frontiers*, Vol. IV, No. 3 (Fall, 1979), 28.

16 Rich, "Vesuvius at Home: The Power of Emily Dickinson," *On Lies, Secrets, and Silence: Selected Prose, 1966-1978* (New York: Norton, 1979), p. 175. See also Foster, pp. 75-76.

17 Hall, *Miss Ogilvy Finds Herself* (New York: Harcourt Brace, 1934); reprinted in Seymour Kleinberg, ed., *The Other Persuasion* (New York: Vintage, 1977).

18 Os-Anders, *The Little Review* (Spring, 1922), p. 24.

19 Os-Anders, p. 27.

20 Os-Anders, p. 28.

21 Bryher, *The Little Review* (Autumn/Winter, 1924-1925), pp. 35-39.

22 Bruce Nugent published "Smoke Lilies and Jade" in *Fire* (1926). Wallace Thurman, editor of *Fire*, wrote a satire on the Harlem Renaissance, *Infants of the Spring* (New York: Macauley, 1932), which also has explicit gay male content. I am indebted to Gloria T. Hull for bringing these works to my attention.

23 Madeline Davis, "Multiple Images: A Study of the Lesbian Character in Fiction and Non-Fiction of the 1940's" (Pittsburgh: Lesbian-Feminist Study Clearinghouse, 1981), p. 5.

24 Kavan, *Asylum Piece* (Garden City: Doubleday, 1940). Bolton, *New Yorker*, Vol. 23 (July 26, 1947), 21-24. Bowles, *Harper's Bazaar*; reprinted in *The Collected Work of Jane Bowles* (New York: Farrar, 1966).

25 Routsong originally self-published the novel under the title *A Place for Us*; McGraw-Hill published it as *Patience and Sarah* in 1972. See Jonathan Katz' interview with Routsong in *Gay American History*, ed. Katz (New York: Crowell, 1976), pp. 433-443.

26 The complete *Ladder* has been reprinted by Arno Press (New York, 1975). Discussions of the creation and development of *The Ladder* can be found in Grier's introductions to *Lesbians Home Journal, Lesbian Lives*, and *The Lavender Herring: Essays from The Ladder*, all co-edited by Grier and Reid (Oakland: Diana Press, 1976); Del Martin and Phyllis Lyon's *Lesbian/Woman* (New York: Bantam, 1972); the interview with Barbara Gittings in *Gay American History*, pp. 420-433. Along with Helen Sanders, Gittings, Grier, Lyon, and Martin served as editors of *The Ladder*. See also Grier's *Lesbiana*, the only one of the *Ladder* anthologies still in print. *Lesbians Home Journal* published only later stories, not the early ones which depict butch-fem relationships.

27 Fran Koski and Maida Tilchen cite Valerie Taylor as having said that "a man named Paul Little ... claims to have written over 500 such novels under the name of Sylvia Sharon" ("Some Pulp Sappho," *Margins*, No. 23 [August, 1975], p. 42).

28 Bannon (Greenwich: Fawcett Gold Medal, 1959), p. 138. This and three other Bannon books have been reprinted by Arno Press (1975).

29 Martin's book (Beacon) is described in Roberts' *Black Lesbians*. In "The Lesbian Paperback," Grier surmises that since the author never published a second novel, despite *Twilight Girl*'s "excellent quality," "Della Martin is the pseudonym of an established author" (*Tangents*, 1966, pp. 4-7; reprinted Lesbian-Feminist Study Clearinghouse). See Jones, *The Ladder*, Vol. 2, No. 12 (September, 1958), 8-10, 20-26. On the basis of personal knowledge of the author, Grier confirmed my impression, based on Jones' story, that she is white. For a later short story about a Black lesbian, see Lin Yatta's "Fitting," *Evergreen Review*, Vol. 13, No. 66 (May, 1969), 23-24.

30 I am grateful to Barbara Grier for sharing with me this information about the history of *The Ladder.*

31 Joan Nestle, "Butch-Fem Relationships: Sexual Courage in the 1950's," *Heresies No. 12* (1981), p. 21.

32 Nestle, p. 21.

33 Nestle, p. 22.

34 Letter signed "L.N." [Lorraine (Hansberry) Nemiroff]. *The Ladder*, Vol. I, No. 11 (August, 1957), 30. In her February-March, 1970 "Lesbiana" column, Grier identifies Hansberry as the author of this and another letter (*Lesbiana*, p. 184). See also Adrienne Rich's "The Problem with Lorraine Hansberry," *Freedomways—Lorraine Hansberry: Art of Thunder, Vision of Light*, Vol. 19, No. 4 (Fourth Quarter, 1979), 247-255.

35 Michaels, "Funeral," *The Ladder*, Vol. 16, No. 5 and 6 (June/July, 1972). Like Michaels' "Phoenix," Daily's "There Are No Gypsies in New York City" and Fullerton's "Lincoln Park" are in *The Ladder*, Vol. 16, No. 11 and 12 (August/September, 1972). "Phoenix" was reprinted as "The Bath" in *Lesbians Home Journal.* Rule, "My Father's House," *The Ladder*, Vol. 15, No. 3 and 4 (December/January, 1970-1971). Rule was a frequent contributor to *The Ladder* beginning in 1968.

36 Editorial note, *The Ladder*, Vol. 15, No. 3 and 4 (December/January, 1970-1971), p. 15.

37 Boucher, *Assaults and Rituals* (San Francisco: Mama's Press, 1975); Dykewomon, *They Will Know Me by My Teeth* (Northampton: Megaera Press, 1976); Rule, *Theme for Diverse Instruments* (Vancouver, B.C.: Talonbooks, 1975). Complete ordering information for books by all contributors is listed under Work by Contributors.

38 Lorde, *This Bridge Called My Back: Writings by Radical Women of Color*, eds. Cherríe Moraga and Gloria Anzaldúa (Watertown, MA: Persephone Press, 1981), p. 248.

39 Macdonald, "Lesbian Short Stories: Fantasy, Romance, Reality," *New Women's Times Feminist Review* (June/July, 1981), pp. 8-9.

40 For a discussion of one mid-seventies view of publishing, see Daughters' co-publisher June Arnold's "Feminist Presses and Feminist Publishing," *Quest*, Vol. III, No. 1 (Summer, 1976), 18-26. Also Lois Gould's article on/interview with Arnold, co-publisher Parke Bowman, Charlotte Bunch, and Bertha Harris, "Creating a Women's World," *New York Times Magazine* (January 2, 1977), pp. 10-11, 34, 36-38; Marina Franchild offers a lengthy critique of this article in "Just What Can Feminists Afford?" *Big Mama Rag*, Vol. 6, No. 4 (April/May, 1978), 5-8, 12. See too Jan Clausen's "The Politics of Publishing and the Lesbian Community," *Sinister Wisdom 2* (1976), pp. 95-115.

41 Brady and McDaniel, "Lesbians in the Mainstream: Images of Lesbians in Recent Commercial Fiction," *Conditions: Six* (1980), pp. 82-105.

42 A bibliography of writing on the fiction of Jane Rule is in *Canadian Fiction* (Autumn, 1976).

43 *Azalea*, A Magazine By & For Third World Lesbians, c/o Gibbs, 306 Lafayette Ave., Brooklyn, NY 11238; *Conditions*, A Magazine of Writing by Women with an Emphasis on Writing by Lesbians, P.O. Box 56, Van Brunt Station, Brooklyn, NY 11215; *Feminary*, A Feminist Journal for the South Emphasizing the Lesbian Vision, P.O. Box 954, Chapel Hill, NC 27514; *Sinister Wisdom*, A Journal of Words and Pictures for the Lesbian Imagination in All Women, P.O. Box 660, Amherst, MA 01004.

44 See too *Lesbian Poetry: An Anthology*, eds. Elly Bulkin and Joan Larkin (Watertown, MA: Persephone Press, 1981), which contains work by sixty-four lesbian poets, an introduction, and a list of work by contributors.

45 Lorde, "Age, Race, Class and Sexuality: Women Redefining Differences," (Pittsburgh: Lesbian-Feminist Study Clearinghouse, 1980), p. 5.

46 Boucher, "About This Book," p. i.

47 Arnold and Bertha Harris, "Lesbian Fiction," *Sinister Wisdom 2* (1976), p. 29.

48 Millett, "The Shame Is Over," *Ms.*, III (January, 1975), pp. 27-28. Julia Stanley, "Fear of FLYING?," *Sinister Wisdom 2* (1976), pp. 52-62; and Stanley and Susan Wolfe, "Toward a Feminist Aesthetic," *Chrysalis No. 6* (1978), p. 58.

49 Brady, correspondence with the author, July 22,1981.

50 Rule, "Sexuality in Literature," *Outlander* (Tallahassee: Naiad Press, 1981), p. 152.

51 Boucher, letter to the author, July 15,1981.

52 Allison, questionnaire response, March, 1981.

53 Allen, "Beloved Women: Lesbians in American Indian Cultures," *Conditions: Six* (1981), pp. 67-87.

54 Noda, letter to the author, October 4, 1978; quoted at length in Bulkin, "Introduction: A Look at Lesbian Poetry," *Lesbian Poetry: An Anthology*, p. xxviii.

55 Carrillo, letter to the author, November, 1980.

56 Smith, "Toward a Black Feminist Criticism," *Conditions: Two* (Fall, 1977), p. 39, available from the Lesbian-Feminist Study Clearinghouse.

57 See, for example, Cherríe Moraga's "La Güera" (pp. 27-34) and Gloria Anzaldúa's "Speaking in Tongues: A Letter to Third World Women Writers" (pp. 165-174) and "La Prieta" (pp. 198-209) in *This Bridge Called My Back*.

58 Linda J. Brown, *The Rainbow River* (New York: Iridian Press, 1980); Andrea Dworkin, *The New Woman's Broken Heart* (East Palo Alto, CA: Frog in the Well Press, 1980); Ruth Geller, *Pictures From the Past* (Buffalo: Imp Press, 1980). The other books are listed under Work by Contributors.

59 Brady's book is *Folly*. Lorde's book is *I've Been Standing on This Street Corner a Hell of a Long Time* (forthcoming from Persephone Press).

60 Routsong, *Gay American History*, p. 442.

61 Grahn, "Love came along and saved me," *The Work of a Common Woman* (New York: St.Martin's, 1978), p. 140.

62 Noda, letter to the author, December 9, 1980.

Lesbian
FICTION

an anthology

Pat Suncircle

A Day's Growth

"Why in the world can't that child stop dancing?"

"Demons."

"Now don't start preaching. I just want to know why she can't be still. Everytime I come over here she got the stereo on shaking the house. Tell her she ought to cool it, children can have heart attacks too, you know."

"Well, I guess she got to pass the time somehow."

"Hasn't she got any friends?"

At eight o'clock when I woke up they were resting on my mind. The two women living down the street who nobody talked about anymore, the joke having died down. I lay there for awhile watching beneath my eyelids the quiet-appearing expressions and tailored suits that I wished I could wear. Miss Katheryn's brown eyes and Miss Renita's smokey grey ones under sharp brows that nearly met in the middle. The only women on the block whose voices I didn't hear straining out the names of children. I hardly heard their voices at all, even though they'd lived on this street since before I came.

But there was Aunt Cynthia's voice carrying up through the crack in my door now, raising at intervals and even if I couldn't make out the words I knew that she was talking to Doris about the revival at church that night and the whole shitload came back. Miss Katheryn and Miss Renita and their cool breeze presence fled and there stood Aunt Cynthia calmly pointing out passages in the Bible to me.

She talked soft and level never getting angry, never letting anything flash in her eye, while I sat stiff, squeezing my thumb inside my fists, waiting for the blow of Miss Katheryn's and Miss Renita's names. What was amazing to me was that she never mentioned them. She merely turned the tissue pages of her book as if nothing else mattered.

"Doris, now this ain't going no further than us. I found Leslie last night and some white girl I never seen before up in her room. I walked in on them. I didn't say nothing, but I told her little friend to 'git' and I went and prayed. Now this ain't going no further than us . . . and we don't even have to say anything about it anymore . . . ."

3

I am fifteen and I want to be like Miss Katheryn.
I'm fifteen and I want to be like Miss Renita.
I'm fifteen and I want to be like Miss Katheryn . . . .
Like a chant over and over because I could not stand to think about the revival.

I had told my aunt that I would go because she had sat me at the kitchen table and she and the Bible sat across from me and I didn't know what she would say when she finally did speak. She used silence like expanding gas. So I promised I'd go. But the very next instant I regretted it and in the days that followed I could only defend myself by acting 'evil' to Aunt Cynthia's every move. She ignored this. Finally I had come right down to the day and could worry about nothing else so just lay across my bed, mouthing cursewords like soft farts, and thinking about how the only thing worse than bringing home a white boy was to bring home a white girl.

I fantasized that when the starships returned they would all be driven by black women, seven feet tall, landing and reducing to rubbish all the earth's ammunition and the bishop of our church to flyshit. I imagined the look on world leaders' faces when they saw they were completely helpless and the looks on the people's faces as they watched the 5:30 news and all of the church women getting naughty winks from Amazons who walked upright. As a choice victim for the latter I concentrated on Doris, Sunday school teacher and my aunt's confidante for years, savoring her terror as she ran about searching for a man of god. I knew who would save me. I'm fifteen and I want to . . . .

And when I felt that I would explode I got up and put on War and danced. Danced like I had been when that girl first saw me and I looked so fine and pranced like I was showing off again when I saw her watching me danced like I danced with her like the whole world was watching and I was fifteen and bad and yeah! dancing with a girl danced like we were nervous danced when we got to my room and couldn't think of anything to say danced through the silence between the records as fast as hard as we could high as platforms and adidas could take us stomping down kicking around around around Aunt Cynthia's quiet voice . . . .

"Leslie. Leslie. Leslie you gonna fall out dead one of these days. Turn that thing off and come on down here and eat!"

I was about to get into a grumble about how she always ran up and told me to stop my music when I looked over at the clock and it said

11:00. But three hours of dancing would not exhaust me, only dispose
of a troublesome block of time that I did not need anyway.

Young people's night at spring revival. I sat on the back step completely surrounded by a dog and a cat who always struck up an intelligence
network whenever anybody ate something around them. Today they were
getting impatient because I paid them no mind at all while I ate, and instead tried to get lost in our yard which blossomed and smelled of dogwood at this time of year.

Young people's night at spring revival was held during spring vacation
so that us young people would surely come. I had gone every year since
my mother died, so that outside of home and school, church was the place
I knew best. Last year Dennis Sands had got religion.

It was kind of sad to look at Dennis because he had gone to Vietnam
and lost both legs. If I saw him sitting at a desk or behind something, he
looked just like he did in school when he was a senior, his face serious
and staring into the book like a dark aristocrat. But that night they lifted
him out from the pew and carried him to the mourner's bench, they sat
him before it on a cushion and began to pray. They prayed and prayed until his features began to quiver and he finally broke down. I watched him
calling out something over and over again that was lost underneath the
prayers of the congregation as he sobbed and tried to wipe at his nose, his
head bobbing up and down, his shoulders shaking. A jack-in-the-box in
funeral attire. The crowd ebbed in and out about him allowing me to see
Dennis small and apart from his desk. A strained amount of time later
they lifted him from the floor and returned him to his seat and I couldn't
see his face because his hands covered it.

We all got to our feet then, and there was clapping and tambourines and
exuberance and bright sweat all over everybody's face as we praised and
clapped and shouted.

I was jarred back from this memory by some bird's song and dog's
chilly nose against my hand. The sun had just enough of summer to feel
pleasant and I pushed the last crumb of cornbread into my mouth. The
dog and the cat, in a mild state of shock over my discourtesy, sat perfectly
still and glared at me.

At 3:30 I went for a walk. My church dress was ironed and spread
across my bed, my patent leather shoes were dusted and under a plastic
bag, and the hot comb had been brought out and placed on the dresser
next to a bottle of grease. After standing and observing all of this for a mo-

ment I had dashed past my aunt's humming and out to the shaded side-walk, barefoot for the first time this year. I think that I heard her tell me to be back by five.

My thoughts finally settled to where they had been this morning when I awoke, pondering Miss Katheryn and Miss Renita. For all of the time that I gave them I really didn't know the women at all. Aunt Cynthia answered questions concerning them with either a yes or a no or a shrug and if I persisted, which I had done only once, she looked at me sideways and said nothing. The two women never talked to me because I was only a teenager and they were in their forties, and once when I'd pulled myself up and said hello they merely replied and had walked on before I could think of what to talk about. I really had nothing to talk to them about, I thought, but one thing. So instead, I dreamed of going to LA with Miss Renita and dancing slow dances.

I walked out past the edge of Duncan Road, where the country crept in, and leaned on the worn fence of somebody's pasture. The wood was warm and smelled strong of animal sweat; I leaned my body against it and relaxed. A few insect sounds blended with the sun's heat which had grown softer, and occasionally a car passed somewhere too far away to disturb my slow dance with Miss Renita in the LA twilight.

We're out on a beach and the portable radio sets in the sand and there is no one around for miles. Miss Renita's body is tender yet very firm; she feels just like she looks in those lean, tailored suits. She holds me against her with the look I sometimes notice in her smokey grey eyes, mischievous and a bit sad. My throat is dry and I'm sweating, but not from the heated afternoon for B.B. is going through my head and "Lucille" and "rock me baby" . . . sweet and warm and rock me . . . quiet and warm as I'm held between sleep and daylight all night long baby . . . .

He is new in town and I would probably never notice him if I didn't see him so often talking to Miss Katheryn. He gets off the bus by her side and walks her halfway home, until she turns to him and after exchanging a few words they part, or he is outside the grocery store when she comes out, or he turns up to join the two of them at the café. I don't want him there any more than the two women do, for my image of them alone is complete. Still he keeps appearing, gentlemanly and aggressive and ignorant of matters. Until one evening they are at the bus stop on their way uptown and he approaches. He is slightly drunk. He stands a couple of yards off and addresses them clearly.

"Ain't you got time for no man? Hey, I'm talking to you two men. Mr. Katheryn. Hey, Mr. Renita."

I see Miss Renita holding her eyes and her body stiff and Miss Katheryn is clutching her hands in front of her until she turns fully around and gazes him directly in the face. But she doesn't say anything.

"Mr. Renita with the lipstick. Hey Mr. Katheryn with the 32 triple A. You want that delicate youngblood over there don't you." And he points directly at me. "Sweet ain't she? Mr. Renita. Hey Mr."

I grip the telephone pole supporting me tighter and tighter and don't even feel its hardness. The bus is nowhere in sight. The man goes on and on with the barest hint of a slur in his voice, talking to the women and to the crowd that is gathered quietly somewhere between shame and humor. I look out on Pay Street and it is one of those long spaces between cars that streets sometimes have, so quiet you can hear brakes screeching far out on the highway. Another to-do in the neighborhood, somebody's business out in the street. Oration time.

I want them to go home and I want them to stay and most of all I want them to say something. But I cannot move either, because he has pointed at me, however ignorantly, and because I have never before seen such absurd torture. (At school I can look at the boys and say they'll grow out of it when they point at the white dykes and say, "Sick, sick, you people are sick.")

Finally Miss Katheryn cuts away and her friend follows her, but as they head for home the man keeps pace with them and the crowd comes hesitantly along behind. Just then another man finds his way through the crowd and I recognize him as Brother Henderson, a deacon at our church. He delicately accosts the man and stands talking to him quietly for a few minutes as my two friends go further and further away. Finally the man is persuaded to go back about his own business. The crowd breaks up. I imagine every street sissy for miles around has gone into the woodwork, but I stand watching the man's back disappearing haughtily into a doorway and I conjure up tortures too heinous for words.

That evening Doris is over to supper.

"Leslie, did you see that mess down on Pay Street, what happened?"

"Nothing."

When I awoke clouds were gathering and I imagined it must be nearly five o'clock so I found the road again and trotted home. I ran into the house just as the rain fell and up to my room where I closed the door, turned on James Brown and danced. Somewhere down below I knew that my aunt was biding time with the belief that this was the last day she had to listen to my 'satan' music because I would soon be saved and too busy for things like that.

My stereo was off and the rain was gone leaving only a few droplets to fall peacefully from the eaves. I sat on my bed fully dressed but not even feeling like reaching over to switch on the light though it was darkening.

"Come look at this sunset, Leslie. It's beautiful."

"No ma'am."

"I ain't seen one like it since last summer, it's really pretty."

I did not move, only brushed my hand across my skirt hearing the whistly soft rustle of the cloth. After services tonight the skirt would hang with sweat.

"Leslie, you almost grown now, it's time to make your choice for the Lord."

"Yes ma'am."

"You know I love you and I don't want to see you lost."

"I know."

I was deep into pondering some mysteries about degrees of love when I heard Doris's voice downstairs. It was all excited and high-pitched in anticipation of the doings tonight. I knew that as soon as I walked downstairs she would start asking a myriad of questions and commenting on the girls my age whom we both knew. Actually she knew more about them than I did because she'd been one. My aunt would listen to all of this because she never carried on so with me, but she was interested. My aunt talked calmly to me, always with soft directness, so that all I had to do to sound unreasonable was raise my voice. Even after she'd seen the girl in my room she came back later and calmly, looking at me a little sideways, made me promise again to go to the altar tonight. She continued reading her Bible then and I went upstairs and danced, wondering what she was wondering.

I was filling up to exploding again so I lay back on the bed and took some deep breaths. If I could I would escape into dancing. I would turn it up as high as James could scream and go crazy like Doris said I was go mad and dance dance flinging my body slinging the shit away with my head like a crazy girl sling the shit against my walls for everybody to see all over my schoolbooks and gym shoes the songs I knew and even my Easter hat sling it girls ain't supposed to fight but girls can sure dance hit and scratch the air like sisters stepping in the aisles shadow boxing with the spirit every hit as serious as Saturday night slinging away opponents so ugly they can't be seen and they sure can't be described in the English language dance and look good dance and chunk it away feel good dance. So I got up.

I pulled off my shoes and socks and walked like a ghost down the stairs, through the hallway and straight out the front door. I walked through the darkness away from my aunt's lighted kitchen purposely blocking thoughts from my mind, listening hard to the night sounds and still humming the tune under my breath.

Mrs. Taylor, in the choir at our church, was just leaving, her husband and children already in the car. Down at the end of the street Mr. and Mrs. Henderson were warming their car engine, and the Herbert children were still playing, calling from corner to corner. Blocks away the traffic light at Pay Street blinked and carlights streamed back and forth past. Voices laughed and called in greeting and then softened to comment on the pretty night, raising again to sparkle mildly when jokes were told. Voices as familiar as the faces. I was in front of Miss Katheryn's and Miss Renita's, walking back and forth when I looked up suddenly and saw someone coming down the sidewalk. Before even recognizing her I dashed into their yard and hid behind the hedge. The woman, still in her maid's clothes, walked slowly past.

It was then that I sat down in the grass and came nearer to crying than I had in days without even thinking about it. So I tried to dream of Miss Renita and me on the beach again, but the scene kept running out and so I just lay back and let my mind cut up. For awhile it assembled all sorts of horrors at my running away tonight. From Aunt Cynthia's cold, still anger to a real god and real hell fire. What if I were wrong? What if I did have more than my aunt to fear? I turned my head slowly away from the sky to look at their house. Dark brick with an upstairs, not different from most others on the street. Their yard was small and hedged and in late summer would have primrose and Black Vesuvius in geometric designs. Even Doris said how pretty their yard was. The windows up front were darkened, but there was a small light somewhere near the back. I did not feel like moving because I knew that I would never go to their door now, especially barefoot, wearing a church dress. There was something else too: I felt tired like I had been dancing tied to the earth. Aunt Cynthia would be searching the house now and Doris would be carrying on like Watson. I hugged my arms about me and lay very still as if I were hiding under the bed. The spring night voices grew fewer, the children were called in, no more cars pulled out from driveways. When I sat up my dress stuck to my legs and chilled me, but I stood and after a few minutes followed the hedge around to the side of their house. I moved cautiously up to the window and looked in. They were not there.

I was relieved and took my time looking about. I had never seen the inside of their house before. The room which faced me resembled our frontroom, only here the furniture matched. It occurred to me that I had heard once that they were well off because Miss Renita's father was a doctor and Miss Katheryn had had a good civil service job for years.

The carpet and couch were a dark red and two large chairs were draped with a patterned fabric of the same color; there were cream-colored curtains and a rocking chair of some beautiful reddish-brown wood and there were statues and vases and things like I'd seen in an antique shop uptown. The room seemed to be capable of quietly absorbing anything. The quietness made things hesitate, the redness warmly pulled them in, whatever they were. I studied the room, touching piece after piece with my gaze. The room floated into and out of some dreamscape. I appeared miraculously in one spot and then another and the two women were there with me and then they were not; we said things to each other and laughed and then listened for the echoes in the silence. The room was, quite simply, Miss Renita and Miss Katheryn. It was clean and pretty.

"Girl, you had me almost crazy. Do you realize you were gone all night long? Look at that dress and what happened to your shoes? Leslie . . . Lord I hope nobody saw you looking like that."

"Everybody saw me. They looked at me like I was an Amazon in a tailored suit."

"A what!"

Finally I moved away, back into the hedge below some dogwood that leaned over. I pretended that I was a Buddhist and concentrated on the smell and when that didn't work anymore I just sat snuggling as close as I dared get to the windowlight flooding a square of dew beside me. I did not think about the past or tomorrow or the present moment across town. Time had stopped for a minute and I felt fine. Everybody saw me . . . and I felt fine.

Judy Grahn

Boys at the Rodeo

A lot of people have spent time on some women's farm this summer of 1972 and one day six of us decide to go to the rodeo. We are all mature and mostly in our early thirties. We wear levis and shirts and short hair. Susan has shaved her head.

The man at the gate, who looks like a cousin of the sheriff, is certain we are trying to get in for free. It must have been something in the way we are walking. He stares into Susan's face. "I know you're at least four-teen," he says. He slaps her shoulder, in that comradely way men have with each other. That's when we know he thinks we are boys.

"You're over thirteen," he says to Wendy.

"You're over thirteen," he says to me. He examines each of us closely, and sees only that we have been outdoors, are muscled, and look him directly in the eye. Since we are too short to be men, we must be boys. All the other women at the rodeo are called girls.

We decide to play it straight, so to speak. We make up boys' names for each other. Since Wendy has missed the episode with Susan at the gate, I slap her on the shoulder to demonstrate. "This is what he did." Slam. She never missed a step. It didn't feel bad to me at all. We laugh uneasily. We have achieved the status of fourteen year old boys, what a disguise for travelling through the world. I split into two pieces for the rest of the evening, and have never decided if it is worse to be thirty one years old and called a boy or to be thirty one years old and called a girl.

Irregardless, we are starved so we decide to eat, and here we have the status of boys for real. It seems to us that all the men and all the women attached to the men and most of the children are eating steak dinner plates; and we are the only women not attached to men. We eat hot dogs, which cost one tenth as much. A man who has taken a woman to the rodeo on this particular day has to have at least $12.00 to spend. So he has charge of all of her money and some of our money too, for we average $3.00 apiece and have taken each other to the rodeo.

Hot dogs in hand we escort ourselves to the wooden stands, and first is the standing up ceremony. We are pledging allegiance for the way of life—

11

the competition, the supposed masculinity and pretty girls. I stand up, cursing, pretending I'm in some other country. One which has not been rediscovered. The loudspeaker plays Anchors Aweigh, that's what I like about rodeos, always something unexpected. At the last one I attended in another state the men on horses threw candy and nuts to the kids, chipping their teeth and breaking their noses. Who is it, I wonder, that has put these guys in charge. Even quiet mothers raged over that episode.

Now it is time for the rodeo queen contest, and a display of four very young women on horses. They are judged for queen 30% on their horse-*man*ship and 70% on the number of queen tickets which people bought on their behalf to 'elect' them. Talk about stuffed ballot boxes. I notice the winner as usual is the one on the registered thoroughbred whose daddy owns tracts and tracts of something—lumber, minerals, animals. His family name is all over the county.

The last loser sits well on a scrubby little pony and lives with her aunt and uncle. I pick her for the dyke even though it is speculation without clues. I can't help it, it's a pleasant habit. I wish I could give her a ribbon. Not for being a dyke, but for sitting on her horse well. For believing there ever was a contest, for not being the daughter of anyone who owns thousands of acres of anything.

Now the loudspeaker announces the girls' barrel races, which is the only grown women's event. It goes first because it is not really a part of the rodeo, but more like a mildly athletic variation of a parade by women to introduce the real thing. Like us boys in the stand, the girls are simply bearing witness to someone else's act.

The voice is booming that barrel racing is a new, modern event, that these young women are the wives and daughters of cowboys, and barrel racing is a way for them to participate in their own right. How generous of these northern cowboys to have resurrected barrel racing for women and to have forgotten the hard roping and riding which women always used to do in rodeos when I was younger. Even though I was a town child, I heard thrilling rumors of the all-women's rodeo in Texas, including that the finest brahma bull rider in all of Texas was a forty year old woman who weighed a hundred pounds.

Indeed, my first lover's first lover was a big heavy woman who was normally slow as a cold python, but she was just hell when she got up on a horse. She could rope and tie a calf faster than any cowboy within 500 miles of Sweetwater, Texas. That's what the West Texas dykes said, and they never lied about anything as important to them as calf roping, or the differences between women and men. And what about that news story I had heard recently on the radio, about a bull rider who was eight months pregnant? The newsman just had apoplectic fits over her, but not me, I was proud of her. She makes me think of all of us who have had our insides so overly protected from jarring we cannot possibly get through childbirth without an anesthetic.

While I have been grumbling these thoughts to myself, three barrels have been set up in a big triangle on the field, and the women one by one have raced their horses around each one and back to start. The trick is to turn your horse as sharply as possible without overthrowing the barrel.

After this moderate display, the main bulk of the rodeo begins, with calf roping, bronco riding, bull riding. It's a very male show during which the men demonstrate their various abilities at immobilizing, cornering, maneuvering and conquering cattle of every age.

A rodeo is an interminable number of roped and tied calves, ridden and unridden broncos. The repetition is broken by a few antics from the agile, necessary clown. His long legs nearly envelope the little jackass he is riding for the satire of it.

After a number of hours they produce an event I have never seen before—goat tying. This is for the girls eleven and twelve. They use one goat for fourteen participants. The goat is supposed to be held in place on a rope by a large man on horseback. Each girl rushes out in a long run half way across the field, grabs the animal, knocks it down, ties its legs together. Sometimes the man lets his horse drift so the goat pulls six or eight feet away from her, something no one would allow to happen in a male event. Many of the girls take over a full minute just to do their tying, and the fact that only one goat has been used makes everybody say, "poor goat, poor goat," and start laughing. This has become the real comedy event of the evening, and the purpose clearly is to show how badly girls do in the rodeo.

Only one has broken through this purpose to the other side. One small girl is not disheartened by the years of bad training, the ridiculous cross-field run, the laughing superior man on his horse, *or* the shape-shifting goat. She downs it in a beautiful flying tackle. This makes me whisper, as usual, "that's the dyke," but for the rest of it we watch the girls look ludicrous, awkward, outclassed and totally dominated by the large handsome man on horse. In the stands we six boys drink beer in disgust, groan and hug our breasts, hold our heads and twist our faces at each other in embarrassment.

As the calf roping starts up again, we decide to use our disguises to walk around the grounds. Making our way around to the cowboy side of the arena, we pass the intricate mazes of rail where the stock is stored, to the chutes where they are loading the bull riders onto the bulls.

I wish to report that although we pass by dozens of men, and although we have pressed against wild horses and have climbed on rails overlooking thousands of pounds of angry animalflesh, though we touch ropes and halters, we are never once warned away, never told that this is not the proper place for us, that we had better get back for our own good, are not

safe, etc., none of the dozens of warnings and threats we would have gotten if we had been recognized as thirty one year old girls instead of fourteen year old boys. It is a most interesting way to wander around the
world for the day.

We examine everything closely. The brahma bulls are in the chutes,
ready to be released into the ring. They are bulky, kindly looking creatures
with rolling eyes; they resemble overgrown pigs. One of us whispers, "Aren't
those the same kind of cattle that walk around all over the streets in India
and never hurt anybody?"

Here in the chutes made exactly their size, they are converted into wild
antagonistic beasts by means of a nasty belt around their loins, squeezed
tight to mash their tender testicles just before they are released into the
ring. This torture is supplemented by a jolt of electricity from an electric
cattle prod to make sure they come out bucking. So much for the rodeo as
a great drama between man and nature.

A pale, nervous cowboy sits on the bull's back with one hand in a glove
hooked under a strap around the bull's mid-section. He gains points by
using his spurs during the ride. He has to remain on top until the timing
buzzer buzzes a few seconds after he and the bull plunge out of the gate. I
had always considered it the most exciting event.

Around the fence sit many eager young men watching, helping, and getting in the way. We are easily accepted among them. How depressing this
can be.

Out in the arena a dismounted cowboy reaches over and slaps his horse
fiercely on the mouth because it has turned its head the wrong way.

I squat down peering through the rails where I see the neat, tight-fitting
pants of two young men standing provocatively chest to chest.

"Don't you think Henry's a queer," one says with contempt.

"Hell, I *know* he's a queer," the other says. They hold an informal spitting contest for the punctuation. Meantime their eyes have brightened and
their fronts are moving toward each other in their clean, smooth shirts. I
realize they are flirting with each other, using Henry to bring up the dangerous subject of themselves. I am remembering all the gay cowboys I ever
knew. This is one of the things I like about cowboys. They don't wear
those beautiful pearl button shirts and tight levis for nothing.

As the events inside the arena subside, we walk down to a roped off
pavilion where there is a dance. The band consists of one portly, bouncing
enthusiastic man of middle age who is singing with great spirit into the
microphone. The rest of the band are three grim, lean young men over
fourteen. The drummer drums angrily, while jerking his head behind himself as though searching the air for someone who is already two hours late
and had seriously promised to take him away from here. The two guitar
players are sleepwalking from the feet up with their eyes so glassy you
could read by them.

A redhaired man appears, surrounded by redhaired children who ask, "Are you drunk, Daddy?"

"No, I am not drunk," Daddy says.

"Can we have some money?"

"No," Daddy says, "I am not drunk enough to give you any money."

During a break in the music the redhaired man asks the bandleader where he got his band.

"Where did I get this band?" the bandleader puffs up, "I raised this band myself. These are all my sons—I raised this band myself." The redhaired man is so very impressed he is nearly bowing and kissing the hand of the bandleader, as they repeat this conversation two or three times. "This is *my* band," the bandleader says, and the two guitar players exchange grim and glassy looks.

Next the bandleader has announced "Okie From Muskogee," a song intended to portray the white country morality of cowboys. The crowd does not respond but he sings enthusiastically anyway. Two of his more alert sons drag themselves to the microphone to wail that they don't smoke marijuana in Muskogee—as those hippies down in San Francisco do, and they certainly don't. From the look of it they shoot hard drugs and pop pills.

In the middle of the song a very drunk thirteen year old boy has staggered up to Wendy, pounding her on the shoulder and exclaiming, "Can you dig it, brother?" Later she tells me she has never been called brother before, and she likes it. Her first real identification as one of the brothers, in the brotherhood of man.

We boys begin to walk back to our truck, past a cowboy vomiting on his own pretty boots, past another lying completely under a car. Near our truck, a young man has calf-roped a young woman. She shrieks for him to stop, hopping weakly along behind him. This is the first bid for public attention I have seen from any woman here since the barrel race. I understand that this little scene is a re-enactment of the true meaning of the rodeo, and of the conquest of the west. And oh how much I do not want to be her; I do not want to be the conquest of the west.

I am remembering how the clown always seems to be tall and riding on an ass, that must be a way of poking fun at the small and usually dark people who tried to raise sheep or goats or were sod farmers and rode burros instead of tall handsome blond horses, and who were driven under by the beef raisers. And so today we went to a display of cattle handling instead of a sheep shearing or a goat milking contest—or to go into even older ghost territory, a corn dance, or acorn gathering . . . .

As we reach the truck, the tall man passes with the rodeo queen, who must surely be his niece, or something. All this non-contest, if it is for anyone, must certainly be for him. As a boy, I look at him. He is his own spitting image, of what is manly and white and masterly, so tall in his high heels, so *well horsed.* His manner portrays his theory of life as the survival of the fittest against wild beasts, and all the mythical rest of us who are too female or dark, not straight, or much too native to the earth to now be trusted as more than witnesses, flags, cheerleaders and unwilling stock.

As he passes, we step out of the way and I am glad we are in our disguise. I hate to step out of his way as a full grown woman, one who hasn't enough class status to warrant his thinly polite chivalry. He has knocked me off the sidewalk of too many towns, too often.

Yet somewhere in me I know I have always wanted to be manly, what I mean is having that expression of courage, control, coordination, ability I associate with men. To *provide.*

But here I am in this truck, not a man at all, a fourteen year old boy only. Tomorrow is my thirty second birthday. We six snuggle together in the bed of this rickety truck which is our world for the time being. We are headed back to the bold and shaky adventures of our all-women's farm, our all-women's households and companies, our expanding minds, ambitions and bodies, we who are neither male nor female at this moment in the pageant world, who are not the rancher's wife, mother earth, Virgin Mary or the rodeo queen—we who are really the one who took her self seriously, who once took an all out dive at the goat believing that the odds were square and that she was truly in the contest.

And now that we know it is not a contest, just a play—we have run off with the goat ourselves to try another way of life.

Because I certainly do not want to be a thirty two year old girl, or calf either, and I certainly also do always remember Gertrude Stein's beautiful dykely voice saying, what is the use of being a boy if you grow up to be a man.

Jo Carrillo

María Littlebear

It was either 1939 or 40. It was the year that God's image appeared on the chapel wall in Hollman. I remember because we all climbed into the back of Tio Cholo's truck on the night of the full moon—you could only see God when the moon was full—and we drove the 30 miles north from Mora. The road was bumpy, the air was cold, we forgot to bring our pillows, well I guess we didn't have any real pillows, but none of this mattered. We could see for miles and miles. The moonlight just hugged everything: trees, bushes, Pike's Peak, and I suppose I felt like it was hugging us too.

It must have been 1940; *that's* the year that we went to see God. People came from Santa Fe, Socorro, Belen, Raton, Las Vegas, Gallinas . . . and just about everywhere else even though it took a long time to travel in those days. It was worth it to know if you were damned or saved and believe me, you knew. Everyone who saw God or the Virgin was safe, if you saw a saint you still had a chance, but if you saw the Devil you were damned. Then you'd be better off giving up everything you owned to save your soul.

The gringos thought we were all nuts. They wrote an article about us in the Journal. Something like "there were Mexicans standing around just staring at the Hollman wall. They claim to see God but they say that this is only possible when the moon is full." It was in the back by the obituaries. Can you *believe* they put God by the dead people?

Oh, but that wasn't even the worst of it. They sent some painters down— you know, the kind that paint the outside of their houses—to cover God's face right up. Then when the next full moon rolled around, they payed José Gallegos to go up to Hollman and look for God. Of course, poor José saw the Devil for trying to sell out his people and he went running into the night, never to be seen again. To this day I wonder if his name was even José. They call everyone José or María, which is my name anyway so they wouldn't be too wrong. At least with me.

That was the year that Elisa Antonia Alvarado was born in Mountain View, New Mexico. She was the oldest out of twelve and the only girl too. Can you imagine that? Well, all she could remember was feeding and

17

changing, yelling and crying, you know, all those things that mothers usually do alone. She would try to remember dolls or some other kinds of
toys too, so it wasn't like she was faking it. Right up until a few years ago,
she'd sit right there in that chair that you're in now, she'd wrinkle her face
up—sort of like a baby will do one second before she starts wailing—and
you could tell that she was really trying hard. Still, no toys. The fact was
that she had too many responsibilities to be wasting time like a normal kid
would do if its papa was rich.

Poor Elisa, when she was only five she had to help her mama have Pablito—
he was her third brother—right there in their house. You see, Elisa's papa Esteban drinks. He is a real cabrón. He'll probably go to hell because Elisa told
me that once when she was sitting there trying to think of a doll she might
have owned, she remembered the night they went up to Hollman, you know,
to see God? Well, while he was sitting there looking at the wall, with the
help of Tequila, he turned all green and sick. Not like when you're in Sears
or Penney's and those funny lights shine on you, but like when you eat
too many capolín.

Elisa just laughed and laughed. She could have jumped all the way up
Pike's Peak for joy. She used to *pray* that he'd leave or die or something
like that, but she never thought, *never*, that she'd be lucky enough to
know beforehand that he'd be stuck with his favorite compadre the Devil.

Where was I? Oh, never mind, I know. We're with Elisa when she helped
her mama give birth. Bloody stuff kept dripping down her mama's legs
while she was helping her get to the back room so that the boys wouldn't
see. Then pop! Little Pablito slid right down the tube. Elisa had never seen
a thing like that before. She used to laugh when I brought it up because
she told her mama when they were having Pablito, that he looked like a
long, hard caca except wrinkled like his grandpa.

Esteban, if you remember the cabrón, wasn't even home. He was out
drinking or with Mande or maybe playing cards. There was never no telling. He didn't come back for days. After all the hard *work* was finished.
That's when my Elisa decided to love women, not men. It's not that she
didn't like them, it's just that seeing her mama's body without clothes
and all really stuck in her mind.

Her grandma could have died the day she found out about Elisa's . . .
feelings, you know, about women and all? She was one for stories. Give
one word, just one, and she'd race off weaving this story that just covered
everything that ever happened to the Alvarado Family. And, that was no
easy job. I remember from the family reunion that there must have been

cabrón (Spanish)—old goat.
capolín—choke cherry.
compadre—relative by marriage or ritual, not by blood.
caca—shit.

at least a thousand, and that's not counting all of the cousins that moved to California! So anyway, she'd tell stories of the gardens that everyone in their family had starting from 1850. And she'd tell stories about how everyone honored their parents and their grandparents and their great grandparents and she would go like that forever. We never tried to stop her. It was like watching someone weave a blanket right there under your very nose.

The day she found out about Elisa and me, she cried and cried. Her nose got puffy and purple just like those plums in the orchard when they get too ripe. It's funny because cheeks are usually the ones that swell up like that. After at least a week of crying and a month of penance she calmed down. Like nothing ever happened. Ay! She just came into our kitchen—we were living together then—plopped down a bag of flour and started to make tortillas. All she ever said about our being together from then until the morning she died was "you think you're so great? You're not the first two people in the world to fall in love."

We were in love too. From the very first day we met. It was at Angel View—the truckstop down by I-40, right before you turn off to go to Albuquerque. Have you ever been inside that place? They have these six little tables covered with red and white checkered tablecloths. They're so funny!

Inez Trujillo, she owns Angel View—well I guess the bank owns it, Inez just pretends she does—she used to love to go through everyone's garden and steal a geranium here, a lilac there, maybe some of those little pink flowers, see them? They're right out there by the porch. She'd do this for the truckstop. We finally got it through her head, Elisa and me, that those truck drivers hate anything pretty so she'd be better off leaving our flowers alone. For los prietitos, that's what we told her.

That did it! Inez has five kids and she cried a little bit. "How can I take my babies' flowers away?" And we kept saying *"Yeah,* that's how they learn about our land, by the plants and besides what would God think if he knew you were giving our flowers to people who didn't even give a damn?"

Elisa was the waitress and Inez used to tell her to act real shy like, when she was working. There were lots of these big guys—truckdrivers. They'd come in from all over. Sometimes loud, sometimes quiet but always mean. They thought they owned the place and everything in it. You couldn't even breathe on them. You were just supposed to treat them like big babies, which is just lots of shit.

One day, the day that I first ate there, this one guy was yelling at Elisa calling her "senorida" and saying things like he'd give her ten big ones if she'd go with him. Since she was the only waitress, no one else could help her. Inez was in the back cooking. So she kept going over to see what he

los prietitos—the little brown/dark ones.

wanted and of course, he didn't want anything but trouble. About the fifth time she went over there, he slapped her real hard, right on the ass. I could even hear the smack over the juke box and I could tell that Elisa's ass hurt. Elisa was just standing there, her face was all twisted and she looked like she was going to start crying any minute. I just couldn't take it. Not because I already loved her, I did, but that wasn't the reason. It was because I hate to see a woman treated like meat. Some women get chewed on a million times and then all they are is all over the place. I just can't stand it.

Me being who I am, I got up, stuck my thumbs in my pockets and walked over there real cool like. I was shaking, but I would never have let *him* know it. And I told that guy in *Spanish* that he was a cabrón who didn't even know how to shit much less treat a woman. He died! Mostly because Elisa was standing behind me sort of laughing and he didn't know what I was saying. When he left, there was a fifty cent piece—that was a big tip back then—still, he should have left the ten big ones he was bragging about. You know, nowadays, since I'm a lot stronger and smarter, I think that I'd just go up to him and punch him right in the nose.

That was the day that I got back from Albuquerque and I was *full* of stories. I thought that I was so cool—you know like well traveled? I had stories about the airport, the planes, how they were full of rich people who were visiting for the first time and were afraid to drink the water—things that I had seen. They'd get off the planes and the first question they asked was "where are the Indians? Are they going to hurt us?" I'd shrug my shoulders and say I didn't know, a lot of gringuitos just disappeared.

They didn't know whether to believe me. After all, I was just there to help them with their suitcases. Have you ever noticed that the more money people have the smaller the tip? Que tites. Anyway, those people would sort of grab their little fat kids. They still weren't sure if I was telling the truth or not and probably their friends had warned them right before they left wherever it was they were coming from, that Mexicans were just a bunch of liars. Besides, it should have been true—not the part about Mexicans being liars, I mean the part about the toys. They were worth more than the kids! Dolls with lace dresses, big stuffed animals, airplanes, cars, boats . . . toys that would have kept any of us eating for weeks.

Elisa loved my stories. They reminded her of her abuelita. I'd tell her how soon it would get better for us if we just stuck together and how maybe we'd be able to build a nice house down by the river, and then how everyday after a great big dinner, we'd have a nice coffee from say, down

gringuitos—little white ones.
que tites—how selfish.
abuelita—term of endearment for grandmother.

south somewhere. But *nooo*. We were supposed to sit around like dogs waiting for the gringos to decide if we were human or not. They just weren't sure if they even wanted us to live on God's earth with them. No matter. We had our own ideas. We shared our land and look where it got us. I used to tell Elisa "never again. If we had it to do all over, we'd just tell them *no way*. Go find your own land."

They would say that they were bringing jobs and lots of money and how *this* was the U. S. I remember this one lady from the job office who told me that there was money for the taking if "you people would just learn not to be lazy." Well, she didn't bother me. I just said "Lady? If there is so much money for the taking, then why the hell do you sit behind that funny window all day long?" And we never believed any of those lies about us being lazy. Never!

You know, Elisa and me finally did build a house. Not as close to the river as we would have liked but a house all the same. This one right here. We shelled the logs, we found the stones, we made the adobe, we layed the concrete . . . we did everything.

I have some pictures of that right here. Took them myself with a camera I found sitting on a chair at the airport. Ah, here they are, shots of Elisa. She took some of me too, but you don't want to see them. I came out with my eyes closed or my mouth open in every single one. Anyway, this camera is the best thing I ever found since now that Elisa's dead I can still see her just like she was.

This one is of Elisa mixing mud and straw—it's my favorite. You can see her hair, black and shiny like a crow's feather. Her skin sort of looking shiny too from sweating out in the sun. In this picture, you can even see her left chiche. That was the smallest of the two.

And this one here . . . by the time I took it, Elisa had muscles just like me. You could see them move whenever she did. And she'd be singing church songs while she worked. Christmas hymnals, those were her favorite. Such a strong woman, my Elisa, small and built like a cat. She wouldn't let no one walk over her in the end.

This one here is after we finished for the day. Out sitting in the evening breeze, Elisa cutting her brother Lito's hair—even though she'd never done it before—Lito playing chords on the guitar we got in Juarez, and me making up words. I sang about Elisa mostly, about her eyes, her strong muscles, her laugh, her dimples, how she used to walk through the fields looking for flowers and herbs . . . all about her. After a few cold beers, we'd all join in the chorus. Elisa always cried. She was really touched by my singing. That's not in the picture.

Here's one of Elisa peeling potatoes on Christmas day. This one makes me cry the most because the Christmas Eve before Elisa died she had to

chiche—breast.

work graveyard at Angel View. I didn't want her to go—after all, we were supposed to have gone to Las Posadas as the shepherds—still, I walked her to the bridge by the truckstop. All the way there, I kept saying little things to bug her like, oh . . . "I guess you'd rather be a waitress than a stinky shepherd like me."

But that didn't work. She just said "María, when you've got to work, that's all there is to it and besides, who's going to buy that hoe you want for Christmas if I don't work?" After that I sort of admitted she was only doing what she had to do so I kissed her goodbye and I walked home alone.

When I got home I went to the kitchen to finish sewing my shepherd costume and I noticed a little package on the kitchen table. She had left me a present. It was small and instead of a bow there were dried flowers taped on to the paper. Those were flowers that we gathered in the fields. Just like spring. Well, I was real careful not to break anything just in case, and I took the flowers and all into the other room.

You know what she left me? A gold ring! And inside, Rex—the jeweler— had engraved "a María Osita, mi amiga más preciosa. Elisa." I knew it was Rex because he's the only one who does those fancy letters. It hurts to talk about it since she must have saved every extra penny for months just to pay for the letters alone. And maybe too, because Elisa died six months later—three months ago this Saturday. She didn't die of anything special; I guess she decided just like that, to go up and visit her mama.

At her funeral, everyone was crying except me. They brought lots of food and flowers, the kind she hated, the kind she always said looked too sad—like little kids who can't even run around without getting in trouble. Oh, and I didn't get to ride in the limo with the "immediate family" either— that's what Gonzalez, the funeral man called her brothers and her papa. Didn't bother me none. I was the one who loved her and I was proud of it.

Just before she got buried, after the last rosary, I put a little box I made out of velvet into her hands. Those dried wild flowers that she gave me were in there. It made her happy. I'm sure. I whispered to her "don't you worry Elisa, we'll be together soon because we're family, how else can it be? Until then, you keep these flowers, I'll bring some more up later. And don't let your mama scare you. God might know what we are, but then, we know what he is too."

Los Posadas—a pastoral reenactment of the birth of Jesus, that takes about eight
    weeks, beginning at the time when Mary and Joseph first entered Bethlehem
    and ending in a celebration at the time when Jesus was born.
a María Osita, mi amiga más preciosa—to María Littlebear, my most precious friend.

Jane Rule

In the Attic
of the House

Alice hadn't joined women's liberation; she had only rented it the main floor of her house. It might turn out to be the alternative to burning it down, which she had threatened to do sober and had nearly accomplished when she was drunk. Since none of the four young women who moved in either drank or smoked, they might be able to save Alice from inadvertence. That was all. And the money helped. Alice had not imagined she would ever be sixty-five to have to worry about it. Now the years left were the fingers of one hand. She was going to turn out to be one of the ones too mean to die.

"I'm a lifer," she said at the beer parlor and laughed until her lungs came to a boil.

"Don't sound like it, Al. If the weed don't get you, the traffic will."

"Naw," Alice said. "Only danger on the road is the amateur drunks, who can't drive when they're sober either. I always get home."

The rules were simple: stay in your own lane, and don't honk your horn. Alice was so small she peered through rather than over her steering wheel and might more easily have been arrested as a runaway kid than a drunk. But she'd never caught hell from anyone but Harriet, rest her goddamned soul. Until these females moved in.

"Come have a cup of tea," one of them would say just as Alice was making a sedate attempt at the stairs.

There she'd have to sit in what had been her own kitchen for thirty years, a guest drinking Red Zinger or some other Koolade-colored wash they called tea, squinting at them through the steam: Bett, the giant postie; Trudy and Jill, who worked at the women's garage without a grease mark under their fingernails; Angel, who was unemployed; young, all of them, incredibly young, killing her with kindness. Sober, she could refuse them with, "I never learned to eat a whole beet with chopsticks," or "Brown rice sticks to my dentures," but once she was drunk and dignified, she was caught having to prove that point and failing as she'd always failed, except that now there was the new test of the stairs.

23

"Do you mind having to live in the attic of your own house?" Bett asked as she offered Alice a steadying hand.

"Mind? Living on top of it is a lot better than living in the middle of it ever was. I don't think I was meant for the ground floor," Alice confessed, her spinning head pressed against Bett's enormous bosom until they reached the top stair.

"You all right now? Can you manage?"

"Sleep like a baby. Always have."

Alice began to have infantile dreams about those breasts, though awake and sober she found them comically alarming rather than erotic, eye-level as she was with them. Alice liked Bett and was glad, though she didn't hold with women taking over everything, that Bett delivered the mail. Bett had not only yellow hair but yellow eyebrows, a sunny sort of face for carrying the burden of bills as well as the promise of love letters and surprise legacies. And everyone was able to see at a glance that this postie was a woman.

Angel was probably Bett's girl, though Alice couldn't tell for sure. Sometimes Alice imagined four-way orgies going on downstairs, but it could as easily be a karate lesson. It was obvious that none of them was interested in men.

"We don't hate men because we don't need them," said Trudy, the one who memorized slogans; who, once she could fix a car, couldn't imagine what other use men were ever put to.

Hating men, for this crew, would be like hating astronauts, too remote an exercise to be meaningful. Alice knew lots of men, was more comfortable with them than with women at the beer parlor or in the employees' lounge at Safeway, where she worked. As a group, she needed them far more than she needed women. Working among them and drinking among them had always been her self-esteem.

"Aren't you ashamed to sit home on a Saturday night?" Alice asked.

"We don't drink; the bars aren't our scene."

Alice certainly couldn't imagine them at her beer parlor, looking young enough to be jail bait and dressed so badly men who had taken the time to shave and change into good clothes couldn't help taking offense. Even Alice, with her close-cropped hair, put on a nice blouse over good slacks, even sometimes a skirt, and she didn't forget her lipstick.

"Do you buy all your clothes at the Sally Ann?" Alice asked, studying one remarkably holey and faded tank top Jill was wearing.

"Somebody gave me this one," Jill admitted irritably. "Why should you mind? You're the only one of any sex who has a haircut like that."

"Don't you like it?" Alice asked.

"It's sort of male chauvinist," Trudy put in, "as if you wanted to come on very heavy."

"I don't come on," Alice said. "I broke the switch."

At the beer parlor someone might have said, "Then I'll screw you in," or something else amiable, but this Trudy was full of sudden sympathy and instruction about coming to terms with your own body, as if she were about to invent sex, not for Alice, just for instance.

"Do you know how old I am?"

"We're not ageists here," Jill said.

"I'm old enough to be your grandmother."

"Not if you're still working at Safeway, you're not. My grandma's got the old-age pension."

"When I was young, we had some respect for old people."

"Everybody should respect everybody," Angel said.

"I have every respect for you," Alice said with dignity. "Even about sex."

"You know what you should do, Alice?" Angel asked. "It's not too late . . . is come out."

"Come out?" Alice demanded. "Of where? This is my house after all. You're just renting the main floor. Come out? To whom? Everyone I know is dead!"

Harriet, rest her goddamned soul. Alice mostly pretended that she never spoke Harriet's name. In fact, she almost always waited to do it until she had drunk that amount which would let her forget what she had said so that she could say it over and over again. "Killed herself in my bathtub. Is that any way to win an argument? Is it?"

"What argument?" Trudy would ask.

"This bathtub?" Jill tried to confirm.

"How?" Angel wanted to know.

Later, on her unsteady way upstairs, Alice would resent most Bett's asking, "Were you in love with Harriet?"

"In love?" Alice demanded. "Christ! I lived with her for thirty years."

Never in those thirty years had Alice ever spoken as openly to Harriet as she was expected to speak with these females. Never in the last twenty years had Alice and Harriet so much as touched, though they slept in the same bed. At first Alice had come home drunk and pleading. Then she came home drunk and mean, sometimes threatening rape, sometimes in a jeering moral rage.

"What have you got to be guilty about? You never so much as soil your hand. I'm the one that should be crawling off to church, for Christ's sake!"

Sometimes that kind of abuse would weaken Harriet's resolve and she would submit, whimpering like a child anticipating a beating, weeping like a lost soul when it was over.

Finally Alice simply came home drunk and slept in a drunken stupor. She learned from the beer parlor how many men did the same thing.

"Scruples," one man explained. "They've got scruples."

"Scruples, shit! On Friday night I go home with the dollars and say, 'You want this? You put out for it.' "

"So what are you doing down here? It's Friday, isn't it?"

"Yeh, well, we split . . ."

Harriet had her own money. She was a legal secretary. Alice remembered the first time she ever saw Harriet in the beer parlor wearing a prim gray suit, looking obviously out of place. Some cousin had brought her and left her for unrelated pleasures. After they'd talked a while, Alice suggested a walk along the beach. It was summer; there was still light in the sky.

Years later, Harriet would say, "You took advantage. I'd been jilted."

Sometimes, when Alice was very drunk, she could remember how appealing the young Harriet had been, how willingly she had been coaxed from kisses to petting of her shapely little breasts, protesting with no more than, "You're as bad as a boy, Al, you really are." "Do you like it?" "Well, I'm not supposed to say so, am I?" Alice also remembered the indrawn breath of surprise when she first laid her finger on that wet pulse, the moment of wonder and triumph before the first crying, "Oh, it must be terrible what we're doing! We're going to burn in hell!"

Harriet could frighten Alice then with her guilt and terror. Once Alice promised that they'd never again, as Harriet called it, "go all the way," if they could still kiss, touch. Guiltily, oh so guiltily, weeks later, when Alice thought Harriet had gone to sleep, very gently she pressed open Harriet's thighs and touched that forbidden center. Harriet sighed in sleeping pleasure. Three or four times a week for several years Alice waited for the breathing signal that meant Harriet was no longer officially aware of what was happening. Alice could mount her, suck at her breasts, stroke and enter her, bring her to wet coming, and hold her until she breathed in natural sleeping. Then Alice would go to the bathroom and masturbate to the simple fantasy of Harriet making love to her.

It wasn't Harriet who finally quit on it. It was Alice, shaking her and shouting, "You goddamned hypocrite! You think as long as you take pleasure and never give it, you'll escape. But you won't. You'll be in hell long before I will, you goddamned *woman*!"

"We're looking for role models," Angel said. "Anybody who lived with anybody for thirty years . . ."

"I don't know what you're talking about," Alice said soberly on her way to work, but late that night she was willing enough. "Thirty years is longer than reality, you know that? A lifetime guarantee on a watch is only twenty. Nothing should last longer than that. Harriet should have killed herself ten years earlier, rest her goddamned soul. I always told her she'd get to hell long before I did."

"What was Harriet like?" Bett asked on the way upstairs.

"Like? I don't know. I thought she was pretty. She never thought so."

"It must be lonely for you now."

"I've never had so much company in all my damned life."

To be alone in the attic was a luxury Alice could hardly believe. It had been her resigned expectation that Harriet, whose soul had obviously not been at rest, would move up the stairs with her. She had not. If she haunted the tenants as she had haunted Alice, they didn't say so. The first time Trudy and Jill took a bath together probably exorcised the ghost from that room, and Harriet obviously wouldn't have any more taste for the vegetarian fare in the dining room than Alice did. As for what probably went on in the various beds, one night of that could finally have sent Harriet to hell where she belonged.

Alice understood, as she never had before, why suicide was an unforgivable sin. Harriet was simply out of the range of forgiveness, as she hadn't been for all her other sins from hoarding garbage to having what she called a platonic relationship with that little tart of a switchboard operator in her office.

"If you knew anything about Plato . . . ," Alice had bellowed, knowing only that.

Killing herself was the ultimate conversation stopper, the final saying, "No backs."

"The trouble with ghosts," Alice confided to Bett, "is that they're only good for replays. You can't break any new ground."

Bett leaned down and kissed Alice good night.

"Better watch out for me," Alice said, but only after Bett had gone downstairs. "I'm a holy terror."

That night Harriet came to her in a dream, not blood-filled as all the others had been but full of light. "I can still forgive you," she said.

"For what?" Alice cried, waking. "What did I ever do but love you, tell me that!"

That was the kind of talk she heard at the beer parlor from her male companions, all of whom had wives and girl friends who spent their time inventing sins and then forgiving them.

"My wife is so good at forgiving, she's even forgiven me for not being the Shah of Iran, how do you like that?"

"I like it. It has dignity. My old lady forgives my beard for growing in the middle of the night."

They had also all lived for years with threats of suicide.

"She's going to kill herself if I don't eat her apricot sponge, if I don't cut the lawn, if I don't kiss her mother's ass. I tell her it's okay with me as long as she figures out a cheap way of doing it."

Alice was never drunk enough or off her guard enough until she got home to say, "Harriet did. She killed herself in my bathtub." Nobody at the beer parlor or at work knew that Harriet was dead.

"I didn't ever tell them she was alive," she said to Bett. "So what's the point of saying she's dead?"

"Why do you drink with those people?" Bett asked. "They can't be your real friends."

"How can you say a thing like that?"

"They don't know who you are."

"Do you?" Alice demanded. "What has a woman bleeding to death in my bathtub got to do with who I am?"

Bett was pressing Alice's drunken head against her breast.

That night Alice fell asleep with a cigarette in her hand. When she woke, the rug was on fire. She let out a bellow of terror and began to try to stamp out the flames with her bare feet.

Jill was the first one to reach her, half drag, half carry her out of the room. Trudy and Bett went in with buckets of water while Angel phoned the fire department.

"Don't let the firemen in," Alice moaned, sitting on Harriet's old chair in their old living room. "They'll wreck the place."

The fire was out by the time the truck arrived. After the men had checked the room and praised presence of mind and quick action for saving the house, the fire chief said, "Just the same, one of these nights she's going to do it. This is the third time we know of."

Jill, with the intention of confronting Alice with that fact, was distracted with discovering that Alice's feet were badly burned.

The pain killers gave Alice hallucinations: the floor of her hospital room on fire, her nurse's hair on fire, the tent of blankets at the foot of her bed burning, and Harriet was shouting at her, "We're going to burn in hell."

"Please," Alice begged. "I'd rather have the pain."

In pain, she made too much noise, swore, demanded whiskey, threatened to set herself on fire again and be done with it, until she was held down and given another shot.

Her coworkers from Safeway sent her flowers, but no one she worked with came to see her. No one she drank with knew what had happened. From the house, only Bett came at the end of work, still dressed in her uniform.

"Get me out of here," Alice begged. "Can't you get me out of here?"

In the night, with fire crackling all around her, Alice knew she was in hell, and there was no escape, Bett with her sunny face and great breasts the cruelest hallucination of all.

Even on the day when Bett came to take her home, Alice was half-convinced Bett was only a devilish trick to deliver her to greater torment, but Alice also knew she was still half-crazy with drugs or pain. There the house still stood, and Bett carried her up the stairs into an attic so clean and fresh she hardly recognized it. Alice began to believe in delivery.

"This bell by your bed," Bett explained, "all you need to do is ring it, and Angel will come."

Alice laughed until her coughing stopped her.

"It's a sort of miracle you're alive," Trudy said when she and Jill came home from work and up to see her.

"I'm indestructible," Alice said, a great world-weariness in her voice.

"This place was a rat's nest," Jill complained. "You can't have thrown out a paper since we moved in—or an empty yogurt carton. Is that all you eat?"

"I eat out," Alice said, "for whatever business of yours it is. And nobody asked you to clean up after me."

"It scared us pretty badly," Trudy said. "We all came close to being killed."

"Sometimes you remind me a little of Harriet," Alice said with slow malice. "That's a friend of mine who killed herself."

"We know who Harriet is," Jill said. "Al, if we can't talk about this, we're all going to have to move out."

"Move out? What for?"

"Because we don't want to be burned to death in our sleep."

"You've got to promise us that you won't drink when you're smoking or smoke when you're drinking," Trudy said.

"This is my house. I'm the landlady. You're the tenants," Alice announced.

"We realize that. There's nothing we can do unless you'll be reasonable."

Bett came into the room with a dinner tray.

"Get out, all of you!" Alice shouted. "And take that muck with you!"

Jill and Trudy were twins in obedience. Bett didn't budge.

"I got you out because I promised we'd feed you."

"What you eat is swill!"

"Look, Angel even cooked you some hamburger."

"You can't make conditions for me in my own house."

"I know that; so do the others. Al, I don't want to leave. I don't want to leave you. I love you. I want you to do it for yourself."

"Don't say that to me unless I'm drunk. I can't handle it."

"Yes, you can. You don't have to drink."

"What in hell else am I supposed to do to pass the time?" Alice demanded.

"Read, watch t.v., make friends, make love."

"Don't taunt me!" Alice cried into the tray of food on her lap.

"I'm not taunting," Bett said. "I want to help."

Until Alice could walk well enough to get out of the house on her own, there was no question of drinking. She kept nothing in the house, having always used drink as an excuse to escape Harriet. There was nothing to steal from her tenants. She was too proud to ask even Bett to bring her a bottle. The few cigarettes she'd brought home with her from the hospital would have to be her comfort. She found herself opening a window every time she had one and emptying and washing the ashtray when she was through.

"You're turning me into a sneak!" she shouted at Bett.

"It all looks nice and tidy to me," Bett said. "Trudy says you're so male-identified that you can't take care of yourself. I'm going to tell her she's wrong."

Alice threw a clean ashtray at her, and she ducked and laughed.

"You're getting better, you really are."

Alice returned to the beer parlor before she returned to work. She wasn't walking well, but she was walking. She had been missed. When she told about stamping out the fire with her own bare feet, she was assured of more free beer than she could drink in an evening even when she was in practice. How good it tasted and how companionable these friends who never asked questions and therefore didn't analyze the answers, who made connection with yarns and jokes. Alice had hung onto a couple of the best hospital stories and told them before she was drunk enough to lose her way or the punch line. She only laughed enough to cough at other people's jokes, which, as the evening wore on, were less well told and not as funny. Drink did not anesthetize the pain in Alice's healing feet, and that made her critical. Getting a tit caught in a wringer wasn't funny; it hurt.

"And here's one for those tenants of yours, Al, hey? How can you stem the tide of women's liberation? Put your finger in the dyke!"

It was an ugly face shoved into her own. Alice suddenly realized why a man must be forgiven his beard growing in the night, forgiven over and over again, too, for not being the prince of a fellow you wished he were. Alice didn't forgive. She laughed until she was near to spitting blood, finished her beer and her cigarette, and went out to find her car. As on so many other nights, even a few minutes after she got home, she couldn't remember the drive, but she knew she'd done it quietly and well.

"Come on," Bett said. "Those feet hurt. I'm going to carry you up."

Drunk in the arms of the sunny Amazon, Alice said, "Do you know how to stem the tide of women's liberation? Do you?"

"Does anyone want to?" Bett asked, making her careful, slow way up the stairs.

"Sure. Lots of people. You put your finger . . ."

"In the dyke, yeah, I know."

"Don't you think that's funny?"

"No."

"I don't either," Alice agreed.

Bett carried Alice over to her bed, which had been turned down, probably by Angel.

"Now, I want you to hand over the rest of your cigarettes," Bett said. "I'll leave them for you in the hall."

"Take them," Alice said.

"All right," Bett agreed and reached into Alice's blouse where she kept a pack tucked into her bra when she didn't have a pocket.

Alice half bit, half kissed the hand, then pressed herself up against those marvelous breasts, a hand on each, and felt the nipples, under the thin cloth of Bett's shirt, harden. Bett had the cigarettes, but she did not move away. Instead, with her free hand, she unbuttoned her shirt and gave Alice her dream.

As in a dream, Alice's vision floated above the scene, and she saw her own close-cropped head, hardly bigger than a baby's, her aging, liver-spotted face, her denture-deformed mouth, sucking like an obscene incubus at a young magnificence of breast which belonged to Angel. Then she saw Bett's face, serene with pity. Alice pulled herself away and spat.

"You pity me! What do you know about it? What could you know? Harriet, rest her goddamned soul, lived in *mortal sin* with me. She *killed herself* for me. It's not to *pity!* Get out! Get out, all of you right now because I'm going to burn this house down when I damned well please."

"All right," Bett said.

"It's my hell. I earned it."

"All right," Bett said, her face as bright as a never-to-come morning.

Alice didn't begin to cry until Bett had left the room, tears as hot with pain and loss as fire, that burned and burned and burned.

Katherine Sturtevant

Photographs of Energy and Color

Maline Corliss, twenty-eight year old lesbian and feminist, felt a need to leave San Francisco. First of all, she was tired of typing insurance policies. Second of all, she was tired of arguing about separatism, art, class, the politics of shoplifting and the authenticity of astral travel. Third of all, she had just broken up with her lover, Kathleen, and could not bear to see her anywhere.

Fortunately, there was somewhere to go. Maline's sister Iris and Iris's husband Alan owned a small but sleek second home on the shores of a Northern California lake. Maline had money enough for an extended vacation—say, six months if the food stamp program proved cooperative. It did. Maline turned the bar into a darkroom and settled down to solitary bliss. It was there at the lake that she met Carol Pine, thirty-four, married, no children.

Carol was the most talked about woman in the small winter lakeside community. The men thought that she was a bitch, and half the women agreed unequivocally. The other half of the women agreed but loved her in spite of her outrageous bluntness and quick, catty tongue. Carol knew that she was controversial, and felt both proud and hurt because of it. She knew that she was strong (armored). She also knew—and hid from the community, yet felt injured that her friends did not realize it—that she was hopelessly dependent upon her husband, Kent. The community thought he was hen-pecked. He *was* hen-pecked. Carol demanded a thousand tiny services from him in order to make up for the fact that she needed him more than he needed her. She needed his constancy, and she needed his money—he was in construction. She drew her strength from the high-beamed house that Kent built, from the blue lake glinting through thermal glass in the living room. Microwave oven, crock-pot, the freedom to read *Newsweek* and *Sunset* and *Gourmet* magazines in peace.

They had decided, six years back, not to have children (Carol had a tubal ligation). She thought children were like kittens, marvelous to watch, but a nuisance after awhile. Cats were different. The Pine household was always full of them: remarkably colored, aloof, almost hostile animals; variations on their tense, dignified mistress. When Carol went into the bedroom and shut the door, they cried until she let them in.

The lakefront was crowded with houses (long panes of glass, multi-layered redwood decks) but when Maline arrived, shortly before the first of the year, she counted only twelve occupied houses in the two-mile stretch between the market and her new home. The other houses stood hollow and elegant, and Maline experienced a rich, satisfying feeling of solitude. New Year's Eve she spent mixing screwdrivers in the darkroom/ bar and carrying them over to the couch, where she sat with her feet on the coffee table, gazing into the fire before her (she was rather proud of it; it glowed bright orange in the midst of dark ash, and, when she poked it, splintered obediently into yellow flame) or at the dark plate glass to her left. There she could see her round white face reflected, and a faint, shadowy movement of needled branches settling. At eleven she wrote her New Year's Resolutions. There were two of them.

1. I resolve to explore the issues of political pressure and political responsibility, and their relationship to each other in my life.
2. I resolve to discover and understand the true reason that Kathleen broke up with me.

"Because you never let me alone!" Kathleen cried in one of their last arguments. "Even now, you keep *pushing* me!"

"I've been pushing you for two years! That the way I *am*, that's what you value about me! Why should it suddenly be so terrible? Because of Paula?"

"Yes, because she's helped me to see that it's not what I need after all. I need space." Kathleen was crying. "Please see that. Loving you has made me less and less myself. It's made me shrink instead of grow, I'm only half a person."

At two in the morning she called Kathleen. She called to say: Are you growing, Kathleen? Are you bigger, taller, fatter? What are your measurements? Have you become an Amazon yet? She called to say: You talk about wanting your own space but what you mean is that you don't want to have to look at yourself, at who you are and how you are in a relationship. *That's* what I push you to do, and you can't face it.

When the phone rang, Paula answered, sounding sleepy. Pain shot through Maline's body, comprehensive. Propriety and territory. Paula had answered the phone.

"Are you living there now?" she asked.

"What? Who is this?" Paula demanded angrily.

Maline hung up, humiliated, wondering if Paula had been able to recognize her voice.

A week later the landscape was magnificently leveled by a record-breaking snowfall. Maline used snowshoes to reach the top of the driveway

where the Volkswagen sat half buried; she swung her legs in large, stiff circles, gathering fuzzy clumps of snow around the ankles of her Levis. For
mail and groceries, she hiked to the market, carrying a canvas pack on her
back. The ploughs had scraped the snow into a tall, clean crust on either
side of the road, and she felt as if she were walking through a tunnel.

The market was owned and managed by Roy and Nancy Dock—Maline
had met them previously when vacationing with Iris. When Maline entered
the store Nancy was at the counter, looking friendly and efficient, with
her grey hair smoothed and sprayed behind her head. They exchanged ex-
clamations about the storm while Nancy got Maline's mail from the postal
window (a letter from her friend Jill, nothing from Kathleen). Maline
bought stamps. Then she prowled the aisles of the little store, gathering
together vegetables and red winter apples, Cream of Wheat, bread, milk,
and liverwurst.

Carol Pine came in, wearing a burnt orange sweater. Maline was attracted at once to the fullness and bluntness of Carol's body, and to her rich
coloring: tight dark skin, glistening black hair and brows, shoulders that
drooped forward and breasts that slumped comfortably against her chest.
Nancy introduced them.

"Carol lives just beyond you, where the road goes up to the golf course.
I'm sure she'd be glad to give you a ride home."

"Oh, did you walk? That's why your cheeks are so red!" Carol said.

Maline reached automatically to feel her cold nose, hot cheek. "Yes.
It's not so bad a hike, really. Invigorating." She made her voice put quotes
around the word.

Carol drove a copper colored van. "Four-wheel drive," she explained as
Maline climbed in beside her and lifted in her pack full of groceries. "I
wouldn't live up there without a van."

Maline told Carol that she was a free-lance photographer. She had never
even tried to sell or publish a photograph, but she needed an identity and
wanted to represent something independent and artistic.

"How interesting," Carol said. "People have told me that I'd make a
good photographer's model, because of my coloring, but I don't know . . .
what do you think?"

"Yes, it occurred to me right away," Maline agreed. "Unfortunately, I
haven't got the equipment for developing color photos. But of course,
even black and white portraits would reflect the . . . ," she faltered, nervous.
"Individuality of your face," she finished at last, glancing sideways at the
curve of Carol's large, soft ear.

"I'd love to have my picture taken. I don't think I've seen a picture of
myself since my wedding, and Kent is always saying I should have a studio
portrait done. How much do you charge?"

"Actually, I wasn't meaning to fish—"

"Oh, I know that," Carol assured her. "But I'm interested, really."

"Well, why don't you look at some of my work, and if you like it I'll try a couple of pictures for you at cost."

Carol didn't want to come in with Maline to see the photos. She had frozen foods to put away, and besides, no snowshoes. "Can't you drop off your groceries and grab some pictures, and we'll have coffee at my place?" she suggested. "I'll be glad to take you home afterwards." She waited in the van with the engine running while Maline, wanting to hurry but unable, labored on snowshoes over the deep reservoir of snow.

Inside the house she ran to her bedroom and began untacking photographs from the walls. Pictures of the ocean and the park, of women hugging each other on Gay Pride Day, of Jill, of Kathleen, and Kathleen's dog, and Kathleen's back yard. Carol looked at them one by one as they sat at her glossy wooden dining table. Maline looked from the photos to the white mist over the lake and back again.

"That's my friend Jill," she said. "And that's my friend Kathleen." Kathleen naked, Kathleen in overalls with a paintbrush (the day they redid the kitchen in yellow), Kathleen crying, her face dark and shrivelled and wet. Maline looked at the photo, remembering the odd, painful argument during which she had taken it, in cold revenge, while Kathleen in vulnerable anguish had faced her through the separating, magnifying lens.

Carol glanced at the picture of two women hugging and put it aside without comment. The tension in Maline's stomach (the lake is not San Francisco, she thought) eased.

They made a date to take photos, and Maline walked home after all, wanting the cold, stiff air as a conductor for her energy and excitement. She liked the strength Carol seemed to infuse into conventionality.

At home she read Jill's letter, detailing the political struggles of a food co-op, arguments about fundraising, Jill's personal economic problems of the moment—and hi from Kathleen. She glanced around at the blue and blond living room, at the bar, the knick-knacks on the mantle, trying to pin down affluence. The true wealth was the lake, of course: the mist darkening over it, shadows sliding across it, bordered by a row of silver icicles and a redwood window-sill.

Carol and Maline became friends. Maline took pictures of Carol in slacks and sweater, or in a hostess gown slit to the knee. Pictures of her holding a cat, stirring a soup, looking out at the lake—stern, blunt-chinned. Maline told her to look contemplative, but she could not. Carol was built of conviction without a gap.

Maline came out.

"I thought you might be," Carol said.

"Did you think I was attracted to you?"

"Well, I certainly hope so. I think *you're* attractive."

"Yes, but finding someone attractive is a matter of aesthetics, *being* attracted to someone is a sexual thing."

"Oh, I see what you mean. I hadn't thought about it like that—are you?"

Maline grinned. "Oh, my appreciation is mainly aesthetic," she said. "So far."

"Terrific," Carol said. "From now on I'll think of myself as a work of art."

"What about me?" Maline said, hating herself for asking.

"Oh, you're a work of art too," Carol assured her.

Maline hesitated. "How do you feel about my being a lesbian?" she asked finally.

"Well, all right. I mean, I can understand women sleeping together. You know the way men are at cocktail parties, always leering." She shrugged and got up to let one of the cats in.

But Carol was not a feminist. She had no sympathy for women who, unlike herself, were trapped in unhappy marriages, or stuffy kitchens, or waiting on tables. "I chose my life and it's what I want," she said. "They should have done the same."

"Not everyone has the same choices," Maline insisted.

"That's not my problem. I mean, I believe in equal pay for equal work and all that, but don't expect me to think all women are wonderful because most of them are very silly. You take Violet Jackson—I play bridge with her. She's always fluttering about Kent's marvelous blue eyes and talking about sex like it was the be-all and end-all of existence. I mean, I like sex too, but I try not to be adolescent about it. She thinks I'm a bitch—I know because Nancy Dock told me. But she won't say it to my face. That's one thing no one can accuse *me* of, everything I'm saying to you I've said to her."

Maline was scandalized and half-envious of Carol's dismissiveness, her refusal to take responsibility at any level for the oppression of other women. She tried to make Carol see, pushed her to see the ways women are oppressed, and to recognize the limits of her own life.

"Frankly," she said finally, "I don't see how you can find this life fulfilling. You're removed from reality, isolated with your toys. Bridge, cooking, television. Don't you want something more?" She expected to shock Carol, to offend her. But Carol was neither yielding nor resistant.

"No," she said, shrugging. "I have everything I want."

And for a moment, Maline could see it. Lakeside beauty, idle fulfillment, and Kent. The three of them had dinner together one evening at the Pine house, and Maline found him likeable. He was mildly witty, easily gratified, affectionate. Maline analyzed rapidly: Kent thrived on Carol's power, Carol on Kent's playfulness.

One morning in March (while the snow was peeling away from the manzanita under the sun's pressure, leaving twiggy little holes) Maline received a letter from Kathleen.

> Now that we have had time and distance, and can write without anger, perhaps we can exchange helpful feedback about our relationship and where it failed. I know that I closed myself off to you a lot, and that you pushed me too hard—those two things. But what else? How did we fail to connect so often, why were the missed connections so electrical, so painful?

Maline wanted to write: We never failed, it was you who failed—faltered—could not endure (a suitably dramatic reply). Or to quote: "The unexamined life is not worth living." But she was beginning not to believe in those answers. She thought of writing instead: The guilt that we collectively impose upon ourselves as individuals when we insist upon political responsibility killed our love. But that did not seem true either.

Finally she wrote:

> How can I answer you? You've gone on to a new part of your life, and are looking back in peaceful, intellectual consideration. I am still trying to encompass my solitude, to believe in the fact of our separation, to understand the truth that you no longer love me (as you see, I am unchanged—still frankly vulnerable).

Adding: P.S. We failed because you were too yielding and too resistant.

Maline began to want rather badly to become lovers with Carol, so that she could feel herself superior, a conqueror, a seducer, and so that she would not be alone anymore. And so that she could write Kathleen: I have a new lover. Or better yet: I am having an affair with a married woman. She knew all this (continually self-challenging, continually self-critical) and was ashamed, but not closed off to the actualization of her shabby needs if it proved possible. And it was—because Carol was flattered and curious, and perhaps, in spite of what she said, a little bored with her life. And, finally, in this stew of unromantic motives—because they were attractive to each other: Maline's energy, Carol's color.

So they became lovers, invariably making love in Carol and Kent's big bed, throwing aside the deep blue bedspread. Carol did not consider herself unfaithful to Kent because Maline was not a man, but did not tell him

about the relationship "because of his prejudices." Maline gave up trying
to pierce the solidity of Carol's vision. She allowed herself to feel politically superior to Carol and gave up arguing with her. Instead, she lavished all
her energy—nervous energy, artistic energy, political energy—upon the appreciation of Carol's body. She let her camera savor Carol's brown flesh as
well, took pictures of Carol lying on the bed, naked; holding a cat, naked.
But Carol was uncomfortable. "My clothes give me confidence," she said.
"Even now I'm being more vulnerable with you than I've ever been with
anyone—even Kent."

Maline could hardly believe this. "You don't seem vulnerable," she said.

"Maybe you're insensitive."

"I don't think so," Maline said, angry but controlled. "Maybe you're
just so used to keeping things in, being repressed, that even when you want
to you can't let loose, can't express the vulnerability you feel inside."

"Who wants to?" Carol said, shrugging her naked shoulders. Maline
watched her breasts roll against her chest.

"Why don't you ever come to my house?"

"Same reason."

"Carol—don't you think you're being awfully insecure? Maybe you'd
find you don't need the trappings you think you need."

"Maybe I'd find you and your rhetoric ahead of me at every turn if I
dared to set foot outside my—domain."

"I don't think I'm as awful as all that," Maline said, beginning to feel
miserable, as though everything were spoiled. "Look, Carol—" knowing it
was a ploy "—you seem awfully defensive. Maybe you'd be more comfortable—maybe it would be wiser for both of us, if we just quit now—
called it off?" Feeling Carol's flesh still beside her, and then:

"No . . . let's don't do that."

And so they continued being lovers into the spring, now that Maline
had the evidence, verbal: No, let's don't do that.

She wrote to Jill: She is casually competent, lazily creative, shrewdly
intent on power, and absolutely without guilt. This last, of course, is the
real attraction. Being with her eases me. And at least now I know it's not
just me.

She did not write to Kathleen. It seemed unnecessary; she would hear it
from Jill.

The hours that Maline spent with Carol were dictated by Kent's schedule. Maline expected to be infuriated by this but wasn't. She was anxious
for her hours alone, they were what she had come for. She photographed
landscapes, read volumes of women's autobiographical writings, and began
an autobiography of her own, synthesizing and enlarging journals kept for
over five years.

When Maline and Carol were together they shared meals, watched TV, played cards, went (after the snow melted) on photographic expeditions, and once rented a boat, taking it out to the middle of the lake where they drifted, swam, ate a picnic lunch, cuddled and caressed, wet then hot—

Carol drove the boat. Maline watched her at the propeller, watched her bare arms on the steering wheel. She admired Carol's competence; remembered Carol in her kitchen or in the copper colored van. At the dock Carol made quick loops and knots with nylon cord, then repeated them slowly, so Maline could watch and learn.

Carol paid for the boat rental, and Maline began to think about money seriously. "Another month is all I have funds for," she told Carol. "What do you think—should I look for a job in town?"

"I don't know," Carol said. "Do you want to?" She was sitting in a lawn chair on the deck, looking dreamily out at the lake. Maline stood behind, playing with the long dark fabric of Carol's hair.

"I don't know," Maline returned. "How do you feel about it?" *Do we love each other, or are we just playing, killing time? Shall I go back and face the community now—untangle the political issues I keep tripping over when I fall in love . . . shall I learn to be like you, Carol, closed, calm, at peace?* "Ever think of leaving Kent and moving with me to San Francisco?" she inquired of Carol finally.

"I thought of it, yes. I mean, it occurred to me. I would never do it, of course."

"Why not?"

"Oh, I like it here." Carol waved a hand at the flat blue water before them. A boat buzzed and skimmed at its center. "The city's so dirty," she said.

Maline was quiet, hurt by the casualness of Carol's reply. She let go the hair; it fell down the back of the chair.

It was spring. Chains of carpenter ants wound their black, glistening way through both houses, and the cats brought home mice and shrews. There was a bird's nest in Carol's mailbox, so she and Maline walked to the store daily to get their mail. It was a ritual, a way of fabricating a little of the routine of marriage for themselves.

Maline got a job in a restaurant in town that was taking on extra help for the tourist season. She wore a dress and white apron, and flowers in her hair. It was part of the restaurant's motif. She hated it, but smiled politely at jovial men and their irritable wives, scooped the tips into her apron pockets.

One evening Carol and Kent came to the restaurant with Roy and Nancy Dock. Maline saw the hostess seat them, and her stomach sent up ribbons of protesting acid: anger and humiliation that Carol should bring affluence and convention to mock her. She took their order sullen-faced.

"What's the matter, Maline? You look like you have a toothache!" Kent teased.

"My feet hurt," she said, giving him a slight, obedient smile.

"Ah, that's the working life. What'll it be, Sweetheart?"

Maline looked steadily at Carol, who looked calmly from the menu to her lover/waitress. "The veal scallopini, I think," she said. Maline chatted with the Docks, and promised to send their regards to Iris.

The next day at Carol's, sitting cross-legged before the fireplace while the wind played the evergreens like pipes outdoors, Carol said, "I tried to talk them into another restaurant, but they were determined. I didn't want to be obvious."

"How could you just sit there as though I were nobody?"

"What did you want? Did you want me to throw you tragic, romantic glances?"

"Oh, I suppose so." Maline gave a tired smile. The fire's heat was giving her a headache. Her anger felt forced; months of hurt, desire, and energy seemed artificial.

"Don't look like that," Carol said. "You know I love you." She said it confidently, complacently.

"Do you?"

"Yes," Carol said, rolling across the rug to where Maline sat, reaching her head up like a snake to kiss Maline's forehead, lips, breasts underneath Maline's polo shirt. They made love, Maline passive under Carol's slow hands and tongue.

Two weeks later Maline got a letter from Kathleen. Carol was with her at the store the day she got it, and when they were outside she said, "What does Kathleen have to say?"

Maline, who had read aloud to Carol letters from Jill and Iris, slipped the envelope into her back pants pocket, saying "I think I'll read it later." Carol raised her heavy brows, then tossed her head (the long hair skittered on her back) and began to talk about summer vacation: she and Kent were going to Los Angeles to see Kent's parents.

Maline did not read the letter until she got home from work that night. It said:

> Paula and I have broken up. I'll always be glad she came along, because of what I learned from her about what I need in my life. In my next relationship, I think I'll be able to stand firmer, more solidly for what I need, and not let myself be bullied by my lovers . . . like you, like Paula.

Sometimes I get sad, think of you and me and how we can never get back to what we had—the finest of what we had was the finest I've *ever* had. I don't think anyone will ever mean as much to either of us as we've meant to each other (correct me if I'm already wrong!). But I know we can never go back.

I hope, though, that when you come back to San Francisco (you haven't settled there permanently, have you?) we'll be able to see each other in new ways, relate to each other with more health and more strength.

She signed it love.

Maline called her up immediately. "Do you have any idea how manipulative the letter you sent me is?" she asked.

"Yes," Kathleen said. "But there are no lies in it."

"The whole *letter* is a lie," Maline said.

"No it's not. Are you going to come back?"

"I don't know," Maline said stubbornly, knowing that she would.

She told Carol the next morning, while they sat with coffee at the dining table. "I'm going back to San Francisco," she said gently. "I have to."

Carol stared into her coffee cup, then out over the water, choppy today, blotted and mottled blue and grey. "I've been expecting it," she said steadily, "but I really don't know why you're going."

"Because I need the culture, the support . . . and total commitment instead of a piece of someone's life." *And because I still love Kathleen and she and Paula have broken up.*

Carol pushed her chair back but did not get up. She looked down at her knees—blue slacks—and closed her eyes.

"You have Kent," Maline said.

"I *hate* Kent," Carol said, childish for the first time, and began to make a sound, a high wailing, with an abandonment of which she was incapable, scarring her peace, the glass, the lake. A skinny tortoise-shell came bounding across the room to Carol's feet, then stood, round-eyed and tense. Maline put her arms around Carol's broad shoulders and comforted. "And it's too late for me to come with you, isn't it?" Carol sobbed.

A wave of shocked blood rocked through Maline: a chain of disbelief, desire, fear. She thought of Kathleen and her dog, the two of them in Golden Gate Park, and of Kathleen singing around the house. Of Carol's hostess gowns—then felt their breasts together and Carol's tears on her neck, and said, "No, it's not too late."

"Yes it is, yes it is." Her sobs were coming chunky now, softer, final. The cat jumped up to the table, and Carol pushed Maline away to take the cat into her lap. "Hello furry-purry," she crooned. The cat purred as she cuddled it to her chest. "Will you love me forever?" Carol asked it.

They said their last goodbyes, for Maline planned to leave the following morning. Maline presented Carol with a dozen beautiful photographs of herself, and went back to Iris's to pack.

At midnight that night, in a final moment of panic, Carol left Kent drowsing over Johnny Carson and hurried through the blackness to Iris's house. She found it dark, and the Volkswagen gone. Maline had become restless, and by that time was miles down the Feather River Canyon, going home, feeling guilt-burnt, but as strong as she had ever been.

Sandy Boucher

Kansas in the Spring

I

On Easter morning we drive out across the countryside until we arrive at a low concrete block structure painted pale green. On a bench next to the front door sits a young man in overalls, his skinny knees pressed tight together, his face knotting with anxiety as he watches us get out of the car. Arlyn speaks gently to him. "How you doin'? Windy out here, eh?" And the young man's face smooths in a grateful childish smile.

This is the rest home where we will visit Bess, Arlyn's sister. Bess was the favored child in the family—a plump young woman grinning saucily out of the photographs. Her hair was fastened with tortoise shell combs into smooth dark cones and buns; she wore silks under a fur coat. They sent her to college to be a home economics teacher. But something happened away at college. Arlyn doesn't know exactly what. Bess was sent home. She became very strange, and no one spoke anymore of her teaching. For the next fifty years she stayed out there on the farm where she had to be taken care of by Arlyn and his other sister Emmeline, until Emmeline died.

Bess turns to us as we enter the dayroom. Hers is the same pouchy pink face as Arlyn's with eyes of China blue. Her white hair falls down snowy and straight next to her cheeks. "Oh I am so glad you came," she says.

She asks our names, repeats them to herself, clasps our hands. She leans toward me, murmuring, "I am so glad to see you, Sandy," and her eyes are like those of a lover, so open and tender, so hungry. Sitting with her, I feel the wild fluttering of her being, the uncontrolled energy that might tip her in any direction. She is aware of the dangers; she hesitates often. It is like being with someone on acid, knowing that each thing I say goes through many transmutations in her head.

Now she must repeat the names again, asking for the surnames this time, spelling them, nodding with satisfaction when she has mastered each one. Her voice is an odd monotone like the sounds from a phonograph record that turns too slowly, the needle dragging.

"Bauer," she says, holding Mary's gaze. "B - a - u - e - r, is that right?"

"Yes," Mary answers.

"Mary Bauer," Bess repeats, her eyes dreamy, and then she slips away, her face suddenly empty of all expression.

Arlyn sits turning his cap on his knee. He has told us he does not understand Bess; she refused to help with the farm work or care about farming. He blames her for that. And he cannot quite forgive her for throwing away her chance to become a teacher, when she might have made a salary that would have helped them out during the terrible hard times of the Depression. So he is uneasy in her presence. But this place itself makes him uncomfortable, for some of the townspeople tried to get him committed here last year, and he had to fight for his freedom. He sits staring at the floor, and glances up in exquisite discomfort when one of the old people in the room speaks to him. Many of them here, like Bess, are younger than he, some lived their whole lives in a neighboring town, on a neighboring farm, known to him, but he maintains his stubborn separateness from them.

Este has brought the still camera (we would never have dared to bring either of the movie cameras), and now she asks, "May I take a picture of you, Bess? I could send it to you later."

Bess rouses herself, looks at Este for a time as Este holds up the camera for her to see. She nods. "Oh yes, you can do that for me. I've been wanting my picture—the one from the Pledge commercial. If you could get that for me . . . Yes, I'd be grateful. You know, it's me in the Pledge commercial, where I'm polishing the table. I'd like that one."

Este's expression does not change, but I notice the skin tighten around her eyes. Slowly she lowers the camera to her lap.

All Ann's efforts to coax Bess into talking about her past have failed, leaving Ann silent and perplexed, and the rest of us secretly amused, for we know about the miniature microphone taped to Ann's middle finger inside her cupped hand, the cord traveling up the sleeve of her shirt to the tiny tape recorder hidden in the inside pocket of her down jacket. We had helped her make these preparations back at the house so that she could steal an interview for the film.

Bess does remember Ann. When we entered, she greeted her with her childhood name, Ann-Marie, but she refuses to talk about those days back on the farm when the child, Ann, would come to visit. She ignores Ann completely to turn all her attention to Mary, Este and me. She touches us, tells us again in that one-tone throbbing voice how happy she is to see us, how she hopes we'll come visit her again. She looks at us so intently it seems she wants to memorize us.

I think of Genevieve, Arlyn's wife, her long years of illness, her early death—Ann's father writing in a letter "I do believe that if Genevieve had been blessed with good health to go with her natural drive she could have given Arlyn leadership and direction and they could have had a really good life."

When so many survived, why were these two destroyed? Genevieve, after all, simply did what was expected of her, like the women in the cafe, saying, "No, see, we all got married. There never was anything else."

And Bess? They lied to her about the world; they coddled her and dressed her up fine and gave her airs, prepared her for destruction.

Arlyn endures. "I love life!" he declares. Genevieve is dead now twenty years. While Arlyn awakes each morning, enjoys his food, tells stories, visits his beloved cattle. Lives his stubborn unwashed eccentric existence in the midst of his fellow townspeople.

Once, speaking of her, he frowned and shook his head. "I never could please her," he said. "Hard as I tried, I never could please her."

It was so long ago.

After sitting through an Easter mass served by a visiting priest, we take our leave. "Come back again," Bess urges. "You, Mary Bauer, and you, Este Gardner, and you too, Sandy Boucher," still ignoring Ann, who stands awkwardly by. "We will," I promise, and then think, why did I say that? and try to find a way to make it be true—perhaps if Ann gets more funding and we come back in the fall to film the townspeople, perhaps . . .

"Goodbye Arlyn," Bess says, her manner growing more formal. "Thank you for coming."

Ever the lady, even in this most distressed and desperately vulnerable state.

Outside the front door of the home, Arlyn takes a long relieved breath, squinting against the sunlight. We follow his waddling, humpty-dumpty figure to the car.

II

I have climbed partway up the ladder on the side of the windmill and cling dizzily there, my head thrown back, while far above me, filling my field of vision, the blades of the windmill spin in my direction. The whole structure seems to move back over me. Much as I try I cannot convince myself it is only the wheel that moves, that the wheel is anchored to the structure on which I stand, whose spindly metal legs were driven deep in the Kansas soil little less than forty years ago and have not moved since, that this tapered frame of windmill, as seemingly brittle as the thinnest of dried bones propped here, may strain against its crisscrossed wires but does not run with the wind or fall before it. Here where I expected to stand still—an eye only, a sharp observer's eye behind the camera—instead I am carried off in this rushing, this uncontrolled movement and opening of that which I had long ago closed away.

There is a whirring sound, and an occasional snap. The blades of the wheel race madly. The wheel itself seems to flow across the sky as I look up at it. Just as the new wheat flows in the field, a tide of short bright-green blades merged in their motion and then separating in ripples and torrents. A wide green rushing broken by the brown strips of road, the high ground of pasture where the cows stand blinking their pinkrimmed eyes against the wind that lifts the hair on their backs in stiff whorls.

We come back from an afternoon of shooting out at Uncle Arlyn's farm, unload the equipment from the back of the stationwagon, and carry the boxes and tripod and equipment cases up the broken sidewalk, over the porch and into our rented house.

We are here in Morrisville, Kansas, in the early spring—an all-woman film crew from California—to make a movie about Ann Hershey's family. Ann's mother and Aunt Genevieve grew up here, children of a big joyful prosperous French family in a house on Main Street. Her mother, Marie Comte Hershey, is dead, having suffered for years, like Genevieve, from rheumatoid arthritis. The townspeople remember the two sisters as carefree girls, show us photographs of them clowning on a stepladder, wearing bloomers in the line-up for the high school girls' basketball team.

To the townsfolk, Ann, now 38 years old and an independent film-maker, is still "Marie's little girl," remembered for her visits here when she was a child.

In the living room of our house, Este, camera assistant, sits on the couch with her hands inside the black bag, unloading exposed film from one of the magazines. Mary, sound woman, and Ann sit on the floor with the Nagra tape recorder, playing back a tape of Uncle Arlyn telling us how the old house used to look when his mother was alive. I am at work on the production notebook, filling in details.

"Take 4: Sync sound. Arlyn opening gate, approaching and turning on windmill. Yellow road grader coming right to left on road behind him.

"Take 5: Same, except for road grader.

"Take 6: Close-up of Arlyn turning on windmill. Sync.

"Take 7: Arlyn feeding dogs. Then throws bag over fence with the other trash.

"Take 8: MOS of broken tractors and other junk in the field around the house."

(MOS, Mary Bauer told me, stands for "without sound." The term came from a German director, who of course said "mit-out sound.")

Ann explains once again where the emphasis must be. "This time around, it's Arlyn we have to get. He's eighty-one years old. He might be dead when we come back in the fall."

"I would like to make a request," says Este. "Do you think you could get him to take a bath?"

Arlyn Lundborg. Short, round old man in overalls and a filthy yellow shirt fastened at the collar with a large safety pin. On his feet he wears black high-top tennis shoes; on his head a brown, billed cap, but this he always removes when he comes inside, revealing a head covered with white stubble, just like his chin. His face is Santa Claus plump and ruddy; his little eyes are a bright pale blue, now innocent, now sly.

Ann remembers his kindness to her when she was a child. He had let her ride his old horse alone about the farm, in long summer days of freedom. He had laughed when she drank from the horse trough, had shown her how to care for the animals she loved. He had been the one grownup from her childhood whom she remembered treating her with respect.

For the last few years now Arlyn has lived in a dilapidated house in town. There is no bathroom or kitchen in his house, and few unbroken windows. He lives, essentially, in one front room. Out in the weedy yard several dogs are chained amid an astonishing welter of junk, tractors and wagons, four or five big old cars, four pickup trucks. "How come you have so many pickup trucks, Arlyn?" I asked him. "Well," he said, "if I take one of them out to the farm and get it stuck in the mud, I just leave it there and come back here and get another."

One day Este came downstairs from taking a bath, swathed in a bathrobe, her long hair tied up in a towel on her head, with a gift for us. In the near-authentic country western twang that she slips into now and then for comic relief, she told us that she had just composed a song about Arlyn—and promptly sang it.

> Well I'm smelly and dirty
> I ain't very purty
> and people don't like me around
> I'm weird and encrusted
> I'm feared and mistrusted
> by half of the women in town
>
> I seen some hard times
> and I've heard some harsh lines
> But I ain't gonna give up not yet
>
> Cause I won the battle
> got my land and my cattle
> And I ain't gonna change now, you bet!

Cause I'm a survivor a smart old conniver
and I don't need no toilet or bath
My wife used to plague me and badger and beg me
But you know that I had the last laugh.

I'm sitting on a rusted refrigerator in the yard of the farm, waiting for
Arlyn to arrive. The sun is falling; a bitter wind claws at my jacket. Cows
moo hungrily. It's depressing out here. The ruin of Arlyn's life. The neg-
lect. The debris. The shit.

Mary talks about how everything here is dying. This is a dying culture—
the small farmer, the family farm. All the young people go off to bigger
towns, get jobs. The land at Arlyn's farm is strewn with rusting broken
machinery, dead animals, objects from the past.

The ancient siding of the house, warped away from its nails, all color
and sap and life drained from it by the decades of weather, taps randomly, gently against itself in the wind. Inside the house a closet door creaks,
a rag of dress squeaks on a hanger, singing to itself. There is almost no inside to this house now, all apertures torn or smashed or simply left open.
The piano stands foot-deep in cow manure on the living room floor. The
ivory of its keys curls up like the fingernails of a Chinese empress. All the
small noises of the house are quietly indifferent—sounds of a ship be-
calmed and abandoned in this great flat land stretching out to a smear of
color where the sky lifts up from beneath it.

In this house Arlyn lived with Genevieve. We have wandered through
looking at the objects here. Old flat metal bedpans, an ordinary wooden
straight chair with small wheels attached to its legs to make a wheelchair
for Genevieve. The bedframe piled over with rags, boxes, rusted objects,
jars, photographs, papers flapping in the wind. The broken mattress upstairs spills brittle yellow corn shucks. It is the beds which shook us most,
their desolation arousing thoughts of the woman who lay suffering year
after year, her body curling inward, in that house without electricity or
running water.

Ann realizes that in those happy childhood visits she had known so little of what went on in this house. Even then, apparently, it had been full
of trash and falling apart—once with a big hole in the floor—in winter. And
Arlyn did not bother to fix it. Genevieve was crippled by then, sitting in a
wheelchair. She was Catholic, saintly; on her face was a smile of sweetness
and resignation.

Once when Ann's uncle, Genevieve's brother, came to visit from California, he found flammable oil spilled all over the floor near the cooking
stove. And Genevieve not able to walk, with no way to get out if the place

caught fire. Arlyn hadn't noticed, didn't seem to register the danger even when the brother pointed it out to him.

> He who has seen the sufferings of men has seen nothing.
> Let him look upon the sufferings of women.
>   (Victor Hugo, as quoted in *Kansas: Prelude to the War for the Union*)

Ida, proprietress of the Morrisville Cafe, has invited us to dinner, *sans* Arlyn. Her two sisters and her niece will be there. Ann decides this is the time to record the women's side of what happened in this town back when Genevieve was alive.

That evening Este and I position the light stands across from the line of booths in the cafe. We tape the big reflector sheets to their stands. Cables are laid across the floor to the power sources. I help Mary tape the microphone to the ceiling, so that it will hang over the booth where the women will sit. We set up the tripod, attach the camera, snap on a magazine of film. The two black magazine boxes sit on the counter, ready. The place is cluttered with equipment now; we can barely squeeze through. Ida and her sisters and her niece observe this preparation with anxious glances. Now everything must stop while Este plies her light meter and we hook up a new battery to the camera, just in case.

And then Ida is talking, haltingly at first, while she works at the grill. She tells about her life after her husband left her. The difficulty of supporting and caring for her six children by herself, when she started to run this cafe. Her operations over the years. Major surgery more than once. "But the cafe always gave me something to come back to."

Out in the booth, Ann begins to question the women about Genevieve. "When Genevieve came back from California," says one of the sisters, "when she had just married Arlyn, why she was real good-lookin'. She was tall and I remember she wore a white coat. She had real nice clothes and she looked nice."

"Yes, I remember that," Ida says. "Then I went off to Oregon to live for some years, and when I came back, why, it was a shame! I couldn't believe it was her. She was all bent over sideways and so crippled she could hardly walk—and the clothes she had on, well, I don't want to say anything about them. But it was a terrible sight."

The sister nods. "But over the years, for all she went through out there on that farm—and I never went out there to see for myself—but for all she had to suffer out there, I'll say one thing for her: she stuck with him!"

The second sister remembers, "When she came to town, no matter how bad off she was, she always had that smile."

III

Our rented house dates from the 1890's. It is actually quite small, but is, as Arlyn points out, "conspicuous," set by itself on a lot a little out from the center of town, toward the grain elevator and railroad tracks. Dormers are built out from each window upstairs; on the first floor is a deep wraparound porch; up on top, a tiny attic room.

Inside, the ceilings are high, and the place is a mixture of the original finishing and the remodeling done since. Old heavy woodwork, new cheap plywood paneling. Fluorescent lights in the kitchen. A bathtub upstairs that takes an hour to fill. Heat from a floor register in the dining room.

In the front room our camera and sound equipment hunches around the walls and sprawls over the couch. Lightstands lean like streetcorner loafers in the hallway. A battery belt coils over the arm of one of the three chairs in the dining room.

My production notebooks rest on another of the chairs along with my small library that is meant to be consolation and escape: Annie Dillard, *Pilgrim at Tinker Creek; Womenfriends,* by Walton and Newton; *Kansas: The Prelude to the War for the Union,* by Leverett Wilson Spring. The last, in its battered library binding, was published in 1885, and happened to be in my apartment in San Francisco. I am of the literal cast of mind that requires when coming to Kansas one ought to read a book about Kansas. There would be some security in knowing how many bushels of wheat the state produces annually, how many U. S. presidents grew up here—these facts to place over my own more immediate awareness of this Midwest. I know these people; my aunts lived in such towns as this all their lives, my former husband's mother came from a Kansas farm town. She carried its morality and its social expectations with her wherever she went. Statistics, then: Morrisville is a town of one thousand inhabitants. Uncle Arlyn is worth a quarter of a million dollars, thusly: he owns five hundred acres of farm land, each worth $500. On this land he has a herd of about one hundred fifty cattle. It was for such numbers that I looked in the Kansas book, but found instead the ugly story of the struggle between the pro-slavery people (mainly from Missouri) and the abolitionists (mainly from New England) to colonize and control the Kansas territory before the Civil War. Lies, violence, greed; the fight over abolition in the Kansas territory was a disgusting, shameful series of events.

After days of cold and even snow, one day the weather surprises us with balmy spring warmth. We eat lunch in the kitchen. Salad in a yellow plastic bowl we bought at the dry goods store, a cheese omelet, beer. I tease Mary, babbling to keep my spirits up. I choose Mary to tease because she is the most distant of us, the most ascetic.

In the hour before we must get back to work, Mary goes out to lie in the sun in the side yard. I follow her out, lie down about ten feet from her. We had a discussion two days ago about a book she was reading, which detailed the process of going crazy. Lying there on the prickly grass under the hot sun, I ponder that. Finally I ask, "Have you ever felt on the edge of insanity?"

Silence from Mary's direction. I become aware of the hum of the grain elevator, the twitter of birds in the trees near the broken sidewalk.

Mary says from behind a frown, "I am trying to sleep."

Why am I so vastly lonely, lying here looking up at the scrolls and curlicues of our house, the trees just coming to bud, the lovely house across the street that looks as if it belongs in Southern France, with its Mansard roof and subtle greenish color like the patina on bronze. It is the loneliness I felt growing up in Ohio, as if I was locked away from the life I sought, that must be more passionate then the one I lived, more full of meaning.

The land stretches out—the miles of wheat fields, of pasture, of milo for feed. I seek out treasures like the house across the street, like the definition of "milo" that I copied from the dictionary. Americanization of a Bantu word, "maili." It is "any of a group of grain sorghums with somewhat juicy stalks and compact heads of white or yellow soft grains." How did this word travel from the black tribes of equatorial and southern Africa here to Kansas? I occupy my mind with such questions, in defense, for that which I did not expect is beginning to happen to me. A wound is opening, an old wound, to reveal the thing hidden deep inside. We grew our layers of denial over it; we grew passivity like a covering of spongy fat, hoping it would protect us. We became complicit with the lying. Here in the heartland, the requirements have not changed. I lied to Bess in the rest home. I said blithely, we'll be back.

IV

SCENE: 5   LOCATION: Cattle auction, county seat

This shot with the Bolex   SOUND ROLL: 18

PRODUCTION NOTES: Camera footage of animal pens, restaurant (sign on wall reads "Cowgirls need love too"), auction hall from the audience, auction hall from the auctioneer's booth.

This is an octagonal building, pine-panelled, with bleachers surrounding the arena floor, rising step-fashion up its sides. The animals are driven in clusters past the auctioneer's booth into the central enclosure, where the bidding takes place. Then a cowboy using a stick with a nail on the end, drives them out again and slams the gate. Pigs squealing. Cows pissing noisily. The cowboy accidentally slams the gate on a pig's snout, and the pig is imprisoned there, shrilling loudly in pain. When the animal is released, it staggers away from the door, blood streaming from its nostrils.

"My god, now I know why I'm a vegetarian," Este mutters beside me.

Ann is on the other side of the arena with the Bolex. A much smaller camera than the Eclair, it is easier to handle in a crowded situation like this one, but it cannot be synchronized with a tape recorder, so that she is shooting silent footage.

Mary, with the Nagra tape recorder slung on a strap over her shoulder, earphones on her ears and the long foam-covered mike held out before her, is getting "wild sound," the random noises going on around us. She is tall and thin, small-boned, delicate appearing. In her rimless glasses she can look grandmotherly or like a skinny bespectacled child.

Uncle Arlyn pays close attention to the babble of the auctioneer, peers intently at the animals. He tells me how the bidding is done. The farmers do not want each other to know who is bidding on what, so each bids covertly with a subtle gesture. A finger raised to a hatbrim, one leg crossed over the other, hand brushing nose—all the while they try to look as casual and indifferent as possible. The auctioneer and the cowboy in the ring must be constantly alert to catch these secret bids. As he sees each bid, the cowboy gives a great whoop.

It's fascinating trying to see who's doing what, while they try to hide it. The older men seem to be doing most of the bidding. They are in general more dominant: probably they have more land and more stock and more money. This is the patriarchy, seemingly intact. The hall is filled with farmers of French and Swedish stock. Many have their male children with them. There are very few women here (though there are two cowgirls working in the stalls), and no brown or black faces in the crowd around me. This is a tight community, held together generation after generation.

At first we had been uncertain how the farmers would react to our filming them, but we needn't have worried. The auction hall is so much their environment and they are in general having such a good time, that the presence of these "girls from California" with their cameras and other equipment is only another occasion for fun. "Watch out," yells a man when Ann aims the Bolex at his seat-mate, "you might break your camera!" That and other tired witticisms make the rounds. The men tease each other about looking good, ask Ann if she wants their phone numbers, and laughter ripples about the hall.

Earlier, when Arlyn and I were in the restaurant section, we sat against the wall watching Este roam the room with the Bolex. She has long thick lightbrown hair, enormous blue eyes in a wide face. "That Este," Arlyn chuckled, "she looks more like a cowgirl than any of the rest of you girls— with them patched jeans. She must've been raised up pretty common."

Has he been taken in by Este's phony country accent? He blinks in surprise as I tell him that Este was, in fact, raised up pretty upper middle class, as the daughter of a professor.

At the restaurant in the county seat where we eat lunch, Mary happens to burp, and claps a hand to her chest. Arlyn, catching this gesture, looks up at her from watery blue eyes. "I guess my table manners aren't too good." "No, no," Mary explains, "I just had to burp. It had nothing to do with you." It's clear he doesn't believe her. The rest of us chime in, trying to help. "She didn't mean anything, Arlyn."

He isn't sure. He is quite aware that the sensibilities of most people are offended by his person, that his neighbors disapprove of the junkyard in which he lives, that his miserliness is a town joke. He suffers from these attitudes, yet it's clear he would change no facet of his behavior to make himself more acceptable. When approached on the subject he retreats into acute discomfort.

Ann starts trying to convince him to install electricity in his town house. Arlyn becomes very ill at ease, his eyes looking hangdog and suspicious.

"But if you had electricity, you could have a television and you could watch the baseball games," Ann says.

Arlyn shifts in his seat. "Uh ... no ... the wiring's bad ... it'd have to be all rewired ..."

"But wouldn't that be worth it?" Ann asks. "Then you wouldn't have to sit in the dark at night, and watching tv would give you something to do."

"I listen on the radio," he mumbles, and now we can't even see his eyes, he has receded so far. Finally his hand lifts to brush awkwardly across his face. It is a hand like a club, deformed by work—the knuckles swollen, the fingers twisted almost sideways at the joints. All of us stare at that hand, behind which he hides his embarrassment.

Only when we change the subject does he return to us. He watches us warily for a time, then begins to participate once again in the conversation and ends by telling a rousing story about a farmer who got drunk and drove his tractor into the pond on Arlyn's farm, in the middle of the day, and Arlyn had to pull him out or he would've drowned. And he laughs at his own story, glancing around at us. Now he is innocent as a child, his eyes mischievous and shining.

When we get up to go, Arlyn scoops the chicken bones from the plates and without bothering to wrap them, shoves them into the pocket of his corduroy coat. "I'm takin' these for the dogs," he explains.

"But Arlyn," I ask him, worried, "isn't it bad to give chicken bones to dogs?"

He nods good humoredly at me. "Well, they say so. You betcha they do. They say they can puncture their stomachs, but I've never had it hap-

pen." And he walks ahead of me out the door of the restaurant, wiping
the chicken grease from his fingers onto his overalls.

SCENE: 7   LOCATION: Cattle feeding Arlyn's farm

CAMERA ROLL: 28   SOUND ROLL: 20

STOCK: 7247
ASA: Normal
LENS: 10 mm
FILTER: no

PRODUCTION NOTES: Take 1 — Este shooting from the road to get the
sunset out across the flat fields of wheat.
    Take 2 — Este inside cab of Luke's truck — sync sound. (Luke is the
man Arlyn employs to feed the cattle now that Arlyn is too old to do it
himself.)
    Take 3 — Este riding in back of truck — sync.

    The cattle feeding is exhilarating to film, out in the cold wind just at
sunset, bumping along in the back of a truck. At Arlyn's house in town,
Luke and his son Kledis load thirty-five bales of hay and two bags of pro-
tein pellets onto the back of Luke's pickup. Then, with us following,
they drive out to the farm, unlatch the gate and go past the dilapidated
house into the open field. The cattle see them coming, begin to low and
hurry toward the truck. Luke drives very slowly over the ground, which
is bumpy with prairie dog holes, while in the back of the truck Kledis
opens the bags of pellets and strews them on the ground. The cattle have
gathered into a great stumbling herd behind the truck, pushing each
other, jockeying for position, leaning to eat the pellets. There are many
new calves—wobbly-legged and curious, a bright redbrown, with white
faces—who stumble in the midst of the hurrying grown-up cows and
somehow never get knocked down.
    Now Kledis begins to drop the hay behind the truck. First he cuts the
twine holding the bale together, then lets the bale flake off and fall to
the ground, where the cows begin to eat. There are two horses in among
the cows: one runs around the edge of the crush, its mane lifting in the
wind, looking wild and free.
    Ann has agreed to let Este shoot the cattle feeding this time. (We will
come back several times more to make sure we get it.) We have strapped
the bodypod to Este's waist and shoulder and have attached the big

heavy Eclair camera to the bodypod. Then we helped her up into the back of the truck where she braces herself on the tailgate, trying to hold the camera steady and stay out of Kledis's way, trying not to be knocked off by the cows who crowd up against the truck. Mary runs beside the truck with the Nagra to get sync sound, and I run behind Mary in case she needs me.

All this is very hard work and tremendous fun. I carry the magazine boxes and the filters and the production notebook. The weather has turned cold again. The wind is icy, and even wearing long underwear, two sweaters and a down jacket, plus a wool hat and scarf, and gloves, I must keep moving to stay warm.

When all the hay has been dropped from the back of the truck, we look out to where more than a hundred cattle are scattered in a long waving line across the land, their heads lowered to the hay strewn on the ground. Behind them, the sky has turned vermilion.

V

From the bathroom window I can see out across the open field to the grain elevator. In fact that's just about all I can see—that great high rounded building filling the space within the windowframe. Just beyond it is the railroad track, some scraggly trees. Now and then a train comes clacking along the track, screeches to a stop on a separate little side track near the elevator; a chute is moved into position, and the contents of the elevator slide down into the boxcars of the train. One by one they clang into position to receive their cargo. So all the way across the great flat central plains, each tiny farm town has its grain elevator on the railroad track, and the freight trains snake their way across, picking up the crops grown by the farmers and taking them to the big cities. Who in New York or San Francisco ever thinks about this vast flat land where the wheat for their daily bread is grown? I sit gazing out the window, a book open on my knees. The low roar of machinery comes from the grain elevator. It starts up in the morning and goes all day. Not a soothing sound like the ocean or even the flow of traffic on a highway, that you live with and forget most of the time—this is a factory noise, whine of metal on metal, loud thumps and groans of weight being moved. It invades our house. I think of how it would be to live here as a wife and mother, caught in the house, surrounded by that noise all day every day.

The bathroom smells of mildew. I sit in here because of the little gas heater in the corner. On the wicker hamper under the window lies the Annie Dillard book, but the book open on my lap is called *Womenfriends: A Soap Opera*. It is a series of communications between two women who have been friends since college—a dual journal over a period of several

years examining the development of their friendship. Pauline, college in-
structor and political lesbian. Rebecca, working woman, wife and eventually mother. Reading, I am often annoyed at the extreme self-absorption
of these women, their competitiveness, their endless self-examination; yet
at other moments I am won by their willingness to expose those parts of
themselves which are least attractive, to risk making of their friendship a
process of discovery.

But now in the quiet afternoon here in our rented house, under the roar
of the grain elevator, with the little town spaced out in yards and houses
around me, and the vast flat empty land beyond, I find the writings of
these two articulate women as foreign as, for instance, would be a Mexican
restaurant on the main street of Morrisville. Pauline and Rebecca live in
the largest, most densely populated, most sophisticated city in this country. The thoughts expressed by them come out of who they are in that
particular New York City environment, the relationship itself is one that
would probably exist only among sidewalks and subways and artists' lofts
and expensive cramped apartments. That women should be ego-centered
and intensely questioning, seeking full intellectual lives and professional
fulfillment for themselves, *as well as,* in Rebecca's case, the raising of a
child—this would be heresy indeed in Morrisville. And that there are
women like Pauline who love other women to the exclusion of men—well,
that would call down the fury of these Kansas patriarchs.

The independent women who surely existed in frontier times—the
entrepreneurs and adventurers, the scratchy cantakerous separate women—
their history is not felt in Morrisville. The ones who surely exist right now
are not visible here. And yet the ideas of options for women are seeping
out even here to the prairie. Listen to this interchange from our evening
at Ida's cafe.

Jackie-Lynn, Ida's niece, who is in her twenties and the mother of two
children, asks of her mother and aunts: "Did it ever cross any of your
minds though, that you would ever be anything other than a wife and
mother? Did you believe that was your role? Your destination?"

They answer in a jumble, all talking at once: "There never was anything
else . . ." "No, see, we all got married." "You have to take what comes in
life." "Who had the time to sit around making decisions?"

Jackie-Lynn: "Take girls today just coming out of high school—they
can go to college and they have a choice. They can at least *think* about it.
They may end up that way too, but you guys didn't really have a choice."

"We did what we had to do," says the mother.

Jackie-Lynn (determinedly): "My daughter is real small now, but as she
grows up I'm going to let her know that she can be anything she wants."

We are drawing close to Genevieve now, as surely our forbear as if all of
us, like Ann, were Marie's little girls. That big-featured face, long and skull-

like with jutting nose, the dark eyes, the black hair hanging straight to just below the ears. Genevieve in her wheelchair, placed at center-front of the group at the family reunion. Wasted face gently smiling. Her body, bony and contorted, leans sideways in the chair.

The women in the cafe speak of her suffering. First for arthritis, then later for cancer, she had sixteen operations. During one early surgery something was left inside her body when the incision was sewn up. They don't remember what exactly—a pair of scissors? some packing? Its presence inside her caused terrible complications. Later the surgeon opened her up again and found it. Arlyn did not sue the doctors or try to get any restitution from them. As is usual with such torture, there were no consequences to the torturers.

On the days when we must film out at the farm, we stumble about glum and angry. The wind whipping through the broken windows of the house murmurs to us of Genevieve. What was it like to come back from each surgery to this house without lights, without a bathroom?

And the summers. Arlyn has never planted a tree. The house has no shutter, awning, porch, and never did. It is a tall box with gaping holes for door and windows. There would have been no shade, no relief from the heat.

Yet the past is slippery. What can we *know* of Genevieve, dead since 1952. Ann remembers a woman in a wheelchair. Genevieve died when Este was only one year old, when Mary was eight years old, Ann thirteen, I sixteen. So we arrive at her from different historical perspectives (a fifties teenage was different in crucial respects from those years lived in the seventies) and lifestyles (two of us are heterosexual, one now living with a male lover; two of us are lesbians). But Genevieve is a wound in all of us by now, torn open. Inside is found the object, the perception, the anguish we thought we had buried or that we never knew was there.

Este adds two more verses to her song.

> Now me and Genevieve we had a hard life
> And she got more sickly with fear
> I can't understand it I treated her good
> And gave her a bath once a year
>
> Had no water nor heat, but she was so sweet
> That she kept all her suffrin' inside
> She smiled every day, seemed to make it okay
> And I can't understand why she died.

Arlyn told a story set in the Depression, a cruel time for him and Genevieve: "Genevieve and I, we got started to, during the hard times . . . we had her dad to take care of and we couldn't and uh, work was scarce then, we had to do something! And we'd go make these trash piles and pick out stuff to wear, shoes and whatnot. You know, now Genevieve was, you might say, raised in wealth . . . she was . . . and that was an awful comedown for her. As a girl she had everything she wanted, about . . . she wasn't forced to work and go off and make these trash piles, that was quite a comedown for her. Well, one day Genevieve and I were in the trash pile looking for things. The bus and preacher came by and they stopped to see who it was, and he saw it was us. Well, he just stuck his head up and drove on, like he didn't even recognize us. And Genevieve says . . . ." Arlyn lifted up his head and laughed in admiration. "She says, 'Well, go ahead, it doesn't matter to me, if that's the way . . .' She didn't care who saw us."

Ah, she must've been a feisty one, we tell each other. She must've given that Arlyn a hard time. But we have begun to perceive the breadth and depth of Arlyn's stubbornness, this obduracy slyly masked by the appearance of yielding. (How come you never brought that piano into town when you left the farm? Mary asked. Arlyn glanced at the ruined piano standing in its layer of cow shit, and said serenely, Oh yeah, you bet, one day I'm gonna do that. And he believes he *will*, while of course having no intention of doing it.) So it comes to us that Genevieve, isolated out here with only Arlyn for company, had to live *around* that immovability, had to make the best of what little there was in that stark, barnlike house, of comfort, of companionship.

Mary has a theory. "Think of the illness as resistance," she suggests. "If she was sick she couldn't breed; if she was crippled she couldn't work."

To resist by destroying oneself, to sacrifice one's body, is a gruesome idea, but it is better than the thought of Genevieve as passive victim with *no* control over her destiny.

—or "destination," as Jackie-Lynn put it.

(Excerpt from a letter from Ann's father):

"Arlyn came of old, basic Swedish farm stock. Stolid, unimaginative and rather insensitive. Never vicious, mean or cruel. . . . I suppose to Arlyn and the men of his family women simply endured the frailties of their lives. It was Genevieve's misfortune to have more than most to endure."

VI

SCENE: 10   LOCATION: Barn Sale, neighboring town
CAMERA ROLLS: 25, 26, 27   SOUND ROLLS: 19, 20

STOCK: 7247
ASA: Normal

LENS: 9.5–95; 25 mm (cam roll 27)
FILTER: 85 (cam roll 26)

PRODUCTION NOTES: Begins with long shot of farm from the road; snow on red roof of barn; pickups and cars lining the road approaching farm.

Takes 1 through 6 — Auctioneers auctioning junk from a flatbed wagon. Arlyn in among the crush of farmers bidding for items and buying them.

Takes 7 and 8 — Women inside barn, selling sandwiches and pies and coffee to the farmers coming in from the sale.

End of roll 26 is just outside the barn, where auction notices are tacked to the barn door. Men stand looking at the notices, which lift and flutter in the wind.

On the way to the sale, Arlyn explained. The owner was giving up his farm to move elsewhere; probably he had already sold it. Now he wanted to sell all his equipment and farm vehicles, everything he had used to work with over the years.

In the back seat, as we drove out into the bleak snowy morning, Este and Ann and I sat crammed together, film gear piled on our laps. I looked out across the open fields to the occasional lines of trees, wondering if Este and Ann were as aware as I was of Arlyn's manure smell here in the closed car. When Este reached to open the window a crack, I smiled.

At the sale, now, there is a sharp wind, and the two auctioneers at work up on the flatbed trucks among the piles of junk are bundled up to the ears. Mud everywhere. Scattered snow. The farmers with their bright billed caps—orange and yellow and red and green—given to them by farm machinery companies and feed companies.

While Este and Mary and Ann are getting the equipment out of the back of the station wagon, strapping the bodypod onto Ann's shoulder, I retreat to the barn. Inside, a dozen women are busily at work. Before them are board tables loaded with homemade pies and sweetrolls, urns of coffee. Behind them are the makings for ham sandwiches, barbecued beef, hotdogs.

The farmers stamp about the doorway, huddling half-in, half-out, drinking coffee. A raw wind enters among them.

While I know I should hurry back out to help start the filming, there is something in this shadowy barn of much more urgency for me. I stand in a corner eating a piece of warm apple pie, watching the women busily setting out the food. There is not one woman here under the age of fifty. Their eyeglasses, their headscarves, their thick wool coats draw my gaze; their mouths are tight with all the years of doing what was necessary, their eyes shy and curious behind the glasses, noticing me as a stranger, even as I am feeling so much a part of them. I am so relieved to be here among them. They can't know this. Possibly they would not want it. Nor understand my affection for them, how much I want to talk with them, come back in the fall to hear their voices, let them speak their lives. And the cowgirls at the auction hall, the waitresses in the cafes, the wives on the farms—that society of women hidden from us this time around.

I should go outside to help with the equipment; I know Ann will be impatient with me. But I am not yet ready to relinquish this good feeling. I want somehow to take it with me, and I think of the still camera I am carrying in my pocket. Yes, perhaps a picture.

When there is a lull in business, I approach the table. Will they let me photograph them all together, I ask, to the women in general. They look embarrassed. I tell them I am from California, I've never been to an event like this barn sale and I really want to have a picture of them, if they don't mind. There are some moments of hesitation, in which I feel ridiculous, aware of how conspicuous I have suddenly become. But then the women cluster together for the portrait. Looking through the viewfinder at the faces of these stolid survivors, I understand why Bess and Genevieve cannot be here, they who carried the weight of madness and pain.

Now I really must leave the barn and go out to help the others. The women return to work again, arranging food on the table, stirring the barbecued beef in the steamer, slicing the pies.

Outside, the wind is a knife ripping at my clothes. Across the barnyard I see the "girls from California," heavyladen with equipment, making their way through deep squishy mud toward the crowd of farmers around the flatbeds. I hurry to join them.

Barbara Noda

Thanksgiving Day

We stand loosely gathered in a circle with our heads bowed and mumble blessings to the clouds. Grandpa lies below us simmering in the ground. The crisp air of November rushes through the empty rooms of the young and thickens in the dark chambers of the very old. Grandma's hands and feet are numb and the cold is lodged between her stiff bones like a bank of fog. She applies a white cold cream to her face each morning and night, and in the soft glow from early winter her wrinkled skin has an almost wooden sheen like a worn puppet that has been rubbed with oil for centuries by strong and gnarled hands. She is the last of her generation.

Her hair is grey as the season and propped limply on the head with bobby pins and a fine black net that she untangles with spotted hands. The bristles of her brush dig into the scalp while the meager strands of hair are merely pushed aside. When she stares into the mirror, her image fades and disappears. There is only the cluttered reflection of Grandpa's desk strewn with calendar pages of years past, scraps of paper he saved for writing. On the wall is the blood-stained Christ preserved on parchment.

Husband and wife, a Japanese arrangement of flowers, they dragged their plow like a samurai's sword through muscles hard as rock, the stomach of young California, and made the valley bleed.

We stamp our feet on the ground like horses and feel him pumping down there. Without a marker we recognize the plot of still cemetery grass. The fatherless sons are balding and the fatherless daughter's hair is brittle from black dye. The grandchildren, their memories sticky with peach fuzz blown from everlasting orchards on hot summer days, are full grown and broad shouldered. The black shocks of hair are stiff as hay, like helmets woven thick and coarse, testament of the ancestral blood. Held in her young father's arms is a child with eyes liquid and musical as a waterfall. Her deaf ears are forgotten. She is the first of her generation.

In the slow rhythm of a Buddhist chant, we faithfully trudge after Grandpa along the heavenly trail from Mt. Fuji to the Sierra Nevadas. From the inside of the mountain, he taps a cryptic code with his wooden cane. We farm the land that he farmed, we give birth to his children, and we conjure new prayers before our meals. We cross new oceans as willingly as he crossed his, and when I trespass the no-man's land with my lover, I think of him—a young man who ran away from Yamanashi-ken to settle in the barren dust of San Joaquin.

Grandma shakes a tired head. Like a cold wind, she leads us away. Invisible leaves fall, silent as tears.

Diana Rivers

Family Reunion

I

Her children are scattered all over now. And so is Sheila. In the past two years she's gone from New York to New Orleans and involvement in women's politics, to a commune in Arkansas, to a California film group and back to Arkansas again. And her possessions too are scattered. Rugs left with her ex-husband—she's going to repossess them as soon as she has her own place. Furniture in the attic of a New Jersey barn that might be sold by now. Boxes of books—how many, three boxes, four, six, she doesn't remember anymore—with a friend in San Francisco, the books she can't live without. Clothes, jewelry, paintings, photos left in a winding trail across the country and more important, parts of herself, deep parts of herself caught tangled in people's lives and endeavors, torn off by departures, hers and others'.

When she comes back again to Arkansas her friends are surprised. "We thought you'd stay in San Francisco. It seems like everything's happening there."

"It is. There's everything there you could possibly want or imagine and more and too much. Everything but a peaceful space to sort it all out. I had to come home for that." So for the first time in her unmarried life Sheila calls a place home and comes back to it—but to town, not to the struggle on the commune.

She rents a tiny house with a big yard. "I've got to have a garden even if I'm not in the country." And she isn't going to live collectively for a while, she says. She has too much to think about and needs time to be alone.

But then the question of loving women, the question that's agonized her since New Orleans and chased her across the country, moves in with her. Nancy, sick with some undiagnosed illness, comes to share the house and they fall in love. Nancy, who was only going to stay a week or so while she found another place.

"Oh yes, time to be alone," Margo says mockingly. "Well, people say all kinds of things about relationships but when it comes to it, I believe what I see."

"Well I meant it when I said it, Margo. I thought I'd had enough of relationships for a while."

"That's different, that was with men. Anyhow, like I said, I believe
what I see." Margo is careful to remain alone.

So the question comes and lands in Sheila's hands as gently as a small
bird. But the small bird has a beak and can use it and sometimes draws
blood.

"You think you're better than me because I've always been gay and
you're just learning to love women," Nancy shouts at her. "You think I'm
queer and you're not." Sheila cries and feels deeply cut, not because it
isn't true but because it is. And lying wakefully in the dark with one of her
anxiety attacks she thinks, Nancy's right, she's right about me but how can
I change that? And do I want to? The central root question of her identity
floating in the shifting fluid of her life. But I love her so much, she says
silently, passionately to the night powers and curls tight against Nancy's
body, always lighter, thinner. "Leave her alone you monsters," she says to
the darkness, to whatever it is that saps and sucks away at life. She feels
herself sleeping between death and love, her body like a shield.

But mostly Sheila finds it easy loving another woman. Even in their
angriest fights there are some lines not crossed, some respect for the person that remains. She never feels that threat of annihilation at the core
and realizes how often in fights with Tom it was not her ideas she was de-
fending, not the correctness of what she was saying but her very survival,
her right to existence. And even Ian that she lived with for a while at the
commune. He'd been so different, a much gentler man, wanting peace in
the world but when he was hurt he fought that same way. How do men
learn that, the words to destroy with and more than that, the will to use
them? Sheila can think quick enough of things to say but women are train-
ed not to use words that way. It's castrating, that terrible word—castrating.
And men have no such restraint. Women after all don't have balls, so men
can say anything, words to crush the ego, the heart, the soul. Symbolic
castration, words to break the spirit—the very thing women value in each
other.

Living with Nancy is a gentling experience. Sheila can feel hard little
crusts and scabs, grown for protection, scaling away, soft parts of herself
expanding. Sometimes, coming down in the morning, she sees the light
falling in just a certain way on flowers Nancy's picked or stones that she's
arranged and Sheila's filled with a sense of warmth and safety. Friends
tease her for being so stable. Charlotte says, "You haven't moved in three
months. Are you settling down? Getting conservative? Where will I get my
vicarious adventures now?" But they're glad for her.

A house, a lover to share it with, a job. She drives a bus for a government agency, taking old people on errands—doctors' appointments, shop-

ping, sometimes a movie. A funny job but she loves doing it. It's mostly women. They like and trust her. It makes her feel useful and pays enough to live on. Not much, it's only four days a week but she doesn't need much and it leaves her some time free. And Nancy stays home and does indexing when jobs come in but the work is sporadic, sometimes nothing for a while, sometimes so much that Sheila has to help. (They've just struggled through a three-volume American history.) Nancy sleeps a lot or rests upstairs by the big window that looks out over the yard toward the hills. They send for Sheila's books. When the boxes come it's like Christmas. The books are lined up now on the low shelf under the window, waiting for Nancy. "I've never had so much time to read before." There's not much furniture but they paint the house white and fill it with big brightly covered cushions. And now that the weather's getting cold and they hardly need it, they finally manage to get a working refrigerator from the landlord.

The roof is the real problem. It's leaking more with each rain, tiny veins of water, probing, probing . . . . But the landlord is stubborn. When Sheila calls up he says, "No way. Not going to put on a new roof. That's crazy. The whole place is falling apart. It's going to be torn down in a year or so— garden apartments."

"Well, for right now it's leaking. At least get someone to patch it."

"I can't. Nobody wants to do that kind of work."

"I'll do it myself, then. Just get me a ladder, the materials and take some off the rent."

"I can't. The insurance . . . ."

"Damn the insurance!" she's shouting into the phone, enjoying it. Nancy is clapping. "That damn roof of yours is leaking all over. Our clothes, our books, everything's getting ruined. Are you going to pay for that?" She hangs up feeling satisfied and not expecting much. After three more calls he brings it all, a ladder, tar, shingles, rope. He mumbles and shuffles and gives terrible warnings, " . . . never saw a woman do such a thing." And finally he leaves.

Sheila stands straddling the roof peak, her arms up, fingers like arrows in the blue sky. "I'm queen of the air," she shouts.

"If you fall off before you get that roof fixed it's going to be a wet winter."

"It's okay. I'm spider woman. I can't fall. Nancy, I love it up here. I do. Do you want to be up here? Is this something you wanted to do?"

"Don't worry, I haven't the slightest desire to be up there. And I don't feel at all deprived or oppressed holding the ladder."

But it's not easy maneuvering with a rope on the steep roof and more than once she feels herself slipping before the rope snugs up on her. Later she wonders what her sons would have thought seeing her up there. She often does that, seeing herself over again through their eyes, giving her life a peculiar complexity, the quality of double exposure coming at the strangest times.

"They'd be proud of you and if they weren't they should be. The hell with them anyway. Who cares? I'm jealous of your past. It doesn't leave us alone. I feel like it's peering into our lives, into our beds. They've had your time. It's my turn now."

The next night they lie together in the dark, safe and dry, listening to the rain. "I love the sound of rain when it's outside." They sink back into that deep voluptuous body comfort, shared warmth and safety from the elements. And for days afterward Sheila feels a warm sense of accomplishment.

"A few years ago I wouldn't even have tried that. I'm amazed at how well I did it. Do you think it's alright or am I becoming too male, turning into the man of the house?"

Nancy makes a sound like a laugh and cough combined. "Look—a year ago I could have out-run and out-climbed and out-danced you easily and a year from now I'll probably be able to again, so don't get too uppity. Just enjoy your glory while it lasts. And besides I like my women tough." Nancy is lying in the upstairs bed looking particularly fragile with the quilt pulled up high around her.

The house is dry now but drafty. Sheila is talking about getting one of her rugs back from Tom when she goes up north for Thanksgiving.

"If he'll let go of it. He'll probably moan and groan about how I'm taking it away from my children too and tell me again how he's kept the home together for them—the twist of guilt. But we need it here."

She wants the rug because the house is old and hard to heat and the dampness is especially bad for Nancy but more than anything and without her knowing it, she wants it because it was her grandmother's. Somehow having that rug on the floor will make her own life seem less bizarre to her and more familiar.

Going to New York for Thanksgiving—the first time she's been there in two years. Back . . . back into a primeval time, a different geological era. And they'll all be there, all her sons, home from the various places they've scattered to. Josh up from Florida where he works in a marine lab, the other two from schools in Michigan and Vermont. She's seen them separately a few times since she left but never together. And of course Tom will be there. She pictures his bulk standing in the doorway as she comes up the walk. All of them—together—that solid male presence, so loud and absolute, the way they talk, how they occupy space, sit in the chair, in the room, in the house, in the world. Will there be space for her in that scene?

Women in New Orleans used to say—three sons? Why'd you have three sons? Why indeed, a feminist with three sons, as if she'd done it on purpose. What hurt was having no daughters to share her new life with. But these are my children and I love them. I carried each one in my body for nine months—alien seed. She remembers how they each had stopped being fluid and light, had hardened, solidified, moved away from her love. Josh had kept it the longest, that loose flowing quality of the new child. That was because he was part reptile. He was the one who caught frogs and toads and turtles and most of all snakes. Snakes that he carried in his pocket and up his sleeves, wore casually around his neck. Memories of her own childhood. She'd taught all three of them about the woods. But Josh had gotten more of it. He was most hers, softhearted, cried easily—until it was beaten out of him, over years. And she'd had to watch helpless. That man's world has no place for a boy that cries. He's learned to toughen up. His brothers aren't ashamed of him anymore. He's with them now, part of that block of maleness, the old flowing rivers parched dry—cracked and hard.

Going back . . . going back . . . She'll have to meet their judgments on her life, on herself. Two years, two years and how can she account for them? "Nancy, I'm scared. Why did I ever agree to do this? How can I be with them and stay myself? Keep hold of my new life, of this reality?"

They're up in Nancy's room visiting with Margo. Nancy is lying with her head on Sheila's lap. The room is filled with sunlight and tiny rainbows flash from the crystals hanging in the window. The whole space seems to float in light and color.

"I'll be there with you," Nancy says. "Even though my body's here, my love will go with you."

"That's right, we'll all be there with you, all our spirits, any time of night or day. And this rotten old atheist will even light a candle for you every night, send you energy. How about that? Just don't tell anyone else or they'll think I'm going soft." Margo's pacing around the room, unconscious of the rainbows slipping across her face.

Sheila shakes her head. "I can see Tom standing there with his square bulk, saying, 'Well, you got rid of your husband, left your children, you had the freedom you wanted. What did you do with it?'" The accounting, what have you made of yourself? Have you scored in the world and how?

She'd been a waitress, an apprentice typesetter, taken a carpentry class, tossed around fifty and one hundred pound bags of food for the co-op in New Orleans and also helped form and felt driven out of the women's collective there, been on unemployment, food stamps, welfare, learned as much about movie cameras and editing as the women at SkyFilms could teach her. And what was she doing with it all? Driving old people around in a bus. "And what does all that amount to anyway?"

"It's your life and you're living it," Margo says sharply. "That's what it amounts to. Why does it matter what he thinks?"

"But look at it. I have no profession. There's nothing I'm good at, not really. I've spent two years just going around in circles."

"He's still in your head, isn't he?" Margo's voice is getting louder. "You've got that fucker out of your life but he's still in your head, sitting there making his fucking judgments and you're letting him, damnit! You're letting him!" She stamps to the end of the room and hits the wall.

Nancy sits up with a groan. "Margo, can you rant more quietly? This house can't take it and neither can I. Privileges of the sick."

"Sorry." Margo comes to sit by them on the bed. "But I'm right aren't I? You're still letting him tell you what to do, how to see yourself."

"No," Sheila says shaking her head. "It has to do with how I feel about myself."

"That's bullshit—pure bullshit! You don't even believe that." Margo's shouting again.

"So you're going to push me around instead and tell me what to think and that's better because you're a woman." Now Sheila's shouting too. "Is that what you feel, Margo? That it's okay for you to bully me because you're a woman?"

"Look, you two. I need some rest or at least some restful space and this isn't it." Nancy lies down again, sighing wearily.

"Sorry." Margo stands up. "I have to go back anyway and work on Charlotte's truck." Stomping downstairs, she calls back, "If you want to keep that man in your head you're welcome to him. Just don't bring him back here with you."

After she's left Sheila asks, "Nancy, is she right? What do you think?"

"You know she's right."

"You don't think it's my own feelings too?"

"I don't think you know what your feelings are yet. Sometimes you are like a child. Your life is very new to you still. And sometimes in different ways we're all like children."

Sheila strokes Nancy's hair gently, watching the colors from the crystals flicker on her face. She sees the knowledge of death there, not just the paleness but a subtle inwardness and wonders as she has so often, what it really feels like to be inside that other person.

"I'm so confused at times," she says softly. "I feel all caught and mashed up between different values."

"Do you like what you're doing? Do you think it's worthwhile?"

"Of course I do."

"Then why are you asking some man up in New York if it's okay?"

"Nancy, I'm scared of going. My whole past is waiting there to swallow me up. I was married to that man for 23 years. I'm really scared."

"I know you are. I've been watching it." Nancy turns her face away so her expression's hidden and asks very quietly, "Will you come back?"

"Nancy—of course! Why the hell wouldn't I?"

"I thought maybe you'd marry them all again."

"Not likely." She hugs Nancy close against her. "No chance."

And anyhow they're gone, scattered now, the family she left doesn't exist that way anymore. But she dreams about them still, young and together. For the week before she leaves she dreams about them every night, her boys as little children and Tom, younger, less cynical, less hard—dreams full of warmth and anxiety.

II

This familiar room but so unfamiliar, as if seen from underwater, blurred and wavy and at the same time solid—so solid—everything massive, appropriate furniture in its appropriate place, no empty corners. Furniture she'd helped select, refinish, arrange, and now it's oppressing her. Unmoving material ghosts of oak and maple stare out blindly. Sheila feels stifled, suffocated here. No—it's more like drowning, going under, her bones turning soft. She's actually spent years of her life in this room and here it still is, a monument, a museum kept in living order. Longing for her bright pillows and quilts and cozy disorder, she thinks, he should have burned it all and started over.

They're all greeting her, talking at once and it's hard to understand the heavy rumble of their voices. She's not used to male voices anymore and can't distinguish the words. She answers or tries to answer, tries to say what will seem normal, tries not to show her panic at the terrifyingly familiar-unfamiliar, not to let them see she's drowning, that parts of her life are colliding and ripping apart, that floods of feelings are rushing through the gap.

Out of the din Sheila can hear Toby saying, "Looks like you lost a lot of weight Mom." And she's able to answer, "That's because I've been moving so fast." She laughs and they laugh with her and that steadies her a little. Tom's watching her intently—studying, waiting. She avoids his eyes. He wants to know who I am and I'm not ready for that yet, not ready. But she knows it's coming soon.

Sitting down to eat they take the same places at the table they've always had except for Josh and Toby who trade jokingly. Sheila automatically sits with her back to the kitchen looking out at the pine grove. Those trees were little seedlings when they first bought the house. They need to be thinned, she thinks. Someone should take care of that. Then she realizes that she's had the same thoughts almost every time she's sat there—years. Well it won't be me now that does it . . . .

Marty's telling a story about school, rambling through people and buildings and places that are endless and unfamiliar to her. Then somehow Josh is talking about reptile collecting in Florida. Sheila feels absent, unconnected to it all, hearing them at a distance from herself as if they were a television program playing in another room. Some part of her Is annoyed that they've shut her out so easily but underneath she's in a frozen panic, thinking, soon they're going to ask me, soon . . . soon . . . .

Tom is still watching her, hasn't stopped since she came and when there's a pause he says loudly, "Well, now, tell us, what on earth are you doing in a place like Arkansas?" As if it's Tibet or Hungary, as if only someone as crazy as Sheila would go there.

They're all looking at her. Now that the questioning's started she's actually relieved. "Just living there," she says as casually as she's able. "Everyone has to live some place and Arkansas is no stranger than anywhere else." They're still quiet, leaving her space to talk, not even eating. "I've rented a little house. I'm driving a bus for the E.O.A."

"You live by yourself?"

"I was for a while. That's what I thought I needed. Now I'm living with a woman named Nancy. We're in love with each other." It's been said, the words that can't be undone, irreversible, irretrievable, dropped like a rock on the table, humming, humming in the air around them. Into that reverberating silence she says quickly, "She's very sick. The doctors don't know what it is," and thinks, I'm throwing them Nancy's death like a bone, to keep the wolves from my throat. How shameful. She'd meant to say it all clearly and cleanly. But she's feeling calmer, steadier than she'd expected. When she can collect herself, she looks around from face to face, each arrested, silenced in personal surprise or embarrassment or confusion.

"We've been to lots of doctors. She's getting worse." Judas, she tells herself, traitor, as if only some great tragedy could make their love forgivable. Is she a traitor for even being there alone? Would Nancy have come with her if she'd been well? Would Sheila have wanted her to? Well, I'm not saying another word into this silence, she thinks stubbornly. I want to be out of this room, out, away from here, away from them all—in the pine grove or walking away down the road. But before she can actually move Josh says gently, "That must be very hard for you." He's watching her with concern. She realizes that only a few seconds have passed.

"I knew she was sick when we got together but it's still hard."

The others don't look at her. They focus on eating. Forks and knives against plates seem very loud. The food gets passed around several times. Finally Marty asks, "What were you doing in California?"

"Mostly learning to make films. There's a women's movie collective there called SkyFilms." She tells them movie stories and they're able to relax and look at her. She even gets them to laugh. But when she runs out of stories Tom says dryly, "Well, you didn't have to learn all that just to end up driving a bus."

Sheila feels the old anger rise in her, rise and subside like a breath. She looks right at him and laughs, "That's right. I didn't. That's not what I learned it for," and she's thinking, he's just where he was when I left, not changed at all. Thank heaven I'm not living with this man anymore. The sense of relief is so intense she blushes.

Tom doesn't ask her any more that night about her life, but next morning he meets her in the doorway, a tight smile on his face. "I always wondered why sex was so rotten between us," he says in that hard, mocking way she'd always hated and been so afraid of. "Now I know. It's just that my wife was a little bit queer. Now I don't have to worry anymore that it was me." He makes a grab for her arm but she steps back. Absolution, he's found absolution for their whole tangled past. Before she would have had to argue with him, struggle, relive the past, try to fix the blame, the ever shifting, never quite fixed blame. Now she just says, "No, you don't have to worry," and thinking of Nancy she smiles with potent, secret warmth. Maybe he's really right, maybe I've been there all the time . . . .

She steps past him into the living room and is standing on her grandmother's rug, in the middle of stiff traditional angular birds and flowers. Being on it gives her a curious strength. "Our house is cold and drafty so I need the rug now." When he starts to protest she says again, "I need it now. I plan to take it back on the plane with me."

"Look, I don't have a whole lot to say to you. It was the boys' idea for you to come. It certainly wasn't mine."

"I'm glad they wanted to see me."

"Maybe they're not so glad now. What kind of effect do you think it's going to have on them that their mother's a Lesbian?" He says that last word almost with a hiss.

"I don't know Tom. That's going to be up to them." She walks out of the house, trying to keep herself centered. It's been said—the worst has been said. On the back porch she sees a plant she'd started years ago, big now and overflowing the pot. I'll take back some cuttings, start a new one. I'll take back cuttings from all of them, but secretly, like a thief. She could not bring herself to ask him for anything.

"Hey Mom, put on some boots and walk down to the pond with me."

Staring into the pond with Josh she sees him again as a little boy, squatting over a puddle full of pollywogs, his cupped hands filled with black wiggly life. "Baby frogs, baby frogs." "Put them back Josh, they'll die." "But I want to take them home." The house was always full of things that wriggled, crawled, squirmed, slithered and mostly didn't stay in their containers.

"Do you still like snakes?"

"I have a boa-constrictor in Florida. My roommate Joel is feeding it for me. How about you?"

"I still like them but I don't keep them anymore, I just pick them up to hold and let them go again. I guess I don't keep anything much anymore. Besides, Nancy's afraid of snakes."

"You just have to show her how nice they are." He says it playfully, in a child's voice. They both laugh. Once, long ago, they'd decided it would be their secret mission in the world to change people's fear of snakes. Feeling really close to him at that moment, she puts her hand on his arm.

"Mom, is it very different to be loving a woman?" Josh, over six feet tall and still the straightforward child, still in some way innocent.

She smiles at him. "It's gentler. There's less conflict at a root level. And for me right now there's shelter and comfort that I need, no put-downs. And I can be as open and loving as I want."

"I think I can understand that," he says dreamily. "It sounds nice for you."

"And I still love you all," she says quickly, "I haven't changed. I'm still the same person at the core." She reaches up tentatively to touch his face. But is it true? At the core she may be the same but for the rest she's shed her past life like the old snake skins they used to find together in the woods.

For the next day or so, talking to old friends and neighbors, she has a weird sense of dislocation, like putting on clothes that are ten years old. She goes to visit Marsha who lives down the road and it's a strain. It's always been easy between them. Now she feels distant and polite. Finally she says, "Marsha, I feel like my own ghost."

Marsha nods and says slowly, "And I don't think I know you anymore."

Telling the bare facts of her life tells nothing of its essence, its real meaning to her. It's as frustrating as trying to tell a dream by the fragments of remembered events and having no words, no vocabulary at all for that great spectrum of mood and emotion that is the real drama.

They're all invited to a party at the Beal's. Sheila is particularly urged to come. Clarence Beal corners her in the kitchen. "Ho, ho, so you've been having a great time playing the middle-aged hippie these past two years and just left the rest of us here in our ruts. Bet you've had a lot of fine adventures along the way." He winks and puts his hand on her arm. She feels revolted and can't believe that she used to find this man slightly attractive and flirt with him at parties. Jack Tate appears over her shoulder. "Hey, I hear you're doing films in California. D'you work on . . .?" and he names three or four current films none of which she's seen or wants to. She shakes her head, smiling, smiling, more like a grimace. She feels them looming over her, repulsive and predatory. Smiling and shaking her head, she slips under Clarence's arm and backs away.

"Don't think she used to be so shy." They laugh together. They're amused by her. She's part of the evening's entertainment, that's why she was invited. She could probably tell them she was gay. They'd find that amusing too and still try to make out with her. Sheila has a quick flash of punching them both in the stomach, that sharp hard punch Lila taught her, seeing their faces turn red, their drinks splashed on the wall, seeing them slowly doubling forward together. But she's more bored than angry, flat heavy boredom. Everything in this scene is stale, the jokes, the bragging, the flirtations—and the cigarette smoke is hurting her eyes.

She leaves early, walking up the familiar road in the dark, rubbing her arm where Clarence held it. You should have just punched him out, she hears Margo saying. That man's a pig for sure. You should really have punched him out . . . .

He is and I should have. I'm just not ready yet. But maybe next time. Then out loud to Margo, to the night, "Next time, next time I'll punch them."

She misses them so much, Lesbian sisters, women she can talk to. Being here in this foreign country she sees clearly that she's one of them. The stars bend over her in the cold air and she's wishing she were back in Arkansas. They probably all went out to Mindy's farm for Thanksgiving. She sees Mindy with no shirt on, her leather vest open to the fall cold, chopping wood, and Margo tossing it in the wood pile. If Taurus is there they'll play drums until late at night and maybe sit out by a fire. Sheila feels isolated, cut off—a plant without water.

She calls Nancy as soon as she gets to the house. The phone rings across all that space—our lives strung out on singing wires, she thinks, like a line from a poem—and then Nancy answers. Nancy's voice is right there in the room with her. Sheila's past and her future and Sheila with the charged connection between them in her hand. The phone seems almost too hot to hold.

Nancy sounds tired but cheerful. She's gotten a kitten, black and long-haired, for company. The roof leaked in another place, lots of rain, ". . . but I got the landlord to fix it. Told him how sick I was and that you were away. Scared the old bastard . . . . Margo's living with a woman from Chicago. Terry and Linda have split up and Linda's going back to the west coast. And I've got an index here that's too big for me. Come home. I miss you." Behind the words there's a weariness.

"Soon. I'll be home soon. I don't belong here anymore. I probably never did. I miss you, I love you."

When she hangs up the house seems tensely quiet around her, alien and waiting. She goes up to her old sewing room somehow expecting it to be the same, the things that need mending piled up in corners waiting for her, and the rest a litter of bright fabrics for making collages and quilted pillow covers. Sometimes all of them, even Josh, outgrew the shirts before she got to patching the elbows.

But it's all changed, the only room that has. Tom's made it into an of-fice-study, male and orderly. All the soft brilliant clutter is gone, her de-signs taken down from the walls. She feels rebuked for intruding here and quickly shuts the door.

That night she sits up sweating from a dream. She remembers struggling to climb a stone wall with broken glass embedded in the top. Her hands are ripped and bleeding but she keeps trying. She has to. On the other side is a huge meeting of women, shouting in anger. Everything is permeated with fear. She knows she must get to the meeting but she can't climb the wall. She's terrified.

Even now, sitting up in the early gray light, that fear is with her in the room. She feels very alone, wraps her arm around herself and wishes for Nancy.

New Orleans—the dream is about New Orleans. There are walls like that in the French Quarter for keeping out prowlers. She looks at her hands for blood. New Orleans and Bonnie saying, "I only have energy for my Les-bian sisters. Straight women can get support from men." Shut out by other women when she tried to be part of the struggle. That six months in New Orleans was the hardest time of Sheila's life. She wouldn't live through it again for anything. And she wouldn't trade it for the world. The first time she's ever felt another woman's flesh pressed against hers, hot and wanting, another woman's tongue in her mouth. Women loving and sitting in judgment and caught in the tides—women shouting at each other, screaming, a roaring chaos, everything going down, anger and tears, accusa-tions so terrible they burn the air, even physical fights, the sisterhood she's just found ripped apart in bleeding shreds and Sheila's terrified vulnerable self running for shelter to a commune in the Arkansas hills, refugee from the women's wars, finding comfort with a softspoken bearded hippie. Liv-ing with women's rage, surviving it. When she'd talked to Josh about loving women she hadn't mentioned New Orleans. She's still trying to come to terms with it herself.

"That was a time wasn't it?" Margo likes to laugh about it. They'd been there at the same time but hadn't met till later. "Shit, I thought somebody was going to get killed for sure. And you left before it really got hot." Margo loves to tell New Orleans stories, the worse the better, but always ends by saying, "But we all came together at the end. It was worth it."

Sitting up, hugging her knees, Sheila says to Bonnie's strong round face in the air before her, Well Bonnie, I'm a Lesbian now. I'm not a dyke yet but I am a Lesbian. It's the first time she's really been able to say that to herself. Bonnie had loved her and wanted her and been afraid of being be-trayed by a "straight woman" and pushed her away. "Bonnie, Bonnie, good morning Bonnie, this is your sister up in a suburb of New York—our lives are strung out on singing wires—I have just this morning declared myself to be a Lesbian." And thank you Clarence Beal—she rubs the spot on her arm where he held her again. You'll never put your hands on me again. When she walks downstairs later she feels different, more solid.

Josh helps her roll up the rug and tie it like a long helpless body. It seems as if every piece of furniture in the room has at least one leg on it. They puff and struggle, laughing together.

"I feel funny taking it."

"Why should you? It's yours. Dad's going to grumble. So what? That's his way. You got little enough out of this house." That's true—little enough.

Marty's driving her to the airport so they can get a chance to talk alone, something he's been asking for. Before she leaves Tom calls her aside.

"I see you took the rug."

"I said I was going to."

"Look, I don't ever need to see you back here again. If you have any business with me you can do it by letter."

"That's fine by me, Tom. I don't fit here anymore. I have no reason to come back." The pond, the flowers she's planted around the house, the grove of pines in back—never is a long time but she wouldn't fly half way across the country for that anyhow, especially not with her finances. She's had to borrow most of the money from Charlotte to come this time. "The boys can come see me in Arkansas next time."

"If they still want to see you at all." He says it so fast, a quick cut. The old game, silent merciless dueling with no blood showing, hiding your hurt while you think of what to say that's hurtful. I'll never have to play this game with him again, she thinks. "It's up to them, Tom." No sign of feeling in her face or voice, the blood dripping inside . . . .

Sheila's glad she took the cuttings from the plants she grew, a living connection with her past self. They're safely wrapped in wet paper towels and tinfoil ready for their journey. Already she can feel Nancy's pleasure at seeing them growing on all the window sills.

She hugs Josh and keeps hugging him, afraid to let go and for a lurching moment it's a little boy she's hugging. Toby gives her a kiss on the cheek and a nod. Tom stands watching, silent in the doorway as they stuff the rug in the car.

On the way Marty talks about everything except what's on his mind but when they're almost at the airport he finally says, "I'm having a hard time accepting it, you being with a woman. It bangs into all my prejudices."

"I bet it does. Don't try accepting. Don't think about it so hard. Just let it be. I'm glad you could finally talk. I thought you were just going to pretend I hadn't said anything. It felt pretty weird. Look, I want you to understand that it took a lot of courage for me to tell you all, a lot of courage. I just want you to hear that. And if I hadn't told you then nothing else I said would have been real."

"Yeah, I guess that's true." He laughs, "Maybe I should be glad you have someone who loves you. Maybe that's how I'll think about it."

"That's a good way." She leans back relaxing and watches the airport sweep in around them.

When he has to leave Marty starts to give her a little kiss like Toby, then changes and hugs her tight.

"Mom?"

"Yes."

"Be happy."

Do it, do it, do it. She urges the plane forward and up, up with her will, up with mounting sexual excitement—then, airborne, she feels a soaring sense of relief and accomplishment, that absolute instant of transition, of not being any longer on the ground.

Immediately the familiar anticipation of disaster hits her. How many times and in how many ways has she seen the plane she's in come hurtling out of the sky, into the ocean, into snowy mountains, flaming into cities. She loves the takeoff but she's always relieved to get back from where she's been, safe at least for this time.

The plane tilts up, the city turning at a crazy angle below her, then flattens out over the clouds. Going home, her blood sings, going home. She feels stretched thin as if her very flesh were stretched out across that space. Somewhere, safe in the belly of that plane, is her grandmother's rug.

Julie Blackwomon

Kippy

We were all sitting down the street on Miss Lottie's newly washed steps when Jaimie came by. I think Nikki saw Jaimie first because she yelled, "Hey Jaimie, bring your ass on down here!" when Jaimie was still almost half a block away. Nikki and Jaimie both play basketball for Southern and have gym and home ec together but it isn't that they're really that tight or anything. It's just that Nikki likes a lot of attention—that's the way Nikki is.

"If you lived on this block you wouldn't be doing all that cussing all up and down the street," Angela said. Angela was sitting on the top step beside Karen.

"All what cussing?" Nikki said in mock innocence. "All I said was ass."

"See, you think it's funny," Angela whined, "but somebody'll be telling my mother we were all down here cussin' and she'll be getting on my case . . ."

"Yeah, beanhead," Sheila chimed in. "Cut out the goddamned cussin'."

"Aw shut up, pepperhead," Nikki said cheerfully.

"You shut up, fart face," Sheila snapped.

"I'd rather be a fart face than a pepperhead," Nikki said.

"Least my family didn't find me on the dump," Sheila said.

I stopped listening to them squabble and turned to watch Jaimie as she approached the steps where we all sat: Nikki, Sheila, Karen, Angela and me. My name's Kathleen but they call me Kippy. School had let out early and we were just hanging out on Miss Lottie's steps shooting the breeze. Earlier we'd been playing hot cold butter beans but Karen's little brother Boo Boo kept standing across the street telling where everyone was hiding. We'd chase him but he'd run and duck behind the parked cars and come right back to pester us again. We would have been jumping doubledutch, but the rope was in Angela's house and Angela's mother was home. If Angela went in now she'd have to stay and finish her homework instead of waiting until seven o'clock when we'd planned on doing it together.

Jaimie was holding her left arm slightly above her eyebrows, shielding her eyes from the three o'clock sun. She must have just left school because she still wore her gymsuit with "Jaimie" stitched in thick yellow thread across the front. Her books were tucked under her arm.

77

Jaimie doesn't come over to hang out with us too often because she's got a part-time job working behind the counter at the Gino's at Broad and Snyder. And then there's basketball practice. Jaimie plays guard for Southern. She's good too, wiry and fast—a blur of blue uniform and flashing brown arms. I'm always glad when Jaimie comes over to hang out with us though, because I like Jaimie a lot. Nikki says Jaimie's a lesbian, only 't's bulldagger when Nikki says it but I don't like to use that word because my mother's a lesbian—which means mostly that my mother has a bunch of women friends and works for the women's bookstore and goes to lots of meetings and demonstrations and stuff, and the only men who get invited to our house for dinner anymore are Grandpop Jones and Uncle Ralph. Only Uncle Ralph isn't really my uncle but the man Mom lived with before she decided she liked women better than men.

"Least my family ain't so poor we gotta eat roach sandwiches," Nikki was saying now. Nikki had an unsharpened yellow pencil behind her left ear. She was sitting on the third from the bottom step and was turned sideways with her back to me, looking up at Sheila who was leaning against the wall beside the steps.

"Least we don't drink snot for kool aid," Sheila said, then looked over at me. I smiled and winked at her. Sheila's my best friend. She and Nikki live over in the projects about five blocks from here, but Sheila comes over and we walk to school together every morning. Sheila used to live in Harlem with an aunt. That's because her Mom used to be on junk but she went into the hospital and got herself straightened out, and now she's o.k. I taught Sheila how to bust and she taught me how to fight—how to duck and slide punches. I don't fight much because I'm really too old for that kid stuff. Besides, I don't like to fight and I don't have to anymore because I'm strong and because I showed them as soon as I moved around here that I've got heart so they don't be messin' with me.

"Least I don't have to steal stuff out the garbage can to wear for Easter," Sheila was saying now. Sheila wasn't supposed to have gotten another bust in before Nikki, but I was glad she did. Sheila isn't too good at busting because she keeps taking stuff personal and starts denying. When you're busy denying that keeps the conversation on you. To win you gotta forget about defense and just attack. So if someone says your father's a wino, you just say "least my father don't eat scabs" or something like that. It's not fair to say anything that's really true or to talk about somebody's Mom 'cause that means you really want to fight. Like Karen's Mom's on welfare and Nikki's Pop's in jail but nobody ever brings that up. Nobody talks about my mother being lesbian either.

"You kids make sure you take all your shit off my steps!" Miss Lottie stuck her head out the second floor window and glared down at us. She had a grey scarf tied around her head with a bunch of thick plaits sticking out the top.

"Yes ma'am," Angela said and balled up her potato chip bag and stuck it in the pocket of the blue jacket she had tied by the sleeves around her waist. Miss Lottie kept glaring at us from the second floor window until Jaimie took Karen's empty coke bottle and handed it to Karen. Then Miss Lottie pulled her head back in the window and closed it.

Before we moved to Pierce St. my Mom and I lived in a women's collective in West Philly. A collective is a house where five or six women shop for food, cook, do laundry and pay bills together just like a family even though some are black and some are white and some have college degrees and make a lot of money and some don't make much money at all. The first year we lived in the collective four of our housemates took me camping at a women's music festival in Michigan while Mom and Terri went to a black women's conference in N. Y. I liked living in the collective. It was like one big happy family. Only most of the family was white. Shortly before we moved here I got into this rift with this kid and ended up calling his Mom a black dog. And it had nothing to do with bad feelings about being black either. It's just that when someone busts on you and you aren't friends with them or anything, the best thing to do is to bust back on their Mom—either that or punch them in the mouth, because if you don't, the kid'll think you're chicken and they'll mess with you until you prove you aren't. So when this kid called me a black dog I just said, "Your Mom's a black dog!" Just like that. I mean, it was automatic. But I knew I shouldn't have said it. The moment the words passed my lips I got this strange uncomfortable feeling; then when I looked across the street and saw Mom and Terri standing in the doorway I could have just squeezed through a crack in the pavement. I expected Mom to start bombarding me with books about Sojourner Truth and trips to the African History Museum again but she didn't and I thought the thing was over until about a month later she started talking about me moving in with Grandma and I said I didn't want to unless she went too, then Mom said although she and Grandma loved each other, they could never live in the same house again but that I needed to live in a black community and she needed to live in a lesbian feminist community. We compromised by moving here which is three blocks from Grandma. Mom still spends a lot of time over at the collective house, especially when they're doing layout for the newspaper, and sometimes they have meetings at our house. I don't get to go to many women's conferences and stuff with Mom anymore but I still like it here. It's fun spending time with Grandma and Karen lives right across the alleyway from me. Karen's the first person I met when I moved over here. Sometimes she spends the night over my house. I can never spend the night over hers because there's no room. She got six sisters and brothers.

Anyway, after Sheila and Nikki finished busting on each other Nikki went back to the story she was telling before Jaimie came up. Nikki was standing on the sidewalk now with her foot on the bottom step and she was telling us about the lady who rents a room in her mother's house. Nikki's always telling the woman's business. This time she was saying the woman boarder and some man were in the room with the door locked doing it.

"How do you know the door was locked?" I asked suspiciously. You gotta check on Nikki's stories sometimes, keep her honest. "Did you try the door?"

"Whenever the door's closed it's locked," Nikki said as if she were talking to a four year old.

"So how'd you know they were doing it?" I persisted.

"Well, what else could they have been doing in there with the door locked?" Nikki said.

Then Karen interrupted to say that yesterday Boo Boo was outside on the steps blowing up a rubber.

"What's a rubber?" Angela asked, and everyone started laughing.

Sometimes I feel sorry for Angela. She's kinda quiet and has really short hair that she hardly ever combs so that sometimes it beads up into little knots and it usually takes a long time for her to figure out when someone's putting her on. They were calling her Pepper for almost a year before she put it together that Pepper was short for pepperhead. Mom says that sometimes when black people don't comb their hair it's because they're getting in touch with another part of their ancestral heritage and that's called dreading or wearing dreadlocks but when I told the kids on Pierce St. this they just laughed and said that might be true for some people but that Angela just wasn't into combing her hair.

Anyway, Karen was saying that everybody was busy laughing at Boo Boo who was outside on the front steps blowing up a rubber until her older brother came home, hit Boo Boo up side his head and snatched the rubber. Then when Karen started teasing him about it her older brother lied and said the rubber wasn't even his.

Man, it was really funny the way Karen was telling it—she was running back and forth, first being Boo Boo in his high-pitched whiny voice and then her older brother in a deep growly voice. I'm sure she was making some of it up but that's probably why it was so funny. Karen can really make you crack up.

Then we got to talking about who'd seen a rubber and who hadn't. Everyone said they'd seen one, even me, although I hadn't really. But it was o.k. though, because I had seen a penis, or two if you want to count the Christmas when Uncle Ralph still lived with us and the buttons of his old red pajamas came loose. The other penis I saw just last summer. It belonged to my cousin Kenny who's fifteen and just starting to shave. I was helping him pick corn in my Grandfather's cornfield in Virginia when Kenny just pulled it out and peed as if I wasn't even there. I turned my head at first then snuck another peek. Kenny looked over his shoulder and said, "What you lookin' at squirt." Then he laughed and shoved it in his pants and we went back to picking corn.

The sun had gone down and the steps were getting chilly under my butt and I wanted to go home and get my jacket but I didn't want to leave because it was getting late and everybody would be going in for dinner soon anyway. Besides, Jaimie might be gone when I got back. So I just got up off the chilly steps and jumped around on the sidewalk a little. I was trying to work up enough nerve to ask Jaimie if I could put on her jacket which was still lying on the steps on top of her books, but before I'd gotten it together to ask, Karen had picked it up and draped it across her knees without even asking Jaimie if it was o.k. first.

Then somebody started talking about doing it and nobody was saying much because Karen was doing most of the talking and Karen's a smart ass. Karen'll tell you a really good story, let you tell one, then turn around and say hers wasn't true at all and that she'd only just now made it up. Then she'd crack up. She's a real comedian.

I think Jaimie was getting restless. She'd put on her jacket which she'd taken back from Karen and was standing around with her hands making lumps in her jeans like she was ready to go. I was getting pissed with myself because I hadn't said anything at all to her except "hello" and then Nikki startled me by calling my name.

"Hey Kippy," Nikki yelled, "some dude's going into your house."

I followed the direction of her gaze and sure enough, someone was standing on my steps and leaning on the side railing with their back to us. From the distance I couldn't tell who it was at first but then I recognized Terri's pea jacket and white tam.

"So what?" Angela said. "You a newspaper reporter or something?"

"Ain't nobody even talking to you, Angela," Nikki said.

"That ain't no dude anyway," Karen said with a little giggle. "That's a woman."

"That's a dude," Nikki said.

"That's a woman, stupid," Angela said.

Nikki turned to me. "Ain't that a dude on your steps, Kippy?"

"Terri ain't no dude!" I said.

"Well, if it ain't no dude, it's got to be a bulldagger," Nikki said.

"And what's a bulldagger?" I asked sarcastically.

"You don't know what a bulldagger is?" Nikki giggled, and elbowed Karen in the ribs.

"No, what's a bulldagger?" I said, my hands on my hips, my nose now only inches away from Nikki's.

"Well," Nikki said equally sarcastic, "a bulldagger's a freak."

"And what's a freak?"

"A freak's a woman who wants to be a man."

"Well, Terri don't want to be no man. She doesn't even like men."

"Then why she dress like a man?"

"She don't dress like no man; she's just got on pants. Everybody wears pants."

"Right," Nikki said. "Everybody wears pants—including bulldaggers. '

Somebody snickered and Karen said, "Nikki, why don't you shut up?"

"You shut up," Nikki said without turning to look at Karen. The other girls were now in a circle around us and Boo Boo and some of the younger kids who'd been playing down the street had now come up to stand around and watch.

"Your mother wears pants," I said.

"Yeah, my mother wears pants, but my mother's got a boyfriend too."

Nikki looked over at Karen, then quickly back at me. Karen looked down at her feet. Suddenly it dawned on me: we weren't talking about Terri; we were talking about my mother.

"Look," I said slowly—I felt sad and kinda tired. "Just because you don't have a boyfriend and wear pants doesn't mean you want to be a man . . ."

The words trailed off and stopped. I wanted to add "Yeah, my mother's a lesbian but she isn't a bulldagger; she doesn't want to be a man." I wanted to say "Yeah, Terri's a lesbian and most of my mother's friends are lesbians but there's nothing wrong with that—it doesn't mean anybody wants to be a man." But it just didn't seem right to say it right then and there in front of Nikki with all the other kids gaping on and probably agreeing with Nikki that lesbians and bulldaggers are the same thing when it isn't that way at all. But I didn't know how to make them understand that it was really o.k. and I felt kinda dumb and stupid because I didn't know how to make them see. And I felt disloyal to my mother, kinda like I'd feel if I were high yaller and in an all-white class and someone said something nasty about blacks and I didn't say anything back. And then I was really mad at Nikki all over again because I felt like she'd busted on my Mom on the sly and because I was scared I was gonna cry right there in front of everybody and it was all Nikki's fault. And I wanted to punch her in the mouth but she was skinny and I knew I could beat her. I wanted to call her a barrel of blitzing bitches but then I didn't want to because Mom says it isn't nice to call girls and women bitches, but mostly I wanted to anyway because I was really mad and sometimes when you're really mad at someone, calling them a few bitches or mother-fuckers is as good as a swift rap in the mouth—though I don't usually cuss unless I'm really mad or just showing off. And now I was just standing around with my teeth clenched trying to decide what to do, and my left leg was trembling so bad I was afraid someone would see it and think I was trembling because I was scared and not just because I always tremble when I get real mad. But before I decided what to do I heard Jaimie's voice from behind me.

"Nikki, why don't you just shut your face and go home."

"This is a free country!" Nikki said.

"Look, Nikki," I said, totally ignoring Jaimie's interference, "you and me can go settle this in the schoolyard!" I took off my sweater and threw it to the sidewalk.

Nikki hesitated, then took half a step backward. "You better get out of my face, girl," she said.

"It ain't your face I'm interested in," I said, both hands on my hips and patting my foot. "I'm gonna kick your ass."

"It ain't about no fighting, Kippy."

"Oh it's about fighting alright. Sounds like you been talking about fighting real loud." I inched up closer until I was right up in her face. Her nose was blurred from being so close and I could feel her warm breath on my cheek.

"Sounds like you'll be thinking I'm some kind of chickenshit if I don't knock you on your skinny ass!"

"I got no reason to fight you, Kippy," Nikki said and stuck her nose up in the air like she was Cleopatra and I was a fly buzzing around her head. This made me madder.

"Yeah, you want to fight me alright," I said. "You want to fight me real bad!" I gave her a little shove on the shoulders.

"Look, I'm going home," Nikki said and turned and started weaving her way through the circle of kids behind her.

"You come back here, you bitch," I said and grabbed her by the back of the sweater. But she pulled away.

I skipped a few steps behind her and pushed her but she kept walking. I wanted to call her another bitch, wanted to go after her, maybe push her again but I was beginning to feel mean, like I was picking on her or something. So I just stood there and watched her walking off with her nose in the air like everyone else had disappeared and she was the only one on the street.

Sheila picked up my sweater from the sidewalk and handed it to me and I brushed it off and draped it across my arm. I was still cold but for some reason I didn't want to put the sweater on. Then Angela mumbled something about getting her butt on home and then she and the rest of the gang kinda wandered off one or two at a time until only Sheila, Jaimie and I were left standing in a half-circle with our hands in our pockets. A kid whizzed by on a bright yellow ten speed bike and I could smell chicken cooking in somebody's house.

"You should have punched her in the mouth," Sheila said.

"Yeah, I should have," I said softly and without much conviction.

"I don't know that it would have done any good," Jaimie said.

"No, I guess not," I said.

"But it might have made you feel better," Jaimie said with a smile.

"Yeah, I guess so," I said.

I was agreeing with everything everybody said and for some reason that struck me as really funny, so I just burst out laughing. Sheila and Jaimie looked at each other and started laughing, too, mostly at me, I think. And then we were all laughing hard, much harder than anything was funny but for some reason I just couldn't stop. It was getting dark and people were walking by and giving us strange looks and that only made us laugh some more.

Jan Clausen

Daddy

I like my Daddy's best. It has more rooms. Mommy just has an apartment and you have to go upstairs. The bathroom is in my room. Daddy has two bathrooms. He owns the whole house. Mommy used to live there when I was a little baby. Before they got divorced. That means not married anymore. You get married when you love each other.

Mommy loves me. Daddy says I'm his favorite girl in the whole world, sugar. He always calls me sugar. We like to go to a restaurant for breakfast. Sometimes we go there for dinner if he has to work in the city. I went to his office lots of times. He has books there. You go way up in the elevator. Sometimes I feel like I'm going to throw up. But I don't. Then you see the river. There's no one there except Daddy and me. Sometimes Ellen comes.

My Mommy works. She goes to meetings. First I have to go to school and then daycare. You can make noise at daycare. At school you have to be quiet or you get punished. But I didn't ever get punished. Mommy helps me with my homework. Sometimes we read a book together. Daddy asks me add and take away. He says sugar you're so smart you can be anything you want to be when you grow up. A doctor or a lawyer or a professor or anything. My Daddy's a lawyer. I don't know if I'll get married.

Daddy said maybe next year I can go to a different school where they have lots of things to play with. You can paint and go on trips and they have nice books. The kids make so much noise in my class. Some of them talk Spanish and the boys are bad. I got a star for doing my homework right.

My Daddy takes me on Sunday. Sometimes I sleep there if Mommy goes away. I have to be good. Daddy says he'll get me something when we go shopping if I behave. I have to take a bath before I go and brush my hair. Daddy says he likes little girls that smell nice and clean. Sometimes Ellen lets me try her perfume. Once she let me put some powder on my face and some blue stuff on my eyes. That's eye shadow. But I had to wash my face before I went home. Mommy doesn't wear makeup. Or Carolyn. They said it looks silly.

Once in the summer I stayed at my Daddy's for a whole week. Ellen was there. She helped take care of me. You're so helpless David she said.

She laughed. We all laughed. I had fun. We went to Coney Island. During the week I just call my Daddy two times because he works hard. Sometimes if he goes on a trip he can't see me. Daddy and Ellen went on a trip to Florida. They had to fly in an airplane. They sent me a postcard every day. You could go swimming in the winter there. Mommy and me went to the country but the car broke.

Sometimes Carolyn stays overnight. We only have two beds. She has to sleep in the same bed with Mommy. When I wake up I get in bed with them. We all hug each other. Carolyn and Mommy kiss each other all the time. But they aren't married. Only a man and a woman can get married. When they want to have a baby the man's penis gets bigger and he puts it in the woman's vagina. It feels good to touch your vagina. Me and Veronica did it in the bathtub. When the baby comes out the doctor has to cut the Mommy's vagina with some scissors. Mommy showed me a picture in her book.

I saw Daddy's penis before. Mommy has hair on her vagina. She has hair on her legs and Carolyn has lots of hair on her legs like a man. Ellen doesn't. Mommy said maybe Ellen does have hair on her legs but she shaves it. Sometimes I forget and call Carolyn Ellen. She gets mad. Sometimes I forget and call Mommy Daddy. I have a cat called Meatball at Mommy's but sometimes I forget and call Meatball Max instead. That's Daddy's dog.

Daddy is all Jewish. So is Ellen. Mommy is only part Jewish. But Daddy said I could be Jewish if I want. You can't have Christmas if you're Jewish. Mommy and me had a little Christmas tree. Carolyn came. We made cookies. I had Chanukah at my Daddy's. He gave me a doll named Samantha that talks and a skateboard and green pants and a yellow top. He says when I learn to tell time he'll get me a watch.

I wish Mommy would get me a TV. I just have a little one. Sometimes it gets broken. Daddy has a color TV at his house. It has a thing with buttons you push to change the program. Mommy said I watch too much TV. I said if you get me a new TV I promise I'll only watch two programs every day. Mommy said we're not going to just throw things away and get a new one every year. I told her Andrea has a color TV in her house and Veronica has a nice big TV in her room that you can see good. Mommy said I'm not getting a TV and that's all. Mommy made me feel bad. I started crying. Mommy said go to your room you're spoiling my dinner. I said *asshole* to Mommy. That's a curse. Sometimes my Mommy says a curse to me. I cried and cried.

Mommy said get in your room. She spanked me and said now get in your room. I ran in my room and closed the door. Mommy hurts my feelings. She won't let me watch TV. She always goes to a meeting and I have to stay with the baby sitter. I don't say a curse to my Daddy. My

Daddy isn't mean to me. I screamed and screamed for my Daddy and Mrs. Taylor next door got mad and banged on the wall.

Mommy said go in the other room and call him then. Daddy said you sound like you've been crying. What's the matter, sugar. Nothing I said. Daddy doesn't like me to cry. He says crying is for little babies. I can't stand to see a woman cry, sugar, he says. Then I laugh and he tells me blow my nose. What are we going to do on Sunday I said. Oh that's a surprise Daddy said. Is it going somewhere I said. Yes we're going somewhere but that's not the real surprise Daddy said. Is it a present I said. Daddy said just wait and see, what did you do in school today. Daddy always asks what did I do in school. I told him the teacher had to punish Carlos. Daddy said listen isn't it about your bedtime. I have work to do. Ellen says hi. Blow me a goodnight kiss.

I hugged my Mommy. She hugged me back. She said she was sorry she got mad. But don't beg for things. A new TV is expensive. We don't need it. Mommy always says it's too expensive. I said I wish you were married to the President. Then we could live in the White House. I saw a picture in school. You could have anything you want. They don't have cockroaches.

The President is a good man. He helps people. George Washington was the President. Veronica gave me a doll of his wife at my birthday. It has a long dress. Mommy said he was mean to Indians and Black people. But we studied about him in school and he wasn't. They had voting once. You could vote for Ford or Carter. My Daddy voted for Carter. I'm glad my Daddy voted for who won. My Mommy didn't vote.

Mommy doesn't like things. She doesn't like the President and she doesn't like Mary Hartman like my Daddy. I told her to get Charmin toilet paper like they have on TV because it's soft to squeeze. She said that's a rip-off. She only takes me to McDonald's once every month. I got a Ronald McDonald cup to drink my milk. She said that's a gimmick. I like milk. Milk is a natural. I told Mommy that and she got mad. I said you don't like anything Mommy. She said I like lots of things. I like plants. I like to play basketball. I like sleeping late on Sunday mornings. I like to eat. I like books. I like women. I like you.

Do you like men I said. I don't like most men very much Mommy said. Some men are okay. My Daddy likes women I said. Does he Mommy said.

I asked my Daddy does he like women. He said extremely. Some of my favorite people are women he said. Like you. And Ellen. Why do you ask. I said I don't know. Daddy said do you like men. I love you Daddy I said. I bet she gets that you know where Ellen said.

On Sunday we had breakfast at my Daddy's house. We had pancakes. Daddy makes them. He puts on his cook's hat. Then we went shopping. Then we went to a movie of Cinderella. Ellen came too. Then we went to a restaurant. I had ice cream with chocolate. Ellen and Daddy held each other's hand. Daddy said now I'm going to tell you the surprise. Ellen and I are getting married. How does that sound, sugar. Ellen said for god's sake David give her a little time to react.

Daddy said I can be in the wedding. He said Ellen will wear a pretty dress and he will break a glass. He did that when he and Mommy got married too. Then Ellen will have the same name as Mommy and Daddy and me and I can call her Mommy too if I want. I won't have to see my Daddy just on Sunday because Ellen will be there to help take care of me. She only works in the morning. It will be like a real family with a Mommy and a Daddy and a kid. But I can't say that part because Daddy said it's supposed to still be a secret.

I didn't feel good when Daddy brought me home. I felt like I had to throw up. Mommy held my hand. I lay down on the bed and she brought Meatball to play with me. She asked what did I do with Daddy today. She always asks me that. I told her we saw Cinderella. It was okay. She rode in a pumpkin. Some parts were boring. The Prince loved her. Daddy and Ellen are going to get married.

I started crying. I cried hard. Then I had to throw up. It got on the rug.

Mommy got the washcloth. She brought my pajamas. She hugged me. She said I love you. She said it won't be so different when Daddy and Ellen are married. You like Ellen don't you.

I love you Mommy, I love you, I love you I said. Why don't you like my Daddy. I love my Daddy.

I don't dislike your father Mommy said. We don't have much in common that's all. I'm happy living here just with you. You're special to me and you're special to your Daddy. You see him every week.

I cried and cried. I love you Mommy. I love you and Daddy both the same. And I love Ellen because she's going to be my Mommy too. I'll miss you. I'll miss you so much when I live there. I'll cry. I'm going to have a big sunny room and Daddy said he'll paint it and I can pick a color. I'm going to have a new kitty so I won't miss Meatball. Next year I can go to that nice school and Ellen might have a baby. It would be a brother or a sister. Daddy's going to get me a bicycle. I can take anything there I want. I'll just leave a few toys here for when I come to visit you on Sunday.

Maureen Brady

Grinning Underneath

School wasn't even out yet and already it was so damn hot and muggy the new flypaper over the kitchen table had curled up. Folly sat in front of the fan in the old wicker rocker. She could feel the small, broken pieces of wood pushing into her legs below her bermuda shorts. She stared at a page of her new mystery story that Martha had just finished and loaned her, but she couldn't read. She thought maybe after the summer she'd start on a new budget and try again to get them out of the rotten trailer and into a house. They were all tripping over each other, all the time, tripping over each other. Especially with that Mary Lou getting hotsy-totsy. It was no good. Mary Lou in there bungling around. She'd leave the bedroom a shambles. How could you read a mystery with such a disrespectful kid in the next room and that wall between you so thin if you put a tack in the one side, it'd come out the other.

Skeeter was out mowing lawns. Now there was a good kid for you. He wanted some money of his own, and he wasn't scared of working a little. Mary Lou'd drop her allowance on the first thing that came along and then hitch from town when she didn't have change for the bus. Worries about that girl as regular as clothes gettin' dirty. With Tiny it was too early to tell. He still minded. He was only ten. She remembered nursing them all in the wicker rocker. Seemed like Mary Lou'd been born with a mean bite. The other two'd taken more easily to it.

Mary Lou came out in her cut offs that she'd sat fringing for two hours the night before. She wore a skimpy T-shirt and a scarf tied around the crown of her head like she was going out to sweat in the fields. "Did you sleep some today, momma?" she asked.

"Not much. Too hot." Folly worked the night shift at the factory putting zippers in polyester pants. She looked back down at her page.

"Yuck. Do we have to have that stupid flypaper right over the table?"

"Mind your business, sister. I don't see y'all working out with the fly swatter, ever. That's the reason we need it."

Mary Lou stood sneering at the yellow strip and didn't answer. She had to admire the way her daughter's body had grown so nice and tall and lean. Graceful too. Mary Lou did a sort of reverse curtsy, going up on her toes and putting her hands behind her back. Then said, "See ya later."

"Where you goin'?"

"Out."

"Out where?"

"To town."

"You stay away from that A & P, you hear, child?"

Mary Lou didn't answer.

"I don't want you hangin' around with that Lenore. She's too old for you."

"Mom, she's only nineteen," Mary Lou said, exasperation puckering the corners of her mouth.

"That's too old. You're sixteen."

"You don't have to tell me how old I am."

"Who told you she was nineteen, anyhow?" Folly asked. "She's been around that store at least four years now."

"I know. That's cause she dropped out of school in tenth grade."

"That's what I mean. I don't want you runnin' with that sort. She'll be givin' you ideas about droppin' outa school."

"But mom, she's smart. She's so smart she can study on her own. That's why she dropped out of school. She had to work anyway so she figured if she worked all day she could get her some books and study what she wants to at night. She does, too. You should see all the books she's got."

"I don't care how many books she's got, she ain't smart," Folly said, her voice rising. "People don't drop outa school from being too smart . . . and I don't want you around her. I want you goin' to school and lookin' for a job for the summer." Folly placed her book face down to keep the place, leaned forward so the chair was still and tried to penetrate Mary Lou with her eyes as if to stamp the statement into her. It was too hot to fight if you could help it.

Mary Lou held on to the back of the dinette chair and matched her stare. She was thinking of what to say. Finally she said, "School's stupid. There's no way I can explain to you how stupid school is."

Folly rolled her eyes up in her head to dismiss the point. "You're goin' to school, that's all. You get you a job for summer and then you'll know how easy you got it. I oughta send you to the factory a couple nights. Let you sit in front of that damn sewing machine for eight hours." She wiped the sweat from her forehead. Jesus, she didn't want to fight. She was just scared for Mary Lou that she'd end up like her or worse. She tried to lower her voice and it came out scratchy. "Look," she said, "I'm working my ass off to try to get us out of this damn trailer. I run off with Barney when I was sixteen cause I thought he was hot shit with his tight pants and his greased back hair and his always having change to buy me a coke at the drug store. They kicked me outa school cause I was pregnant, but I figured sweet shit on them, I already knew everything. Then I had to work cause

Barney kept on goin' out with the boys and gettin' drunk and losin' his job, then I was pregnant again .... Then, you know the rest."

Folly looked at the flies stuck on the flypaper instead of at her daughter. She felt embarrassed. That wasn't what she had meant to say.

"Ma. It ain't my fault you married a motherfucker," Mary Lou said.

"You watch your mouth. You watch how you talk about your father."

"Well, he was." Mary Lou kept her mouth in a straight line though both mother and daughter were aware that she was probably grinning underneath. She'd always had a grin to go with her defiance. Folly had pretty much slapped it off her face by the time she was twelve, and now she was sorry. She'd rather Mary Lou would just grin, and then she'd know for sure it was there. Instead she picked up her shoulder bag and made a sort of waving gesture out of the way she hiked it up on her shoulder.

"Anyway, Lenore's trying to get me on at the A&P for the summer," she said at the door. Then she was gone.

Mary Lou was gone and Folly was left with a picture of Lenore standing behind her meat counter, quartering the chickens, her strokes swift and clean. She had always kind of liked the girl. She got up from her rocker and moved the fly paper to an old nail stuck in the wall by the kitchen window.

She took the wash off the line out back and called across to Martha to come on over. The two women sat at the table on the concrete slab they called a porch and Folly folded the laundry into two piles. She folded neatly, trying to keep the ironing pile low. On the other hand, she didn't want the kids going to school looking sloppy poor.

"How's your ma?" Folly asked.

"Oh, she's getting back to her old crabby self. She woke me up at noon to make sure I wasn't hungry ... you know, in my sleep I'm gonna be hungry and not feeding myself. Then all afternoon it's, 'Go lie down, you didn't get near enough sleep.' I couldn't go back, though, with her bungling around with the cane. She's not near as steady on her feet as she was before the pneumonia. I can't help myself from peeping out at her, waiting for her to fall down. Lotta good it's gonna be if she does, me lying there peeping."

Martha had brought her mother there to her little two-room trailer after she'd had her second stroke. Folly had a lot of respect for what she'd put up with but whenever she said anything like that Martha would say, "Look at your own load, Fol, and the way you take care of it." Once she'd even said, "I swear you were born a solid rock."

Folly thought about how Martha always seemed like the rock to her. She kept her awake at work making jokes about the boss. She'd touch her shoulder when Folly was really nodding out and say, "I wish I could just give you a pillow but you know old Fartblossom'll be making his rounds soon." Coming home in the early mornings they always came back to life for the fifteen-minute drive and concocted tricks they would do on Fartblossom once they were ready to quit the factory. That was Folly's favorite time of day. Once you'd come out into the sun and sneezed the lint out of your nose, the air always seemed so sweet and fresh. She often wished they lived a little further from the factory so the drive wouldn't be over so fast.

"Did you finish that mystery yet?" Martha asked.

"No . . . . Hardly got started on it. I been tryin' to figure that Mary Lou again."

"Yea. What's she been up to?"

"I don't know if it's anything or not. You know that girl behind the meat counter at the A&P? Short, dirty-blond hair brushed back, kind of small and tough?"

"Lenore? Is that who you mean?"

"Yea, you know her?"

"Not much. Only from going in the store."

"She's queer. Least that's what the guidance counselor down at the school says. She called me in to tell me that Mary Lou's been hanging out with her."

"I didn't think Lenore went to school."

"She don't. The guidance counselor says she comes by in her car when school lets out and picks my Mary Lou up every now and then. What do you think?"

"I don't know, Fol. Did you talk to Mary Lou?"

"I told her I didn't want her hangin' out with no one that much older. She's a smart ass kid, got an answer for everything. She ended up callin' Barney a motherfucker."

"What's he got to do with it?" Martha asked.

"Good question." Folly shook out a pair of jeans, then placed one leg over the other and smoothed them with her hand. She could hardly remember how Barney got into it. "He sure was a motherfucking bastard," she said. "Serve him right if his daughter turned out queer. Him runnin' back, just stayin' long enough to knock me up with Tiny." Her face felt hot. The anger always rushed to her head when she thought of him.

"I sure have to agree with you," Martha said. "It never sounds like he done you any favors."

"I was pretty stupid," Folly said. She tried to get back to thinking about Mary Lou. She didn't want her mind wasting time on that bastard. The thought struck her that at least if Mary Lou was messin' around with that girl she wouldn't be gettin' herself knocked up. She didn't say that to Martha, though. It was a weird way for a mother to think.

Martha sat quiet and patient, waiting for Folly to get back on the track. She ran her fingers through her hair. It was then that Folly realized Martha's hair was cut just about the same as Lenore's. It was the same color too except for the temple parts where she had most of her grey. Folly looked away and tried to pretend she was immersed in her laundry. Ever so strange, the feeling that had crept up on her. How could it be that you live next door to this woman, you know exactly how she looks, you know she came up to North Carolina from Florida seven years ago when her ma first took sick. She works all night in the same room with you, she sleeps mornings in the next trailer, she knows every bit of trouble you ever had with the kids. They mind her like they never minded you. She loves them. She's like family. Folly was realizing that Martha never had talked about sex. Never. She'd never talked about any man. She'd never talked about not having children. She'd talked about her girlfriend in Florida when she'd first come up, about working citrus groves with her; then Folly'd become her best friend.

This all slipped furtively through her mind in a few seconds and she could only glance sideways at Martha. She was husky. She flicked her cigarette ashes with a manly gesture. "For Christ's sake," Folly said to herself, "so do I." Then it hit her that she never talked about sex to Martha either. Except to bitch about Barney. But that was because she didn't have any. She didn't want no man within a clothesline length of her. No thanks. She did just fine living without.

Folly stooped forward and fished around in the laundry basket for more clothes but she was down to the sheets. She sat back again and scrutinized the ironing pile just to make sure she hadn't put anything in it that could go right on over to the other pile and be done with, but she didn't find any mistakes. Then she searched out two corners of a sheet and Martha came around and took the other corners just as she would always do if she were around when the wash was taken in. They stretched it between them.

"Listen here. I just don't want no trouble for Mary Lou," Folly said. "You know, she seems cut out for gettin' herself into things."

"Yea, but she's pretty smart about getting herself out of trouble too. Least she don't come crying to you most times. I bet she didn't go to that guidance counselor on account of wanting guidance."

"Uhn't uh. Matter of fact if you ask me I think that counselor is a snoopy bitch. She'd probably like to have somethin' on Mary Lou. Said Mary Lou is a rebellious girl, that's what she told me."

"What of it?" Martha said. "Ain't nothing wrong with that. I bet this counselor don't like any kid that don't run around with a runny nose and whiny voice asking for guidance." Martha shook her end of the sheet vigorously as she spoke. "That's a fine girl you got there. Reminds me of someone I know real well."

"What you mean?" Folly said.

"You know what I mean. I mean you. Remember when you ran around getting us all ready for presenting that petition to Fartblossom's boss. They tried to give you some guidance. Remember that? You saying, 'Piss on them, they'll never get me outa here till I'm ready to go.' "

Folly tried to keep her mouth down to a flat line but the grin was there anyway. You could see it if you knew her as well as Martha did.

Pat Suncircle

Mariam

From where Phoebe stands, just outside the door, only Mariam's back is visible as she leans forward in her chair to point something out to the little sister, her broad, stretching back and the long black leather coat like a scholar's robes or bat wings momentarily obstructing Phoebe's view of the girl. Phoebe smiles, but that fades as quickly as if it has been met by a frown. The girl is fascinated by Mariam's stories of Georgia, or her army days in France, or her coming out on the southside of Chicago in 1953, and if Phoebe could read lips it would only take a few words for her to recall which story. She'd listened to Mariam and heard them all. Three years ago, when she was only eighteen and unsure what to say to strangers Mariam had filled their hours by talking about herself. She took Phoebe and they wove back through the beauty and repulsiveness to the time she lost her eye in a fight with her first lover to the houseparties and rentparties and marriages and how she performed a ceremony herself in '58 and the couple was still together. Sometimes she talked so softly that it seemed she spoke to herself but Phoebe listened to the older woman and learned things that other women her age never knew existed.

At the time Mariam's words had been golden; they still were she knew by watching in the girl's eyes a subdued kind of awe that only escaped from adolescents in the presence of an adult they truly respected.

She walks slowly back to the desk, pulls out the chair but then just walks past it and over to a shelf of neatly arranged books and begins to straighten them. Nothing will get done in the store today she knows, so she won't even attempt it. Laughter comes from the little office. It angers her. Not because she isn't part of the laughter, jealousy could be dealt with. This is something that the thought and sight of Mariam, and even recalling her words, stirs. A keen anger at the woman who has taught her so much and scary wishes that she had never learnt it. And then a thick shame at having this anger towards another black woman.

She whirls abruptly and goes into the office with them, slamming the door purposely to scatter their words. But Mariam and the girl have an energetic rap going about Cuba and Phoebe knows how it is, for a couple of years ago when she was only interested in style and the latest dances, Mariam could coax her to Brooklyn and the lament of the Haitian refugees there. Mariam is a history teacher and Phoebe's anger softens a little. She sits listening to them for maybe a whole half hour before her gaze rests on the older woman and she stops hearing her words and grows sour again. "Goddamn butches." She says the words far beneath a whisper and as close to tenderness as to anger.

The first time that she saw Mariam the woman was enfolded in butch like a bat inside its wings and upside down, leaning against the bar with the patch over one eye which sucked attention to her stern chocolate face. Phoebe's gaze had traveled over Mariam's vest and black leather coat down to the pair of cowboy boots keen enough at the toe to go up a rat's behind; Phoebe had decided now here was a butch with class at least, and had forgiven her a little. But not quite enough. Walking down the street people stared, did double-takes at the woman they thought was a man. It angered Phoebe that they thought she wanted an imitation man—any man—and she became silent and didn't talk to Mariam. And did not answer Mariam's questions.

A customer comes into the store and Phoebe goes out to wait on her, but the woman only wants to browse so Phoebe paces the room, swinging her arms like a bored child, blanking her mind, trying to savor only the sweetness of Mariam.

The word bulldyke was something that she could not deal with, its connotations violated every sensitive thought that she had ever had about herself; she was lesbian and she was gay. She was not what the sisters in her family called 'bulldyke' and pronounced only in hushed or sneering tones. 'Bulldykes' were tightlipped and when they spoke every other word was a curse word, 'bulldykes' got puking drunk everytime they set foot in a bar, they beat women with their fists, they looked at women like men did, and, of course, they dressed like a man. The sisters said all this about 'bulldyke'; the words lesbian and gay weren't in their vocabulary until Phoebe put them there. She called herself a lesbian and acted like she always did and treated them like she always had; their keen sense of threat had nearly been laid to rest, and then along came Mariam. The sisters saw her and shot Phoebe an 'uh huh' look and went quiet.

'Bulldyke,' of course, was a part like 'sissy' or like 'preacher,' but when Phoebe cautiously mentioned this to Mariam all she did was chuckle and talk about being 'old-fashioned.' If Phoebe insisted she said less and less, so, afraid that Mariam would start avoiding her, or worse, get tightlipped, Phoebe accepted the 'bulldyke' part, always weaving past it anyway to the woman she called her friend. Then last winter, when she quit work and returned to school, she moved in with Mariam to save money.

She walks towards the door, stares through it at the street, stares until her eyes strain and squint and stares until they pull and become wet with pain because for the second time that afternoon, to remedy an anger growing scary, she is recounting the detail of last winter.

They became tight. They went to movies together, they barhopped and danced and looked at women together and they gave each other time apart when Phoebe went to meetings and classes and Mariam watched television. Phoebe was becoming more and more involved in politics and the two of them talked for hours about black politics, but when she mentioned gay issues the conversation waned. She talked then and Mariam nodded and smiled. The time or two that she practically dragged Mariam to gay rallies, the older woman merely reared back in her chair and looked and made unsettling remarks about the 'white boys' who ran it. Sometimes she fell asleep and displayed her scorn by snoring. But when the meeting was over and everybody filed out they all somehow meshed with the other people on the street and Mariam was the only one who resembled the issues discussed. Mariam was who all the eyes followed. And sometimes Phoebe would walk down the sidewalk shoulder to shoulder with her friend and sometimes she would walk as far apart as she dared.

In the apartment just below Mariam's lived Thompson, a gay brother with his hi-fi speakers on the ceiling and usually loud enough for their whole end of the building to hear. The reason that nobody complained, it soon became obvious, was that he played the right kind of music. Mariam had long ago made his acquaintance. She would occasionally even make special requests by stomping on the livingroom floor, three stomps for Al Green, four for the Emotions, and he would cut short whatever he was playing and comply immediately. Sometimes Thompson came over with Sonia and she brought Mexican soul food and she and Thompson would put on salsa and invent new steps and teach them all at the same time. Mariam would call to Phoebe from the kitchen, "This is the gay rally right here baby, gay tarry meeting, gay revival meeting, Sunday go-to-meeting meeting it's all right here and no white boys allowed." Phoebe partied too.

Sisters. Thompson said he was tight with the sisters. He stopped the sisters of their building on their way from the grocery store, the day care center, on their way to pick up the mail and introduced them to Phoebe. They smiled coolly. Phoebe was familiar with the nature of that smile; a sissy kept abreast of all the latest fashions and knew how to rap what the New York models were doing with their hair like a beauty pageant moderator and he invited them over for elaborate meals and movie star gossip. Sissies were fun; but the women didn't have no use for lesbians.

Phoebe hurt. She would wear her brother's air force jacket then, and say that they were going to look at her funny anyhow so why leave any doubt in their minds and she and Mariam would be 'butch' together. But it was easier not to, because then she could talk to sisters on the street, on the bus, at the laundromat, sisters she'd never seen before and it would be alright to. She pulled off the jacket, walked differently and looked at Mariam more and more disconcertedly out of the corner of her eye.

An old stray cat took to following them around and when they went in he would lay outside their door sometimes all night. He would disappear for a few days and then turn up at the kitchen window and they would make a circle place in the frost there for his moon face to stare in. Then one morning Phoebe went downstairs and almost stumbled over him lying dead on the front steps with a car aerial jammed halfway up his ass. She numbly chipped away with her boot at the ice freezing him to the steps and pushed him over the side. When she came back the body was gone. But when she got to their door she recognized laying there the aerial sticky with blood. Perhaps the hallway was just quieter in winter, but now it seemed listening quiet.

Mariam, when she was told, shook her head and cursed under her breath. That was all.

Phoebe had seen in the older woman's eyes flickers of the same pain that came to the surface when she told her horror stories. Phoebe had expected her to be outraged at least. Wearing cowboy boots be a crazy cowboy shoot up the building especially the sisters. But all that Mariam did was hold her and cradle her wet face and for just a little bit she lost herself in Mariam, becoming aware of the firm flesh which was almost hard on her upper arms and grew softest down around the breasts and she felt herself in one of Mariam's history stories and that was the closest they'd ever been. But the anger came back when she insisted to Mariam that they start confronting the people in their building—especially the sisters—and Mariam reacted like she really had suggested shooting up the building. When she insisted Mariam set her face and said less and less and finally grew silent—big butch immovable-black matriarch lie cohabited and gave birth to so much chickenshit, to Phoebe's way of thinking. She wanted to say so, but already Mariam sat facing the window.

Phoebe remembered the massages. How when there had been warm times, that was the core. How Mariam's hands took her farther and farther out like a string unwinding from the top of her head working her until finally she was a big chunk of dough under Mariam's great big hands molding her into any shape she desired and back out again and rolling her over and over and over spinning her tossing her in the air squeezing her between the fleshy palms until she felt as amicable as the fabric of a sweet dream as light as the airhole in a biscuit. Mariam's hands massaging were simply the hands of a mother working on the family supper.

Mariam sitting back in her robe and her yellow, green, red, purple, patterned headrag, her Jamaican headrag, talking on the phone to her brother.

"I'm the only daughter," Mariam said, "when somebody gets sick I have to go home."

Her first night in an apartment by herself, Phoebe heard the sounds very clearly. The footsteps of neighbor boys just inside the door, women's voices whispering in fear, the scratching of the cat at the window. For one hour just before the sun rose, she slept.

The next morning when she opened the door, three sisters were standing in front of 219; they hushed their conversations as she stood locking the door, fumbling a little because their fishhook eyes caught at her skin. She walked away without looking at them.

"Ummmmmm, her girlfriend left her you know, saw her moving out yesterday."

"She be on the lookout for another one, Marcy you better watch out."

"Huh, I ain't worried. I got my man, he'll stomp that little scrawny ass scandalous he catch her eye on me."

"Well me, I carry a blade . . ."

She would not run she would not let them see that, but if she had run she would not have heard what she heard. They were talking to her as sure as her mother had, as sure as her grandmother when they went about the kitchen putting things back in their proper place again after dinner, after company, not looking her way often but with a steady stream of good advice and gossip about poetic justice; calling to her as she ran out the door to school telling her to avoid so-and-so and she better not do such-and-such, for her own good.

A week later when she heard Mariam's heavy boot on the hallway she knew that all of the other women heard it too and was ashamed. A goddamned lumberjack; no wonder they were scared. Mariam's key turned in the lock and she did not even look towards the door. A week after the first day of spring, she moved into her own place.

She looks at her own reflection in the door; slender, dark and the 'you put me in mind of my niece' of an elder sister who lives in her new building. There are elder brothers and sisters and some younger sisters with children in the new building and everyone has told a story and had it listened to carefully by the others. They are a family. Phoebe has told a story . . .

"Where's your man today?" a grey-haired brother asks her jestfully.

"I don't have one," she replies.

The simple, unsmiling reply does not lend itself to another joke and so the brother nods to himself and a minute later smiles quietly . . . . but Mariam has never visited her there.

She opens the door to get a lungful of smoked autumn air from the university campus, and stands there awhile watching the people. College students and the black children from the community that is surrounding gradually seeping color onto the fringes of the academic pale green. Mariam often speaks of this area years ago when you didn't even see black street cleaners here.

She turns to pace the floor again, but instead walks to the office to ask Mariam to watch the store. She hurries out intending to get a quick breath of air. She walks the rest of the afternoon thinking that if she had not met Mariam things might be much simpler, however to love Mariam is to be unable to lie.

Someone comes behind her and puts their arm around her shoulder. It is Mariam.

"I closed early," she says, not moving her arm. Phoebe looks about, it is a busy sidewalk, late afternoon classes are letting out, dinner is beginning in the student dining hall.

Right away she hears snickering, they are young brothers around nine and ten having passed going the opposite direction now doing a leprechaun dance and poking each other laughing. A very proper white professor carrying a briefcase goes by, looking down his nose at them, but he would probably do that anyway, they both know. Everyone is either looking at them or making it a point not to. Phoebe's anger subsides a bit as she genuinely wonders how Mariam has managed all these years. She wonders if her walk has always been steady like this, like a graceful, proud lumberjack, even when children carefreely tossed epithets at her so often that sometimes they slipped into her own mind in place of her name, so that when she got up and looked into the mirror on Monday morning she would think of the worst name she had been called that weekend.

"Why do you put on an act?"

"What act?"

"Dressing like a damn gangster or a cowboy . . . walking like you John Wayne."

"That's the way I am, baby. I remember when I first bought this coat . . ."

"No." Mariam would edge her way into a story and never answer. It was scary, demanding things of Mariam, it seemed nearly disrespectful to someone who had taught you so much, but only Mariam could help her to clear her mind of everything the sisters said—the mother, the grandmother, the aunt, the daughter—only Mariam was closer to her now.

"Mariam no. I've seen people severed . . ." She is trying to place together the words that explain how there are millions of people in the world but they are of the chosen few. And alienation is unhealthy.

"I got my eye on you all the time, Phoebe. I'm watching what you do. I really am."

She smiles an assurance then, and will say no more and does not look at Phoebe, only keeps her arm tightly around her shoulder. "Okay." Mariam has listened to every word she ever said, every story she has ever told too; even the ideas of the white boys at the gay rallies, so long as they came through Phoebe's mouth. Mariam is listening. Okay. The anger at her friend that has been straining for an entire summer now loosens, leaving a fine dull ache in every single muscle in her body ... She takes a deep breath and without thinking about it, puts her arm around Mariam. It is nice. The warmth of her flesh is either coming through the big coat or has over the years and stories become meshed with it. It is a worn, smooth old skin, sweet to her fingers. Phoebe thinks about nothing else for awhile. Then she considers what they are doing now, walking directly to her new home—two women in the situation of lovers, a simple guerrilla action.

She strokes Mariam's arm gently, almost lingeringly as if they sat already in her apartment with no one looking but two women in a mirror. The thought of the sisters is painful, but worrying about that brings exhaustion and costs precious things. They are nearly home.

There are distinct voices and words that she will hear inside her head for weeks to come and ringing out constantly like the rhyme in a poem is the classic 'bulldyke' playing on itself 'bulldagger.' She realizes that she is biting her lip ... someone tall and muscular, larger than Mariam, is walking on her other side, pressing against her, stepping on her heel but she does not turn her head and finally he falls away behind laughing at the top of his voice ... and she is afraid that her fingernails might be tearing through Mariam's tough coat-skin, she is clutching so hard.

There are distant silences, mostly in the eyes of women her mother's age. There are the voices of children that most times she would not even hear. She looks over at Mariam's hard profile and feeling her eyes the woman turns and gives her a gentle look that nearly warms her into a smile. Mariam is here. Again and again.

For a few moments, Phoebe holds the eyes of a young girl of about ten, not fearful eyes, nor angry nor scornful, instead eyes that simply search their faces.

Another Place to Begin

This is the beginning of my story. I plan to get up at six every morning and come here to write, alone, at the typewriter, while the day is fresh. It will be hard to manage this. For one thing Regina isn't very encouraging. When I told her my plan she assumed I wouldn't be able to do it and therefore would just blame myself. I feel I will do it and I know, even if I don't, I would blame myself more for not trying. Gina doesn't realize that writing must be *done*, that it doesn't just happen. I shouldn't expect her to understand right away, after all it's taken me this long to figure it out myself. For just a few minutes this morning when I could see that I would not be here as early as I wanted, I began to feel the frustrated anger. Starting tomorrow I will be working full-time. I need time to read, to be with Gina, to keep the house together. When am I going to write? What makes me think I can do so much? And even if I did crowd in my writing, wouldn't that cramp always be there? I want my writing to be free. I felt that frustration only a minute, then I said, simply: No, absolutely, no. I have had enough of that anger. That was my experience most of last year, all of last summer, and now I don't care how difficult my situation is, I will write, I will enjoy it, no frustration anymore. I will be hopeful. Wide open. It is really very simple. Get up at six, get ready and come here, work on my story until nine o'clock when the work day begins. The only thing that bothers me is being afraid to be here at work alone. I will lock the doors and go into all the rooms to make sure no one else is here. No discontent now. Mustn't feel that, must just go ahead. In fact, as I write I am very happy. I like to think that morning after morning stretching into the future, I will be writing.

There was a dream Regina and now there's a real, day by day Regina. I feel that I hold out on the everyday Gina. I'm not as brave as I might think and much too afraid of losing things for myself. Sometimes it bothers me that I can't tell how Gina looks. It's like listening to a language you know and not being able to hear how it sounds—her face has too much meaning. We've been friends for thirteen years.

Gina was very happy last night when she came home. Peacefully happy. And very tired and wanting to go to sleep but I was in her bed and hadn't gotten out yet, so we talked. She'd been talking to the man who fucked her the night before. He was supposed to withdraw and didn't. She was upset yesterday, couldn't decide to take the morning-after pill because they require her to sign a paper saying if it doesn't work and she is pregnant that she will get an abortion. Yesterday she decided she *would* get an abortion if she were pregnant. It was a big decision for her to make. I talked to her about getting a diaphragm. She was thrilled to imagine not being a victim anymore. How sordid it all looks to me now. It's because I have this other experience, this other knowledge of how nice things can be, how we don't have to have anything at all to do with men. Of course, the whole thing makes me hate that man and hate Gina too in a way. Damn it.

This anger in everything I do, everything I think. Ironically enough Gina particularly understands the source of that anger, Gina knows *why* I hate men, white, rich so much. But now I'm hating brown, poor, incompetence, pain. I want nothing to do with it. I want money, ease, *space*. I want to cry. I can't. I feel the struggles of my whole life pushing out through my eyes. And here at work I'm expected to be the secretary. To be pleasant! Pleasant! Fuck that shit! Here to keep my job, the only thing going for me right now, I'm to be polite, calm and certainly not angry! Not even sad! I'm to be efficient. I'm to smooth the way so that these fucking *men* can get a good day's work done—and *my* work, what of that, what about *my* work! I want to write too and to read and to think and to be involved with other women who are writing and thinking and reading. No room for that in this scheme of things. Lucky to get this job. Great! A job copying down notices for the professors of what their salaries will be next year—most of them around $20,000. Twenty thousand dollars. If I made that much money I would have gotten to my writing class at the Women's Building last night. I wouldn't have been anxious the whole long bus trip, anxious first of all about having to change, having to wait around as it got darker and darker, afraid of men, men who tease at violence and rape, not that they intend to do anything, too much energy required for that and a bit too much risk most of the time, but still it isn't too much energy to make me afraid, so they'll do that. Walk right up to me, feel the fear rise, walk on by! I do know if I were making 20,000 a year I wouldn't have been that sort of anxious last night, the eagerness, the anxiousness making my stomach upset, being hungry too but no time to eat, didn't know what to eat in any case. Then getting off the last bus, seeing from the numbers I was still blocks away, already late by now, getting darker and darker. Deserted places, parking lots, warehouses, few people, walk,

walk, my legs being pushed, their tension, my whole body tension. Trying
not to sense I'm defeated, that I'll never make it. My $1.29 paint-scraping
razor tied around my wrist, held in my fist, opened, determined I'd use it,
wish it weren't so nothing; if only it were a gun. Ahead of me rows and
rows of train tracks, trains standing still, fenced-in roadway, and I'm not
sure how far I have to go, how safe I can be, I can't face it, I resist acknowl-
edging defeat—I cross over to the next street (out of my way), the relief of
seeing people going into restaurants, getting out of their cars, going into
restaurants.

Last night I dreamed of Jay. She'd bought a house in the country. It
was a new house, hadn't set yet, didn't have living in it yet. I went there
when she wasn't expecting me, I cooked, I was happy. I loved looking at
the animals and smelling the country smells. I was about to leave and she
came in. I knew she was happy to see me but she kept saying other things,
pretending I should leave and I pretended I would. Then she kissed me,
said she wanted to give me a baby. I yelled, *"What do you think I am, a
test tube?"* I was happy to leave that house with the yellow walls, and
walk in the evening down the country road going to my own home.

Also dreamed of Regina, her having something to tell me, being afraid
to tell me. Finally she told me—how ugly it was to her that I don't shave
under my arms. Oh, how angry I was, how disgusted with her for not being a lesbian. In fact, the dream was like being with her this morning. I
hated when she came and got in bed with me, explaining it was because of
the cold. I really don't want to touch her. That getting in bed with me sort
of thing more than anything I know makes me angry with her for all her
interest in pricks. Oh, I'm working my way back to last night, to just
before we went to sleep. I'd changed the sheets on the bed (we traded,
now she's sleeping on the floor and I have the bed, I was quite happy
about it until I realized this morning what a bad soft bed it is, aches and
pains, and Gina laughing saying now you know why I wanted to switch).
I'd changed the sheets, used white sheets. I couldn't sleep. I started reading about witchcraft. Mostly my mind was working on my essay, the poli-
tical/spiritual realities. I kept thinking the contradictions to everything I
was reading while I was agreeing too. I began to feel that everything was
possible, that I would be able to travel. I lit candles and started making a
tiny dream pillow out of muslin, stuffing it with mugwort, sewing it with
pink thread. Gina wanted to make one too. How she laughed and laughed
when she saw how tiny my pillow was! She calls it a checker. With black
thread she embroidered a life sign and a flower with stars shooting out. To
stuff hers she dumped the herbs right onto my bed and started stuffing
in her messy way. We commented on how each one's pillow looked like
who made it—mine orderly and neat, plain, hers disorderly, crooked, in-

spired, and dirty. We traded dream pillows. She made us saffron tea. She forgot we had a teapot. How can she forget we have a teapot! We use it everyday and talk everytime about what a nice teapot it is. I think it was because last time we made saffron tea there were roses in the teapot, nine lovely salmon roses.

I was shocked to find myself writing that I didn't want to touch Gina. And yesterday when she wanted to hold my hand it was alright with me and we held hands for awhile. I could easily remember then the very early days of our being together and how we always held hands, held each other in bed, gave each other baths. How without tension it all was for me, how I knew Gina'd balk at love-making or rather more of it so I never expected it. But neither did I expect that when she'd heard Rose and I'd been lovers in the Navy she'd quit coming home, quit snuggling, quit holding hands so naturally. That was years ago and that rejection cut so deep into both of us we could never tell exactly how to be with each other after that and now there's yesterday and the rose garden and holding hands. I loved smelling the invitation roses.

I have what's almost one single image of my life at Miss Annie's where I lived for a year and a half and where I was living when Jay and I became lovers. And that single image is of the big room, its row of wide windows above the wooden box, the sheer white curtains and how alone I was, how happy. I'd read, I'd write, I'd get ready for work in the early morning and walk there noticing every tree and every flower; in the evening I'd walk home again, wonderful to feel the strength to walk the two miles home though I was tired from cleaning and recleaning Ms. Halden's already sterilely clean house, coming home and being alone, how deep that solitude became, it became my joy, my pleasure and my pain and then knowing a new friend. She'd come early, before the sun, later give me a ride to work and suddenly I wasn't so alone. She found an old bicycle in an alley and fixed it up for me and I timidly began to ride it a few places, all the time really wanting to be walking and four of my plants were stolen off the porch and the roses bloomed and bloomed and I'd get cranky with Miss Annie for watering them before I got a chance to, she'd always beat me to it and that wonderful morning when she called me outside at 5:30 to show me a long row of plants all violently blooming in wonderful purple, all those old cans of flowers strung across a wire and how ever after I called them the Paris flowers because how I felt right then, that morning, was in love, loving Miss Annie, sharing the love of the flowers with her, and how that in love was all of me, the inside out of me, the air I breathed and why am I remembering Springtime now when it wasn't Spring, not at all, when Jay came into my life, how she'd come over, I'd listen for her motorcycle

and then she'd be there thin and smiling, smelling like squashes and cauli-
flower, her lankiness would be there, that flopping down on the bed, her
black sweater, new jeans, leather motorcycle gloves, how she'd swish
around her blond strands of baby hair, how she wouldn't talk and I'd
want her to, how she'd smile and I'd feel that happiness coming out of her
like the being in love was coming out of me, and those Paris flowers and
the morning Miss Annie called me into the green house to see the blooming begonia the "just a talking doll" it was to her; she hardly knew how to
be that happy, her energetic seventy-four year old dyke self, us together
loving that begonia, and Jay with me, Jay coming on the blue motorcycle
and my solitude disappearing, beautifully disappearing, I'd buy more groceries, I'd think of her when I bought food, I'd try to have things for us to
eat, but she wasn't satisfied, said she'd bring things from home, it'd be no
trouble, and how sad that felt, I'd pushed back into being alone but so
cruelly this time because she was right there, in the kitchen, looking into
the refrigerator, laughing, making jokes at how little there was—and I
thought of Ida how she never did anything *but* joke and play tricks but
never would Ida have joked or even let on she'd noticed if someone's refrigerator wasn't as full as hers, she never made fun of panties that were
old the elastic stretched completely out—and Jay who hardly ever let me
laugh, who'd threaten with her asthma the minute I started to laugh, Jay
throwing me so cruelly back into a solitude that she'd shattered for me,
throwing me back there with her jokes about how empty the refrigerator
was and I knew there were three meals there, I knew exactly what was in
the refrigerator, and I knew those three meals were meals for sharing. Her
laughing and then coming back into the room and offering me three dollars worth of food stamps. It was my turn to be silent, for her to want me
to talk, didn't I want the food stamps, why shouldn't I take things from
her? *Fuck you,* I was feeling good, food in the refrigerator, food to share
and you because you have more money, more food saying you'll bring
your own from home, giving me three dollars worth of food stamps, there
now, we'll be equal. *Fuck you*—keep your damn food stamps and leave me
my pleasure my sharing why can't you fucking learn about me, why can't
you fucking learn how I know every piece of fruit every vegetable I
buy like I know every rose I pick, why can't you learn about me how I
hardly eat at home how I eat in the houses where I work because it's free
because they only pay me $15.00 a day and they spend twice that each
day on groceries alone and when they offer me lunch I take it and if they
leave the house during the day I go to the refrigerator and I eat and I put
oranges into my knap-sack and when they say "These vegetables aren't
fresh, would you like them?"—I take them. Why don't you learn about
me damn you how Miss Annie brings me eggs back from the country and
I share them with my sister and with Ida and then I have six wonderful

country eggs and I love the shape of them, I leave them out in the sun so I can feel their warmth, how I loved them, growing up, hunting for them in the lots among the straw in the sheds, how sometimes I'd find them in the bright sunshine hardly hidden at all, I'd gather all the warm eggs into that rusty coffee can that we used to measure the cottonseed meal and I'd take them in to Mother with such absolute pleasure and how she'd make her little speech, the little speech of appreciation she always made— "Oh, am I glad to see those eggs, put them right here, we can certainly use those fresh eggs, my girl's got bright eyes." Learn about me *damn you* don't go laughing because your refrigerator has more in it than mine's got and stuffing your damn three dollars worth of food stamps down my throat when *I'm* the one working, *I'm* the one with four days of work a week. It never seemed to Jay that I had a job, and later on when our tensions couldn't bear themselves any longer she'd yell how I should have gotten a job, all along I should have had a job! And I'd yell "All along I *did* have a job, I *worked*, I *know* I worked, I feel every clean floor, every clean dish, every made bed in my *blood*, I *worked dammit!*"

And now it's the smell of Jay, always the smell of her and that unexpected closeness, just that having her there, the ever miracle to me that was, the sound of her motorcycle and she'd be there, take up space in the room, lie in the bath-tub, tub full of water, me on the toilet seat listening to her talk, finally Jay begins to talk and I try to piece things together, grope around, know I'm not doing a good job, keep thinking well that isn't all—she's left something out. Jay there, relaxed, unselfconscious, strong arms, her smiling silence and blue eyes, small breasts, vulva exposed, nothing buried, no churning muddy rivers. Jay there. Jay in the kitchen, Jay eating the food she'd brought from home, Jay allergic to tomatoes but liking the eggplant with cheese, my joy of actually sharing food with her, loving the dark purple of the eggplant, the funny greenish yellow of the inside, eggplant always making me think of long ago Julie, Julie telling me it wasn't even a food, it was a *poison*, Aunt Zell telling how her aunt pulled up her uncle's eggplants never having seen them before, thought they were weeds, threw them over the fence to dry up in the sun, eggplant and scraping the skin off with the potato peeler and remembering Mother crying, Mother's heart breaking while she scraped the carrots at home, making our supper, Mother's caring and caring and caring and always feeling that tenuousness about it, never taking it for granted, never letting us, always reminding us she was taking care of us because she could now she might not always be able to, Mother growing up in those Federal schools, making her own way, on her own, from age three and before that when Grandma'd leave her in the upstairs room to care for her brothers, little Mother worried one day, worried when Grandma didn't come home, knew she'd have to get food, taking down the flat tin pan, tiny Mother deciding she'd wash her hair before she left her brothers alone, before she left to find Grandma or find food whatever she could manage, Grandma hadn't come home when she usually did and they'd watched for her from the window, watching for Grandmother coming home, and then the Indian schools, those earnest years, those silent years, then crying scraping carrots and crying and scraping and crying, the slivers falling onto the old newspaper where she'd collect scraps for the pigs' slop, Mother crying, Mother's heart breaking and my not understanding, not knowing what to do, not knowing, wasn't I there with her, why was she crying, wouldn't I take care of her always, didn't I love her, hadn't we walked together in the evening like we did every night, hadn't she told me then the things she always told me, hadn't I run ahead eager to make sure the nest and little birds were where I'd found them, were still where I was taking Mother to see them, running ahead, too eager, leaving her to walk more slowly, should I have walked slowly too, should I never never never have left her side, Mother crying, Mother's heart breaking and Mother fixing our supper, the carrots she'd scrape and cut in half and then each half in long quarters and place in the shallow glass dish with radishes, Mother who never cooked the carrots, never served us cooked carrots, that was much later, years later, coming home to see her, both of us women together then, both of us able to share the secrets of that, those unspoken secrets those unspoken secrets of woman loving woman, woman happiness with a new recipe, a recipe for cooked carrots, a recipe called copper pennies, how beautiful the orange carrot circles the green pepper circles were to her, much later that, years later. And Jay *there*, Jay in the big doorway between the bedroom and the hall, that joy in me, that almost disbelief at the *company*, and then I knew she'd move, she wouldn't be framed there, not for long, just a few seconds and then she'd move, she'd say something, she'd want something, she'd suggest something, my life buoyed up, lifted beyond itself, Jay there and us together, rainy evening, tired of being in the house, tired of love-making— what pleasure—and walking in the misty evening, her under bright orange poncho, me getting wet, wishing it were wetter, taking our books, going to the ice cream shop, going to sit and read, going to find the tiniest distance for the shortest time, going to read different books, going to step into different worlds and every now and then return to say the smallest something to the other—"Do you want another Dr. Pepper?" "Do you want some more coffee?" "Are you liking your book?" "Are you happy?" and then reading again, raining outside, at first hard to read, hard to want to leave her, hard to want to separate and then my mind catching hold, my mind jumping with its freedom, wanting to be away, wanting to read, not wanting her to interrupt, hoping she doesn't tire first, hoping I get to read for hours and hours and for her to still be there, wouldn't want to adjust to her absence, just let her stay there, across the table, Jay's red and white face reading, quiet, there, Jay across the table, Jay looking out the window, Jay watching the rain, Jay there, there, there, with me, not alone, for awhile not alone, how strange, how I'm not nervous, how I'm sure, how I'm happy, Jay there, and then later in the dark, walking back to my house, she'll spend another night, walking beside her in the rain, rain puddles, street lights in the puddles, loving her for being there, how long since I've been out at night, not since I was raped, so long since I've felt the silence, the nighttime, unafraid, glad she's there, glad I'm there. Jay—there.

I need to start all over, to find another place to begin. I'm so sleepy. I didn't get to sleep till after three, I was excited. So was Regina. She cooked us green beans, told me I'd been creative last time I'd gone shopping, and laughed when I told her I was tired of hommos. She'd been to her calligraphy class, had a bottle of black ink and pen, showed me what they'd done, the lines and circles. She'd left behind the sample of writing her teacher'd passed out. "See, there I was taking care of everyone else and forgot my own things!" I laughed and she called out, "Your ink! Here's your ink! You're forgetting your ink!" like she'd done in class and then it was clear to me that *she* had been in that class. Strange how I forget how real Gina is, if she's not right under my nose.

I'm ashamed now of how I told how we quit living together years ago. Gina was pregnant. On the train to the house after she'd met me at Greyhound she told me. She told it like a happy surprise. She wanted to get an abortion. I said, "Oh, no, don't do that, we'll take care of the baby." She laughed, said she knew I'd say that but no she wasn't going to have the baby. All nineteen-year-old me knew was that it was wrong to kill and I certainly didn't know how to go about getting an abortion. We didn't have money and we didn't know anyone. Finally she made friends with Rachel, another Puerto Rican woman, who knew someone. All this time passing though, four months, and Gina'd say look and show me her breasts how full they were, how happy she was to be pregnant. And then Rachel went with her. I heard about it later. A woman had done it for $75.00. Gina said she was "like a man" and there had been pictures of women covering the walls and the ceiling. Rachel took her to her own house where Gina'd been living most of the last two months anyway. They went home by cab. Gina lost alot of blood and was in a great deal of pain. After two days Rachel took her to a city hospital. When I went to see her I took a chocolate bar which Gina had me eat; she said she could tell I hadn't eaten lately, my hands were shaking the way they did when I was hungry. I ate the candy. She was pale and far away from me. There were bottles of liquid, tubes going into her hand. The ward was green and dirty, noisy, the beds close together. I sat for awhile in the hall on a splintery bench and talked to another woman. She asked me what was wrong with my friend. I said she'd lost a baby. How clearly I remember that woman's face, so wrinkled, so New York, so poor and her smirky knowing nod, "Oh, lost a baby." It was illegal then to get abortions I suppose. Gina stayed in the hospital a long time but she got better, little by little. Her hand where they'd fed her through the tubes was the last to get well—for months it would swell up and hurt. She lived with Rachel after that. Rachel had a baby girl and sometimes I'd go over there and babysit while they went out, just because I wanted to, they were quite used to leaving her alone in her crib. I remember Rachel carrying the girl on her hip to the beach. How tan Gina got during that time, how beautiful. She and Rachel busy hustling and shop-lifting, going dancing, living that fast-pace. I'd gone to live with another woman then and Gina hardly ever came over.

How could I write about the time we quit living together in that up-stairs apartment without mentioning the chickens—Gina brought home four chicks and kept them in the bathtub with wire fixed over the top. Whenever we wanted to take a bath we had to manage to get the chickens into a cardboard box, set the box out the window onto the roof, and clean out all the smelly chicken shit. They grew so fast and soon the whole apartment smelled bad and when I'd call Gina and ask why didn't she ever come home anymore, she'd say how bad it smelled there and laugh and laugh! How much time we spend making each other laugh. I suppose that's the most characteristic thing about the two of us together—we make each other laugh, on purpose and as often as possible.

I dreamed there isn't much food to go around. The maid has a little food. She keeps it for herself. She doesn't hand it over to the rich people. I pat her on the back. I want her to know I agree. Why should she give up those few cucumbers? But our hearts know different. We know she is in the right to keep the small portion of food. And yet. She is able to give it up. She knows its value. And she knows she can give it up. And she does. But sometimes she'll be hungry. Sometimes she'll wish there were someone to know that those few cucumbers had been rightfully hers—after all, they did belong to her. And at those times she'll not want to be with Jay any-more. She'd rather walk alone where the hill slips down to the water and in the river she'll see floating trees, whole trees sometimes, and she'll find minnows near the edge. Sometimes she'll want to be interested in how big the water can be and at the edge how small—why, not even big enough to cover her fingernail, sometimes she'll choose not to be interested in Jay, or in anyone. For the maid it's a matter of being stumped, not wanting to have so much in her own hands. Here, take some of me, look into my face, see what it's like to give up those two cucumbers, here, take all of this. I'll talk and talk and talk, I'll tell Jay everything, she'll see how angry I can be, she'll see how far under I can go, she'll see how being locked out after the long bus ride when I was ready to clean your house, you rich people's house, and you didn't leave the door open and I went home again without the money for the day's work and you didn't call until you wanted me to clean again, you didn't get your house cleaned but you did save yourself $15.00, Jay'll see how one of those days and I don't know how to go on, when we go to the store I really have no idea *what* I want her to buy for our supper, I think about it and feel well whatever Jay wants I guess I'll want that too, and I get worried thinking I won't know when I'm hungry but it's bound to be more often than Jay, and then what will I do—go hungry? Yes, I guess that's the best way, I don't have my $15.00 to put in and I've lost myself somehow, too many similar circumstances I suppose, slipped back in one day to those times with men, those hungry times, when I'd eat what they wanted to eat when they wanted to eat because I didn't have my own money and I couldn't hold out against the flood of them. Sure I worked I had money too but even all of it was so little and we always lived within *their* means. Oh, yes, I lived better, learned about proper ways to eat, but I didn't eat what I wanted when I wanted it and now I'm desperate and there's this awful cloud like I'll never even *know* what I want to eat again. I left to go talk to my sister. Not about what was happening, I was too fogged up in that to think I could talk about it, but just to go see my sister. Oh and then I got things right. Then I could see again and talk again and feel hungry again. Damn it, I hate you rich people. You're the ones with the cars, the houses, all the furniture to clean, kitchens dirty from all the damn food you've eaten—I go over there, long bus ride, up hours before I even start working, then hours of cleaning. I hate you. And always I start loving the work about the time I'm too tired to want to finish. Just about the time when I start to think I just can't finish, I want to sit down, damn it, just about that time that understanding that isn't in my mind, that knowing, that stretched out place will come to me and I'll finish my work, and your house will be clean, I'll want to look and look and look like when I write I want to read and read and read but I'll pull myself away and I'll go home. I'll have spent all day *caring*, perhaps in spite of myself, but caring even so, wanting the bathtub spotless, wanting all the shelves and books dusted just so, and I'll go around seeing the house through your eyes, the beds changed, your funny water bed that if I were still riding the maid van we'd all laugh about together. The newspapers scattered all over the floor, someone knocked a trash can over this morning and didn't pick it up, I guess you thought, "Oh, the maid comes today." That's what hurts, not honest work for honest pay, but that thinking I'm *supposed* to do for you what you're too lazy to do for yourselves. Some of you won't even throw your underwear in the hamper, won't even pick it up off the floor, and that's what *hurts*, what makes me angry, if I have energy enough, just kind of knocks off a part of my heart if I don't. I'll clean your house, I'll care about it all day long, I'll really try to get the kitchen floor clean, and I'll want the stove and counter tops shining, I'll feel bad if I can't get everything done before you come home, and what is your part? Well, leave the door unlocked so I can get in and pay me $15.00. I'd like Dr. Pepper but that's really something extra and if I have the money I'll buy my own and bring it in my knap-sack. No, just leave the door open and leave $15.00 on the table. You won't have to learn about me, it'll never have to occur to you to wonder what *my* house looks like, how I have things to do just like you, how my days mean something to *me*, not just to you in how clean your house is when I leave, none of that, and those of you who spend the day at home with me you'll talk all day long about yourselves, my heart will love you, feel bad at your imprisonment, feel bad to know you pay me half to listen to you since no one else will (of course you expect the house to be cleaned too), you'll talk every-day I come for weeks and weeks and it'll never occur to you to wonder what's on my heart, whether when you're talking to me I might not have my own head full of things to say. No, none of that required. All that is required is that you leave the door open and the money on the table. (You went away once for three weeks and expected me to clean without getting paid. You paid me when you got back, as though I didn't have to buy food and pay bus fare while you were away.) I keep harping. I just mean to say—leave the door open, the money on the table. I'll do the rest of it, I'll take into myself whatever needs to be taken in, I'll do the work. And then you lock me out! You don't call later to say you're sorry, that you'll bring the money over anyway. Alright, not bring the money over, but just to call and say you're sorry, that you'd intended to leave the door open! Some-times on those days the pain covers me over and I get lost and for days I can't even be with Jay, can only just float along there beside her, feeling that I'll manage if I just eat when she's eating. But we'd planned to go to the ocean. She'd even borrowed her friend's car. We'd *planned*. I can't go. I can't decide to go. I can't decide to stay. *I WANT MY TWO CUCUM-BERS BACK*. I need them now. I can't ride on the top of this wave. If on-ly I could yell my anger! If only I could march over to your house and start screaming.

I'd gone to the Friday night coffeehouse. The newsletter had just come out with some awful slander against the separatists and since most of us were at the coffeehouse there was lots of talk, alot of excitement. I was very tired. I'd cleaned Ms. Keese's house and then waited an hour on the bus. I don't even know why I went to the coffeehouse except that it had something to do with not being defeated, taking a bath, putting on clean clothes and making the world mine again, no matter how tired, the tiredness would leave, it'd just give me an easiness, a special cloud to see the others through. I sat on the big stuffed pillow, Darlene sat beside me and Linda on the other side, separatists all around me on the floor. I felt like I was the center to the whole discussion, something was making me the center, I couldn't tell what. The articles in the newsletter hadn't affected me much, I saw them for what they were, that was all. The tall weedy wildflowers in the vacant lot had affected me more, my tiredness affected me more, being there with the other women, the triumph for me in that, no more going to strange houses with strange men doing strange things, no more being used, absent—my taking the world, my going to the coffeehouse, sitting on the stuffed pillow sitting between Darlene and Linda, somehow being the center of the circle though I wasn't even talking. Joan was the most upset, it mattered to her so much that she be liked, that she not be misunderstood. I told her *we* loved her, to just consider herself part of the Lesbian Separatist Organization and forget the Lesbian Organization. I told her "water off a duck's back" and thought of buffle-heads on the Hudson near the falls, thought of upturned tails that could make me laugh, thought of those walks by myself through the snow to see the buffle-heads. All of it water off a duck's back, the body tiredness I'd defeated, I'd come on my bicycle in the twilight. I could hear women's voices, I loved to look at us, to see how we looked, felt Darlene about ready to curl up into a tiny kitten on my lap, and Linda wanting to hear from me what separatism meant, did I just mean no men, and I remember her face pushing into my face, not actual physical closeness, and yet her face squashing into mine, like my first memory of Regina, Gina squashing her red-cheeked face into mine. Later everyone leaving, I sat on the desk by the door, I said good-by, that evening beautiful to me, some sort of actual embodiment of my triumph over the tiredness of the whole week, of the day, of the long wait on the bus. I said plenty when I got to Jay's house. I wouldn't let her get a word in, I had an opinion about everyone, about everything said. I loved the flatness of her bed on the wooden platform, loved being next to the wall, on the inside, loved the half-Vicks, half-garden vegetable smell of her as we went to sleep.

Last night I spoke to Regina on the phone. Her mother had gathered nine dozen gladiolas into the house to welcome her! I'm looking now at the bricks laid to form patterns and thinking how the most I have "built" is my altar from time to time. There was the altar I built beside the ocean once, a part of the ocean I got to by finding my way through a coconut palm forest. Big rocks carried through the forest and pressed against the sand. This morning my body has a dignity. I feel very beautiful and even wearing clothes is alright with me.

I carried Gina's plant here in its round glass bowl. I'll take care of it. Through loving it, repotting it into something clay, something more porous, I'll return to my love for her, I'll weed that love of our too-close contact of the last few months, our too-great differences. Such a melody in me this morning. The bushy green plant that even so needs care, is glad to be here with me, watching the birds on the round brick roof and feeling the breeze. I stayed home this morning, burned the purple candle, the temple candle of work, of writing. I read Jay's letter, not the reading that makes sense, just the reading of words skipping around, skipping toward some sort of fountain, some sort of happiness in me.

Dorothy Allison

I'm Working on My Charm

I'm working on my charm.

The other day at a party a woman told me, "Southerners are *so* charming." She had a wine glass in one hand and a cherry tomato in the other, and she gestured with the tomato—a wide witty 'charmed' gesture I do not remember ever seeing in the South. She leaned in close to me. "We just have so much to learn from you—you know, gentility."

I had the most curious sensation of floating out of the top of my head. I seemed to look down on all the other people in that crowded room, all sipping their wine and half of them eating cherry tomatoes. I floated there, watched myself empty my third glass of wine, and heard my mother hiss in my left, my good ear, "Yankeeeeeees."

When I was young I worked counter with my mama back of a Moses Drugstore planted in the middle of a Highway 50 shopping mall. At that time I was trying to save money to go to college and ritually every night I'd pour my tips into a can in the back of my dresser. Sometimes my mama'd throw in a share of hers to encourage me, but mostly hers was spent even before we got home—at the Winn Dixie at the other end of the mall or the Maryland Fried Chicken right next to it.

Mama taught me the real skills of being a waitress—how to get an order right, get the drinks there first and the food as fast as possible so it would still be hot, and to do it all with an expression of relaxed good humor. "You don't have to smile," she said, "but it does help." "Of course," she had to add, "don't go around like a grinning fool. Just smile like you know what you're doing, and never *look* like you're in a hurry." I found it difficult to keep from looking like I was in a hurry, especially when I got out of breath from running from steam-table to counter. Worse, moving at the speed I did, I tended to sway a little and occasionally lose control of a plate.

"Never," my mama told me, "serve food someone has seen fall to the floor. It's not only bad manners, it'll get us all in trouble. Take it into the back, brush it off and return it to the steam-table." After a while I decided I could just run to the back, count to ten, and take it back out to the

115

customer with an apology. Since I was usually just dropping rolls, squares of cornbread and baked potatoes—the kind of stuff that would roll on a plate—I figured brushing it off was sufficient. But once, in a real rush to an impatient customer, I watched a 10 oz. T-bone slip right off the plate, flip in the air, and smack the rubber floor mat. The customers' mouths flew open and I saw my mama's eyes shoot fire. Hurriedly I picked it up by the bone and ran to the back with it. I was running water over it when mama came in the back room.

"All right," she snapped, "you are not to run, you are not to even walk fast. And," she added, taking the meat out of my fingers and dropping it into the open waste can, "you are not, not ever to drop anything like that again." I watched smoky frost from the leaky cooler float up toward her blond curls, and I promised her tearfully that I wouldn't. I'm sure it was magic but I didn't.

The greater skill she taught me was less tangible. It had a lot to do with being as young as I was, as southern, and working by the highway that so many travelers came down. The lessons began when I was hired. Harriet was the manager and her first comment on hiring me was cryptic but to the point. "Well, sixteen," she said, "at least you'll up the ante." Mama's friend, Mabel, came over and squeezed my arm. "Don't get nervous, young one. We'll keep moving you around. We'll never leave you alone."

Mabel's voice was reassuring, if her words weren't, and I worked her station first. A family of four children, parents and a grandmother took her biggest table. She took their order with a wide smile but as she passed me going down to the ice drawer, her teeth were point on point. "Fifty cents," she snapped, and went on. Helping her clean the table thirty-five minutes later I watched her pick up the two quarters and repeat "50 cents," this time in a mournfully conclusive tone.

It was a game all the waitresses played. There was a butter bowl on the back counter where the difference was kept, the difference between what you guessed and what you got. No one had to play but most of the women did, and the rules were simple. You had to make your guess at the tip *before* the order was taken. Some of the women would cheat a little, bringing the menus with the water glasses and saying, "I want ya'll to just look this over carefully. We're serving one fine lunch today." Two lines of conversation and most of them could walk away with a guess within 5 cents.

However much the guess was off went into the bowl. If you said 50 cents and got 75 cents, then 25 cents to the bowl. Even if you said 75 cents and got 50 cents you had to throw in that quarter, so that guessing high was as bad as guessing short. "We used to just count the short guesses," Mabel told me, "but this makes it more interesting."

Once Mabel was sure it would be a dollar and got nothing. She was so mad she counted out that dollar in nickels and pennies, and poured it into the bowl from a foot in the air. It made a very satisfying angry noise and when the people came back a few days later no one wanted to serve them. My mama stood back by the pharmacy sign smoking her Pall Mall and whispered in my direction, "Yankees." I was sure I knew just what she meant.

At the end of each week, the women playing split the butter bowl evenly.

My mama said I wasn't that good a waitress but I made up for it in eagerness. Mabel said I made up for it in "tail." "Those salesmen sure do like how you run back to that steam-table," she said with a laugh but she didn't say it where mama could hear. Mama said it was how I smiled.

"You got a heartbreaker's smile," she told me. "You make them think of when they were young."

Whatever it was, by the end of the first week I'd earned $4.00 more in tips than my mama. It was a little embarrassing. But then they turned over the butter bowl and divided it evenly between everyone but me. I stared and mama explained. "Another week and you can start adding to the pot. Then you'll get a share. For now just write down $2.00 on Mr. Aubrey's form."

"But I made a lot more than that," I told her.

"Honey, the tax people don't need to know that." Her voice was patient. "Then when you're in the pot, just report your share of the pot. That way we all report the same amount. They expect that."

"Yeah, they don't know nothing about initiative," Mabel added and she rolled her hips in illustration of her point. It made her heavy bosom move dramatically and I remembered times I'd seen her do that at the counter. It made me feel even more embarrassed and angry.

When we were alone I asked mama if she didn't think Mr. Aubrey knew that everyone's reports on the tips were faked.

"He doesn't say what he knows," she replied, "and I don't imagine he's got a reason to care."

I dropped the subject and started the next week guessing on my tips.

Salesmen and truckers were always a high guess. Women who came with a group were low, while women alone were usually a fair 25 cents on a light lunch, if you were polite and brought them their coffee first. It was, after all, 1966 and a hamburger was 65 cents. Tourists were more difficult. I learned that loud noisy kids meant a small tip, which seemed the highest injustice to me then. I've decided since that it was a kind of defensive arrogance that made them leave so little, as if they were saying, "Just because little Kevin gave you a headache and poured ketchup on the floor doesn't mean I owe you anything."

Early morning tourists who asked first for tomato juice, lemon, and coffee were a bonus. They were almost surely leaving the Jamaica Inn just up the road, which had a terrible restaurant but served the strongest drinks in the county. If you talked softly you never got less than a dollar, and sometimes for nothing more than juice, coffee and aspirin.

I picked it up. In three weeks I started to really catch on and started making sucker bets like the old man who ordered egg salad. Before I even carried the water glass over, I snapped out my counter rag, turned all the way around, and said, "Five." Then as I turned to the stove and the rack of menus, I mouthed, "Dollars."

My mama frowned while Mabel rolled her shoulders and said, "Ain't we growing up fast."

I just smiled my heartbreaker's smile and got the man his sandwich. When he left I snapped that five dollar bill loudly five times before I put it in my apron pocket. "MY mama didn't raise no fool," I told the other women who laughed and slapped my behind like they were glad to see me cutting up.

But mama took me with her on her break. I walked up toward the Winn Dixie where she could get her cigarettes cheaper than in the drugstore.

"How'd you know?" she asked.

"Cause that's what he always leaves," I told her.

"What do you mean *always*?"

"Every Thursday evening when I close up." I said it knowing she was going to be angry.

"He leaves you a five dollar bill every Thursday night!" Her voice sounded strange, not angry exactly but not at all pleased either.

"Always," I said and I added, "and he pretty much always has egg salad."

Mama stopped to light her last cigarette. Then she just stood there for a moment breathing deeply around the Pall Mall, and watching me while my face got redder and redder.

"You think you can get along without it," she asked finally.

"Why?" I asked her. "I don't think he's going to stop."

"Because," she said, dropping the cigarette and walking on, "you're not working any more Thursday nights."

On Sundays the counter didn't open until after church at one o'clock. But right at one, we started serving those big gravy lunches and went right on till four. People would come in prepared to sit and eat big—coffee, salad, country fried steak with potatoes and gravy or ham with red-eye gravy and carrots and peas. You'd also get a side of hog's head biscuits and a choice of three pies for dessert.

Tips were as choice as the pies, but Sunday had its trials. Always some tight-browed couple would come in at two o'clock and order breakfast— fried eggs and hash browns. When you told them we didn't serve breakfast on Sundays they'd get angry.

"Look girl," they might say, "just bring me some of that ham you're serving those people, only bring me eggs with it. You can do that." And their voices clearly added, "Even you."

It would make me mad as sin. "Sir, we don't cook on the grill on Sundays. We only have what's on that Sunday menu. When you make up your mind let me know."

"Tourists," I'd mutter to my mama.

"No, Yankees," she'd say and Mabel would nod.

Then she might go over with an offer of boiled eggs, that ham, and a biscuit. She'd talk real nice, drawling like she never did with me or friends, while she moved slower than you'd think a wide-awake person could. "Uh-huh," she'd say, and "Shore-nuf," and offer them honey for their biscuits or tell them how red-eye gravy is made, or talk about how sorry it is that we don't serve grits on Sunday morning. The couple would grin wide and start slowing their words, while the regulars would choke on their coffee. Mama never bet on the tip just put it all into the pot, and it was usually enough to provoke a round of applause after the couple was safely out the door.

Mama said nothing about it except the first time when she told me, "Yankees eat boiled eggs for breakfast," which may not sound like much now, but then had the force of a powerful insult. It was a fact that the only people we knew who ate boiled eggs in the morning were those stray tourists and people on the T.V. set who we therefore assumed had to be Yankees.

Yankees ate boiled eggs, laughed at grits but ate them in big helpings, and had plenty of money to leave outrageous tips but might leave nothing for no reason that I could figure out. It wasn't the accent that marked Yankees. They talked "different," but all kinds of different. There seemed to be a great many varieties of them, not just northerners but westerners, Canadians, black people who talked oddly enough to show they were foreign, and occasionally strangers who didn't even speak English. All of them were Yankees, strangers, unpredictable people with an enraging attitude of superiority, who would say the rudest things as if it didn't matter.

Mabel plain hated them. Yankees didn't even look when she rolled her soft wide hips. "Son of a Bitch," she'd say when some fish-eyed, clipped-tongue stranger would look right through her and leave her less than 15 cents. "He must think we get fat on the honey of his smile." Which was even funnier when you'd seen that the man hadn't smiled at all.

"But give me an inch of edge and I can handle them," she'd tell me. "Sweets, you just stretch that drawl. Talk like you're from Mississippi and they'll eat it up. For some reason Yankees have odd sentimental notions about Mississippi."

"And other things," my mama would throw in. "They think they can ask you personal questions just cause you served them a cup of coffee." Some trucker had once asked her where she got her hose with the black thread up the back and mama hadn't forgiven him yet.

But the thing everyone told me and told me again, was that you just couldn't trust yourself with them. Nobody bet on Yankee tips, they might leave anything. Once someone even left a subway token. Mama thought it a curiosity but not the equivalent of real money. Another one ordered one cup of coffee to go and twenty packs of sugar.

"They make 'road-liquor' out of it," Mabel said. "Just add an ounce of vodka and set it down by the engine exhaust for a month. It'll cook up to a bitter poison that'll knock you cross-eyed."

It sounded dangerous to me, but Mabel didn't think so. "Not that I would drink it," she'd say, "but I wouldn't fault a man who did."

They stole napkins, not one or two but a box full at a time. Before we switched to packets they'd come in, unfold two or three napkins, open them like diapers, and fill them up with sugar before they left. Then they might take the knife and spoon to go with it. Once I watched a man take out a stack of napkins I was sure he was going to walk off with. But instead he sat there for thirty minutes making notes on them, then balled them all up and threw them away when he left.

My mama was scandalized by that—"And right over there on the shelf is a notebook selling for 10 cents. What's wrong with those people?"

"They're all living in the movies," Mabel said.

"Yeah, Bette Davis movies," I added.

"I don't know about the movies," threw in one of our regulars, "but they don't live in the real world with the rest of us."

"No," my mama said, "they don't."

I take a bite of cherry tomato and hear her again, "No."

The woman who was talking to me has gone off across the room to the buffet table. People are giving up nibbling and going on to more serious eating. One of the men I work with every day comes over with a full plate.

"Boy," he drawls around a big bite of cornbread, "I bet you sure can cook."

"Bet on it," I tell him with my Mississippi accent. I swallow the rest of the cherry tomato and give him my heartbreaker's smile.

Jan Clausen

Thesis: Antithesis

> But we have different voices, even in sleep,
> and our bodies, so alike, are yet so different,
> and the past echoing through our bloodstreams
> is freighted with different language, different meanings—
> though in any chronicle of the world we share
> it could be written with new meaning
> we were two lovers of one gender,
> we were two women of one generation.
>
> —Adrienne Rich, *Twenty-one Love Poems*

for Jean

Two women were friends; then they quarreled over politics. But, though the period of their silence and anger with each other lengthened until soon it had been going on for considerably longer than that of their original friendship, oddly enough they did not grow farther apart, did not gradually become indifferent to one another. In the normal course of things they would have realized, on one of their chance meetings (for years they continued to live in the same half-decaying, half-renovated urban neighborhood, moving often but usually ending up within several blocks of each other), that they no longer cared enough to maintain their feud. Then they would have gone out for a cup of coffee, smiled for an hour at memories of youthful folly, and parted amicably with hearty admonitions to "keep in touch." Instead, each found that the momentary encounter, the other's closed face glimpsed in a crowd, continued to inflict acute pain. They avoided one another.

But I have begun badly. In making it appear that I'm competent to give you both women's perspectives on what happened (even that, in a sense, they shared a perspective) I misrepresent my position. In fact, their almost desperate need to understand one another should not be confused with a similarity of outlook. They were so unalike in their approaches to their common experience—and I am so deeply involved in the issues with which they were grappling—that it is probably beyond me to understand them equally or to present them objectively.

121

Take, for example, my first sentence: "Two women were friends; then they quarreled over politics." Neither Jean nor Amanda would have used the word "quarrel." Amanda would have said that her friend Jean had simply become impossible; that she, Amanda, had had to draw the line somewhere. Or this is how half of her, the rational, injured half, would have explained it. The guilt-ridden, remorseful half would have retorted sarcastically, "Yes, she got to be too much trouble, so you ditched her. You didn't want to be bothered." To be fair, most of Amanda's friends would have corroborated the first explanation; they too found Jean, or rather her politics (but it became increasingly difficult to separate Jean from her politics; this was part of the problem), insufferable.

Jean's view, corroborated by *her* friends, was closer to the second explanation: she had been ditched. After all, Amanda was the one who had come out with, "I don't think we have anything productive to say to each other right now." Jean had made it plain that she wanted to continue their dialogue. For, as she had carefully pointed out, honest and productive relationships are impossible without struggle; isn't that part of the meaning of dialectics? It was unfortunate that Amanda had felt so threatened by Jean's politics, or rather by the politics of her Organization, since their current line had been forged in struggle with other groups on the Left, represented the culmination of a difficult process of learning to take leadership from the proper quarters, and was proven correct on the most basic level by a host of national and international developments. Not that Jean was surprised; she had lost other friends lately. But none of them had been so close to her as Amanda, either politically or (she hesitated slightly before using the word) "personally."

I am assuming, by the way, that we all share a basic, intuitive understanding of the difference between the "political" and the "personal"; despite the feminist proverb which equates the two, I think you will find that, in this story at least, they are hardly interchangeable. It may simply be noted that whereas, in the women's movement in general, the blurring of distinctions between the personal and the political often signals a desire to dismiss the strictly "political," for Jean it was an assertion of the irrelevance of the purely "personal."

In summary, then, while Amanda, in her self-critical moments, faulted herself for having abandoned a *friend*, a "personal" responsibility, Jean emphasized Amanda's evasion of "political" responsibility. But Amanda also had her moments of wondering whether she had not been guilty of political cowardice: perhaps she ought to have been strong enough to continue to subject her every opinion and motive to the grim, battering scrutiny which Jean called "struggle." And Jean, I suppose, felt abandoned and wronged on a personal as well as on a political level, but she tried to set such feelings aside since they were insignificant compared to the much more serious fact of Amanda's political intransigence.

I say "I suppose" because I don't know for sure; of the two, Jean is the one I find much more difficult to understand. The thing is, though, that I try, and in that sense I am, it seems, like Amanda, like Jean; from the beginning their friendship had been based on "understanding," on long conversations in which they sorted out their psychological, aesthetic and political perceptions and values, each attempting to come to terms with the other's point of view.

Their divergent personalities cannot very well be explained by their backgrounds, which appear nearly identical. Their ancestors had immigrated from the same two or three Western European countries in the same decade of the nineteenth century. Both were born, in one of the bleakest years of the Cold War, into white, middle-class, Christian families by whom the Cold War years were not perceived as particularly bleak. They were raised in the suburbs by women who saw motherhood as a profession, and claimed to desire no other. From the first grade on they were tracked into the "gifted" classes. After high school came college; there were no alternatives. The backdrop to higher education was the Viet Nam War which gradually attracted their attention, pointing up the irrelevance of everything they were supposed to be doing. They demonstrated, dropped out, hung out, bummed around, went back, dropped out again, collected food stamps, took money from their parents, stopped taking money from their parents, worked in factories and fast food joints and offices, fled to the inner city. They became "artists," first tentatively, then with increasing dedication, but they never stopped attending political meetings. They learned to identify themselves as feminists, then lesbians. Both were socialists, a term they avoided using because they felt it had become so vague as to be almost meaningless.

We are the same person, Amanda said to herself occasionally, liking the sound of it, not at all sure what she meant. Yet from the beginning they had focused on their differences. Were these really so great, or did they simply loom larger than differences in less important relationships? "Thesis and antithesis," Amanda had once dubbed them, at a point when it was still possible to make such jokes.

"But which of us is which?" Jean had asked. And she had swung into one of her clowning imitations of Broadway routines:

> *You say po-tay-toes*
> *And I say po-tah-toes*
> *You say to-may-toes*
> *And I say to-mah-toes*

Amanda was compulsively punctual, Jean chronically tardy; Amanda was a writer who claimed incomprehension of all other branches of the arts, Jean a painter who wrote poetry; Amanda was the oldest daughter in a prim Protestant grouping of three, while Jean fell somewhere in the middle of one of those sprawling Catholic families of five or six or seven; Amanda was serially monogamous out of habit and preference, while Jean held high the standard of experimental nonmonogamy. And though they appeared for a time to share a comparable level of political confusion, Jean one day ushered in a new era with the ominous remark, "You can't remain unaligned forever. I'm joining a study group."

Of course you are curious about the precise content of the political disagreement which ensued. I have, however, decided against going into all the gory, sectarian details. For one thing, Jean's Organization changed its analysis several times, and to follow this development would be extremely tedious. For another, it was precisely Amanda's problem that she could never care really deeply about the particulars of a given "line"; her clash with Jean was not, in essence, one of belief versus belief, but of belief versus skepticism.

Still, it may prove instructive to trace the form of a policy shift which took place several months after Jean's formal reception into the Organization (an event she jokingly referred to as "taking the veil"). This development, which at first cheered Amanda because it seemed to belie the Organization's reputation for rigidity and dogmatism, later alarmed her. The salutary spring cleaning was, so far as she could tell from Jean's reports, turning into a bit of a purge. They had all, Jean revealed, been opportunist and worse. It now appeared that most of the Organization's work to date had been completely worthless, if not downright counterproductive. Only a thorough renovation of their analysis, a radical overhaul of their methods, a ruthless elimination of members who remained entrenched in the old positions, would enable them to move forward.

Heads rolled, but—somewhat to Amanda's surprise—the Organization pulled through, and Jean with it. True, there were now only about thirty members locally, in addition to a handful of smaller affiliate groups scattered around the Eastern seaboard. But they all had so much energy! And instead of the "lowest common denominator politics" in which (as they now said) they had previously indulged, they began "upping the ante," confronting other groups and individuals on the Left with their new, quite drastic view of what was to be done.

Amanda was now singled out as eminently organizable. She was smiled upon at demonstrations and court appearances, invited to dinners, benefits and forums. She went on one dismal country retreat, sitting around a smoking fire all weekend with some other fellow-traveler types while two or three of Jean's "comrades" (they really used this expression) led discussions of such questions as: How can the lesbian community play a progressive role on the Left? Is it possible to give up privilege? and (thank god for this old standby, which has whiled away many a tedious winter evening), What is the primary contradiction?

Amanda argued, expressed her point of view, but later she was to realize that she had been careful to do this in a way that would be acceptable to the discussion leaders. For example, she questioned the evidence for considering this group more oppressed than that, but she did not question the necessity for devoting so much energy to the ranking of oppressions. She was left with an uneasy sense of having allowed terms to be dictated. She resolved to avoid such predicaments; from now on she would discuss Jean's politics only in one-to-one situations with Jean.

It did not occur to her that she and Jean might stop discussing politics. For what, then, would they talk about? Amanda could see for herself that Jean had less and less of a "personal" life.

Jean reminded Amanda of a woman who claims she's getting married merely in order to furnish her apartment with the wedding presents, then becomes hopelessly enmeshed in her wifely role. Gone were the reservations and questions of which Jean had spoken at the time she "took the veil" (an expression she did not use any more). There was no criticism of her Organization for which she did not have an instant rebuttal, whether in the form of a defense or a shouldering of blame which somehow served to encompass and neutralize the criticism.

Amanda made an effort to recall her old friend Jean: demonstrating fifties dance styles in bars; painting in the morning, paint all over her tennis shoes, light streaming in through the dusty windows of the loft she had long since left for a collective house; waiting out a heat wave in nothing but her ragged underpants, a beer in her hand; telling funny horror stories about her Catholic education. That was the real Jean, not this chain-smoking politico who saw "agents" everywhere and refused to discuss anything on the phone; who spent her days silk-screening posters and her nights attending meetings; and for whom the shit was, always, "finally hitting the fan," the contradictions "heightening" or "intensifying." This new Jean talked too fast.

"Does Jean take speed?" someone asked quite seriously one day.

"No, she's just high on History," Amanda replied cynically.

Their encounters now took on an unvarying pattern. Jean would describe her political activities, interlarding the account with generous doses of political theory. Amanda would respond with questions, criticisms or agreement. Amanda was at this time becoming "more political," which is to say that she more often knew what she thought, began to break out of her old habit of wallowing in helpless admiration of lives she considered more radical than her own. Now that she allowed herself to investigate her opinion of Jean's Organization, she realized that she had simultaneously nurtured two contradictory views of it: that it was a collection of heroically dedicated, morally superior individuals (this, though she of course knew with what withering contempt "morality" is regarded on the Left); that it was a gang of fanatics wearing blinders and driven by complicated needs including deeply painful guilt and a lust for power. Perhaps there was something in each of these views, but could she sustain both?

And why did it matter so much? Why couldn't she just dismiss this particular craziness in the same way she would have done had Jean joined up with the Hare Krishnas or Moonies? She knew people with friends who had done such things, and she knew what their response had been. They had cut their losses.

Amanda felt sure that this *struggle* (Jean's word, of course, but she meant it a bit differently) had been going on almost forever, the form identical and only the content shifting with the times. At a period when religion had been impossible to ignore, she, Amanda, would have been the one tormented by doubt, by the example of Jean's belief. (Jean, on the other hand, was clearly the type to have burned for her too-intense, heretical devotion.) During another explicitly political era—the thirties, say—Jean would have joined the CP while Amanda remained the fellow traveler. Or Amanda would have joined briefly, fleeing in dismay at the time of the Nazi-Soviet pact, while Jean only redoubled her dedication. None of this was original. They might have been crude figures counterposed in some dreadful Herman Hesse novel.

Well, she is the Catholic, I the Protestant, Amanda thought. Her liberal parents, for whom "prejudice" was a cardinal sin, had instilled in her the WASP's usual consciousness of superiority to dogma-ridden Catholics. If she closed her eyes she could still see the copy of *American Freedom and Catholic Power* prominently displayed on their bookshelf.

What if she is right? Amanda would think. The question had the dizzy fascination of a view from an open fifteenth-story window. They could not both be right. *Am I saved?* is really what she meant. But, consciously or not, she had already made up her mind. It was only a matter of time before she would precipitate the fatal conversation, come out with the famous words, "I don't think we have anything productive to say to each other right now."

"Speak for yourself," Jean replied when the time came, sullen, unsurprised, lighting another cigarette.

Amanda did not protest. She had assumed for some time now that she would land the role of heavy in this production. She even enjoyed the dramatic moment in which she got up and walked away from Jean's objections. Partly, this was sadistic pleasure: after all the difficulty, there was some satisfaction in having hurt Jean. Partly it was relief: Jean was not omnipotent, then. Within their relationship her power was great, she set the terms. But Amanda had the ultimate power. She could walk away.

Or so she thought; and for a while she enjoyed her vacation from the complications of Jean. Certainly she felt somehow diminished in her range of possibilities; she would never, for instance, be able to call herself a revolutionary. On the other hand, she was beginning to feel better about the issue-oriented political work she was doing. And she had plenty of friends; she did not need Jean. Life was so much simpler now that she had "given Jean up," which was how she came to think of it, as though Jean were some pleasurable vice: cigars, or an expensive country house.

But the thing was that she had not really renounced Jean. Because she remained on the Organization's mailing list, she was able to keep up with its—Jean's—political development by reading through the ten or fifteen points of unity inevitably printed in miniscule type on both sides of the leaflets that flooded her mailbox. And since the Organization was active in the neighborhood, the walls of abandoned buildings and boarded-up storefronts were always plastered with posters—designed, naturally, by Jean—advertising their forums and demonstrations.

Amanda went away in the summer. When she returned her mailbox was full of propaganda, the storefronts covered with fresh posters. She remembered guiltily that Jean never took vacations. Amanda went to a movie she considered frivolous and encountered several of Jean's "comrades" in the lobby. She promptly experienced a ludicrous sense of relief, as though she had received permission to be there.

Amanda's obsession was shared by some of her friends. Small conclaves devoted hours to discussing, criticizing, and complaining about the Organization, which was, everyone agreed, misguided, crazy, divisive, dangerous, and above all irrelevant. Prediction, often disguised as grim humor, was a favorite pastime at these gatherings.

"Not that I might not endorse terrorism under certain circumstances, but if *they* ever use it I'll know there's something wrong with it," Amanda once remarked.

"Won't it be ironic when we all get put in jail for refusing to testify to the grand jury investigating that crew?" someone responded.

All this was pleasurable, the scratching of a chronic itch, but it represented only one aspect of Amanda's ongoing relationship with Jean. Another was the fact that Amanda had begun to search for Jean's characteristics in other women she met. And then there were the dreams.

These dreams were deeply satisfying, some even sexually so, which was odd given that Amanda had never thought herself to be erotically interested in Jean. But the sexual dreams were not more important than the others, the ones in which there was danger, the city toppling all around, an atmosphere of terror straight out of "The Battle of Algiers"; the ones in which Jean, although dressed in contemporary clothing, was undoubtedly a nun, martyr or religious hermit; the ones in which everything seemed quite normal, they were talking about something insignificant, "personal," as they used to do in the old days, except that there was something just below the surface, everything was about to change, some important secret

to be revealed. There was even one dream in which Amanda came up behind Jean as she stood in front of an easel, painting, then stepped aside to
reveal a great, vibrant design which, Amanda realized upon waking, could
only be described as a mandala. She laughed at herself; she did not approve
of Jung. But she found herself waiting to dream this dream over again.

In all these dreams, even the sexual ones, Jean was in some way teacher,
mentor. There was a hint of sternness, a whiff of reproach, but also the
promise of forgiveness, absolution.

All of this might have gone on indefinitely if the Organization, weary of
its righteous isolation, had not relaxed its standards somewhat. ("A lower
level of unity is acceptable at this stage of the struggle," was, I believe, how
they phrased it.) They launched a fresh "outreach campaign" directed at
"all progressive elements" in the local women's community. Amanda began to get phone calls sweetly pressuring her to attend this or that demonstration. Smug as Jesus freaks or Right-to-Lifers, Jean's "comrades" twisted
her arm. "Wouldn't you feel a lot better if you did what you know is
right?" was their basic attitude.

Amanda was vulnerable because she had been Jean's friend. When she
finally grasped this elementary fact, she knew what she would have to do,
and did it. She became brutal and sarcastic on the telephone, wrote "return to sender" on all mailed communications, refused leaflets thrust in
her face at demonstrations which the Organization's members attended
not to offer support but to make converts. The result was that she ceased
to be considered a "progressive element." They let her alone.

Still, she could not be sure of her freedom unless she were willing truly
to divest herself of Jean. In order to accomplish this, she decided to put
Jean into a story, a strategy she had, without realizing it, been saving, saying she did not want to be disloyal.

It worked. She stopped having the dreams. She experienced a bitter
sense of triumph, as though, after long planning, she had pulled off the
perfect crime. But when she saw the magazine in which her story finally
appeared, she understood that what she had written was nothing other
than a long love letter to Jean, an explanation and self-justification, a plea
for understanding and forgiveness.

This story has, it seems to me, at least three possible (and plausible)
endings. Please be assured that my decision to offer you your choice
among them has nothing to do with the hackneyed tricks of certain "experimental" writers. Rather, as I indicated earlier, I am more involved than
I might wish to be with this subject matter, and am therefore incapable of
exercising proper authorial control.

In the first ending, Amanda's half-joking prediction of an extremist
direction for Jean's Organization is proven correct. After many months of

strenuous "outreach" work, mostly unsuccessful, several members initiate a criticism-self-criticism campaign. A scrutiny of past practice reveals errors so serious that the validity of the Organization's existence is once more cast into doubt. At the same time, the country is moving rapidly to the right. It seems that a change of tactics is called for.

One by one, Jean's cohorts drop out of sight. Months go by; then there is a rash of bombings at selected targets throughout the city. The bombs having been timed to go off at night, there are no injuries except for one security guard who is killed instantly. In their note claiming credit for the explosion, the Organization places the blame for this death unequivocally upon the shoulders of the government and the multinational corporations. About a year after the last of the bombings, Jean is apprehended in a large midwestern industrial city.

Of course Amanda works on her defense committee. The positions of real responsibility are reserved for those who are close to Jean politically, but there's plenty of shitwork left for everyone else. Amanda makes a lot of phone calls, posts a lot of leaflets. She is never to know for sure whether Jean was or was not directly involved in either the planning or the execution of the bombings. Not that it matters.

Jean is magnificent. She takes a principled stand, insisting that her defense emphasize the criminality of the government and the illegitimacy of the institutions which had been targeted, rather than focusing on technicalities. Although barred from reading her own prepared statement at the trial, her presence is itself a statement. Her thinness, her pallor, her hair cropped close to remove the remnants of bleach from her year underground, all somehow underline not vulnerability, but strength. She looks like she's *sure*, like she *knows*, Amanda thinks. Like Joan of Arc at the stake. The characterization is admiring, not sarcastic.

The government's case is weak, so Jean ends up doing a few years at a minimum-security facility where repressive tolerance is the order of the day. From breakfast to dinner the inmates are free to wander up and down corridors painted in dingy pastels. There is a "beauty salon" where they spend hours doing each other's hair and nails. They watch a lot of television.

It is like high school, Jean says, when Amanda goes to visit her. "The sisters really want to get it together, but ..." The problem, Amanda sees, is that there is very little overt brutality around which to organize. And the lack of it has diminished Jean; she looks listless and bloated. Amanda is reminded of descriptions she's read of mental patients subjected to insulin treatments and electro-shock. Well, an indeterminate sentence and the prison diet would do it to anyone. Amanda goes back again and again, knowing Jean doesn't have many visitors now that her case is no longer publicized. But she dreads the visits.

After Jean's release—she is recommended for parole on grounds of good behavior—they avoid a review of their history. Once, though, Jean tells Amanda about her year underground. "You can't imagine it, it was tremendous, like not having a face or something." Amanda is a bit shocked by the eagerness with which her friend describes this obliteration. Jean is, she realizes, talking about the happiest year of her life.

Back among the living, Jean's time is once more entirely taken up with political work, but work that is, so to speak, more ecumenical than formerly. She lends her name out to worthy causes, is invited to speak with the likes of Martin Sostre, Morton Sobell, Angela Y. Davis. This broadening of perspective is, after all, what Amanda had once hoped for. Why, then, has she come to think of Jean as a has-been? The two are cordial, but they do not meet often.

I should perhaps mention that there is a variant of this particular ending in which Jean is killed—murdered, that is, as the leaflets for the protest demonstration quite accurately state—by police who claim she drew a gun while they were attempting to apprehend her. But I tend to agree with Jean's own analysis that such fates, in this society, are typically reserved for those "more oppressed" than she. Typically—but not always.

According to the second ending, things remain fairly stable for a period of some years. Jean continues her political graphics work, her endless round of dreary meetings, ineffectual demonstrations, lethal criticism-self-criticism sessions. (But these harsh adjectives represent Amanda's perspective; probably Jean herself considers this life quite rewarding.) Jean and her friends never do anything drastic enough to incur more than routine FBI harassment, phone taps, and arrests for unruly courtroom behavior and illegal postering. The Organization, though disliked, has become a fixture on the Left, and as such is tolerated. Its vitality is as mysterious as that of some fundamentalist sect which keeps predicting the Final Days and is not the least bit chagrined when they fail to materialize. The contradictions—make no mistake about this—are heightening, deepening, intensifying.

Then one summer Jean is killed in a car accident. Amanda, hearing the news, experiences a confused sort of grief. But she does not hesitate in deciding to attend the funeral. There she learns what happens to daughters of the middle class who ignore the petit bourgeois custom of making provision for one's own demise: their remains are claimed and borne away by relatives who install them safely in suburban graveyards. It is the most dismal finish Amanda can possibly imagine.

One of the "comrades" invites Amanda to a sort of memorial party or wake held in Jean's old collective house. Amanda is surprised to see how neat and pleasant everything is, not Jean's old chaos, the irrelevance of housekeeping in the face of impending revolution. The walls are covered with Jean's graphics. Amanda notices how good they are. Oh, she had always known Jean was good, of course, but it had been hard to cling to that knowledge in the face of Jean's deprecation of her own talent.

It's not quite fair, Amanda thinks. What she means is that Jean gained a certain moral advantage by pretending to renounce art, while in fact she renounced nothing. "Did she ever talk about me?" she wants to ask Jean's housemates, but doesn't dare. She imagines she recognizes something like her own face in a multi-ethnic grouping on one of the posters, but she can't be sure.

In the third and final ending, nothing happens. Both Amanda and Jean go through many personal and political changes, some of which appear ludicrous to outside observers, but all of which are experienced as internally consistent. Yet the hurt of their rupture remains long after the circumstances which produced it have altered. They cannot seem to transcend this.

Amanda tries—once. After a lapse of months or years, she has another one of her dreams about Jean. Taking this as a sign, she obtains Jean's current phone number, calls her up. Could they meet to talk things over?

Jean is cool, but agrees. They choose a neutral spot for the meeting, a women's bar. Jean is typically late. Amanda sits alone, nervous, drinking her beer, while around her couples sway, dancing, or sit at small tables gazing into each other's faces, no doubt absorbed in romantic dilemmas with which Amanda feels an overwhelming lack of sympathy.

Finally Jean arrives, apologizing perfunctorily for her lateness; she was at a meeting. She orders a drink. They talk, review their history. But they are not getting to the real point.

"I loved you, I always loved you," Amanda says suddenly, risking. In the pause that follows this non sequitur, she hears the jukebox parodying her statement.

"I think," Jean says finally, staring into her drink, "that you've always been so goddamned involved with what I represent, something I mean to you about yourself politically or who you think you ought to be or something, that you don't have the slightest fucking idea what you feel about me personally. So let's not discuss it, okay?"

The truth, Amanda thinks, *but not the whole truth*. Yet what choice has she other than to accept it?

Aleida Rodríguez

Sequences

Sequence I

she reached a hand into the deep ceramic bowl pulled out a
tangerine in the center of her palm she put the tangerine
down then picked up the nutcracker like a pair of scissors
with her other hand she started choosing the different nuts
in the clear glass bowl sandy colored rough almonds wrinkled
symmetrical hard walnuts the smooth reddish nuts the small
round brown ones with a rough oval face on one end the cat
leaped onto her shoulder watched her sort through the bowlful
of hard shapes following the movements of her hands she held
each nut rolled it in the center of her palm before she splintered
it on the counter the cat waited she ate a few brushed the shells
into one cupped hand with the other flat running across the counter
                              then she picked up the tangerine again
walked to the garbage bag by the open back door started ripping
the peel she stooped from the weight of the cat still perched
on her shoulder the orange tearing skin sent small spurts into
the sunlight that floated down disappeared but the citrus smell
floated up she stood over the brown bag until she finished the
tangerine her hands dripping sticky she licked her fingers walked
over to the sink washed her hands pulled a paper towel down to dry
them
the cat lowered itself to the sink edge licked the last drop of
water hanging from the mouth of the faucet the traveling vegetable
truck passed announcing through a loud speaker tomatoes broccoli
sweet carrots the cat jumped from the sink ran to the livingroom
window avocadoes string beans the cat stretched hooking its nails
into the screen she moved away from the sink where she'd been
staring at the dishes walked into the bathroom
                              her robe opened as she moved she adjusted one
piece of cloth under the other then pulled the sash tighter when
inside she turned her face but not her shoulders into the reflection

132

of the bathroom mirror she didn't look at her eyes with her fingers
curled she pushed back the hair on her forehead then dropped
her hand to the curve of the sink looked at the bitten nails
at the drain the cat came in jumped on the edge of the tub
started licking the pink flesh at the center of a paw

Sequence II

just then the water for tea was boiling and spitting out of the pot. she rose
to make herself a cup. one of the cats ran past her in the kitchen carrying
a ball of aluminum foil in its mouth. she let out a sigh and started chasing
it over the couch in the livingroom under the chest between the wheels of
the bicycles parked inside out of the rain. she finally caught up with the
small white skinny cat in the doorway of the kitchen, gave it a sharp slap
on the head as she wrenched the foil from its mouth. her lips formed
'mongoloid' and 'jesus christ' as she pulled the tin box with tea bags from
the pantry. she watched it rain on the screen while she washed a cup. putting the cup down on the stove without filling it she walked back to the
typewriter. she wanted it to come out already in some form, a piece of
something she could recognize from the beginning and just follow. she sat
down and stared at the humming machine.

you ditch it. dump it. get out. go away. just pull the paper out of the
typewriter turn it off push back your chair go do something get some tea
you know how continental it makes you feel to have tea with cream sit on
the couch and sip your tea slowly listen to the rain pelting the palm fronds
curl your legs up stroke the back of a cat put your empty cup down and
promise yourself that you'll get up for another in a few minutes stretch
out reach over and turn on the heat that's right you won't even notice.

the problem was too much passivity. bring in some characters. but it
would be like having a roomful of the same person in different bodies.
everyone's always saying how, of course, everything you write is *always*
you, yes, and with that kind of inflection. she laughed, enjoying the way
she amused herself. a beer. none of this continental tea business and she
walked into the kitchen, peering around the floor for any cat she could
attack.

the black cat was just then coming in through the broken screen on the
back door, which a few weeks before the calico in heat had torn making

the outside a cinch. and today it was raining. oh, manya, she called out too sweetly and the cat backed away suspicious of this turn of favor. come here, baby, *sweet* manya. that cat always fell for it and she knew it. she grabbed manya's front paws and twirled with her in front of the refrigerator laughing put her down again and scratched her head for being such a good predictable fool. she opened the refrigerator and reached for a beer. she sat on the floor by the broken screen watching it rain lightly now not as hard as before. it felt strange to drink beer and have it be cold, not that it was cold here by the refrigerator even with the back door open, but it was cold out there. she felt vaguely like an alcoholic drinking like this out of season.

she noticed the hum of the typewriter in the other room, took a few more swallows of beer before she got up. when she reached the machine she looked at the writing on it for a while, piecing it together. it started to rain suddenly in a burst the room filled with staccato sounds. she turned around to look for a window to gauge how hard it was coming down as if she were deaf and had to see a solid sheet of water moving down the small surface of the window.

but of course you don't trust sounds if you're alone and haven't heard your own voice in a while you begin to think all the sounds are in your head like your voice which doesn't stop but follows you from room to room.

she stretched her arms behind her back clasped together then sat down and began to pick out letters slowly with two fingers.

Sequence III

she leans on the sill, looks out the window after the rain. the stucco house across the street is yellower, the earth by the sidewalk nearly black. these things are to be expected. the red curved tiles on the roof next door are slick, they make her want to lapse into spanish, write bodega or jamón into the wetness on the window. what she has to say today feels like a seizure, she would shake the floor with her shoulders and elbows and heels, would speak in tongues the private. she would flatten, become the wooden slats, the earth beneath the house dusty and crossed with angled pipes, she would keep shifting through the layers, emerge under the painted desert quickening up the sand like a pulse bursting through the mesas without history or collective unconscious, pulled, gutted from the earth's heat like turquoise or bones or secrets.

she shifts her weight away from the wndow sill, moves closer to the heater. she thinks of the deception of stoves white and slick pretending cool but hiding instead the heat so that from then on heat was the one thing everything kept from her.

in the bathroom this morning, when their bodies maneuvered around each other with the familiarity of water, hands sliding off shoulders and down backs, she had wanted to say that her skin felt thick, the nerve endings were going further under, curling inward, taking comfort instead in the flow of blood through veins, the slight expansion of arteries and capillaries. that as she smoothed cream around her breasts, down the fine line running the length of her torso, she felt stark, separate, felt her body as the place where she began and ended. as she rubbed the orange cream along the curve of her hip she was sure of this, her fingers warming over her skin. she had wanted to explain.

recently, all her movements/gestures were bringing her arms and legs closer to the center. walking through the doorway of the bedroom, tucking a fragment of material under itself near her neck, then letting her fingers retreat along the track of her collar bone, she felt that with each fold, each tuck or bend, she was constructing her shape, was living origami.

now, from her position over the heater, she angles her face to the white light framed in the small window. she can see part of the overcast sky opening to blue inside a cat's cradle of telephone wires. the calico yawns and stretches on the grill of the heater at her feet. the ribbing at the roof of its mouth is stained irregularly with black. she wonders if its stomach or heart are patched with black clouds in the same way, bends to lift the cat to her shoulder, but holds it too tightly and it squirms, jumps to the floor, leaving three red scratches at the inside of her arm just below her elbow.

Sequence IV

there is the dream. an old lover tries to break into the apartment where she now lives with her lover, the good one, the one who kneads her back muscles in the doorway of the kitchen. the old lover splinters fists on the front door and she, on the inside, locks it quietly, tries to avoid the creaks in the floor back to bed to the good one. but once in bed there is the epiphany of the back door maybe not locked. she arrives before the squares of glass at the precise moment when something, no longer the old lover, is rushing up the length of wooden stairs. she looks to her left in front of the refrigerator and finds the good one there, risen out of bed but shrugging, ambivalent, offering palms up. she looks out through the door again, it is an explosion of movement with vague hands on the wooden banisters, the mass suspended and rushing. she awakens to her own questions. there is no glass on the back door, no stairs. her brother.

all the piles of books, the dangling of bells from the doorknob of her bedroom on 6th st. to warn her to wake up in case. it had worked, caused her to wake sweating on the skinny bed by the window. she had heard the bells, the books falling, whispered go away and the fear released the door, the force moved back to his room. she was surprised her own voice could hold him away, couldn't depend on it again, stayed awake until morning. her parents' bedroom was downstairs at the other end of the house, they were there but ineffectual, didn't speak english, worked nights or did laundry, far away. the first time she hadn't wanted to wait for them in the laundromat, had asked to be driven home, to read, didn't want to see her mother sneaking dimes from the bottom of the broken machine or her father grunting loudly in spanish although he almost always told her to be quiet in public. it was the dead-end house on mac arthur, he put on roll over beethoven, starting mincing at her in the livingroom while she read, her cheeks were hot, she didn't want to act as if he were the cause. he had always called her einstein because she read, because she had little bottles of stolen ingredients from the kitchen in her laboratory in one corner of the basement. on the floor she had on her black corduroy pants with the red flannel lining, it was showing. she didn't have much pubic hair, he was holding his cock up to the red lining, it was like clay and she squirmed. she locked herself in the bathroom.

he had always been the favorite, the only son, the brother she had seen after six months in the u.s. it was christmas, he had been in a boys' home in chicago while she and her sister had it good with the presbyterian minister and the seven kids and the orange juice on weekdays, grape on sundays before church. he had been the one she had asked to look at her new doll at the door, just as he was entering, but the last word had come out in english, she was already letting go of his world, had learned white coral bells upon a slender stalk. he was the one who knocked on the bathroom door but she wouldn't open it as she washed between her legs with a warm wash cloth and shivered. her parents worried about her, locked in the bathroom every time she was left at home. she would bring books to the table, not look up. when they moved to 6th st. her parents wanted the bottom bedroom, assured her that no one would get in, wouldn't take the bedroom next to hers. her brother started running out into traffic in his blue swimming trunks in indiana while on vacation, swallowing a bottle of aspirins and curving off the road toward beardstown, getting the reputation of being nervous, as her mother stressed to her, but somehow never losing rank, always able to switch the t.v. channel when she was watching and she sent to her room to be better than he, to be the smart one not the nervous one.

but he wasn't the one steaming up the back stairs. it was the child. the one who wore the black corduroy pants, the one who sweated on that skinny bed on 6th st., the one who hung the bells, the one who wanted a place in her body now, the one who didn't want to be kept walking from her bedroom forever into the livingroom in the first apartment in california, the one with long hair which she had cut when she came out, a ritual discarding but never a cleansing, the one who kept her from having orgasms. this was the one pressing behind her lips everyday now, wanting to tell the good lover, the lover who noticed the reptile crawling under the skin of her back and worked it slowly for her up to the tense neck, the headaches. the one coming up the back stairs had claws, a short nylon nightgown, had her head down and was looking up at her almost through her eyebrows, was about to spring. she recognized her, let her slip from between her lips in bed, named her. she felt an easing away at the inside of her thighs as if she had wet the bed as she had done until she was ten. she had decided, had stayed up all night when she was eleven lying on her hands, that she wouldn't suck her thumb anymore. she had stopped that night because she had wanted to.

the good one was now curled away from her, she fit her belly to the mold of her warm back, started falling asleep hearing the noises of the cats clawing the straw mats, jumping from the window sills, no one was trying to get in.

Ann Allen Shockley

A Case of Telemania

Freda sat on the edge of the bed in the criss-crossed shadows of the night table lamp, restlessly smoking her third king-sized Winston cigarette. The radio/clock facing her showed eight p.m. Kimberly had left an hour ago to attend a faculty committee meeting. The apartment was quiet and entirely too still for her. She thrived on people and talk, sounds and movements. The tranquility gnawed into her like the teeth of a worrisome rat.

Even the usual Friday night traffic noises were halted because of the falling featherlight snow coating the streets. At times, a lone car could be heard moving clumsily down the white frosted road. To her, it seemed to do nothing but snow in this small, campus town nestled in the Pennsylvania hills.

Irritably she drew heavily upon the cigarette, thinking of all nights for Kimberly to have a meeting. They could have had Tonnie and Laverne from upstairs in for a little party. Hadn't the college officials here ever heard of TGIF?

The room breathed a slight chill against her. She could go into the living room and turn up the thermostat, but this was secondary to her thoughts. Instead, she simply fastened the plaid robe tighter around her pajama clad, short chubby figure, while her eyes fastened hard on the telephone beside the bed, cigarette parting a smoldering white line between thick, brown fingers. The yellow telephone, color selected by Kimberly to harmonize with the beige walls and green rug when they first moved in together four months ago, seemed to hypnotize her as she stared gravely at it.

Really, Freda, she cautioned herself silently, you *shouldn't*. Last month's bill was a terror. Luckily she had gotten the mail before Kimberly that day. After all, the phone *was* in Kimberly's name even though she did pay her share. Times like the last, it was a mad race trying to beat Kimberly to the mailbox. On those occasions, she simply told Kimberly that she would take care of it and Kimberly never saw the bill.

She would have rather had the listing in her name, since she used the phone more than Kimberly. Only Ma Bell wouldn't trust her until she finished paying that Greensboro bill left over from last year. Stupid, considering all the money Ma Bell had. But *that* wasn't as bad as her mother. God!

138

Her own *mother* put a lock on the telephone whenever she was home, constantly bitching about the enormity of the past bills she made when visiting, and worst of all, yakking about all the women she called up across the country. Why did she have to call up those *women* all the time? She must have a case of telemania, her mother coined.

She didn't know why her mother bitched so much. She tried to pay the bills, and what were telephones for if not to be *used*? To her, a phone was what a drink was to some people at five o'clock, exquisite cuisine to others, and a good screw to those who needed one. Talking over the telephone was *her* thing, something she *had* to do and *enjoyed* doing. The telephone served as an outlet to family, friends, ex-lovers and potential lovers.

Like right now, she had this urge to call Harriet in Camden. She reached down for the almost forgotten glass of chablis on the floor. A bad habit, Kimberly chastised her, because invariably at sometime or another, the glass was knocked over, adding more spots to the rug. She sipped the wine, feeling its warmth relaxing her, crumbling prudence.

Just *one* little bitty call shouldn't upset the equilibrium. The new phone bill wasn't due for two weeks. Besides, she hadn't seen or talked to Harriet in a long time. Harriet used to be her sounding board, lending a sympathetic ear to her problems. Too bad she never made it with Harriet. If Gloria wasn't always in the picture to keep such a goddam protective eye on her *and* her business, personal and otherwise, she was certain that she would have gotten through. Anyway, she should call Harriet to tell her how much she enjoyed her latest book of poetry. She *owed* her that, considering their friendship throughout the years.

Setting the wine glass back on the floor, she squashed out the cigarette among the dead stems of like ones and got up to get her address book out of the bureau drawer. Running a finger down the R section, she found Harriet Ruse's telephone number. With bare feet flip-flapping in run-over houseshoes, she went back to sit on the bed and dial the number.

There were several rings before she heard Harriet's gentle, low-keyed rich poet's voice answering. Thank goodness it was Harriet and not Gloria. "Hi, Harriet, this is Freda Delaney—"

"Freda! How *are* you?" The woman on the other end seemed delighted. "It's been a long time."

"Un-Hun-n-n—" Freda hummed a musical tune. "It has. I thought I'd call to let you know how *much* I enjoyed your new book, *Black Gems for Black People.*"

"How *sweet.* I'm so glad you liked it."

In the background of the phone's opposite end, Freda could hear Natalie Cole singing *Inseparable.* "In addition," she continued in her husky Yale graduate school affected preciseness, "I wanted you to know that I am now on the faculty of Wilshire College in Willy, Pennsylvania. It's a predominantly *white* school, private and in the middle of nowhere!" she laughed.

"How did you get *there*? I thought you were at that all-girl black school in—"

"I *was*," Freda interrupted, pausing to cradle the receiver between her shoulder and neck to extract another cigarette from the half empty pack on the table. Eyeing it fretfully, she hoped Kimberly would remember to bring some home. Quickly she sparked a flame with the gold lighter Kimberly had given her last month for a birthday present.

"Didn't you *like* it?" Harriet cut into the suspension.

"*Loved* it! My first teaching position out of Yale. I loved going back to my *roots*, so to speak. Being around *my* people for a change. You know, after all those years being exiled at white schools. Scholarships to Putney, Marlboro and Yale."

"I understand."

Harriet *would* understand, for she was a sensitive poet and writer. Although Harriet was forty-five, twenty years older than she, Harriet could *relate*. Furthermore, she got along better with *older* women, even when she was younger and the pet of all the black teachers in her hometown of Anniston, Alabama. "As I was saying, Harriet, it was wonderful being there, teaching history to all my beautiful black sisters—"

"Well, why did you *leave*?"

Freda loudly sucked in a pit of smoke, then exhaled it in one spontaneous cloudburst. "Because the black *male* administration over a *girls'* college, mind you, namely, the Dean, wanted to get rid of me."

"How *awful*. Why?"

She could imagine Harriet's handsome sharp, creole face screwing up into knots, the dark eyes widening questioningly. Harriet's deep, engulfing eyes were the most memorable feature about her. She could hear the record player being turned up. Gloria must be home signifying, she calculated. Gloria could be so ridiculously jealous sometimes for a lover who had lived with Harriet for eleven years. Case in point now when they were merely having a friendly chat.

"Oh, Harriet, because a very *close*—at least I *thought* at the time, friend of mine, who taught in the department with me, spread the rumor that I was a lesbian."

"Really!"

"Un-Hun-n-n. And *you* know how *black* people feel about lesbians. Or bulldaggers to use *our* race's favorite label. They'll tolerate fags, but not people like—" She started to say us, but caught herself. Harriet hadn't actually come out. Silly, since *everybody* knew. "Homophiles—" she supplemented, thinking that was a good aesthetic word to use with Harriet.

"Oh—" Low and thoughtful.

"It *was* a rumor and no one could *prove* it. Of course, if you aren't seen dating a male or letting one go to bed with you, people start surmising."

"Yes, but on what basis—"

"Like I was saying, this *supposedly* close friend, who had taught there for years, was *jealous* of me. Students signed up for my classes more than hers and were always either hanging out in my office or at my house. Plus, I was *younger* than she and the girls could tie in better on my wave lengths—" Christ, she rebuked herself, she had slipped and exposed the generation gap analysis to Harriet. "Besides, I had a degree from Ya—ale," she continued, putting out the cigarette in the congested ash tray. "This person told the Dean, according to *my* source, that I got loaded one night over to her place and made a pass at her. Imagine! And her as ugly as Job's turkey."

The wine glass was brought up to her mouth. Perpetually something to the mouth as if solacing an oral need: cigarettes, wine, telephone receivers. The record player blared Patti LaBelle's group, a phantasmagoria of female bleating rock rhythms cloaked in a nightmarish colorful garden of mind blowing soul motion sounds.

"Now, Harriet, *the* night in question," Freda continued, "I must admit that I *was* drunk, and I *may* have—" She set the glass back on the floor. "In a way, I guess, I *did* rather *like* her. As I look back, it was probably pity. She was so ineffectual—helpless, although Jesus-s, she had *per—so—na—lity*. And, shit, the way she hung around me all the time, rubbing up against me and reading Audre Lorde's poetry, I just *assumed—*"

"Un-Hun-n-n." Harriet at times could be so damn guarded. Freda extracted another cigarette, flicking the lighter angrily as memories began to stir. "I should have *sued* her for damaging my reputation. You don't *know* how uptight and straight-assed those black bourgeois colleges can be. It practically *ruined* me for the rest of the year. Faculty members avoided me like the plague. If they only *knew* a fourth of the student body is gay." She bent to sip from the glass again. "Oh, well, pity all those self-righteous people who can fuck each other's wives and husbands and get students pregnant, yet want to act all pious and knock the other."

"How do you like Wilshire?"

Freda placed the cigarette on the edge of the ash tray to scratch her Afro. "So-so. I'm the only *black* faculty member aside from a Hambuk Toré who goes around all the time in his tribal robes to let people know right off he's not a black American," she giggled. "Frankly, I think he's hiding a swish underneath that African garb. Isn't that a new wrinkle?" Distantly in the receiver, she could hear Harriet whispering her name, probably to nosey Gloria. "I've seen four black students since I've been here. There aren't enough of us black folks here to give this God awful constant snow a color tint," she lamented facetiously. "Furthermore, I *do* prefer warm weather. Wasn't that why we were brought to this country? Because of our ability to sustain and work in heat—"

"Black fruitful labor courting seeds of fertility—" Harriet intoned poetically.

"Actually, I think most of the people here are racists. I had to fight tooth and nail to teach a course in Afro-American history . . ."

"In this point in time?"

"I don't believe they've *ever* heard of a black *or* gay revolution—" The cigarette was retrieved again.

A single female voice singing in a whiplash beat about love love love replaced LaBelle. "Who's that singing?"

"Lib Tolson—"

"Un-Hun-n-n. I hear she's gay. Turn it up louder."

"Wait a minute. Gloria's gone next door. I'll have to go into the living room."

"Ok—" Freda bent down for the wine glass. Seeing it empty, she put down the receiver, got up and started to the kitchen, carelessly dropping a trail of ashes from the cigarette as she went. Opening the refrigerator, she refilled the glass from the bottle on the shelf next to the milk. Then she took one last draw before stubbing the cigarette in the overflowing kitchen ash tray. Returning to the bedroom, she resumed her place on the bed, picking up the telephone. "Ok—back. Harriet?"

"Right here. Can you hear the record better?"

"Un-Hun-n-n. Lo-o-ve it!" she exclaimed, twisting her body sexily in time with the music. "Yeah-h-h, sing it, sister!"

"This call must be costing you a *fortune*."

"Don't worry about it. I called *you*, didn't I? What are phones *for*, if not to keep up with old friends." She gulped the wine, getting a buzz on which began to create a little fire of nastiness. "The more I think about that skinny legged, yellow bitch spreading that malicious tale about me, the madder I get!"

"Did they actually *fire* you?"

"No. Just didn't renew my contract. Isn't that a bitch? That Dean, who'd been trying to feel my legs under the table at meetings all year, ought to be hung. The old gizzard'd probably need a prop to keep it up! Men can sometimes be bastards, can't they?"

"Are you going home for Easter?" Harriet evaded the question.

Freda remembered that Harriet never said anything bad about men in conversation, or her poetry in which she wrote of them as beautiful, strong, black men, while in reality, she lived with a beautiful, strong, black woman. "Un-Hun-n-n. I'd *rather* be in New York with the gang and run over to see *you*. But you know my mother would have a fit if I didn't spend Easter there with her."

"Are you happy there?"

Harriet forever worried about people being happy, her muse's preoccupation with feelings. "I miss my *black* sisters--"

"You may get back in a black college," Harriet said sympathetically.

"Yes, my black sisters *need* me." From the next room, she heard the door opening and closing. "Well, Harriet—sweetie—I must go," she said hastily. "It was wonderful talking with you. I'll be writing soon. Bye, bye."

This time, she carefully set the wine glass on the night table and went quickly to meet Kimberly entering the living room. The stately looking whitewoman with checkered gray in her brown hair looked tired as she threw off her hat and coat. "Meetings can wear you out—"

"I know—" Freda said consolingly, kneeling to help her take off the wet-stained boots. Moving up, she kissed her gently, breathing in the outdoor breath of winter still enmeshed in her face and hair. The closeness to the woman, combined with the wine, kindled a small, familiar flame. "Missed you—"

Kimberly leaned her cheek against Freda's. "I think I'll get a glass of wine—"

"I'll get it for you. You go and get undressed." In the kitchen, Freda got the bottle of wine and a glass, taking it to the bedroom. "Here you are." Handing Kimberly the glass, she refilled her own. "Did you remember to get cigarettes?"

"On the dresser—" Kimberly murmured, fatigued.

"Good. Now, darling, tell me *all* about the meeting—" Freda invited, snuggling into bed beside her, next to the telephone where she always slept just in case.

Irena Klepfisz

The Journal of Rachel Robotnik

> *So all that is in her will not*
> *bloom—but in how many does it?*
> Tillie Olsen, "I Stand Here Ironing"

To the Reader:

Over 10 months ago I received a letter from Ms. Robotnik asking for assistance in editing and finding a suitable place for presenting an excerpt from a journal she had kept while writing her collection of short stories *Kaleidoscope* (Random Books, 1978). She explained that, though pleased with the reception of her work, she had become increasingly uneasy about it. She was "plagued" by the idea that something was missing, and, in hope of pinpointing it, had gone back to her journal from that period. One re-reading made her realize that, though not an integral part of the stories, the journal was a kind of companion piece, almost marginalia, to the fictional work, and she became determined to have it published. She, therefore, asked her editors at Random Books to issue it as a second volume; they refused, as did many other editors over the next year and a half.

Her discomfort over *Kaleidoscope*'s acceptance into the literary world, she explained, stemmed from her belief that most reviewers as well as readers could not understand it if they did not understand how it came to be. Hindsight, she wrote me, enabled her to see a sharp difference between the realism of her stories (which had received such praise) and the realism of her journal (which had been rejected) — a difference which she characterized as that between "fairy tales and hard-won vision."

> At some point I left one reality for another. It was as if I'd journeyed to another planet. The force of gravity was different. Suddenly I had no grace — was clumsy, awkward, moved with greater difficulty — slow, ever so slow. What amazed me though, was that I never intended to go there, never chose it. Yet there I was and I had no idea how and when I arrived. It was a time without solace, except for those brief moments

144

when I thought about that 'other' place — which gleamed like
a dead star whose light I could still see but whose substance, I
knew, had long since burned up and vanished.

Anyone familiar with the *Kaleidoscope* stories must agree they are far
from fairy tales. Nevertheless, the discrepancy between them and the journal is indeed unsettling. As Ms. Robotnik wrote (and rather bitterly, I
think) in another letter:

Lovers of great art are pure poison. They live for the single
moments, for epiphanies, for great revelations. They want to
forget what happens in between; they don't want to see the
process, the conditions, the dead flies stuck to the half-dry
canvas. Yes, they want the journals and the letters — but only
after they've been purified of their 'trivia' — only after they
are comfortably part of history. Those appreciators of great
art — how conscientiously they avoid dealing with the daily
grind, how ignorant they are of the real triumph, of the real
nature of the tragedy.

From the outset, therefore, we had a tacit understanding that the journal
would be edited only for clarity and that no deletions would be made. But
remaining completely faithful to the original proved somewhat problem-
atic.

The manuscript covers the period from September 12, 1974 to March 3,
1977, a period during which Ms. Robotnik wrote *Kaleidoscope* and during
which she earned her living as a medical transcriber at Memorial Hospital
in New York City. It is bound in two black, plastic covers, each containing
approximately 175 unnumbered pages. It is typed — extremely unusual for
a journal; each entry begins on a new page and is single spaced. Besides the
text, it contains numerous *New York Times* articles which are stapled or
scotchtaped at the end of entries or on separate pages between entries.
Since it was impossible to reprint the articles in their entirety, we decided
to provide only the headlines. Underlined passages, however, were repro-
duced to indicate focus. As will be seen, neither clipping nor labeling
(date, page, column) was systematic or consistent.

In addition to the articles, sections from the stories on which Ms.
Robotnik was working are occasionally included. These appear three times
during the two weeks excerpted here and provide a unique opportunity for
comparison with parallel passages in the final version of the title story
(pages 7, 4, 19 and 22; hardback Random Books edition).

The text itself contains numerous abbreviations, all of which have been
retained. The most frequent are: w/ = with; abt = about; cd, wd, shd =

could, would, should; sd = said (used inconsistently); fr = from (used inconsistently); wk = week; $$ = "money," "price," "cost," or "expensive" (used interchangeably); K. = "Kaleidoscope," the story; D = Dia, Ms. Robotnik's lover. Except for "tho" and "thru" I have standardized spelling and corrected obvious slips; words appearing in brackets [ ] are my own, inserted for clarity.

Mary M. Arnold
Chicago
January 9, 1980

DELAY ASKED IN CURB ON ALIEN PHYSICIANS—New York Hospitals See U.S. Law as Threat to Medical Care—by Ronald Sullivan—A new Federal law that will drastically limit recruiting of graduates from foreign medical schools by hospitals . . .

In New York State, the foreign ratio is much higher, 52 percent, with even higher percentages in municipal hospitals and in those that have no affiliation with a nearby medical school. (1/5; A1)

ECONOMISTS FIND PAUSE ENDING: GROWTH PROJECTIONS FOR '77 RAISED—by Paul Lewis—The recent advance of several important economic indicators has convinced many private American economists that the so-called pause in the nation's economic recovery from the deepest recession since World War II is now ending . . . (1/6; 1)

CALIFORNIA HOMOSEXUALS HELD TO LACK JOB RIGHTS—San Francisco, Jan. 5 (AP)—Homosexuals have no legal protection against job discrimination the California Court of Appeals has ruled. "There is simply no constitutional right [for homosexuals] to work for an unwilling employer . . ." (1/6)

FOR $59, A NEW YORKER WINS A DIVORCE WITHOUT LAWYERS (1/6; 22)

Fri. Jan. 7 '77; 6:30 AM: Windows completely iced over. Feels like I cd freeze to death. Turned on oven. Must call Stan. It's the boiler, *not* the valves. How can anyone so big be so stupid? Einstein was tiny. But then D pointed out Einstein probably cdn't fix the boiler either.

Spoke to Barb last night. Wants to get together, but too overloaded. [She] Spent fortune on presents. Dead broke. Found it all pointless. So do I. Meeting her nxt Fri at the D[iana].

Claire back yesterday. Combined coffee breaks & lunch & took Roberta to Brew Burger for her 43rd. Outrageous: $52 w/ tip split 4 ways. Limp salads w/ rippled pickles, drinks—& yes, Marcie's $$ diet burger. Long discussion abt *sculptured* nails. Growth & clipping. Gave me the creeps—thought the plastic nails grew. Everyone hysterical. Claire types w/ nails; Marcie w/ fingertips. Both see a manicurist every couple of wks. $15 a visit. Carmen thought it $$. Claire said no—only $1 a day.

BEAME OFFERS PLAN TO CLOSE THE DEFICIT IN 1977-78 BUDGET—Says It Won't 'Sap' Services—7,500 Job Slots Expected to be Cut—Proposal Needs the Approval of Banks, Unions, State and U.S. (1/7; 1)

PEOPLE'S INAUGURATION TO INCLUDE SOLAR HEATING, BUT NOT FOR MANY (1/7)

Sat. Jan. 8 '77; 6 PM: Dull flat day. Cold. Recycling center. Dragged clothes to laundromat. $$ up again. Shopped. Coffee $$ still impossible. Refused. Tuna on sale (.39). Stocked up. Vowed to make sandwiches for work. Probably won't—too practical. Always forget. D props hers against the door. Vacuumed. Washed kitch flr. Too long.

My turn to call Fla. The same. She's still obsessing he's dirty; he complains she's constantly "rude." Papa's the only person who still uses this word. Both talked abt the strike; disappointed the Steins haven't come down. Leah called last wk & invited them to N.M. [Albuquerque], but Mamma refused. No explanation. More expansive abt kids. Tanya: "remarkable" reading scores. Adam: swimming medal. Best: Alex's article accepted in CE [*College English*]. Certain he'll get tenure. So Alex scraped thru. Felt glad for him/them, but found it painful to hear.

Mamma predictably: how are things at the "shorthand pool"? Moved in another direction. She ignored it. I was doing that 15 yrs. ago. Isn't there some school I cd be a teacher? Snapped & she w/drew. Know she was hurt—why won't she let it alone? Neither asked abt D. 2 yrs & they still ignore her. What makes it so hard?

D went back early [to her loft] to work on new stretchers. [I] Started organizing for income tx. Hope for $300. Went over mutual expenses for Dec. Our food $$ just flows. Owe D. Didn't get to work till 3 & have to leave in an hr.

Tried working on K. & thinking abt it in some constructive way. Seems unmanageable—no beginning, middle or end—keeps going on & on unfocused. Have no idea what to do w/ all the details. Listed them to see if there's a pattern. A maze. Just don't see the connections.

STRUCK HOTELS BLEAK IN MIAMI DESPITE WINTER SUN—by B. Drummond Ayres, Jr.— . . . The union originally

demanded pay increases averaging 10 percent annually plus increased hospitalization insurance and guaranteed tips for some
hotel employees. The union officials say service employees'
salaries exclusive of tips, run from a low $10 daily for bell-
hops to $22 a day for bartenders.

"I make only $400 a month, half what city lifeguards get,"
Gilbert Manzano, a Doral Beach lifeguard complained as he
walked the picket line in front of the hotel's soaring main
building. "I must have dignity."

Sun. Jan. 9 '76 [sic] ; *5 PM:* Ate last night at Sh[ah] B[agh] on E. 6th.
Still only place that's kept $$ down. Brought in brandy & got high. Talked
abt writing & painting, what it means in terms of "feeling right & com-
plete." & again: how to balance work ($$) & art (work), if it's possible,
the general lack of $$ support, grants, etc. D: you can tell how much so-
ciety values individuality, originality by support it gives artists—just like
you can tell how much it values life, human beings by support it gives the
poor. I sd it was the same thing. Long discussion. Confessed I've been feel-
ing like a sham lately—unable to complete anything. D asked what sched-
ule I was on. Still *almost* 41 & only 1 collection *almost* completed. Time.

Thought we'd go to the D[iana], but it was after 9 & we didn't want to
pay the $3 cover. Felt disappointed. Wanted to dance & see if the Santa &
elves mobile was still hanging over dance floor. Walked uptown [to the
loft] watching my breath all the way. Empire State [Building] still lit up
green & red. Checked for lumber [for stretchers] at M[acy]'s trash bins.
Dismantled a display case. Tore my gloves, but got good plywood & 2x4's
that wd probably cost $15-20. Extremely exhilarated at getting something
for free. Had a sense I cd live just by scavenging. Pictured D & me—old
ladies—rushing thru the night—hugging our loot. Giggled a lot over that.
D talked again abt buying a ghost town in Wyoming for $5 & living in the
bank.

Back here this a.m. Cdn't concentrate. Kept seeing Quinn in his cubicle
peering out at all of us. Then suddenly, my last chart on Fri: the boy
w/ sickle cell disease—the neat tables of drugs, dosages, & CBC's—lab tests.
The senseless words & statistics: leukocytes, hematocrit, platelets, reticu-
locytes, lumbar puncture, lymphocytes. Veesey's crisp Indian accent pour-
ing out of the machine: "Bone marrow showed hypocellular marrow with
many blasts." Thought abt the parents—the long days, the watching for
signs.

Don't really understand where all that goes—how I manage to block it out & yet keep it in me, so that if I'm jarred all the pieces fall into place.

Was determined today w/ K. Feel if I don't figure this out, the whole group won't hold & I won't get to anything else. Seems crucial. Must be a form for the lack of focus, the fragmentation. Retyped list. Not much help. Reconstructed the day I got the toy. Better. Can't articulate the importance, tho I'm moving closer. [I] Remember how Haddley had insisted: "Write about what you know!" Seemed obvious at 21. Now the connections, the logic eludes me—a pointless shuffling fr place to place, fr house to office, fr task to task. For example: it's hard to absorb at this moment—almost as if it were one of those incomprehensible laws of high-energy physics that I'll actually *live* thru the nxt 5 days, second by second, minute by minute. That I'll be conscious, awake, alive—& yet I know I will.

Each morning I will get up & eat. I will dress. I will talk. I will go to work. I will say hello. I will plug myself into the machine. Time. I will unplug myself from the machine. I will eat. I will talk. I will plug myself into the machine. Time. I will unplug myself from the machine. I will drink coffee. I will plug myself into the machine. Time. I will unplug myself from the machine. I will say good-bye. I will go home. I will be numb. I will be tired. I will be hungry. I will argue. I will make love. I will talk. I will eat. I will watch the news. I will wash my underwear. I will go to bed. I will dream. I will wake up. I will not remember the dream. I will eat. I will go to work I will plug myself into the machine. And time will pass. And the light will change.

She had never seen anything so wonderful as the patterns in the wooden tube—the endless and effortless regroupings of the colored pieces of glass as they reflected over and over in the angular mirrors. Like the designs formed by the older girls in the maypole dance, she thought after her first glimpse—blue shifting with red and green, then fanning out and allowing the yellow and orange to peek through and then unexpectedly clustering in the center in perfect symmetry.

It had been her mother's gift, presented late one morning when Ania was not quite seven and recovering from her latest bout of a mysterious "lung illness" for which the doctor had no name. Mrs. R. hoped the toy would distract her daughter from the shortness of the visit, and thereby spare her another painful confrontation with the child's loneliness. Rushing into the overheated, shadowy room, the mother was characteristically

breathless, appearing unravelled ("not quite put together," her husband
had once phrased it), her thick black hair slipping out of its net and her
heavy brown woolen coat carelessly misbutttoned.

"I know you thought I wasn't coming, Annushka," she said quickly,
upon seeing the gray flecks of anxiety in Ania's eyes. Pointing to the clock
on the window sill, she defended herself: "It's only 5 after 11. I'm just a
few minutes late. I stopped to get you something." She pulled the kaleidoscope out of the paper bag and immediately saw the child's exhausted fear
vanish. This particular toy had once been a favorite of her own and, before
handing it to her daughter, the mother stopped for one long extravagant
moment to look through it.

"It will remind you of everything beautiful in the world," she murmured almost to herself as she surrendered it to Ania with one hand and placed
a thermometer under her tongue with the other. A few moments later,
calling from the kitchen where she was preparing Ania's tea and mixing
chocolate syrup and milk for Rivka, she added: "You'll never get tired of
it. Nothing ever happens twice. As different as snowflakes."

After returning with a tray of two steaming cups of tea and a thick
piece of black bread covered with a slice of farmer cheese, she checked
Ania's temperature. Relieved it was normal for the ninth day, she began
straightening out the tangled quilts and sheets on the makeshift cot, simultaneously instructing Ania to "stay warm and under the covers." Then, in
a kind of ritual they had evolved, she proceeded to give the child a bunch
of rapid kisses—first one on each eye, then one on each cheek and finally
one special one on the tip of her nose—and to press the small face against
the rough coat. Quite unexpectedly, as she let her go, the mother added a
half-articulate, barely audible excuse: "It's very, very busy today, thank
God! Your father needs me." The visit almost over, she now delivered her
final orders: "Be sure to nap at one! Drink your tea! Remind Rivka to
heat up some soup for you when she gets home! Don't pester her! Wear
your slippers when you go to the bathroom! Don't forget to nap!" And
she was off—to her husband and the store—more out of breath and less
"put together" than when she entered twenty minutes earlier.

It was perhaps the only time during the lonely period of her recupera-
tion that Ania was completely oblivious to her mother's presence, hardly
noticing the rapidity with which she executed her duties and disappeared.
Extremely susceptible to suggestion, the child allowed the toy to draw her
away.from the dreariness of her isolation, from the oppressive silence of
the bleak apartment, towards everything "pretty" she had ever experi-

enced: the spring maypole festival which she had watched from her friend Alice's room, the sunlight as it leaped at her when she stepped outside, the melody of a song her father sang about the poor shoemaker who worked till midnight and then worked some more. And so forgetting her mother's instructions and her own physical weakness, she sat for hours that day turning the tube till her arms ached and her face was numb from squinting. She wanted to prove her mother wrong and failed. There was no way to deny the knowledge that none of the patterns would return or "stay put," and with that realization came, for the first time, an acute sense of loss and vulnerability.

Rivka came home at three. While serving her the bowl of soup, she accidentally bumped Ania's arm so that a particular design she had been trying to balance, suddenly scattered off into the periphery. It did not matter that it was replaced by one equally intricate and fine. Ania was enraged, saying in her most vehement way that she would never, never forgive her. Unaware of her sister's painful discovery, Rivka shrugged her shoulders and told her she had "gone loco." "It would've cracked up anyway," she said calmly drinking her milk. And though Ania knew she was right, knew that her mother was right, she felt defeated for being robbed of a few extra seconds of something so beautiful, so special "that there was only one."

Mon. Jan. 10 '77; 7 PM: Stan just left. Said it was the *thermostat*. Set high enough for the lower floors, not for here. Not allowed to change setting. Was furious. Oven is dangerous. My choice: asphyxiation or freezing to death. He shrugged.

D starts [teaching] new [course] tonight. When I woke up this a.m. she looked calm. Hated to leave the bed, her warmth under the blankets, her skin smooth from sleep. But a wreck all day. Called me 3x fr the center & 2x after she got home. Ostensibly, abt Mr. Antonelli. The same old story: another grossly painted papier-mâché figure of a woman w/ her legs spread. Another major speech by Mr. Fernando abt decency in art & the beauty in natural things like birds & trees. Mrs. Stein & Mrs. Sanders indignant, threatening to quit. Robt. promised to speak w/ all of them.

Saw her [D] briefly before she left [for the course]. Don't know why she gets so crazy. Always at the beginning, then the routine sets in--the complaints abt how young they are, how undisciplined. Wonder how it's going. She's probably introducing herself right at this moment.

We tried the new mid-Eastern place last night. Knew I shdn't, but wanted to get away fr my desk, the sense of failure. Keep saying I'll hold back, then say: what'll I save? $3? $5? What will that get me? So I went. A real rip-off. High $$, small portions. At home, gorged ourselves on Italian pastries.

Feel very close to D right now. There are times when the connection between us is so clear, so obvious. I find it almost painful. When she kissed me last night, I began to cry. Don't quite know why. Fear? Keep thinking this can't last forever & yet we seem to keep going. Can see her right now—trying to look stern & determined. Never quite pulls it off. Think they realize right away she's a pushover, as soon as she says: "Despite what you've heard to the contrary—art was never meant to be an agony."

AIDES OF CARTER TALK ABOUT JOB FOR MRS. AB-ZUG—by Frank Lyn— . . . Friends of the former Representa-tive from Manhattan's West Side said that a regulatory agency would be ideal for her since it would give her an independent forum and a minimum of administrative responsibilities. (1/9; 15:1)

NEGOTIATIONS BREAK DOWN IN MIAMI HOTEL STRIKE— Miami, Jan. 8 (AP)— . . . A key union demand is a guaranteed daily tip for maids from each guest staying on pre-paid plans. The union is seeking wage increases of 10 to 13 percent.
   Union officials say maids are paid about $16 a day, bell-hops $10 a day and food servers about $12.75 a day. All re-ceive tips. (1/9; 26:6)

Tues. Jan. 11 '77; 11 PM: Already overdosed on Quinn & it's only Tues. Seems he'd been to the Coliseum over the wkend for some sort of show & saw 2 midgets there—a couple I presume (why?). Came in this morning, stood in the middle of the room in his shiny blue suit, his hair all puffed up (we heard abt his hair blower last wk) & started describing them: their "wrinkled" faces, the jewelry on their "stubby" fingers. Kept laughing abt how small they were & yet how all their clothes fit perfectly. The woman wore a white fur coat & "cute" leather boots w/ white fur trimming. Every-thing abt them was "tiny, tiny, tiny." He was impressed by the $$ made-to-order clothes & wondered if they might be circus [people] who earned a lot of $$. Claire sat & tapped her fingers impatiently & Carmen made faces behind his back. Roberta decided she had to go to the bathroom & excused herself rather abruptly when he started describing their skin. But Marcie feigned interest & surprise & kept repeating "You don't say!" Whenever he had his back to her, she'd raise her eyes to the ceiling. Once she gave him the finger.

How was someone like that created? What mother, father, school, neighborhood made him possible? He fills me w/ such utter revulsion & hatred. Helpless anger that my life is intertwined w/ his, dependent on him in a bizarre way—all connected w/ the fact that I need to eat. Was left w/ an underlying feeling of nausea—slight imbalance. Took it out on D the second I walked in. The sink was piled w/ dishes & she was pissed because she was ready to go & shop & wanted me to clean up. [I] Just wanted to have a drink & not bother. Suggested we go out. She became furious—on a 23-hour, part-time job & 1 art course she can't afford etc. etc. & neither can I. Knew that, but then she'd been willing to eat out all wkend. Told her I can't keep up w/ what she wants (a lie!).

So we went thru it again. Living in 2 places, neither place ever fully stocked or taken care of. Food spoiling. *& again:* we're not ready to live together, but maybe in the near future, etc. Anyway—*finally*—I did the dishes & she went to 3rd [Ave.]. Made Japanese noodles & fried vegetables. Very good & very cheap. $4—enough noodles for abt 3 more dinners & some vegetables for one.

Rest of the evening (not much left), she glued paper for drawings & hammered on her stretcher. [I] Worked on K. Thought I got somewhere, tho it still seems very, very lumpy.

Wed. Jan. 12 '76 [sic]; *7 PM:* A scene w/ Quinn & Maurry. Realized that in 2 yrs I've never written abt Maurry. Simultaneously memorable & easy to forget. Probably abt 70, slight limp. Face gaunt, emaciated. Waxy yellow-ed skin. Sparse hair—stands straight up so even on the calmest day, he looks as if he just came out of a wind-storm. Hard to imagine his evolution —a strange, sweet creature right out of Dickens or Gogol.

His job: to help Terry in the RO [Records Office] across the hall, main-ly by running errands, delivering charts, etc. (wd love to see job title & description). Also does odds & ends for Quinn, who's predictably con-descending. Calls him "Mr. Maurice," he told Carmen, "to show his respect." Today, for lunch, brought Quinn an $$ hamburger, then went to the RO to eat his own lunch: prefab food consisting of chicken pot pie, chemically compounded pound cake. Suddenly Quinn yelled for him. Came limping in, smacking his lips & twitching crumbs fr his fingertips. Then we heard Quinn quiz him abt the raw onion. There was none & he ordered extra slices & pd for them. So Maurry went out again—in the cold & slush. Didn't seem to mind, tho. Wanted to be obliging. Glad, I think, to be part of a drama (after all, $$ was involved), glad to be of use.

Remember Papa's somber face when he read us *"Bontshe Shweigt"* [Bontshe Keeps Quiet].* How after a lifetime of being a porter, a non-entity, of being abused, of being hungry, of never complaining—Bontshe finally reaches heaven. Here he can have *anything* he wants. To the angel's horror, he asks only for a warm roll w/ butter. Papa explained: some people have to learn to dream.

> THE ECONOMICS OF STARVATION II—The Rats Don't Starve—by Emma Rothschild—"We goofed on Bangladesh," one senior official in the Agriculture Department said, "and a lot of people died."
>
> "It was a man-made famine," another United States official said of the Bangladesh famine of 1974. (1/11; 33:2)

> NEW HOSPITAL PLAN WOULD CURB LAYOFF—Proposal by Advisory Group Offers an Alternative to the Drastic Cuts Suggested to Ease Deficit—by Ronald Sullivan—A special financial committee that was set up by Mayor Beame has tentatively concluded that the New York City Health and Hospital Corporation can cut its financial deficit without imposing the wholesale job layoffs that were threatened last year. (1/11; 23:3)

> DONATIONS ARE URGED BY INAUGURAL PANEL—Plea for $350,000 Is Made to Union Officials and Business Leaders at Fund Raiser in Capital—by David E. Rosenbaum (1/12)

Th. Jan. 13 '77; 10:30 PM: Another bad fight. Had set the alarm early so I cd get up & work. Went off, but I was sleepy & stayed in bed for what seemed only a few minutes. Dozed off. Finally got up & realized it was too late to do anything. So—back to bed. By then D was wide awake, furious. Accused me of *always* setting the alarm & *never* getting up (one of her global statements). Affirmed my right to get up when I felt like it (one of my Bill of Rights statements) whether I actually worked at my desk or not. Pointed out she does a lot of staring at her work & I need time for that too—& I don't get it. Still was defensive. She was tired fr last night. Had to talk to students & didn't get home till after 11. [I felt] Guilty for waking her & having nothing to show for it. Ended up slamming out of the house. Forgot my lunch.

15 minutes after I got in Quinn told Claire she wasn't typing enough charts. His tallies show she's got the lowest record (big news!) in the pool.

*A Yiddish short story by I. L. Peretz. (M. M. A.)

In short—told her to shape up. She was in tears—make-up, mascara blotch-
ed. Suddenly noticed how rumpled she looked—the knit suit seemed worn
& ragged—not her usual clean & prim image. Worn out. Older. & of course
she *is* older, at least 15 yrs older [than Q]. Took some bus[iness] c[ourse]
in man[agement] or something as an under[graduate] & now he's a damn
super[visor] over a woman who cd be his mother.

Claire's sure he'll fire her. But Carmen sd he's never fired anyone in the
last 4 yrs—& quite a few weird ones had passed thru—too chicken—a real
old fashioned bully, i.e. coward. Claire pretty shaken tho. Cindy sick last
wk—lost 2 days—no $$. & she's worried Bert will cut off support. Been
complaining the payments are too much, asking what she does w/ the $$ &
how come Cindy's not dressed "more pretty." She's not sure if he's just
hassling for kicks, or if he really intends to cut down/stop the $$. Have no
idea how much is involved. Can't be much, tho—he's working in a gas sta-
tion. Still any $$ makes a difference.

We were all upset & had lunch together. Claire, nervous & defensive:
she's been typing a lot of foreigners & it slows her down (added she's not
sure she types more than any of us). Roberta: we shd keep our own records & hand in the same # of charts, at least the same # of pp. Carmen:
still not fair since the A[mericans] go faster than the others. Frustrating &
tense. Marcie conspicuously silent—picking at her jello & cottage cheese.
Sd a couple of wks ago she wants to push so she cd ask for more $$. [I]
Wanted to ask how she felt abt equalizing, but somehow cdn't. & it's true.
Claire *is* the slowest one, which clearly means she shd be stood against the
wall & shot.

The whole thing felt very delicate & nothing was resolved. It wd help if
the drs. bothered to enunciate, but they barely go thru the motions & the
A[mericans] are often as hard as the others. Just mumble, suck candy &
eat snacks. Assume we'll get what we need in the charts. Time.

When I got home D sd she'd been evaluated at the center. Her *1st* time,
so she was completely unprepared. Robt. gave her grades! She's 45 yrs old
& she got grades! All A's & B's—rapport w/ workshop members: A-. We
cracked up over Mr. Antonelli. Got 1 C: efficiency in filling out forms.
Cdn't believe it! We were both in stitches.

Made no reference to this a.m. Won't set the alarm for tomorrow tho
tempted. Don't want a repeat performance & I'm exhausted. Enough is-
sues for one day. Am I intimidated?

After supper made lunch. Worked well for a couple of hrs. K. still in sections—unresolved, but some progress.

HENRY FORD 2nd QUITS FOUNDATION, URGES APPRE-
CIATION FOR CAPITALISM—by Maurice Carroll (1/12; A4)

FROM GROWER TO TABLE, COFFEE WILL COST MORE—
by Rona Cherry—Despite the growing boycott of coffee in the
United States, some industry analysts expect prices to rise
steadily at least until early 1978, perhaps reaching $4 a pound
in stores. (1/12)

UNEMPLOYMENT DROPS AND JOB TOTAL RISES:
WHOLESALE PRICES UP—December Rise 0.9%—Volatile
Farm Sector Jumps, but Industrial Goods Climb the Least in
7 months—by Edwin L. Dale Jr.—Jobless Rate at 7.9%—3 Mil-
lion More at Work by End of Year after a Spurt of 222,000 in
December—by Edward Cowan (1/13; 1)

ETHNIC GROUPS ANGERED BY PLANS FOR CARTER'S
'PEOPLE'S' INAUGURATION, FEELING LEFT OUT—by
Bernard Weinraub (1/13)

Fri. Jan. 14 '77; Midnight: Mamma called. [I] Became very frightened.
Late—11:30. But everything's all right. Just keeps ranting—he's dirty—a
filthy man! Asked what was dirty abt him. Everything—stains his shirts &
leaves spots & hair in the bathtub. Got nowhere. Is she having a break-
down?

Can't understand it. All those yrs of talk abt retirement—their only
dream. Wd never look at cheese again, hated the store—the dampness &
cold—cdn't wait to get rid of it. At least that's what *she* said. Wanted
warmth, sun, late morning hrs. & tonight: "You don't know how he is,
how he *really* is. Dirty. Dirty on purpose." Told her to try & relax, pointed out she never thought that before. Classic reply: she'd been too busy to
notice—was seeing him "properly right" for the 1*st* time. Then she cried
how she tries to keep the apt. clean & how he messes things up & she
must have order. Just don't understand her. Didn't know how to respond.
Think it's strange she called me & not Leah. Apparently been trying to
reach me all evening. [Phone] Ringing when I walked in.

Dinner w/ Barb—good! Met for a drink at the D[iana]. Holiday decor dismantled. Reminisced abt the 1st time she brought me there. My confusion because I didn't know (a) if we were on a date; & (b) if everyone in the place was a dyke. Was dumbfounded that so many women looked "perfectly straight." Expected to see a bar full of bull dykes in leather & chains. It was crowded tonight, women coming directly fr work, wearing their working clothes. Increasingly aware of how young they seem. It's unusual to see anyone over 40, almost never over 50.

Barb's doing ok—tho very lonely. [She] Concedes it's a relief to come home & not face one of Annie's numbers. Difficult Xmas—Annie conspicuously absent fr the family dinner. No one asking any questions. An eerie family silence around the break-up.

The usual talk abt work & $$ & the lack of it. But big news: Barb came out at school. Sd she's been nervous & edgy, kids really getting to her. Wanted someone to know what was going on. Thought of course everyone knew by now. Told Anita, who was completely stunned. Funny—Barb's been thru the whole trip—someone I know, a friend of mine, this woman I know, my roommate, the woman I live w/. Still total shock when they finally hear: *lover, lesbian*. Felt envious. Wish I cd bring myself to do it—at least w/ Carmen (does she know, *really* know?). Maybe Roberta wd cut the jokes abt Quinn. Why can't I do it? What stops me? Barb sd I'll do it when I'm ready. When?

Feel anxious. Wish D were home. Don't like her seeing Lisa. Hate straight snobs. Always a toss up abt why they're looking down at you at any specific moment.

Weekend: Taxes. K. Movie w/ Barb tomorrow nght.

Sat. Jan. 15 '77; 10 PM: Mamma called this a.m. Told Papa to move out & he went to a hotel a few blocks away. Perfect timing. Strike's over. "He's wasting all our $$," she told me. Asked her how she expected him to live in a hotel & not spend extra $$. Ignored me & complained I always side w/ him (that's probably true—why?). The crisis: he spilled something (tea?) on the new tablecloth w/ lace trimming. Adamant he'd done it on purpose. "These things are not accidents." So she told him to get out. [I] Was tongue-tied—asked her if she felt ok abt spending the night alone (don't think she's ever done it before). Sd she's "an adult woman" & "it's abt time I shd be on my own." Will call tomorrow. Called the hotel. He sounded extremely tired but ok. Just wants some peace & quiet to read his paper. Sd the bed seemed comfortable, that it was "puffed up looking."

Felt frustrated. Want to side w/ her, or at least feel her side (see it very clearly), but something always stops me. Know she's given up so much for him. But she's so impossible—a broken record, a memorized chant. Can't get past the formula, can't reach the pain. Her rage—why does it put me off so? He's of course, stoic & silent. & there I am: stone.

Started crying the second I put the phone down—like a kid whose parents are abt to divorce & has to choose. Remember how D felt when her parents died—an orphan at 42.

D thought we shd stay home in case one of them called—cancelled w/ Barb. Invited her for dinner, but she wanted to try the D[iana] alone. Sounded disappointed. D went down & bought brie & brandy & food for dinner. Turned the kitchen upside down, used all the dishes. Created an elaborate 10-step chicken curry casserole. Sat around & drank while it was in the oven.

Swapped stories abt our parents, what kept them together. Am constantly amazed how outside our parents we are—outside the bond, the intimacy—in a way we're not w/ friends or even other relatives. How strange to live in a home w/ a secret that will never be revealed. My parents were living together for 44 yrs & at this moment he's in a hotel & she's in an apt alone—& except for the obvious I don't have a clue. Maybe there's nothing more than the obvious.

Feel tired & drunk. Started out as the usual Sat: recycling center, etc. Then Mamma's call. Didn't get a chance to do laundry. Now I'll never catch up on the wk. D stayed all day. [I] Was glad, but also guilty—neither of us did any real work. There's no time to be human.

It came after a long, undefined illness when she was seven years old— something to do with a lung "weakness" inherited from a Russian grandmother who had died of tuberculosis. Mrs. R., who still retained vivid memories of her mother's deathbed, now agonized over having passed on the genetic defect. Each day she watched in terror as the doctor came and felt the hot forehead, listened to the rumbling in the fragile lungs, and puzzled over the fever which refused to be exorcised by penicillin.

When she saw she was ill, Mrs. R. immediately removed Ania from the bed she shared with her older sister and placed her on a makeshift cot created by two overstuffed armchairs facing each other. These she moved near the living room window, close to the steaming, clanging radiator and within arm's reach of the couch where she and her husband slept. For three weeks she sat and watched as the child, lost in a maze of feverish dreams and oblivious to her own danger, diminished visibly in size and sank deeper and deeper into the thick quilts and puffy pillows. It seemed an illness without an end—a futile struggle to force some food into the frail body that consistently refused sustenance.

In addition, there was another worry. Rivka was losing weight and beginning to cough. Her skin looked faded, sallow. The anxious mother consulted the doctor who found nothing wrong. Rivka had managed to contract the symptoms but not the disease. Mrs. R. diagnosed the problem herself one afternoon when she saw her older daughter's face a moment after she had been told to stay out of the living room. It was simple and there was nothing to do about it. She had to nurse the sick one. He had to be in the store. Rivka would have to make do.

* * * * *

But as soon as Mrs. R. became convinced the fever was banished permanently from her daughter's body, she was once again immersed in the details of the store and in the seemingly hopeless battle to pay off the debts incurred during Ania's illness. Initially, Rivka was kept home from school to watch over her "baby" sister. Though only a year older, she was an adept nurse, reheating soup, making fresh tea and concocting a special "goggel-moggel"—milk heavy with honey and melted butter. In addition, she was good at telling endless stories about Smelly Fanny, Ania's second grade teacher and her inept solos at Wednesday assembly. But after a week, when Ania's recovery seemed to have "taken hold," Rivka was ordered back to school and Ania was left alone, staring silently at the clock.

If the illness did not change her, the recovery did—a painful period of confinement and isolation which allowed her to focus on her surroundings for the first time. She quickly developed a kind of aversion to her own home, an unspoken anger at her parents. She did not, of course, articulate it that way. What she expressed was more of a feeling, an uneasiness, which had suddenly made her wary. She complained to her mother that she felt dizzy, that she thought she might fall over, that the sidewalk was unsteady, and repeatedly asked if there were a "safe place" to go to. Mrs. R. now began to worry whether the extended fever had not left a serious mark on the child who, though the doctor said had reached perfect health, insisted "the world is crooked and makes me sick." Things were "tipped," she said angrily, tipped so she might slide right off. She thought about

Columbus, how he went on his voyage unafraid he might "hit the edge and fall off." Maybe—Ania argued with her father—just maybe, Columbus never reached the horizon. How could anyone be sure? Maybe it was still there—waiting.

Sun. Jan. 16 '77; Noon: 1st thing, called Mamma. Very distant. Doesn't like how I talk to her. Thought I'd understand because of my "women's ideas." Asked if all that applied to everyone else. Told her [that] wasn't the point. Almost hung up—sd she needed to vacuum the apt. Coaxed her: talked abt the cold wave, the wind-up of the strike, plants, Mrs. Kravitz's singing. [She] Said it's been quieter lately.

Then Papa: very depressed, somewhat disoriented—doesn't have his things around him. "Do you think she's gone crazy?" he asked. Said I didn't know, but thought perhaps she was very tired & just didn't want to wash another tablecloth.

Finally braced myself & called Leah. Instant hysteria. Kept saying: "I just can't believe it! I just can't believe it!" Promised to call them tonight & me tomorrow. Felt sorry for her—how they neglected her, for work, for $$—made her into the little automaton mamma she is today—& now they can't stand to be In the same room. Keep seeing Mamma at the sink, her red hands wringing out the damn tablecloth, the tight gray bun, the tight lips—no loose ends, no strands. When did she pull herself in like that?

Totally drained by the calls. Bitched to D the whole wkend was shot, K.'ll never get finished. She casually suggested I quit. Go on unemployment or get a loan (where?) & focus on my writ[ing]. Haven't done that since I got this job. 2 yrs. of my life. Seems longer. D thought the business w/ Claire was a set-up. It's possible Quinn's budget's been cut & he's being pressured to fire someone. Hadn't occurred to me, but if it's true, then maybe he'd be content to get rid of me.

Was excited for abt 30 sec—then filled w/ complete, utter panic. To go on unemployment w/ no savings of any sort. I've been thru that—the constant hustling—on the books, off the books. Always trying to be 1 step ahead, at least 1 month's rent ahead. Constantly at the mercy of the phone, unable to turn down any shit job that comes along because there's never any guarantee there'll be another one later. So ultimately the writing came last anyway. I hated, *hated* living like that—never sure where I'd be nxt—no schedule, no order, no routine—working 1 month in the evening, the nxt in the morning. That's why I'd gotten this job. It's steady. It's predictable. It's secure.

But D insists my priorities are all wrong. My writing shd come *1st*—& if I can grab 9 mos. of even marginal existence, I shd. Sounds very reasonable, perfectly sensible. But then overwhelming breathless fear—like running on a floating piece of ice—& suddenly reaching the edge.

Had hoped, wanted desperately to escape this. Can still see Mamma & Papa going [over] accounts & monthly $$, the rent *almost*, but not quite pd. Mamma begging, then insisting Papa [call] Uncle Joe & [borrow] $$. He refusing because Joe was younger & his pride wdn't let him. Then he'd leave the table, his food only half eaten, his face set hard, spitting out the words: "I deserve to eat in peace!" & Leah—ashen—[her] fingers clutch[ing] at [her] skirt, pleading w/ him to come back. Always during dinner—till my stomach was a knot fr anxiety abt the numbers coming [out] right, balanc[ing]. The same knot tonight at the prospect of not [being] able to get thru the month, feeling I'm in a race w/ my checkbook. & the less I have, the more frantic, reck[less] I get. Like Mamma before the maypole dance. How strange she seemed—her voice from somewhere deep inside her: "The few dollars, Jake, what's the difference? For God's sake! Let them have the dresses!"

BEAME CUTS CITY COFFEE BUYING BY A 3rd—by Edward Ranzal—The soaring price of coffee has added to the city's fiscal headache. Mayor Beame yesterday ordered a one-third cut in the purchase of coffee ordered by the city for its hospitals, prisons and other institutions. (1/14; B3)

20-DAY MIAMI HOTEL STRIKE SETTLED—. . . Last week the union was said to have dropped the pre-paid tip demand, but the issue of rehiring the striking workers had not been settled until today.
  Union members, most of whom are Cubans, are expected to approve the agreement, as recommended by the union leadership. (1/15)

NEW ECONOMIC SLUMP FOR INDUSTRIAL NATIONS IS FEARED—by Clyde Farnsworth. (1/15)

Mon. Jan. 17 '77; 7:30 PM: Barb called last night to ask abt my parents. Brought her up to date. Told her D's idea abt unemployment (wonder if D's right abt Quinn). Supportive. Asked what I was saving for. Sd I wasn't saving at all. B: "What's the point? You can always get a job like that." Can I? Took me 3 mos. last time. Thought she was glib.

[She] Lasted exactly ½ hr at the D[ial]. Sd the average age was abt 25 & the whole scene made her feel old, worn out, lonely. Thought the younger women just turned off when they looked at her. Told her she's paranoid, but secretly empathized. It wd scare me to be alone again. When did we become "older dykes"?

David called at the office & sd he'd stop by to have lunch nxt wk. Genuinely shocked abt my parents. Sd he always loved the store & that Papa used to give him extra chunks for treats. Still remembers the crumbs of farmer cheese sticking to his fingers. But he saw it fr the outside. I remember Mamma's rage. "You feed other people's children better than your own," she once said. Have no business giving away food—like giving away $$. "How come," she once taunted, "you're suddenly so big-hearted?" Was she right? Can't find the center.

Bumped into Annie on the way home fr the subway—1*st* time in months. Felt guilty for never calling her. Unemployment up in 3 wks (I clutched). [She] Asked if I knew of any work. Told her I'd think abt it—gave her Sally & Ruth's number. [She] Sd the 9 months had been productive, but rough. Took a lot of pictures. Asked if D & I are planning to live together. Said *no*—there are different ways of being together. Felt defensive. Also somewhat awkward. Know there's always 2 sides, but do think she was unnecessarily cruel to Barb. Never really understood it, because I'd never perceived her that way before they started having problems. But as soon as that began, she seemed to become someone else. Yet today, on the street, she seemed the old Annie.

Tues. Jan. 18 '77; 10 PM: Ironic? Bad fight w/ Quinn. Maybe I *can* get him to lay me off. Came in this a.m. & asked to see me. Checked what I'd done yesterday & told me to change my typewriter ribbon. [I] Pointed out he saw only the carbons. He nodded. So I sd: "You mean to tell me you can look at carbons & know my original is too light?" He became enraged, started pounding the desk—reminded me he was running things. Became frightened, thought he might try to hit me. Left feeling very shaky.

Called D later in the afternoon. Told me to ignore him—just do what I have to & think abt leaving—either getting unemployment or another job—it's not the only hospital that needs transcribers. She sounded irritated, had just gotten home fr the center—only a couple of hrs. left of daylight.

Seemed depressed & distant when I got home. Sd she feels I'm never satisfied, that she doesn't provide me w/ anything. Felt caught off guard.

Told her she was absolutely wrong, that our relationship is extremely important. At the same time, thought that *the relationship is not everything.* It doesn't, can't help me w/ certain things, can't ease my frustration that I'm not doing what I want. Sometimes—today—when I'm so stuffed w/ that idiot at the office, so empty of my own self, I wonder who it is she cares for so much. Is it really me?

Feel stymied abt how to save myself, how to hold on to myself. Am afraid I might drive D away. Am so eaten up w/ anger & bitterness that sometimes I don't recognize who I am. *Know* that I must come to terms w/ $$ & my work. *Know* also that maybe there's really no solution, that this is the way it's going to be, no matter how much I rage. Feel as if I've been pounding my head against a brick wall & finally am beginning to *know* for the first time, that there is no way out—there are no real choices, that the opportunities are narrow, limited. *Know* for the first time that all those dreams, those fantasies, abt who I'll be, what I'll be, will simply not come true. Keep seeing the broken toy—the translucent pieces of colored glass all at the bottom of the tube, lumped together in a dark, opaque heap. The mirrors cracked—no pattern, no design.

Apologized repeatedly to D. Made her dinner. We talked a lot abt our expectations, how to make them realistic. It was good. D grounds me.

ANAIS NIN, AUTHOR WHOSE DIARIES DEPICTED IN-
TELLECTUAL LIFE , DEAD—by C. Gerald Fraser— . . . In ad-
dition to the diaries' pictures of the Bohemian and intellectual
life of Paris in the 1930's and of New York during and after
World War II, her journals became widely known for their
view of the perspective of a Western woman and artist strugg-
gling to fulfill herself.
    . . . . Her life, she said, "covers all the obscure routes of the
soul and body seeking truth, seeking the antiserum against
hate and war, never receiving medals for its courage. It is my
thousand years of womanhood I am recording, a thousand
women. It would be simpler, shorter, swifter not to seek this
deepening perspective to my life and lose myself in the simple
world of war, hunger, death." (1/16)

FIVE-DAY 'PEOPLE'S' INAUGURATION BEGINS IN CAPI-
TAL TUESDAY—By Bernard Weinraub— . . . the inauguration
planners are emphasizing the 'simplicity' of the day.
    For example, the President-elect will wear a business suit
rather than the morning coat and top hat traditional for the

event. For lunch on Inauguration Day, the families of Mr. Carter and Vice-President Mondale will eat sandwiches, buttermilk,
and fruit . . . .
Inauguration Day starts at the Lincoln Memorial at 8 AM
Thursday with an interfaith prayer service . . . (1/16)

Wed. Jan. 19 '77; 12:30 PM MH [Memorial Hospital] : No word fr Leah.
Suppose it's terrible, but I didn't call her. Spoke to Fla before going to
bed. Both the same. They'd talked w/ Leah Sun nght.

Went w/ the others to the cafeteria. Food looked so disgusting (called
"chicken chow mein")—goppy, gooey stuff—abt 3 shreds of chicken—
took one look & my stomach flipped. How can hospital food be so awful
& so unnutritious? It's all corn starch & chemicals. So bought an apple &
coffee & came back. Didn't want to spend the $$ anyway. Have started a
writing fund—i.e. will try to save some $$. Tx refund shd help. Too wiped
out yesterday & this a.m. to make lunch. *Must* get myself to do that. End
up spending abt $15/week in the lousy cafeteria—almost $60/month. Cd
use some of it for vacation & some of it for my writing fund—don't have
to give it to that place. Why are all the daily mechanics, the little details so
draining, so costly? Why am I not more disciplined? Why am I always
forced to choose between time & $$, when time is $$, so I'm always losing?

Quinn tried to be friendly this a.m. Nodded but didn't stop typing.
Later asked him abt W-2 forms. Polite, sd he'd ask. He's trying to improve
relations. Carmen talked to him abt a point system, so we cd get credit for
the more difficult drs. Claire's pushing. Sometimes I can't bear to look at
her, the concentration, the anxiety on her face. Can always tell when she's
stuck, hearing the tape click again & again as she goes over the same words.
& Marcie's just as determined to get her extra $$. Know she's got a right,
but sometimes I'm so angry w/ her. Makes no sense. Am angry w/ the
wrong one.

*It was as if she realized for the first time that the life she was born into
was not universal. There were people who did not live in dingy basement
apartments, so that all they saw was the strewn garbage on the street. A
home was not always three damp, dark rooms. The couch in the living
room was not destined to open every night for parents to sleep in, while
the two daughters crowded in a narrow bed in the room facing the alley.
Not all daughters were exchanged for necessity. All these things, she was
beginning to understand, did not have to be.*

Yet why, how had this particular life come to her? Was it a legacy like the weakness in her body? Was it an accident? Had it all simply fallen into place randomly? Could it be swapped? Altered? Could the world be jostled so that it formed a different pattern for her? Was it possible, perhaps, to wake up in her friend Alice's sunlit room high on the eighth floor overlooking the park and peer down to where the girls danced around the maypole, weaving their long, brilliant ribbons and forming patterns she could never have discerned from the ground? In short, was there a way to open her eyes one morning and find herself inside another life?

The question was both dream and nightmare.

Thurs. Jan. 20 '77; 6:00 AM: Leah finally called last night. Total panic. Kept saying: "What's going to happen? They can't do this? They just can't do it!" Tried to calm her, told her it might be better if they separated for a while. Mamma hasn't had a chance to realize the consequences. Tried to comfort her, but am very anxious. Don't like to think of them as isolated, envision something happening, something physical. Tripping & falling— unable to reach a phone. Am scaring myself, but have always assumed they'd be there for each other (for me?). Leah sd Mamma's still talking abt $$ he's spending. Papa's resigned—eating in the hotel dining room & taking walks. Uncle Joe saw him yesterday. Leah sd Papa was crying. Hard to imagine.

We discussed the possibility of one of us flying down there. Leah implied it shd be me since I have "fewer responsibilities." Meaning: no husband or children—you're obviously free. Growled silently. Wanted to say: I also don't get paid if I don't show up for work! Felt the old rage: a job, a lover, my writing, *my life!* None of that counts. I'm the unmarried daughter—always available, always on call.

D sd Leah's very threatened by it all: "After all, we're the ones who're supposed to have the unstable lifestyle." Probably true. Thought I shd refuse to go, that I just cdn't afford it. I snapped that was easy when it was theoretical. Regretted it the second it was out of my mouth. Knew it wasn't true. Apologized. Feel this is a maze w/ no exit. We finally went to bed. Held on as if I were drowning.

Bad, bad insomnia. Kept thinking abt Leah & Mamma & Papa & the store & what we all looked like 30 yrs ago—the old faded photographs. Who wd have predicted it, any of it? & then kept dozing off & dreaming vaguely abt Quinn—not really able to remember it. & I'd wake up & think abt leaving & writing & the $$. & shd I do it? & cd I do it?

This a.m. got up w/out the alarm at ¼ to 6. Freezing. Exhausted. Decided I might as well get up & write. It's as good a time as any.

COLDWAVE CONTINUES TO GRIP EASTERN U.S.—Two Elderly Men Die of Exposure in Hotel on Amsterdam Avenue— by Peter Khiss—Two men in their 60's were reported by the police in the West 151st Street station to have died during the day at the Hudson Residence Hotel, 1649 Amsterdam Avenue, at 141st Street, because of exposure to the cold. The Police had been told that heat had been only sporadic in the building for several days. (1/19; 1:4)

Kitty Tsui

Poa Poa Is Living Breathing Light

for Kwan Ying Lin:
my grandmother, my closest connection

Aiyah, chien sai loh. My feet, how come so swollen? Aiyah, how come? What to do?

THE OLD WOMAN STOPS FOR A MINUTE, WORRY LINES CREV-ICED DEEP ON HER BROW. SHE PICKS UP A PHONE AND DIALS SLOWLY, SAYING THE NUMBERS OUT LOUD:

Baat look saay, yat yat chat baat.

SHE HANGS UP IMMEDIATELY, WITH A GRIMACE OF DISGUST AND IMPATIENCE.

Ai-yah, bis-see. Must be that no good girl of my daughter, she alla-way on telephone.

SHE EXAMINES HER FEET AS WELL AS SHE CAN, UNABLE TO DRAW THEM CLOSE BECAUSE OF HER SWOLLEN BELLY. SHE SHAKES HER HEAD, PUZZLED. SHE PICKS UP THE PHONE AGAIN AND DIALS A DIFFERENT NUMBER.

I try second daughter.

THERE IS A PAUSE AS SHE LISTENS TO THE RINGING OF THE TELEPHONE ON THE OTHER END.

How come no answer? Not too late? They not working in garden now? Night time. How come no one home?

SHE HANGS UP.

Poa Poa or *Poa* (Chinese)—grandmother.
aiyah, aie—commonly used exclamation.
chien sai loh—it is hopeless.
baat look say, yat yat chat baat—864-1178.

Ahhh. May-be they in Dai Fow eating dinner.

SHE TRIES CALLING THE OTHER DAUGHTER BACK BUT THE
LINE IS STILL BUSY.

Ai-yah, that no good girl talk on telephone allaw time. Three things that
girl like to do: talk on telephone, read too much-ee book, and she allaw
time writing. She say she making up see-tor-ree. Aie, I don't know what
for, mut yeah see-tor-ree see-tor-ree.

SHE SHAKES HER HEAD SLOWLY.

Poa Poa called me last night. First thing she did, of course, was yelled at
me for being on the phone! Wasn't even me! It was dad talking business
with a friend. She said her feet were swelled up and she wanted to go into
the hospital. Ma-mee said it wasn't anything serious and to go to bed and
not worry about it. She said Poa Poa was always getting too excited about
nothing. Ma-mee says it's late and you should go to bed and not worry
about it. See if it's still swollen in the morning, ok?

No ok. You call doctor for me. No reason for feet to swell, I tell you.

Poa, I called the doctor. He said there's nothing to worry about. It'll
probably be gone in the morning. It's ten o'clock, go to bed. He said it's
too late to go into the hospital anyway. He's gonna call you in the morn-
ing. I will too, ok?

My belly already swollen for two, three months now. You know how I like
to eat . . . but now, no appetite, don't want to eat nothing. And my belly,
at first it was small, then got bigger and bigger and tight as a drum. I go see
doctor, he my doctor thirteen year now. I ask him, how come? Doctor say
it gas in there. He giv-fu me pills and tell me it's nothing to worry about.
They allaw say I tai guun jeung, too excited. But how come I no feel good?
I still don't want to eat. And my belly big like a baa-loon. I go back to
doctor. He giv-fu me different kind medicine, pills, two kinds—one to take
before I eat and one to take after I eat. He tell me, don't worry. He take
X-ee-ray. He say it nothing. He send me see another doctor. I call for
'pointment, say I not feel good. He say, got no time, have to wait two
weeks. I wait. He feel my belly like this. He press on it. He too say I got
gas and he giv-fu me medicine make it go away. But I feel like I dai tow. Me,

Dai Fow—San Francisco.
mut yeah—what kind.
dai tow—pregnant.

seventy-eight, how can be pregnant? I cannot eat, I cannot sleep at night. What I do? He say it gas and don't worry. He giv-fu me more pills. He say, eat pills you be ok. But after a few days I still feel bad, feel worse. I call him and say, how come? He yell at me. He say, of course you not better. I giv-fu you one hundred pills and you only eat them for two days. You got to take the whole bottle first. But I no feel good. I want to go to the hospital. I feel like something not right.

AFTER THE OPERATION SHE IS SMALL AND FRAIL, LOST UNDER THE THIN COVERS OF THE HOSPITAL BED, AN IV STUCK IN HER ARM. AFTER THE OPERATION HER STOMACH AND ABDOMEN ARE FLAT BUT TWO DAYS LATER IT IS AS IF SHE WERE SEVEN MONTHS HEAVY WITH CHILD. SHE DOES NOT UNDERSTAND WHY. THE DOCTORS TOLD HER THEY HAVE DRAINED OUT THE FLUID. SHE IS WORRIED. THE DOCTOR WILL NOT LOOK HER IN THE EYE. HE SAYS THE REPORT IS NOT BACK FROM THE LAB.

PEOPLE CROWD IN AND OUT OF THE SMALL ROOM: PEOPLE FROM THE FAMILY ASSOCIATION, OLD FRIENDS FROM HER THEATRE DAYS, FAMILY MEMBERS COME AND GO.

THE DOCTORS HAVE FOUND CANCER IN HER BELLY, CANCER RUNNING RAMPANT IN HER ABDOMINAL CAVITY. AUNTIE DOES NOT WANT HER TO KNOW SHE HAS A MONSTER GROWING INSIDE HER. THE DOCTORS SAY CHEMOTHERAPY IS THE ONLY WAY. THE DOCTORS SAY CHEMOTHERAPY IS THE ONLY WAY AND SHE MUST BE TOLD.

I wait till the people are gone and we are alone in the room with pots of wheat gold chrysanthemums and red purple gladiolas. I sit on the edge of her bed, groping for words. But they evade me. Instead, a steady stream of tears falls down my face. All day she had asked my cousin: hai m'hai cancer? Is it cancer? But no one would answer her. No one would look her in the eye. Yes, they found cancer is all I can say. Then I lie as my aunt has instructed. Yes, they found cancer but it's very small and still early yet.

TEARS SIT IN THE CORNERS OF HER EYES BUT SHE WILL NOT LET THEM FALL. HER EXHAUSTED BODY IS GIVEN TEN DAYS TO REST, TO RECOVER BEFORE THE TOXIC DRUGS ARE SHOT INTO HER VEINS IN AN ATTEMPT TO CURB THE GROWTH OF THE MONSTER CELLS. HOURS PASS SLOWLY FOR A PRISONER IN A HOSPITAL BED; WEAK FROM LACK OF FOOD (A POST-OPERATIVE SEVENTY-YEAR OLD WOMAN WITH DENTURES BEING FED SLABS OF TOUGH MEAT AND CHEWY VEGETABLES), WEAK FROM

LACK OF FOOD AND THE PAIN OF TWO WOUNDS—ONE HEALING ON HER BELLY WALL AND THE OTHER FESTERING INSIDE HER.

The treatment is started on Saturday morning. By mid-afternoon she is knocked flat on her back, her bony limbs rigid, her eyes screaming in silent agony. I try to feed her jook, but she refuses, tasting only the pain. On Sunday she throws up constantly, expelling a gooey dark brown mass. Each time she retches, her tiny body is shaken in spasms. She cannot eat or take any liquid. After three weeks in the hospital, Poa Poa is all bones wrapped in yellow parchment skin.

I stay at the hospital until midnight. Then home to a cold dinner and bed. The night was filled with dreams but there was nothing I remembered. On Monday it was the same—vomiting, retching, choking. In the evening they decided she was vomiting too much. They pushed a tube down her nostril to her stomach to suck out the dark brown goo. As they were about to do it, they drew the curtain and told me to go outside. I asked to stay and hold her hand. A nurse said: "If you can stand it."

PUSHED A TUBE THROUGH A NOSTRIL DOWN THE GULLET. TAPED THE TUBE DOWN ON HER NOSE AND HEAD. SHE HAS NOT EATEN FOR SEVENTY-TWO HOURS. EVERY DAY THERE ARE MORE LINES ON HER FACE, WAVES UPON WAVES IN HER EYE-LIDS, CHEEKS AND CHIN.

Ai-yah, jun chien sai loh. Jun hai sun foo-ah. When I don't eat, my stomach very uncomfortable. When I eat, I throw up. Ai-yah, look at me, allaw bone, so ugly. How can you stand to be with me? Does it make you feel bad to be facing a beng yan, a sick person?

No, Poa Poa, you are not a sick person. You are my grandma and I love you.

Ai-yah, better to die. Me old lady no good. What for like this? Can't eat, can't move . . . Aie, what I do to deserve this? Did I wrong someone in a past life? Ai-yah this my punishment. Aie, better to die. Me no good, no good . . .

Poa, don't say that . . .

---

jook—a soup with a rice base, usually made with fish or meat.
jun chien sai loh—it is very hopeless.
jun hai sun foo-ah—it is very painful.

No good, no good. What for like this? Old lady no good, like me no use. Beng yan better to die.

Poa Poa, you are not a beng yan, you are my grandma. You are the one who raised me from a bebe. You taught me to fold animals from squares of newspapers; rapped my knuckles with a teng tiew everytime I bit my nails; washed and combed my long hair and bought me colored ribbons; took me to Lung Goong Goong's place every summer to pick dragon's eyes. And on Saturdays to the amusement park at Lai Chi Kok and then go yum cha, eat gee mah guen allaw time. Remember?

Hai, you right. And take you to eat chow fahn every day after school too! You remember you like to eat fried rice?

Yeah, still do. Even though you say they use leftover rice.

Hai-ah, that's right. Because only low fan eat fried rice. They fry the left-over for the low fan. They eat allaw same, they don't know what they eat anyway!

THEY LAUGH TOGETHER AND THE GRANDMOTHER REACHES FOR HER GRANDDAUGHTER'S HAND AND STROKES IT.

Ai-yah, your hand used to be so smooth, now too rough. Allaw too many bumps on your hand. You do man's work no good. Not supposed to be for girl to make rough hands. No man want to marry girl with tough hands. You change job, you grandma happy.

Oh, Poa, it's just a part time gardening job, planting trees, digging, weeding. I like to work outside in the sun. Besides, it's fun! And if some man don't want to marry me 'cos of my rough hands, that's just tough!

THEY LAUGH TOGETHER.

---

teng tiew—feather duster.
Goong Goong—grandfather or old man.
dragon's eye—a fruit grown in Asia on trees in grape-like clusters. Hard brown skin, sweet white flesh.
yum cha—usually breakfast or lunch food consisting of various steamed, baked or fried *dim sum* (pastries).
gee mah guen—a sweet black gelatin-like dessert.
chow fahn—fried rice.
low fan—white people.

Ok, ok, hon-ee! Why I feel so tired allaw time? Mow jing sun, mow lick. No energy, no strength. Seems like yesterday I can walk around. Go here, go there, to kitchen, to ba-foo-loom by myself. With only the walker. How come today may may chee? Like I want to go to sleep. Ai-yah, I no feel good today, girl. You do something make you grandma laugh.

Gee Poa, what shall I do? I don't know what to do. I'm too shy to sing or dance and if I told a joke, you wouldn't understand it! I know, why don't we play a game together?

Hey, stupid girl. Me sick, in bed! How me play game?

No, Poa. All you gotta do is guess what I'm pretending to be, ok? Just try it.

Ok, ok.

THE GIRL PUTS HER HANDS STRAIGHT UP ABOVE HER EARS AND HOPS AROUND THE ROOM.

You a rabbit. Hey, girl, you just eat dinner. Don't jump around with full belly.

Alright, alright. How about this one?

THE GIRL PUTS ONE HAND ON HER HIPS AND THE OTHER OUT LIKE A SPOUT. SHE BENDS SIDEWAYS FROM THE WAIST.

Teapot.

Gee, Poa, how come you're so good at this?

THE GIRL SQUATS WITH HER ARMS FORMING A TRIANGLE ABOVE HER HEAD. SHE GETS UP SLOWLY, UNFOLDING HERSELF AS SHE RISES.

I don't know.

I'm a flower, Poa, a flower opening and reaching for the sun. You are the sun, grandma, you are the sun in my life.

may may chee—tired.

No, girl, you are the young one. Me old lady, dying soon. Ngay m'hoo gwa gee ngow. You are the young one. You are the flower opening to the sun.

Thursday's vigil begins at eight. Yee-ma who promised to stay has long left. Poa is all lines and there is the slightest trace of tears in her eyes. I kiss her face. On the table is half a cup of milk, still warm. She has been waiting for me to come feed her. I bend my body parallel to her thin frame, hug her tight in my arms and pull her gently to an upright position. I hold her close as I arrange a nest of pillows. She leans into the circle of my arms and slowly sips the milk. When it is gone, she sinks her head onto my breast. I unpin her hair and stroke the long waves of white and grey. I match my breathing to hers, our hearts sound as one. Leung poa suen, we embrace in a timeless moment, now, as in the beginning of my own life.

Last night I dreamt I was in a wide open space. A rolling countryside all white like it was covered with snow, and I felt really peaceful. It wasn't cold either. I blew air onto my hands and didn't see its trace in front of me. As I walked, I saw Poa Poa standing in the snow smiling at me. She was glowing. Then, I saw a bright white light coming out of her mouth with each exhale.

My Poa Poa is living. My Poa Poa is living, breathing light.

ngay m'hoo gwa gee ngow—don't worry about me; don't miss me.
yee ma—aunt.
leung poa suen—grandmother and granddaughter.

Dorothy Allison

A River of Names

At a picnic at my aunt's farm, the only time the whole family ever gathered, my sister, Billie, and I chased chickens into the barn. Billie ran right through the open doors and out again, but I stopped, caught by a shadow moving over me. My cousin, Tommy, eight years old as I was, swung in the sunlight with his face as black as his shoes ... the rope around his neck pulled up into the sunlit heights of the barn, fascinating, horrible. Wasn't he running ahead of us? Someone came up behind me. Someone began to scream. My mama took my head in her hands and turned my eyes away.

Jesse and I have been lovers for a year now. She talks about when she was a child, her father going off each day to the university, her mother who made all her dresses, her grandmother who always smelled of dill bread and vanilla. I listen with my mouth open, not believing but wanting, aching for the fairy tale she thinks is everyone's life.

"What did your grandmother smell like?"

I lie to her the way I always do, a lie stolen from a novel, "Like lavender," stomach churning over the memory of sour sweat and snuff.

I realize I do not really know what lavender smells like and I am for a moment afraid she will ask something else, some question that will betray me. But Jesse slides over to hug me, to press her face against my ear, to whisper, "How wonderful to be part of such a large family."

I hug her back and close my eyes. I can not say a word.

I was in between the older cousins and the younger, born in a pause of babies and therefore outside, always watching. Once, way before Tommy died, I was pushed out on the steps while everyone stood listening to my cousin, Barbara. Her screams went up and down in the back of the house. Another cousin, Bobbie, brought buckets of bloody cloths out to be burned. The others ran off to catch the sparks or poke the fire with dogwood sticks. I waited on the porch making up words to the shouts around me. I did not understand what was happening. Some of the older cousins obviously did, their strange expressions broken by stranger laughs. I had seen them helping her up the stairs while the thick blood ran down her legs. After a while the blood on the cloths was thin, watery, almost pink. Bobbie threw them on the fire and stood motionless in the stinking smoke.

David went by and said there'd be a baby, a hatched egg to throw out with the cloths, but there wasn't. I watched to see and there wasn't; nothing but the blood, thinning out desperately, while the house slowed down and grew quiet, hours of cries growing soft and low—moaning under the smoke. My aunt came out on the porch and almost fell on me, not seeing anything at all. She beat on the post until there were knuckle-sized dents in the peeling paint, beat on that post like it could feel, cursing it and herself and every child in the yard, singing up and down, "Goddamn, goddamn, that girl . . . no sense . . . Goddamn!"

The others ran away, wise in my aunt's angers. I hid under the porch with the dogs, while the smoke in the yard thinned down and the ashes fell in on themselves.

I've these pictures my mama gave me—stained sepia prints of bare dirt yards, plank porches and step on step of children—cousins, uncles, aunts; mysteries. The mystery is how many no one remembers. I show them to Jesse, not saying who they are, and when she laughs at the broken teeth, torn overalls, the dirt, I set my teeth at what I do not want to remember and can not forget.

We were so many we were without number and, like tadpoles, if there was one less from time to time, who counted? My maternal great-grandmother had eleven daughters, seven sons; my grandmother, six sons, five daughters. Each one made at least six—six times six, eleven times six. They went on like logarithm tables. They died and were not missed.

I came of an enormous family and I can not tell half their stories. Somehow it was always made to seem they killed themselves. Somehow, car wrecks, shotguns, dusty ropes, screaming, falling out of windows, things inside them. I am the point of a pyramid, sliding back under the weight of the ones who came after, and it does not matter that I am the lesbian, the one who will not get children.

I tell the stories and it comes out funny. I drink bourbon and make myself drawl, tell all those old funny stories. Someone always seems to ask me—which one was that? I show the pictures and she says, "Wasn't she the one in the story about the bridge?" I put the pictures away, drink more, and someone always finds them, and says,

"Goddamn! How many of you were there?"

I don't answer.

Jesse used to say, "You've got such a fascination with violence. You've got so many terrible stories."

She said it with her smooth mouth, that chin that nobody ever slapped, and I love that chin, but when Jesse said that, my hands shook and I wanted nothing so much as to tell her terrible stories.

So I made a list. I told her, that one went insane—got her little brother with a tire iron; the three of them slit their arms, not the wrists but the bigger veins up near the elbow; she, now *she* strangled the boy she was sleeping with and got sent away; that one drank lye and died laughing soundlessly. In one year, I lost eight cousins. It was the year everybody ran away. Four disappeared and were never found. One fell in the river and was drowned. One was run down, hitchhiking north. One was shot running through the woods, while Grace, the last one, tried to walk from Green-wood to Greer for some reasons nobody knew. She fell off the overpass a mile down from the Sears, Roebuck warehouse, and lay there for hunger and heat and dying.

Later sleeping but not sleeping, I found that my hands were up under Jesse's chin. I rolled away but I didn't cry. I almost never let myself cry.

Almost always, we were raped, my cousins and I. That was some kind of joke too.

"What's a South Carolina virgin?"

" 'At's a ten year old can run fast."

It wasn't funny for me in my mama's bed with my stepfather, not for my cousin, Billie, in the attic with my uncle, nor for Lucille in the woods with another cousin, for Danny with four strangers in a parking lot, or for Pammy who made the papers. Bobbie read it out loud—"Repeatedly by persons unknown." They stayed unknown since Pammy never spoke again. Perforations, lacerations, contusions, and bruises; I heard all the words, big words, little words, words too terrible to understand. DEAD BY AN ACT OF MAN; with the prick still in them, the broomhandle, the tree branch, the grease gun . . . objects, things not to be believed . . . whiskey bottles, can openers, garden shears, glass metal, vegetables . . . not to be believed, not to be believed.

Jesse says, "You've got a gift for words."

"Don't talk," I beg her, "don't talk," and she, this once, just holds on, blessedly silent.

I dig out the pictures, stare into the faces. Which one was I? Survivors do hate themselves, I know, over the core of fierce self-love, never understanding, always asking, "Why me, and not her, not him?" There is such mystery in it, and I have hated myself as much as I have loved others, hated the simple fact of my own survival. Having survived, am I supposed to do something, be something, say something?

I loved my cousin, Butch. He had this big head, pale, thin hair and big old watery eyes. They all did. I was the dark-headed one. All the rest of them seemed pale carbons of each other in shades of blond though later on everybody's hair went dark or red, and I didn't stand out so. Butch and I stood out, I because I was so fast and dark, and he because of that big head and the crazy things he did. He used to climb on the back of my Uncle Bill's truck, open the gas tank and hang his head over, breathe deeply, strangle, gag, vomit, breathe again. It went so deep, it tingled in your ₗoes. I climbed up after him and tried it myself, but I was too young to hang on long enough, and I fell heavily to the ground, dizzy and giggling. Butch could hang on. He would climb down roughly, swinging from the door handle, staggering and stinking. Someone caught him at it. Someone threw a match. "I'll teach you."
Just like that, gone before you understand.

I wake up in the night screaming. "No, no, I won't." Dirty water rises in the back of my throat, the liquid language of my own terror and rage. "Hold me. Hold me." Jesse rolls over on me, her hands grip my hipbones tightly.
"I love you. I love you. I'm here," she repeats.
I stare up into her dark eyes, puzzled, afraid. I draw the breath in deeply, smile my bland smile. "Did I fool you?" I laugh, roll away from her. Jesse punches me playfully, and I catch her hand in the air. "My love," she whispers and cups her body against my hip, closes her eyes. I bring my hand up in front of my face and watch the knuckles, the nails as they tremble, tremble. I watch for a long time while she sleeps, warm and still against me.

James went blind. One of the uncles got him in the face with home-brewed alcohol.
Lucille climbed out the front window of Aunt Dot's house and jumped. They said she jumped. No one said why.
My Uncle Matthew used to beat my Aunt Dot. The twins, Mark and Luke, pulled him out in the yard one time, throwing him between them like a loose bag of grain. He screamed like a pig coming up for slaughter.

I got both my sisters in the tool shed for safety, but I hung back to watch. Little Bo came running out of the house off the porch, feet first into his Daddy's arms. Uncle Matthew swung him like a scythe going after the bigger boys, Bo's head thudding their shoulders, their hips. Afterward Bo crawled around in the dirt, the blood running out of his ears and his tongue hanging out of his mouth, while Mark and Luke finally got their Daddy down. It was a long time before I realized that they never told anybody else what had happened to Bo.

David tried to teach me and Lucille to wrestle. "Put your hands up." His legs were wide apart, his torso bobbing up and down, his head moving constantly, then his hand flashed at my face. I threw myself back into the dirt, lay still. He turned to Lucille, not noticing that I didn't get up. He punched at her, laughing. She wrapped her hands around her head, curled over so her knees were up against her throat.

"No. No," he yelled. "Move like her." He turned to me, "Move." He kicked at me. I rocked into a ball, froze.

"NO. NO." He kicked me. I grunted, didn't move. He turned to Lucille. "You." Her teeth were chattering but she held herself still, wrapped up tighter than bacon slices.

"You move," he shouted. Lucille just hugged her head tighter and started to sob.

"Son-of-a-bitch," he grumbled, "you two will never be any good."

He walked away.

Very slowly we stood up, embarrassed, looked at each other.

We knew.

If you fight back, they kill you.

My sister was seven. She was screaming. My stepfather picked her up by her left arm, swung her forward and back. It gave. The arm went around loosely. She just kept screaming. I didn't know you could break it like that.

I was running up the hall. He was right behind me. "MAMA. MAMA." His left hand—he was left-handed—closed around my throat, pushed me against the wall, and then he lifted me that way. I kicked, but I couldn't reach him. He was yelling but there was so much noise in my ears I couldn't hear him.

"Please, Daddy. Please, Daddy. I'll do anything. I promise, Daddy, anything you want. Please, Daddy."

I couldn't have said that. I couldn't talk around that fist at my throat, couldn't breathe. I woke up when I hit the floor. I looked at him.

"If I live long enough, I'll fucking kill you."
He picked me up by the throat again.

"What's wrong with her?"
"Why's she always following you around?"
Nobody really wanted answers.

A full bottle of vodka will kill you when you're nine and the bottle is a quart. It was a third cousin proved that. We all learned what that and other things could do, every year something new. "You're growing up." "My big girl." There was codeine in the cabinet, paragoric for the baby's teeth; whiskey, beer and wine in the house. Jeanne brought back MDA, PCP, acid; David, grass, speed and mescaline. It all worked to dull things down, to pass the time.

Stealing was a way to pass the time, things we needed, things we didn't, for the nerve of it, the anger, the need. "You're growing up," we told each other. But sooner or later, we all got caught, then it was, "WHEN-ARE-YOU-GOING-TO-LEARN?"

Caught, nightmares happened. "Razorback desperate," was the conclusion of the man down at the county farm where Mark and Luke were sent at fifteen. They both got their heads shaved, their earlobes sliced.

"WHAT'S THE MATTER KID? CAN'T YOU TAKE IT?"

Caught at sixteen, June was sent to Jessup County Girls' Home where the baby was adopted and she slashed her wrists on the bedsprings.

Lou got caught at seventeen and held in the station downtown, raped on the floor of the holding tank.

"YOU A BOY OR YOU A GIRL?"

"ON YOUR KNEES, KID, CAN YOU TAKE IT?"

Caught at eighteen and sent to prison, Jack came back seven years later, blank-faced, understanding nothing. He married a quiet girl from out of town, had three babies in four years. Then Jack came home one night from the textile mill, carrying one of those big handles off the high-speed spindle machine. He used it to beat them to death and went back to work the next morning.

My cousin Milly married at fourteen, had three kids in two and a half years and welfare took them all away. She ran off with a carnival mechanic, had three more babies before he left her for a motorcycle acrobat. Welfare took those too. But the next baby was hydrocephalic, a little waterhead they left with her, and the three that followed, even the one she used to hate so—the one she had after she fell off the porch and couldn't remember whose child it was.

"How many children do you have?" I asked.

"You mean the ones I've had, or the ones I have? Four," she said, "or eleven."

I used to know all their names, but I forgot.

My aunt, the one I was named for, tried to take off for Oklahoma. That was after she'd lost the youngest girl and they told her Bo would never be "right." She packed up biscuits, cold chicken, and coca cola, a lot of loose clothes, Bobbie and her new baby, Cy, and the four youngest girls. They set off from Greenville in the afternoon, hoping to make Oklahoma by the weekend, but they only got as far as Augusta. The bridge there went over under them.

"An Act of God," my uncle said.

My aunt and Bobbie crawled out down river, and two of the girls turned up in the weeds, screaming loud enough to be found in the dark. But one of the girls never came up out of that dark water, and Nancy, who had been holding Cy, was found still wrapped around the baby, in the water under the car.

"An act of God," my aunt said, "then God's got one damn sick sense of humor."

My sister had her son in a bad year. Before he was born we had talked about it. "Are you afraid?" I asked.

"He'll be fine," she'd replied, not understanding, speaking instead to the other fear. "Don't we have a tradition of bastards?"

He was fine, a classically ugly healthy little boy with that shock of white hair that marked so many of us. But afterward, it was that bad year with my sister down with pleurisy, then cystitis, and no work, no money, having to move back home with my cold-eyed stepfather. I would come home to see her, from the woman I would not admit I'd been with, and take my infinitely fragile nephew and hold him, rocking him, rocking myself.

One night I came home to screaming—the baby, my sister, no one else there. She was standing by the crib, bent over, screaming red-faced, "SHUT UP, SHUT UP!" With each word her fist slammed the mattress fanning the baby's ear.

"DON'T!" I grabbed her, pulling her back, doing it as gently as I could so I wouldn't break the stitches from her operation. She had her other arm clamped across her abdomen and couldn't fight me at all. She just kept shrieking, "That little bastard just screams and screams. That little bastard, I'll kill him."

Then the words seeped in and she looked at me while her son kept crying and kicking his feet. By his head the mattress still showed the impact of her fist. "Oh no," she moaned, "I wasn't going to be like that. I always promised myself." She started to cry, holding her belly and sobbing. "We ain't no different. We ain't no different."

Jesse wraps her arms around my stomach, presses her belly into my back. I relax against her. "You sure you can't have children?" she asks, "I sure would like to see what your kids would turn out to be like."

I stiffen, say, "I can't have children. I've never wanted children."

"Still," she says, "you're so good with children, so gentle."

I think of all the times my hands have curled into fists, when I have just barely held on. I open my mouth, close it, can't speak. What could I say now? All the times I have not spoken before, all the things I just could not tell her, the shame, the self-hatred, the fear; all of that hangs between us now—a wall I can not tear down.

I would like to turn around and talk to her, say . . . I've got a dust river in my head, a river of names endlessly repeating. That dirty water rises in me, all those children screaming out their lives in my memory—and I become someone else, someone I have tried so hard not to be. But I don't say anything, and I know, as surely as I know I will never get a child, that by not speaking I am condemning us, that I can not go on loving Jesse and hating her for her fairy tale life, for not asking about what she has no reason to imagine, for that soft-chinned innocence I love.

Jesse puts her hands behind my neck, smiles and says, "You tell the funniest stories."

I put my hands behind her back, feeling the ridges of my knuckles pulsing.

"Yeah," I tell her, "but I lie."

Judith McDaniel

Present Danger

1

She watched them turn and walk away. Single-file. The way they had walked down the narrow path to her cabin four days ago.

The fat one gestured with his rifle. "Don't follow us." He turned back up the path.

The threat was real. She felt it. Sat silent as the four men heaved and grunted up a small rock face and tromped up the stream.

She paused only until they were out of sight, then tied her blanket in a roll around her waist and moved away from the stream. The forest darkened around her as she entered, pushed back branches, made a place for her head and shoulders to weave through the dense underbrush. She went about fifty yards, then sat and watched the path she had come through.

Her mind focused on the image of their retreating backs. She recreated the picture of them, one by one, climbing the rock face and disappearing. Then she would imagine one turning away from the others, coming back silently to kill her.

But no one came up the path. She must have sat, her back against the rough tree trunk, knees pulled up to her chin, for several hours. If one had come back down the stream, he hadn't seen where she had gone into the woods.

She was alone for the first time since they had come. The first time in four days. As the solitude settled around her, sensation began to return. Her eyes burned from staring up the path. She blinked and looked to one side, moving head and neck cautiously. Green, she registered. Sitting in deep shade she noticed the dark moss, ferny ground cover. A few yellow brown leaves had filtered to the forest floor. No sound of other humans since the men had gone beyond range. Noise. Her own body breathing. Water. Birds. Insects.

She stood slowly and began to move toward the stream again. At the edge of the underbrush she looked around. They were gone. Her eyes burned, her throat was dry. Every muscle felt torn. Her vagina was raw with a searing pain. Taking off her boots, then her sweater, pants and shirt, she put her feet into the icy water. She moved deliberately, ignoring the cold. Slowly she sat and submerged her whole body.

2

As she lay back in the water of the Adirondack stream, her head began to ache from the cold. Water washed over her face. She inhaled tentatively, then blew bubbles of air outward. Her face was an icy mask. She wanted to be numb.

"We're heading northwest," they had said the night before when they had reached the stream. "You can go south. You should find something." Laughter.

At dawn she had wanted to ask for a knife, matches, some of their food, but no words came. They had turned and left her with only a single blanket.

Sitting up in the stream, she looked down at her thighs under the clear brown water. Red scratches ran along the top of her inner thigh from just above her knee to her crotch. The young one, she thought, he'd never take his pants off. His zipper had raked her. She wouldn't ask him to move it. He was ashamed to let the other men see him. He wouldn't drop his pants, just worked vigorously, his zipper cutting her with each thrust. Her limbs felt fragile in their stiffness as she lifted herself slowly out of the water. Pulling her long dark hair back, she wrung the water out of it, shivered, looked up at the late September sun through the heavy layers of pine branches. About one o'clock, she guessed, climbing onto a rock mid-stream where the sun struck more directly than at the woods' edge.

She lay in the relative warmth of the afternoon sun, but could not rest. The acrid odor of burnt logs from last night's campfire lingered under the pine. She was still where they had left her. Better to move, stay warm moving.

The stream bed to the south looked passable. Large rocks had been dropped randomly by a retreating glacier. And gravel. She looked down-stream for a moment, then tied her boots, wrapped sweater and blanket around her waist, and started to pick her way from rock to rock.

She had no sense of destination, knew direction only vaguely. She had no illusions about retracing the direction they had come. The men had bushwhacked through heavy underbrush, using compasses, carrying water. Two landmarks, she thought, the tracks and the stream. The second day they had crossed the railroad tracks, running north and south the length of the forest, a symmetrical steel anachronism, they had seemed, moving in and out of the tangled underbrush. And the stream. She stopped fre-quently to drink, assuaging her thirst and hunger with water, realizing as she did so that she must stay with the stream to survive.

Now she tried to remember what she knew about the wilderness. She wasn't out of place there. But camping and canoeing were things done with equipment, with friends, and food and fire. Survival camping? Even then the survivor got a tin cup, a knife and some matches. She had one blanket. And some knowledge. Don't eat mushrooms and bright colored berries.

But what could she eat? Her stomach contracted in pain, a distinct and familiar pain. She had been hungry before. If she could focus on this discomfort, maybe she wouldn't notice the sharp burning pain in her crotch with each step forward.

3

When they had forced her out of the cabin—two of them, then her, then two of them, single file down the narrow path to the pond and out into the bush—she had gone without protest. She had stopped speaking. The passivity she had adopted, complying mutely with their demands, was her bid for survival. To resist, she saw the first day, was to give them an excuse to kill her, at least to brutalize her more fiercely.

The dynamic was easy to see. Her friend Jamie had two dogs. One, Jamie said, would attack when it was scared. If you didn't scare it, it wouldn't hurt you. The other dog feared nothing, hunted and killed for sport. Startled by a woodchuck, the first dog would bark ferociously, terrified enough to hold the chuck at bay. The second dog would come bouncing up happily, sniff curiously at the hysterical barker, then kill the woodchuck. It was a deadly combination.

She had come to the cabin alone, leaving work early on Friday and driving the hundred miles quickly. She had gone straight to the woodpile for the key Jamie had left her. Instead of unpacking the car, she had begun to split wood in the early autumn twilight. Not because she needed it to burn; she knew Jamie would have left the woodbox full inside the cabin. She needed the stretch of her body, the violence of impact. Before darkness stopped her, she had split nearly a quarter of a face cord. Placing the cut log on the block, swinging the maul behind her, sliding her hand down the smooth handle as it arched over her head and slammed into the log end.

When she had first seen Jamie split a log, she thought it seemed an impossible skill for her to learn. Jamie was a tall woman; Susan was just average height, slightly built with thin hands and wrist bones.

"You put your body weight behind it, Susan," Jamie had explained. "Swing with your whole body."

"But how am I going to hit the top of that little log?" she had asked in exasperation. "How do you hit the center of it each time?" Her ax bounced off the side of the wood block again.

"Just like playing tennis," Jamie had insisted. "Keep your eye right on what you want to hit."

It worked and Susan had loved the sense of powerfulness, of energy directed, released, effective.

Unlocking the cabin in twilight, lighting the kerosene lantern, she felt a sense of peace return. She was glad to be alone, glad Jamie had taken the dogs with her on her short trip south. She poured a glass of wine, then read Jamie's note pinned under the lantern: "Sorry to miss you. Lots of tomatoes ripe in the garden. Make yourself at home and call me next week."

Susan kindled a small fire in the stove for company and then pulled out Jamie's fluffy down sleeping bag. She arranged her back against the sofa and began to read, dozing gradually, and then slept deeply without dreams.

4

Picking her footing as she stepped from boulder to boulder, Susan felt hunger making her awkward. She hadn't eaten a real meal since the Saturday the men had first come. Now it was Tuesday. She had tried to fast once after reading Doris Lessing's *Four-Gated City*. Skipping breakfast wasn't hard, nor even lunch. But when she had come home to her apartment, sipped a glass of water and lemon juice, she couldn't think about anything except the food she might be preparing and eating. She knew it would be days before she experienced the heightened perceptions and insights Lessing had described, and she realized, sitting dizzily on the bed, how silly this was. She had to go to work the next day and the next, could not indulge in a long and quiet isolation in a peaceful room in a house someone else was taking care of. She had gotten up from the bed, fixed a bowl of soup and an omelet, and eaten them too quickly. It was her only attempt at fasting.

Now she recognized the lightheaded and dizzy feeling of prolonged hunger. She supposed there must be something she could eat growing in the stream bed or at the edge of the forest. But summer was past with its abundant variety of berries, and she couldn't think what else there might be. If Jamie were here, if Jamie were here, part of her mind chanted, as she looked vaguely along the stream bed for something to eat. Images of Jamie leading her class of seven-year-olds around the edge of the playground, pointing out the delicate sharp bud hidden under the protective stem of the leaf, naming the trees and plants, putting names and pictures together with finely drawn details. "It's what makes you a good teacher," she'd told Jamie once, "and you'd be a great detective, I'll bet." Susan was joking, but it was one of the differences between them that mattered: that Susan saw only the broader shapes of things, recognized familiar forms and never focused on a detail. She knew the birds by their color, some trees by their shape and a life-long familiarity, had an instinctive liking or disliking of the people she met, but rarely examined her responses to them or looked closely at the texture and environment of their lives.

Vegetable food was green, she knew, and looked at the brown reeds and cattails without bothering to pick one. In a muddy backwash she found some green shoots and broke them off, sniffing tentatively at the stems. Inoffensive. She put her tongue out and licked the smooth white lower stalk. No taste. She bit into it. The flavor was musky and slightly muddy. The reed was sinewy, not tender, and the tough celery-like strings wouldn't chew. But some of the pulp dissolved and she swallowed it and walked on slowly, chewing the stems and looking for other food.

5

When she had awakened that morning in the cabin, curled still in front of the fireplace, she couldn't at first remember why she was there. The place itself was familiar; she had come to the cabin many times in the three years since Jamie had moved there. As she lay looking at the dark rafters overhead and the flagstone chimney climbing up the wall, she felt peaceful, completely rested—stiff from the thin foam pad on the hard wood floor—but rested. Jamie's cabin always did this for her. She loved the freedom of isolation, the physical presence of the mountains, watching the shift of color and tone as the seasons changed. She came for Jamie's companionship but more, she sometimes thought, for the quiet of the country and the sense of knowing herself again that Jamie's cabin and the mountains had always seemed to give her.

She thought again, as she puttered around the kitchen, lighting the gas burner to melt butter, cracking the eggs, that she was glad to have the time to herself. She took the eggs out in the sun on the back porch. The night had been cold, but the sun could still warm the air by midmorning. She sat back on a wide wood porch chair, stretched her legs up to the porch railing and started to eat her breakfast.

She remembered the eggs and her complacency as she climbed around a small waterfall, carefully picking her footing down the broken rock face. She remembered the eggs, not because of her hunger, but because she had been so relaxed, so self-secure as she sat on the porch. What had happened? What had she done wrong? What could she have done differently to escape the horror of the last few days? Alone. Shouldn't have come alone. Careful. Careful? What did I do? What did I do wrong?

It had been so irrevocable from the moment when she heard the branches snapping in the underbrush and then looked and saw the four men walking down the path toward the cabin, rifles slung over their shoulders, too early for any legal hunting season.

6

Retching violently, she vomited back the pieces of long stringy green her stomach rejected. She leaned on a rock, pressed her forehead against the pebbly cold surface and waited for the spasms to pass. Exhausted and chilled, she began to look for some shelter for the night. In the waning light she moved away from the noise of the stream into the shelter of the deeper forest. The blanket—now wrapped around her arms and shoulders—was an old wool army surplus one, warm, but not warm enough for near-freezing temperatures. And the damp. She had been soaked the first night in the forest clearing, sitting defiantly, back against a tree, soaked by the heavy dews that came when days and nights carried such temperature extremes.

When she had walked out of the house that Sunday, she had carried nothing with her. "We'll take her along," they had said, and she had not known what that meant, not understood where they were going, believed really—in that level just below conscious thought—that they were walking her into the woods to kill her, and she had taken nothing but the clothes she had been wearing.

And if she had not kept up, she wondered. If she had not been able to walk as quickly, climb as well, if her shoes had been thin instead of sturdy, if her pace had slowed them, what then? Would they have left her sooner, closer to home? Or would they have just shot her, turned a rifle on her for sport, as one had threatened? "Watch it," he had said when she stumbled, stopped to catch her breath. "I'll tie you to a tree and use you for target practice." Better, she supposed, to be lost this far in, than tied to a tree, even five miles from the cabin, slowly starving. Or bleeding. Or dead.

A more heavily wooded copse to her left seemed promising and she picked her way carefully through the top branches of a tree that had fallen. At the base of the trunk several branches crisscrossed and she pulled others from the ground onto the trunk, creating a small cave, about a foot tall and long enough to crawl into. She wrapped her blanket around the length of her body, sat on the ground and inched feet first into her shelter. The odor of freshly broken pine and crushed moss rose around her shoulders. Shivering, eyes open wide, she watched dark obscure the shapes around her. She tried not to think, not to remember, but as her physical activity ceased, her thoughts moved frantically, repetitiously, staccato.

The whiskey. Must have been that. Always got worse after the whiskey. Why did they do it? Other men think these things. Don't do them. Other men drink whiskey. Already breaking the law. Deer jacking. Do it every year. Got dull. Do they do this every year? Other men have fantasies, but he . . . . The voices stopped. She was sitting with her back to a tree. Cold. Dulled. They had finished eating. They sat at the fire passing the flask.

"What's that you got there, Jack? Something for the girl?" Her brain went grey, winced without movement. She had thought they would forget her.

"Hey, girl, come over here," he commanded. "We got something for you." Laughter. Always the laughter. She sat without moving. Her pulse speeded and she felt the blood heat her face. She needed to swallow, but couldn't. The lackey stood up, walked to the tree and pulled her to her feet, shoving her by her elbow toward the fire. Jack sat, feet stretched in front of him, fly open, cock erect.

"Hey, honey," he grinned, "it's getting cold out here. I want you to take those jeans off and sit down here on top of me and keep it warm." Lackey was grinning, the fat one giggled. The boy swigged another shot of whiskey.

She did not move. Head bowed, this command she could not follow. She could not take part in her own humiliation.

The lackey jogged her elbow, then slapped his hand across the side of her head. When she did not respond, he tore her pants down and, holding her arms above her head, forced her onto Jack's lap.

7

In the dream she was sleeping, but the covers kept slipping away. Her hands were weak as she tried to pull on the edges of the blankets. She knew there was a reason she could not keep the covers up and if she could only remember what it was, she wouldn't be cold. It was her own fault, her own fault, the voice said. Then her bed was on a boat that rocked and rocked and she felt the ocean under her and the voice said hold on, hold on or you'll roll off, hold on, but her hands were weak and numb and she thought if I can only wake up from this sleep, I'll be fine. She opened her eyes. There was only the dark and the sound of the ocean rolling and sobbing, and she saw that her bed was a cradle with sides and knew she couldn't fall out, but only wanted to pull the blankets up so she could be warm.

She woke just before dawn, as the birds started to talk, and turned painfully onto her back. She had slept in a curl on her side all night for warmth and her shoulder and arm had no feeling. As the light returned, she watched the branches move against the sky, the voices silent within her.

Movement made her arm tingle, then shot streaks of pain from elbow to hand. As movement displaced the warmth of her shelter, her body started to tremble violently, a shiver that began at her core and pulsed outward to the extremities. Walk. She knew she had to start walking. Warm up. Wrapping the blanket serape style around her arms and shoulders, she began to move throught the denser forest toward the noise of the stream.

At the stream she drank, then sat and took off her boots. She had carefully removed her socks each night and tucked them around her waist to dry, sleeping with the heavy leather boots unlaced on her bare feet. Now she pulled the dry socks on, laced the boots tight. Standing, she was hit by dizziness so extreme she had to bend down again. She needed food, she knew that, needed food to go on walking, and yet she could see nothing edible. Rising more slowly, she began to step from boulder to boulder down the stream bed.

Susan thought that if she concentrated on seeing something to eat, she was likely to find it. She wanted to believe most firmly in the control of her conscious life. "Accidents rarely happen," she told Jamie, "if you're looking for something, it will come. A lover. A new job. We prepare ourselves, make ourselves receptive, then change can happen to us."

"That's naive," Jamie had countered. "You can't really believe you have that much control."

Susan wasn't sure. But it was an attitude that helped her live.

8

The path of the stream had been growing less and less steep. Gradually there were fewer rocks for her to step onto and she found herself forced to the edge of the stream, to walk on a bank, where footing was less secure and tangled branches made her progress slower and slower. Then she was at an impasse. Water spread on all sides, lying in pools among the limbs of fallen trees. A dam. Beavers chewing, building, backing up the stream.

She walked out on a log to survey the marshy bog confronting her. Sitting on the edge of the log, her feet dangled only inches above the murky water. Exhaustion became fixed in her mind as she began to count the steps around the muddy tangled expanse. She sat slumped on the log, no energy for anger or grief.

She was a child again, lost in the endless tangles of childhood dreams, nightmares of being lost and alone, not fantasies but sleeping dreams over which she had no control. Wandering through the maze of a forest, lost in the midst of thousands of strange adults in a place she could not recognize, she woke calling, heard no answer, no voice answer. Woke in the night not knowing her own bedroom, sobbing and sobbing, until her mother heard and came and stood beside her in the dark. "Did you have a bad dream, honey?" "I got lost, Mommy."

The thought—half-formed and present from the first moment—that she might be rescued, came more to her mind as she sat gazing up into the wide blue expanse of sky. She looked for a plane, someone to come and find her. Why aren't they looking for me? Surely someone's noticed I'm gone. But who? Jamie might have noticed that the cabin was messed up, but one of the men had locked the door again and another had driven her car out of the clearing around Jamie's cabin and parked it a mile up an old logging road. Someone find it. Let someone find it. Mommy, I'm lost.

She had walked through the woods with the four men for two days, looking as they came over a rise or into a clearing, looking for other people. But there were none. Hunting season was weeks away, and summer was over. The enormous expanse of forest seemed deserted. She was alone.

Sitting on the log, she knew vaguely that she had lost the sense of clarity that had carried her through her first day alone. Relief at being alone, free, and alive left little room for fear. Now part of her doubted that she would survive. To survive meant going on, going on alone, perhaps for days. It was never a question of whether to try or not to try. She never envisioned walking out into the marsh until she lost her footing and drowned. She had endured much in order to survive. What she doubted now was her ability to endure.

She reached out a hand and pulled absently on one of the cattails growing out of the mud. Ugly. Then she ran her thumb along the stiff fuzzy brown head. She no longer felt hunger, but knew her body craved food. Pulling the cattail toward her, she thought there might be something inside it she could eat. It came up from the mud, slurping as the mud sucked its roots. Nothing in the head. She pulled apart the stem. It was dry and woody, the leaves tough and fibrous. She looked at the roots, covered with mud and mucous grey slime. Nothing, nothing at all.

But she dipped the roots in the water and swished off some of the mud. On one side of the root clump she saw light colored pointed finger-like roots sticking out. She broke one off and washed it cleaner. Brown petals of leaf covered a glistening shell pink root. She broke it in half and bit the smooth surface. Not bitter. She chewed slowly, remembering her attempt at eating the day before.

She ate two, then stopped, waiting to see what her stomach would do, gathering in other plants as she waited. She walked the length of the log, tugging gently at the cattail stems, coaxing them out slowly, rinsing off the pale pink protrusions and laying them in a corner of her folded blanket.

By noon she had eaten and rested and gathered food for the journey. Finding this food was a gift, she thought. But she felt, too, a renewed confidence. She had found food. The frightening tangle of underbrush around the pond seemed to recede. She tied the blanket in a pouch around her waist and walked back up the stream until she came to dry land on either side. She decided to cut east through the forest, then angle back to the stream below the marsh. She thought the railroad tracks might parallel the stream bed. But if she didn't cross them, at least she'd get back to the stream before dark. Taking a drink of fresh water, she turned then and walked into the forest.

9

"Keep your eye on what you want to hit," she remembered Jamie saying. Spotting a tree 50 feet due east, she began to move toward it. The old pine forest had shaded out most of the undergrowth, making passage seem fairly easy at first. Stepping over fallen branches, ducking under closely woven bare dead pine branches sticking out like spikes from the tall trunks, Susan picked her way toward the first tree. Checking the sun and the clearing where the stream had run, she picked another tree and started toward it. Two, three, four. She had imagined the bog to be about two miles long, a mile wide. Five, six. She paused to pull a briar away from her pants leg. On the 50th tree she would cast back toward the west and pick up the stream. Unless she came to the tracks.

Counting, moving in a chosen direction, munching on the cattail roots, she felt her sense of clarity returning. She was thirsty. But she was on a path of her own choosing.

She loved the smell of the tall conifers, the sense of grandeur she felt in them when she stood at the base of one and looked straight up its trunk to the sky. Solitude, she thought, that's what it was. Surrounded by other pines, yet each one of these huge old trees seemed to stand alone in the forest.

As a child she had learned that all of New England had been pine forest once, that the Indians knew that the deer loved the fresh pine shoots, and that pine trees could only grow in acid soil. So every year the Indians burned a part of the forest back, keeping the soil acid and making new pine growth for the deer. The pine seeds hid in the pine cones during the fire and, when it was over, started to grow.

She had thought it was good of the Indians to do that for the deer, but she was not pleased to learn that the Indians needed the deer for food and clothing. She only wanted to imagine the delicate bodied doe in the spring, stepping daintily through the forest, nibbling with white teeth the new pine growth.

She wondered now, as the undergrowth became thicker and less passable, whether the four men had killed the deer, found them in their passage to winter feeding grounds, and killed them. Killed them before the hunting season, before they had reached their natural protection higher in the mountains. For a moment she saw the blood and torn flesh, and then she saw herself, tied to a tree, torn and bleeding.

Stop. She told her mind, stop. Leaning exhausted against a tree, she realized that the way ahead was more and more difficult. Large trees had fallen, not just dead branches. And thick green undergrowth was coming up in the light left by their falling. She was hot now and the ground was sloping upward. She spotted a tree at the top of the incline and moved toward it, hoping for a clearer view of her direction.

She wondered why they wanted the deer, those gutted carcasses, fur matted with blood, piled up in a truck. Money? What were they worth? Did they use them for food like the Indians? She thought not.

Sweating, she struggled to the top of the hill by pulling herself over a fallen tree. She could look across the gully to the next rise. There, stretching through the forest, were the silver rails lying across the dark railroad ties. She sat abruptly as relief loosened her body. They were there, in front of her, running for miles through the tangle of forest and swamp. She had only to cross the gully.

She started over the rocky ledge and down toward the trees. They were much younger, much shorter now, and they were deciduous, she realized. She saw the shades of brown and light green ahead of her, not the heavy dark green of the older pines. Puzzled, she continued to climb down toward the gully bottom.

Before she reached the young woods, she knew. A windfall. It stretched for miles. Hundreds of large old pines blown down in a huge swath of wind, blown down and lying on the ground, rotting as the young trees grew up in the open light, healing the forest's wound. She stood looking at the hundreds of feet of fallen trees, split, wrenched out of the earth, roots twenty feet tall where they were pulled out of the rocky soil.

She walked back up to the ledge and sat, dropping the blanket behind her, pulling off her sweater. It was warm, too warm for a late afternoon at the end of September. A fine haze covered the sun. She rested her head on her arms. The bog behind and to her right. To the north the men with their rifles. A windfall ahead to cross. And tonight, she thought wearily, rain.

10

Resting, then dozing on the hard rock, she dreamed of going north where the men with their rifles hunted the delicate bodied doe with soft brown eyes. Where the men with their guns and knives shot and killed and dismembered and left bleeding corpses behind. She dreamed of their campfire at night and of their rifles piled together under a tree and of herself creeping into the camp where they slept, whiskey on their breath and blood on their hands. And she dreamed she would pick up one of the rifles and walk toward the shapes of the sleeping men with blood on their hands. And she would raise the rifle and fire it at the four sleeping shapes. Fire it again and again and again.

She woke at dusk, chilled, feeling light rain drops on her face, thinking, I should have done that, I should have followed them that first day and at night crept into their camp and shot them all.

And while she climbed back toward the pine forest, looked for a tree that would give her some warmth for the night and shelter from the coming rain, she imagined the looks on their faces, imagined killing Jack first, and then the lackey. But she wanted them to wake up and see what was going to happen. She wanted them to be afraid of her. And she wanted the fat one to squeal and the boy to look unbelieving as she fired shot after shot into their writhing bodies. She could kill them, she knew she could kill them. She could kill them.

Taking the blanket off her shoulders to move more freely, she remembered that it had belonged to the boy. They had goaded him into taking her that night when she lay on the ground where Jack had dumped her from his lap. He had come reluctantly and worked back and forth on her, his face grimacing as if with pain, his zipper scratching her thigh. When the boy was through, she had stood and pulled on her jeans. Then walked out of the fire light circle and sat again with her back to the tree. The boy had brought the blanket and dropped it beside her. As the night got colder, she had wrapped the blanket around her shoulders, curled with her back against the tree, and shivered until dawn.

Now she carefully pulled small green pine branches off the larger boughs, twisting each stem to avoid peeling the bark. She arranged the branches along the frame of the shelter she had constructed, needles down, to shed the rain. Remedy enough in a shower, she knew, but useless if the rain turned into a downpour. Wrapping the blanket around the length of her body, she inched into the shelter without disturbing the branches, then pulled the fragrant pine boughs closer and wrapped them like arms around her.

Listening to the rustle of the rain in the pines, she lay and wondered what she ought to do tomorrow. No point in going back. She wasn't even sure where back was. She wouldn't go north. The men had probably killed the deer and left the forest by now. But to the north was more wilderness, unpopulated forest. She had to get south. She would have to cross the windfall. That was brutal work. In her condition she might slip, turn an ankle, break a limb, trying to climb over or around the enormous tree trunks.

She told herself she ought to be glad. She knew where the tracks were now, knew exactly what it would take to get out. Tomorrow she would find food and then start across the gully. She should be glad. But anxiety, not relief, pushed blackly against her eyelids, sapping her sense of confidence in her body, her ability to go on. "I should have killed them," she whispered again.

As she thought of her dream, and remembered the feeling of the rifle in her hands, against her shoulder, she wondered again why they hadn't killed her. Had they been so sure she wouldn't find her way out? They had never been threatened by the idea that she might confront them some later day. That she could have them arrested for illegal hunting. Or rape. She thought that second. The anxiety tightened her backbone as she imagined seeing them again, trying to tell someone what they had done to her. She knew she'd rather kill them. It would be easier to pick up a rifle and shoot them than to hike into a village and find a sheriff and tell him what they had done to her. Yes, they had been sure that she would never tell anyone, even if she could walk out of the forest and into a village. They had never been afraid of her.

Hunger knotted her stomach and distracted her thoughts. She needed food; she would feel better if she found more food. But the thought of cattail roots turned the spasm in her stomach to nausea. She wanted food that had an odor, food with flavor, food that was warm or even hot.

Moving her weight off her shoulder, she turned on her stomach. Around her the forest came to life. Nocturnal feeders moved through the underbrush with rustling feet. A raccoon sniffed the pine branches she had spread over her, then moved on. She heard a fox catch a burrowing shrew in the windfall over the ridge.

11

Her sleep was light, dreams scattered. For a moment she drove the car on a wide road toward a place she had to be. And then she realized the car was only a bicycle and she worked harder to pedal up the rolling hills. As she worked and breathed harder, the bicycle became a tricycle with little wheels and she still had to go up the hill and behind her was a wagon tied to her tricycle with a little girl in it, and her legs were stiff and cramped with pedaling. Waking and shifting her body to straighten her legs, she thought of Jamie and imagined herself walking back into the cabin and wondered what she would say. Would Jamie know something was wrong? Or would she have to begin, "Guess what happened the other day?" Her throat ached with wanting comfort and tears trickled down her nose. "Oh, God, I want to get out of here, just let me be home," she whispered into the pine leaves.

She remembered Saturday morning, how she was resting in the sun drinking a third cup of coffee, her feet propped on the porch railing in front of her. The sun was warm on her face. And then there was the crackling in the underbrush and she had looked up . . . her mind refused the memory. No. No. Just the sun and the front porch. But the crackling in the underbrush persisted and she looked up and saw the four men walking single file down the path toward the cottage, rifles slung over their shoulders, too early for any legal hunting season.

She had stood as they approached, stood on the porch with the cup of coffee in her hand, stood on the porch so she was taller than the men who were walking up the path. But they had not stopped. They had not stopped and asked permission. They had walked up onto the porch and lounged against a railing.

"Hey, honey, got a cup of coffee for us?" Jack had asked.

And then she began to lose her perspective, began to lose the small bit of control she had created over the memory by knowing it was past and she was lying wrapped in a pine bough shelter somewhere deep in the forest.

"No," she had said, thinking of the pot she had just emptied.

He laughed. "Yes, you do," he said.

"Hey, a girl like you ought to have some hospitality for nice guys like us," chimed in the shorter man.

She saw that the four of them were around her. She felt them pressing toward her, even while they leaned—apparently at ease—on the porch. They were around her and she felt the menace in Jack's voice when he said, "You'll bring us some coffee, won't you?"

She was afraid. She hesitated, then turned toward the cabin door, thinking she would lock it as she went in. But the smaller man moved first and held it open for her in mock chivalry and Jack had followed her into the kitchen. Moving jerkily, she filled the kettle with water and lit the gas jet with a match. As she shook the match out, Jack grabbed her hand and pulled her toward him.

She jerked her hand away, fear turning to anger. "I don't like that," she said, moving away from him. "What do you think you're doing?"

"Hey, Jack, you're not going to take that, are you?" asked the little one, his voice a goad. "Come on, she's a pretty little piece." Then they both moved toward her, rough hands on her clothing as she struggled to break away and the kettle started to shriek on the stove.

"Hey," Jack shouted sharply, slapping her hard, his knuckles grazing her jaw. "Cut it out, or I'll hurt you." Her teeth ached from the slap and her arms were bruised. He smiled. "I don't want to hurt you. We just want some pussy."

The fat man and the boy were watching from the kitchen door.

"Why are you doing this?" she asked, her voice monotone dazed. No one answered her.

Jack moved toward her. "Don't move," he warned. "Just stand still and you won't get hurt."

He stood in front of her and put her hand on his cock, swollen under his pants. He unfastened her pants and slid them down to her ankles. She did not move. Two of the men took her arms and pulled her backward over the table. No no no, she was saying, but the memory went on relentlessly. Went on while Jack pulled her sweater up over her breasts, stripped her off her ankles, went on while the men grinned and breathed and Jack pushed forward and rammed between her spread thighs, and she screamed with the tearing pain, screamed silently. She was screaming, but no one could hear her, screaming but there was no noise and her tears made everything wet around her.

12

She could still feel Jamie's hand on her hair when she woke, the long gentle caress moving down the side of her face. A dream of comfort and warmth and tenderness.

Rain had soaked her blanket and clothes. She touched her hair. It was wet, clinging to her head. Rivulets ran through the pine needles she was lying on. She was not at home. Jamie was not there. Wearily, she thought for a moment she could not go on. Then her body started to shake with chill and she eased herself out of the wet blanket and stood to stretch. The world around her was green and brown through a filter of grey rainy mist. Leaving the sodden blanket lying on the ground, she began to walk down toward the gully.

Mist rose from the heavy vegetation in the windfall. The rain had stopped and the windless dawn seemed hushed and tentative. As she walked, her body moved sluggishly, half alive, a foreign thing, barely under her control.

She had done nothing wrong, she told herself, nothing to deserve punishment. She did not understand a hatred so deep that it lit on any random victim. She had been there. That was all. It had nothing to do with her. Nothing to do with her.

Then she caught the lie. Yes, it had everything to do with her. It had happened to her. They did this to me. They did this to me. I'll kill them. Jesus, I'm going to kill them. Fury exploded whitely. Dizzy, distracted, she knelt on the ground, her body rocking back and forth, back and forth. They did this to me. I'll kill them, I'm going to kill them. There was anguish and necessity in the thought.

She was caught in a trap of frenzied anger and hatred. Kill them. Kill them. She rocked oblivious to the stones under her knees, the damp hair falling forward over her face. Body clenched tightly, she rocked and the anger washed over her, submerged her. She was no longer separate, her body had no beginning and end, skin no longer separated herself from the forest floor where she rocked and rocked, clenched in a fist of hatred. The tiny kernel of herself dissolved and spread like dye on the water, marking the location for a moment, then merging, floating outward, sinking.

Gradually her pulses slowed. She let her shoulders loosen and began to consciously draw one slow breath after another. Her throat felt sore and a shiver started deep in her stomach. She sat without moving for a long time, then brushed the hair away from her face with a slow motion. The sun came out palely on her left, almost over her shoulder.

She rested in the sun, drained and battered. No context of her own knowledge or experience could explain what had happened. Lost control. I really lost control. It was the only point she could focus on as she sat on the forest floor, staring down at the tangled windfall growing below her at the foot of the ridge. She sat, mentally touching each side of her bruised self, testing, probing, remembering. She felt her body had grown very small.

Her mind played images: I got lost, Mommy. She walked to the wood-pile and picked up the ax. Four men walking up the path. Jamie tucking a note under the lantern, walking out of the cabin. The doe stepping delicately through the underbrush. Four men walking up the path. The ax. The rifles lying stacked under a tree. Jamie's voice, Keep your eye on what you want to hit, Susan. Walking out of the cabin, two of them, then her, then two of them. She crouched on the forest floor paralyzed. She could not think why she should go on walking.

She imagined herself never moving from the forest floor, lying curled, ceasing to breathe after a while, the autumn leaves floating down to cover her in gold and brown. That was not the comfort she wanted. She wanted to be warm and alive and stroked. It was a desire she could not relinquish.

She stood and began to walk again, deliberately, slowly angling sideways down the slope. At the edge of the gully she paused and looked across the young forest. From this height it seemed to her a sea of green and gold, as she looked at the rounded rise and fall of brush. She entered the windfall. The light surrounded her in translucent green, the sun catching fine mist that sprayed off the leaves as she passed.

Under the slanting trunk of a shattered pine, she paused. In its shade were clusters of ferns, damp moss and tall spiked day lily leaves. Digging down, she pulled up the tendrils of the day lily roots. Knuckles, orange knuckles clung to the fibrous root, crunchy and sweet. They grew wherever the shade was too deep for briars and saplings. They would grow here while the young trees struggled for light and filled the scar in the old forest.

She struggled up to the trunk of the fallen pine tree. She looked back for a moment at the other pines, tall, lining the sky behind her, each a solitary splendour. Then she slid down the other side and continued to work her way across the gully.

Lynn Michaels

Oxblood Shawls

Part One

"You're a hardened sinner, bunny, like me," the nine-year-old girl, Leila, whispered into the ear of the snowshoe bunny. At nine, the girl mimed the rabbit. Pale, the quartzlike animal appeared both counterpart and reflection of the Northern Jewish girlchild.

But Bethy froze to marble, in order to be pleasing to the Lord. Bethy, the Christian girlchild, would come out on the right side of the roll call at the end.

Leila, the Jew, told Beth she'd die and go to hell if she "et those three raw chinaberries" from the bush in the yard. Leila was punished. Thousandfold. She must remain on her side of the backyard chickenwire fence for a whole month, cyclone fencing splitting the sky between the two. Leila blinked thru the gaps. Beth was called into her house earlier and earlier with winter twilights shortening, was called away from the Devil's Disciple.

Then there were only the chill red eyes of the penned rabbit, marbly, leftover from last Easter to stare at. She crawled thru the hole in the cyclone toward him from her yard into Bethy's, dusting her pinafore. Shivering in alien earth, gazing into the bloodshot eyes of the white snowshoe bunny, Leila knelt before his cage. There was redemption for the Catholic child but not for her.

"You're a hardened sinner, bunny, like me."

From the time she was five, living on the outskirts of the South, she'd been aware of the Gentile—the suspect other. The Gentile, like Lavinia Meizenheimer, large, impassive, but smouldering over the feisty little Southern Gentile. Jo, Leila and Vin—they came as close to hating each other as women can. Vin had lived with Jo for nearly twelve years, when the Jewish girl appeared, dark eyes burning, a stranger from Lord knows where. She appeared in an oxblood shawl which a great aunt in the east had knitted. (She gave an identical one to Jo the next year.) Their passion was a tinderbox. By the end of the eighth month, the fear had taken hold of the two rivals that they'd run into one another at a library or in a corridor of the college. (Suddenly, one can have an arch-enemy on earth, when one thought she had walked placidly those paths, all her ways pleasantness, and all her roads peace. Avoiding the lures of Satan, one runs into Him, the temptation, the Judas-kiss.)

Three lady teachers, their decorum became like a white hospital gown a doctor wears. They achieved an iron self-control like a mask over the face, a cloak of invisible (irreversible) cloth knit across their backs and shoulders. For when the stranger in oxblood shawl had come, she had loomed like an apparition, in that backwater-town where superstition clung like the Spanish moss to the trees in the bayous. ("A back-drainwater of sad-eyed Junkies," Leila had called it, "dotted by a few brick buildings: brick schools, Gothic, Southern, backwoods temples.")

But for Jo Ellen, it was as if a child had stepped into a garden, to cry out a rollcall of the flowers. Objects burst into color, out of black and white. Maybe Keats' "Softness for the spiritual touch" had descended into her earth, a glove out of the blue, a palm to heal up the hardness of her world, a hardness that had gradually closed in, like a prison window narrowing. The challenge—to carry back that frailty world of the flowers into the real world.

Leila recalled the precise, Quaker-like words she'd used to propose to Jo, "Shall we try the adventure now, Jo?" Teaching in the same department, English, at Natchez College, their interchange was slight—a smile here, a word there. But soon, catching Jo's blond form, flitting cross campus from her office-window, Leila glimpsed a grace of mind, quick like the body, to match Shakespeare's boy-brides. For Jo Ellen had command of repartee, and resembled the bard's boy heroines—Viola answering now with toughness, now with a tenderness to make the heart of stone melt. Jo, a nervy realist masking a poet's mind, a poet's expression, with a singular lack of smiling. She hid behind the mask of the teacher, vulnerable and reticent, puzzling her fair eye over dark gradesheets.

"It's a pure fact," (the thirty-six-year-old Southern woman would whisper to her Hebrew lover) "you've brought joy back into my life. You're more than I hoped for, you hear?" She chain-smoked, with a bad heart, a defect no open-heart surgery could heal. She smoked, reading a book of history, *The Tower of London*. "Look at *her*, locked in," she pointed to Queen Elizabeth, tiny and trapped in the tower.

Try as they would to elope, plans failed. Thru one spring, the next summer and its winter, the adulterous affair burned. Smouldered. Now, it was like a high ship upon the rocks, containing the three of them. Now, its crisis was to break. They were no longer capable of boy-bride ingenuity, not now; nor of stoic innocence.

Leila remembered back to that time in the South, the snowshoe bunny. Was there a pattern to her life, repeated like the snowflake on the winter pane, the footprint in the mud or sand? Thirty years back, Leila and Bethy had lived next door, it was the winter of the divorce, the icy winter whose memories were chained to each other, like those Black men Leila had seen on her way to school in the morning, ankles chained to balls, digging dusty Southern railways.

The memories were linked. That was the winter after World War II ended. She had been compelled, since then, by other pale, rabbit-like Christian girls. But it began during those days, when her daddy, an Army psychologist, tested out the early Rorschach upon her mother and her. The Inkblots. Her mother's face swung up, a lamp, pale as soapstone, underneath a green shaded lamp hung above the kitchen table. Her mother would move hands as if in some sign language to the birds on the sill night after night, her mother would interpret shapes of inkblots. "It's a witch," she'd say, the child's thin, peeled ears catching the words. Or . . . "It looks like nothing to me." Her mother's social life consisted of going to escort her father to dances for inmates of the local mental asylum.

That, perhaps, was when love began to strike Leila as a peculiar brand of sacrifice. So when she fell in love with Jo Ellen, it made common sense.

Leila read Hawthorne. Propped up in bed, a full month that winter with the "Iron Maiden," a brace which ran from her butt up to her neck, blue as a month of Sundays. Leila, unable to teach, read and read, reviving those sharp contrasts between good and evil. Hester Prynne threaded her winter. Paralyzed, confined to a wheelchair, *now* did she epitomize the deformity which her mother claimed was the soul of the South?

"The South could stand some cheerin'," said Jo Ellen, the tall rawboned Louisiana girl who'd come over evenings to visit and make sweetcakes or shortbread, her knuckles shining with shortening, her cheeks flushed to old rose—those porcelain cheeks—from the effort, and from mirth. Jo would set the typewriter on a board, placed on Leila's lap in bed. "You know, my name, it means night, darling," Leila would laugh, "night, in Hebrew."

Leila, typewriter propped on the board on top of a pillow, would be pegging away for hours, then would read the draft of some story to Jo. Sometimes they'd play the Zenith radio, or sit in silence. "You are a young Ingrid Bergman," Leila said to Jo, looking up, smiling. "I took a shine to her, you know, when I was nine—that square jaw, those widespaced eyes, those French-Swedish features. My mother was dragged four times to see *Saint Joan* that winter," Leila said. "Lord, Jo, your short-cakes are good."

"All English teachers are good cooks," Jo said, shrugging off praise. "Hey, you know what, Leila, your front porch would be a superb setting for the first scene of *Romeo and Juliet*."

Sometimes they'd discuss their fear: exposure. "In the South," Jo would say, "you can get by, being incredibly eccentric, so long as you're obvious. But if you try to cross the boundary, you threaten them *on their own ground: then* you'll get burnt."

"Is that what you fear?"

"These are the provinces."

"You mean there's Vin? When I first loved a woman, I imagined that my students could *see* her curled up inside my womb, like a little silver statue," Leila said. She went on, "Superstitions, Jo, I wonder, are they particularly Southern? When I was in fourth grade, the white kids used to rib the black kids in the school cafeteria who drank milk, 'drinkin' that won't turn you white, licorice stick.' I used to believe if I climbed to the top of the garage like Fodderwing, I'd be able to fly clear out of the body. But Fodderwing, he just ended up splitting his spine and was stove-up in the hips for the rest of his life."

Leila closed her eyes, thinking back on the night her father came to the hospital after her illness. Divorced, her daddy made the all-night train journey; when he looked upon his daughter, in traction, in her hospital cot, he'd said, "Never seen you so beautiful, Angel." Silently, she watched the scene unfold before her closed eyes, come into colors again.

She pulled Jo down close to her, kissed her on the lips, and whispered very low in Jo's ear, "Jo, darling, when I was nine, visiting in Florida, I met a little girl whose Gramma had laid her in the casket alongside her just-dead grand-daddy, to give the girl a sense of death. To make her kiss the dead grand-daddy. The child lost her power of speech for three years."

Jo Ellen would laugh, "They think I'm a speedfreak cuz I'm so thin. My heart's just a bag of worms. Leila, that little girl, she lay in the grave; me, they say I'm just looking for the key to my grave." "Seems to me we're both looking for the key to our *lives*," said Leila.

Leila rested up during that month. She thought of gutsy Jo, who had been a Black Jack dealer one summer and had dealt "Twenty-One." That was her other side: the lost glamor. Her dissertation had been stolen from her locked briefcase, in her room. "Packed up, I did, and moved to Vegas where I caught my second wind, completed another dissertation which I turned in for my Ph.D."

"Jo, now I can see why the chairman said to you, you've been teaching like a virgin in a whorehouse all these years. You have a purity to rend the heart—"

They took refuge in literary analogy. Their minds locked, two sides to a ring. When Vin's presence seemed a molesting of their love, indeed a butchery, Jo was able to cry out, "We are not meant to mate one for life, darlin', like the swans."

"Marriage, sweetheart," Leila would wink back, "is a permitted joy."

But, to Leila, who'd been raised amid cataclysm of divorce which bloomed like fields of Southern cotton, it was familiar to wake from nightmares, pushing aside air like currents of rough water. She remembered being turned away from hotels in the deep South because the family was Jewish. She remembered—during this month of her slow healing up—and would draw her oxblood shawl from the night table.

She continued to dream, of course, in New England fashion of a world where women set an example for the Peaceable Kingdom. She read her Hawthorne. She wrestled with her Angel. These bouts were cleansing. More than ever, she felt herself to be a fugitive in the South. Fugitive? She lived in this borderland between the dust, and the light of some kingdom. "We're New Englanders, girl," she heard her mother say, "even in flood, we're lean." Could she redeem her unholy acts? She rose one January night, looked in the mirror from her wheelchair, and said, "Tomorrow's my birthday, and I'm ugly as sin."

The mirror was silent—like silver, or mercury. Why should it answer anymore than the reflecting eye of the bunny? Flicking on her bedside lamp, she read *The Desert Fathers*, a book Jo had brought. Their love, at first, consisted of book-exchanges. There lay Saint Pelagia, her veil rent. Dressed as a man. Only at her death was her body found to be that of a woman. Only then did they uncover her sex—the corpse of a woman, an anointment, easing off a sheath of skin as if to discover the soul.

Leila crossed herself, recalling the old Mexican woman who said (crossing herself) outside a San Antonio church, "Happiness for men, not for angels." Leila lay—in the clay colored dark, thinking of her office mate last year, a Texas Baptist who wanted to become a minister. As a boy, he had dreaded silence more than sound—the night time silence when he imagined if he stopped breathing, if only . . . he would be able to hear all those souls in hell: Burning. And she saw again, flash like a brilliant lantern, the bloodred marble eyes of the snowshoe rabbit.

Huddled under blankets for comfort like birds, Leila and Jo.

"What is it, old Jo? Usually you're euphoric."

But Leila was downright only in her *Night-Book:*

Dear Christened Child:
Ever since I was tiny, I have been warned by my mother and father about the suspect other, that shadowy, bitter suspicious other, the Goy. You . . . have opened a rift to my past, a chasm into that deeper chasm,

the South. Something dire always drew us South. The divorce was in the
South, the War we lived thru in the South, then my illness when my spine
was twisted at twelve, and a warmer climate was good.

Jo, my Bethy created one vacuum—or did she only fall into that deeper
chasm of my own soul? Now, often, Beth comes back to me, shivering, a
stranger in the dust. This memory is like the incision of a wound. Am I
Pip at the edge of the Great Salt Marsh? Why do I once again have the de-
sire to marry the other.

I have felt, from the time I was a girl in State Hospital, I must part with
a portion of life. Jane Austen had an ability not to desire what she couldn't
have. She sought her "two inches of ivory to carve upon."

But you, Jo Ellen, you have driven back the days to that year. These
memories tear me apart like North Wind. Yet, you read me the very words,
from a Japanese novel: "Full, if tragic, circumstances are preferable to a
void. Kazu far preferred the North Wind tearing her body to a vacuum."

O wind, tear *my* body to a vacuum! She pulled the light chain, lay some
moments in dark. She no longer wrote, nor spoke the words. Words lay
embedded, like frozen bodies of Arctic men in ice. But they were buried in
her bloodstream. They were memories more bitter than those of the South.
Locked by ball and chain to the ankle.

Memories of that part of her girlhood spent in hospital; she hears the
rollcall still, some nights, as she falls asleep: Jenson, Brown, Kowalsky. As
in the military, all proceeds according to schedule. She'd earned blood
knowledge of that particular privation to which we cannot put a name.
One must fully *face* a dread, give that dread a face, rend the veil; a faceless
fear is a horror.

"Write it, honey," Jo urged. "You spent part of your girlhood in a
children's concentration camp."

"It'd kill me, Jo."

"The only way to bury the past, darlin', is to relive it."

It would be going on, in some cleft of time, forever. The icy bedpans
would be slapped on the kids' butts at 5 a.m. The children were by twos,
in cubicles, except for those isolated in the single-bed cubicle, closest to
the nightnurse. Ritually, there would be a carting of toy bunnies and
mouses, piled high on some stretcher, to be burned, or scalded in vats,
then returned to the children. Ritually, every Saturday when parents paid
brief visits—some children, like the girl with Rocky Mountain Tick Fever,
had not been visited for years—parents would make a mass exodus, out the
ward door, holding at arm's length before them a brown bag of stinking
fish served weekly each Friday at the State Hospital.

"I wondered," she told Jo that month while she was bedridden, "whether my parents had ceased to love me. One day I was being watched round the clock by twenty-four-hour nurses and my stepmother, Anya. The next, I was driven a long ride, past greenhouses (water-smooth from the ambulance) driven in a glass-windowed casket out of the city, to upper state, this death camp I had never had warning of. Up the mountain, into the cold, where chill fell—like snow. Where the eyes of children had lost power. Their eyes loomed like lamps at nightfall. Albina said to me (in the next cubicle when I was inducted), 'See, I was borned this way'—she waved two stumps, a circus seal's flappers thru the glass. That was my Baptism."

"Were the lights of the ward red at night?" Jo asked.

"I don't know. But," (changing the subject) "did you ever want to turn into an animal?" she asked Jo.

"No."

"Me, I did. A horse."

"You and all the hospital kids?"

"I don't know. Farther. Farther back. When we first travelled South for the divorce—had to leave New York, for adultery could be the only charge there. Mother packed up her two girls—Kate with long hair like yours, she practiced neighing. All the children down South, all the young girls, they tossed their long manes. I said to Caroline (who went off always to religious instruction on Wednesdays), 'Caroline, pray for me. *You* know how. Pray my parents get together again.' We girls loped around with a box of Quaker oats, raw, stashed in our hip pockets. We'd draw out a handful from time to time. And, Jo, we nailed up trading cards with stallions or palominos on them directly above our beds. We dreamed we'd change over in dream."

Form flowing into form. Girl into horse. She saw it now, with Jo Ellen, locked mute in her arms.

"I was a good child," Jo whispered.

"I was wicked."

(From the *Night-Book*):
Dear Jo:
You have only one rival, an eighty-five-year-old woman. Is that why we've been at each other's throats these past few days? All these years, I've been waiting for love. You're right. We're both nervous, highstrung. She's in the apartment directly above me. I lie in bed at night, and think of our bodies, one on top of the other, the light breathing of those bones. She's New England, an Old Greek and Latin teacher. Smart as a bunch of tacks, hard as nails, delicate like birchbark. On the days when I don't see you, darling, I wheel up to visit her, carrying a slice of the caraway cheese, or

*Scottish shortcake you gave me. The slowing-down, deceleration, life has
forced upon us creates a bone-closeness. Retreat from life, they say, de-
forms, but Willa's whole. I say, tell me, Willa, about your first day teaching. I was so nervous, it nearly knocked the breath out of my body. She
ran ladders in her half-silk stockings that morning, not having slept "atall"
the night before. She tells me, now things are slipping; but she recalls history in pristine clarity. Jo, we spent a whole afternoon looking up one
word, "pious." Our meetings become ritual. Sometimes, it's risky for both
of us, moving, me rolling from kitchen to living room, carrying her a scald-
ing cup of tea, "a cup of scald." We meet in confidence, nonetheless, and
cheer, an overflow which isn't recklessness.*

*I don't tire of her telling me the same stories. Like the End of the War,
or Woodrow Wilson's Campaigns. We meet, a Latin and Greek dictionary
at her side on the couch. She gives me roots of verbs, nouns, a rosary, a
Pater-noster. I don't hear the words some days, if there's a lot of pain.
But they sound clear, like rain on a roof. They are like oil rubbed into
wood.*

*"Let's be sure to do this again," she says, every time. Or greets me
at her door, always insisting upon rising, with that painful hip of hers;
"we're in great luck today (she'll say)—two types of Angel Cake; and
brick cheese."*

*The end of the war. Does it ever end? The color flowers she grew in
her back garden, on Euclid Street. Her little boy's twin, burnt to death
in the kitchen by some careless maid who tipped a vat of boiling water.*

*Jo, I notice of late I hustle you out the front door, in order to visit
Willa. Lately, I notice I slip on a fresh blouse to call on her, and even daub
a spot of rouge from Mother's rouge-pot. I feel peaked. I sit in the tall,
horsehair chair, in her living-room, gaze at pictures of Pacific blue skies,
watch the burgundy sparkle of her grey eye, and talk about Mills College
girls.*

*You, grand-daughter of a lost war, you who call me an old-fashioned
girl because I say such things as "icebox; taps; valise"—what would you
say to all this? I go to her. Back fifty years in time. Until our eyes lock,
two sides to a gold band. You tell me I live on the diet of an eighty-five-
year-old woman. One day, I tell you of Willa. "Have her tell you about
Horace. Horace and Catullus. Those two are most important for a lyric
poet."*

Part Two

"Horace? He wrote to, for, all the little people, the country people. He
wrote with polish and earthiness."

Leila took down other spoken poems. She drew forth from Willa her
ideas about history, "the way forces come down." But Willa, who adored

Horace, had negative memories of Catullus. He truly possessed a rude streak.

In her dream, she again shoved Bethy off the front porch; directly into the flowerbed by an elbow-knife. Then, lay awake all night shuddering, as she had done. Again, she saw herself in her peajacket, the year she was twenty-one, and struck her first match, to smoke, in the back bathroom of a summer resort. She wrote that night in her *Night-Book*: "Tonight, I am a fallen woman."

Was her hospital experience the thorn, inverted, transformed into a scarlet cloak?

"I made a little library, Willa, of books stashed on my windowsill, the first hospital room, overlooking the slate-darkened East River. I think of all the different color bindings." (She made a windowsill of books for Jo.) Leila thought: We all want to be Christ, and crucified. Maybe a Jew suffers double-guilt, knowing it to go both against human nature, and one's religion. Did she in fact desire to lie back in her child's cot, in that hospital? She took out the slate-colored *Night-Book*, and began writing.

After that, a dam was loosed. She and Jo spoke a good deal of Hell. The conventional beauties were the beauties of Hell, Jo said. Fire and ice.

"What's a Catholic hell like?"

"More conventional than other Christian hells."

"We don't have one. We rest submerged in our own burning."

She'd waited these 20 years for affection. Waited, as though she were a mongrel posted at the kitchen door. And now this swan, this goose, feathers alight, sailed past the screen door at sunset. She nipped it, but drew blood; or the meat became too sweet, too rich. She didn't like the way her teeth cut into the long glide-feathers. She mauled it by her love. The bird-blood ran, not oxblood . . . She lay, stark-still back in the wooden vat of tepid water. Waiting for the waves of memory to recede, she almost stopped breathing. But they rose, higher.

"You don't look well. You look *peakèd*," Leila's mother said, when she came for a visit, "I think that Southern girl's becoming too attached to you." She was scared, and she kept dreaming about the third woman, Vin. When her mother departed, she doubled the intensity of her visits to Willa. The sensible old Scottish voice. Willa said they'd freshen themselves up by a piece of cheese. But she was fevered these nights. She took a painkiller. Some days, Willa was pale as a figure of porcelain, some she had a girlish bloom to her cheek. And her laughter would be light as burning paper.

The South. This was it. They drifted, between the loss of two wars. Could she be in love with an eighty-five-year-old woman? She wanted to ride ridges at night. To match her anger to the pain.

When Jo asked, "What can I do, darlin'? What?"

Leila said, "Shoot me, Jo. *Shoot*. They shoot horses."

But Jo answered, "They don't shoot horses any longer, honey; it's gone out of fashion."

"If you've been lonely from childhood," Jo would say, "think how far back it goes."

Born to old parents, Jo knew that particular solitude which surrounds an only child. But growing up in the Deep South, or the brownstones of the East, Leila and Jo discovered a common ambiance. Jo opened her Southern photo album to show Leila a child grim-looking as if she'd swallowed cod-liver oil—but with a sweetness, temper underneath, not quite veiled by the immediate disaster.

("Look at her, locked in, tiny," the words seemed to be going on forever, pointing to the chill Tower of London. Jo taught Shakespeare.)

(From the *Night-Book*):

You, Jo, are imprisoned by your sweetness, your wit; it's both the bane and blight of the Southern woman.

"Something dire, something dreadful," she said in actuality, "always drew us South." She said it, setting the light in the oven.

"Seeing earth from coffin-corner again tonight?"

"They say women can know nothing of war," Jo laughed, her low laugh. But the two, Leila and Vin, never did have a run-in. Not in a classroom, nor in the chill corridors of the library. Southern Town, it blazed. Honest John's Pawnshop glistened coldly on Main, its sign out front picturing guns and coins. There was a square dance dress shop. There was a mortuary, by rows and rows of black-green Southern cypress, "Run, not by *gold*—but by the *Golden Rule*."

"What religion would *you* say you are?" Jo asks.

"Jewish-New-Englanders," Leila would answer, steeling herself, recalling what her mother used to say about being lean.

No, the two women never had a run-in. But they didn't escape the wrath of Jehovah. Did the heavens crack open? The Saturday night phonecall broke, like a whip, over the backs of the three of them, making them rear. It was a smoke signal, their meeting round that kitchen table. A sign sent out, by three who had drifted far from civilization.

"Leila, it's Jo," Vin's husky voice came over the wires. "Down. She's bad. Askin' for you."

Leila and Vin had never been in the same house, save for that party last spring thrown at Leila's, which now appeared grotesque. Vin hadn't come, not as a proper guest—although she'd been invited, as Jo's house-mate—but had come later, haphazardly, at the end, to fetch Jo. That was the party where they talked about *The Last Picture Show*, Vin and another woman in the department, sitting side-by-side on the sofa, two lumpish persons.

Leila's nerves were steady as steel, while she drove over in her oxblood shawl, now.

She slid in, by the kitchen door. The radio was playing low, some blues. She caught sight of Vin—just saw the back of the large woman slumped over a cold cup of coffee at the red oilcloth table.

Wherever Vin sat had an ultimate air. It became the Last Bus Stop. The Last Train Station.

When Vin heard the kitchen door bang, she turned round. She never wore make-up. Her cheeks were patchy. She held some of the handsomeness of a Pioneer woman. Her red-brown hair (wound tonight in two braids round her head) shone coppery. It was a face that had crossed the plains. On the back burner of the range stood a soot-blacked teapot.

"We had a tough night," Vin said, without turning round.

A ginger cat sat before her on the table, directly opposite, as if the two were engaged in dialogue.

Vin and Leila now, slowly, were moving with the dignity of two in a Greek play, forward to their curtain lines.

There was an unfried salmon in the pan; the salmon looked like a shoe: there's the heel, there's the big toe. Vin wore a sweatshirt, loose at the hips, hiking boots crusted with dirt. One of her school kids had made her a heart—it was Saint Valentine's day—which she'd folded (big, made of cardboard, bright red) and stuck in her hip pocket. Doubled, it resembled a pair of garden shears. Maybe. Or else wings. Vin was smoking. Her well worn German face steered Leila to the bedroom. The vodka bottle (Leila observed as she moved past) had been set on a small, lace-edged valentine where it stood, nearly drained, on the valentine, on the soapstone tile.

Vin ground out her cigarette in the kitchen sink. Leila crossed the threshold to a shoebox-room. She could hear Vin move about, who had seemed a moment before sunk in her flesh.

Soon came the moment when the three would be locked in icy combat. Dante's moment of paralysis. Soon, round the kitchen table. Now, though, Leila could hear Vin behind her light another cigarette, she could hear the match striking. And could hear Vin pour herself a small amount of vodka. Before her, she heard the light breathing, as if thru gauze.

From the doorway, the bed looked as if no one were in it. A low night-bulb, reddish, burned. The *History of the Tower of London* was on the nightstand beside a glass of water. ("When you grow tired of readin' of the Tower, honey, you grow tired of this world.") A bottle of rubbing alcohol stood on the floor, to the left of the bed.

Leila straightened her back. Jo's hand moved above the bedclothes, with a tiny star of light waving, like an orchestra conductor. Pan hung on a wood plaque above the bed: half-man, half-goat, shaggy, playing pipes.

The face in the bed appeared shining, elfin. (Leila recalled again her father's words after the illness: "You've never appeared more beautiful.")

"Smoking—"

"Yes. I mean to."

Jo's was the most musical voice of the three. Slightly ceremonious, modulated, distinctly Southern. Her voice always sounded pleasant when she'd been thru a siege.

"How are the bones?"

"The bones are nothin'—"

"The bones are everything. I'm hiding the cigarettes," Leila came closer to the bed, laid her hand upon the faded blue quilt with the embroidery on it. "Darling, you've been crying." She laid her cool palm upon the burning forehead, sweeping back tawny bangs cut for a Swedish boy, straight across the brow, cut as if someone had placed a bowl over the skull.

"Let's rest quiet. Vin said you asked for me."

"I don't know what the hell broke over me. But it's quieter. A kind of fear. I saw the white light in the corner of the room. Couldn't sleep for three nights. Christ, Leila, we had a knockdown drag-out last night. She finally asked me outright did I want to go and live with you. I said to give me time. Solitude turns me into a child again. Been phoning the Post Office this past week just to have someone to talk to . . ."

They heard—Vin rise in the kitchen, turn on the tap, run the water hard. That was her anger. But though she stirred, she didn't come in. She was biding her time. They felt the large woman's patience, like a presence, a third presence in the room. A volatile presence.

"Jo, I feel this sympathy for Vin—"

"I know." A shadow of pain crossed her face, flitting like deer thru forestfire. Jo closed her eyes; it was precisely the inability to ask for comfort that makes people commit suicide. Leila unbuttoned the man-styled p.j. top (faded blue; *all* Jo's clothes were the faded blue of prisoner's denim). She cupped her hand round one breast. The nipple turned erect.

"With Vin in the next room—"

"She doesn't mind. She's scared."

Leila laid her hand on a boy-thin shoulder. Those days of last summer, of teasing, "You're my Viola" were gone.

"Not ready to bite the dust yet. But some time . . . I ought to let them do that operation—"

"On your heart? Wouldn't work anyway. You told me."

"Might. There's a shadow of a chance."

These moments. Volatile as that lighter-fluid Vin kept igniting in that lino-floored kitchen down the hall. (Must have run out of blue tipped Diamond safety matches.)

"She says I rise at your name, like the horse to his carrot, or lump of sugar."

Vin's arrival came first in a scraping, shuffling. She'd exchanged her desert boots for mules which padded down the hall. There she was. The height and length of her, in the doorway. She stood, arms akimbo. Then she stretched her arms out, as if she were holding up the door.

"Look at the two of ye."

How far could she see into the dark bedroom? (What Juno-like self-control was she exercising to speak as if she spoke to her students in her chalk-on-blackboard voice?)

"Look here," said Vin, "it's been nothin' but *upset* for well over a year, ever since you appeared. But maybe that's from the Lord. I'm goin' back. To the kitchen. Time we talked."

She withdrew, padding on mules back to the kitchen. There is a peculiar brand of Southern sadism which wears the cloak of chivalry. There is a particular sway and ease which heavy people employ in their movements.

Jo turned over to face Leila. She slipped one foot over the bed edge.

"Move slow, love," Leila said, "how are you feeling?"

"Dizzy. My head swims. But I want the three of us to go inside to that kitchen and have it out. Sometimes I feel I won't be in my right mind till I'm clear of the body."

"Darling, soon it'll be spring," Leila whispered as she helped Jo on with her torn blue robe, "with the warm weather, you'll feel better. You'll be able to exchange that mackinaw of yours, for the oxblood."

Vin had begun pruning the plants along the sink edge with the large garden shears. Burning up strength. Glowing with energy. The big grey quilted garden glove lay on the kitchen table, beside the coffeepot. She was heading toward Leila with the opened shears.

"For my part, there's little to say. Maybe nothin'." She slumped down, into one of the cathedral-back chairs that clustered round the table. She laid the shears at her left elbow. "But it feels good ta front ya, Leila. Beyond that, I don't feel much. You could say I feel numb. Jo, she finds her way to you like the horse to the stable."

"The terms you use for us are for animals," Jo said. "Hitchin', shackin' up."

"Ha!" the ample woman rose, throwing back her head, like a riding mistress, squaring her shoulders. She'd been in the Marines in her youth. The posture hadn't deserted her, nor the tone. Her placid features belied her fiery spirit; her reddish hair was gleaming.

Jo rose, slipped into the screened in sunporch which looked out over snowfields now, to retrieve the oxblood shawl Leila had given her. (It was draped over the old upright piano.) With bravado she threw it over her slim shoulders, on top of the old blue robe. When she sat back down, she and Leila were twins.

"*Well* now—" she lilted.

The blood had gone from her cheek. She appeared deathly-pale. Pale as a rabbit.

Vin came back from strolling around the room. "Look *here*," she fronted Leila, "I want ya to know I'm indebted to ya for comin' over tonight. I bite my pride. I told her you're comin', and the color mounts back into her cheek. But I also want ya to know I'm scared for the both of ya."

"Scared?"

Jo was so silent you could hear her slipper scuff the lino, in rhythmic sweeping. Then silence. She was turning into a quartz rabbit, freezing to marble, not to get whipped, to be pleasing to the Lord. What *I'm* fixin' to do, not one of you knows, her eyes said. I won't blink; my fur's turnin' to stone.

(How many angels can dance on the head of a pin? Leila was stunned by Jo's air of innocence. And how many whores in convents? she thought, staring across at Vin.)

"I said, scared of *what*?"

"Conspiracy. Frailty's catchin'. You let it in your backdoor and soon it's knockin' at your front. With the both of ya, it'd burn like wildfire. Look at ya. *Maimed*."

It was as if the word had been forming on Vin's tongue all her life. As if it had burned in her brain, and grown with her very sinew, in her limbs, from her semi-Southern girlhood, on thru all she read, and her studies, up into her present womanhood. The word matured now: *Maimed*.

Jo and Leila, they sat opposite each other, in their identical oxbloods. Was it as if, in Vin's eyes, they already had the red death laid across their shoulders? Jo bore her fierce expression, of exhaustion, blonde shoulder long hair drawn back by a piece of string, grey—the hair shining. Leila was her precise counterpart, a double. Fair-haired. Green smokey eyes. Delicate. Alert.

Leila was back in that dust, that morning, staring down the snowshoe bunny with red marble eyes, reflecting hellfire. Locked in the barbaric calcine dust. (Had she taken steps forward, or simply run and run, standing in the same place?)

The desire to be *chosen*. Then a smile started. From Jo, and Leila. From one corner of the mouth, a sinister smile. Blush rising in her cheek, Leila pushed over, close to Vin.

"Scared of what?"

"I told you, of *that*." The elder woman laid her strong hand upon the cold silver rim of the wheelchair.

"Thank the Lord," Jo said, bowing her head, "It's out, at last."

Paralysis; the three combatants locked in icy embrace, while the eyes turned into the red chill eyes of rabbits at the end of day; while evening wrecked up, upon snow and blue spruce, leaving these three survivors.

Leila breathed more slowly. Vin was to herself, filling the four corners of night, humped like a rabbit, her head a carving in space. Jo was the child, calling the roll call, bringing the flowers to color, the frailty world. She was tracing some leaf in the dust upon the table, it shone like glass. She stood up, took the fresh vase of flowers Vin had culled, lifted them from the water and, like a child bearing a garland to a funeral, laid them out of the water flat upon the dull soapstone of the sink. She sat down again. They sat breathing, very close, quiet like soldiers in a trench. *Who is the enemy?* Marble turns to fur. The prisoners return. For camouflage, they chose silence, and held to that silence, breathing in unison. That was the moment they sensed the enemy was common.

Jo arose, glided in to the piano on the sunporch. With all that cracking cold of February night, she sat down, began playing as on a Southern verandah in mid-July. She began with Chopin waltzes, agile fingers, thin notes going on and on.

Leila continued to stare across at the big woman. Vin's eyes were long-suffering, steady. In time, they would come to question whether it had all occurred. In time, they would take up their lives again, in fierce monotony, in that border town. Blacks. Whites. The color would drain. Had they truly entered a confessional that night, each calling the shots? For each went back to believing—after the last flow of wrath—that all her paths were pleasantness, all her ways peace.

"You are God's chosen people," Jo said to Leila, months later.

Leila shrugged, "*All* people are God's chosen people."

For now, over the snow and blue spruce, the light dry tunes broke on and on, the Night of Saint Valentine's:

Child, child, child of mine, tonight is Saint Valentine's. Your love for me goes out into the world to be, like him, put to death, the words written on a red heart, like the rabbit dwell close to death, spare breath, I'll spare my breath. Flesh of my flesh, bone of my bone, blood of my blood, my love.

Barbara Sheen

Twins

The twins stood in front of their double size closet inspecting their wardrobe, two of everything hung snuggly together side by side. Anna Mae sighed, u sure u want to wear the blue? I was kind of leaning towards the orange lace, her sister turned to her, they were mirror images, the corsage that Pappy got is pink, it just wouldn't look right with orange, this is our 25th birthday and we really should look nice, I thought u liked the blue dress, besides Mama always said that blue was our best color, brings out our eyes, Anna Mae frowned. I suppose u are right Billie Jean, u have better taste than me anyway. Her sister smiled, nonsense, she reached out to squeeze her sister's hand, u have excellent taste, besides, she moved closer, running her hand along her sister's long white neck, stroking her face, I like to look at u in the blue dress, u look so sexy. Anna Mae breathed heavily, Billie Jean moved closer to her sister, hugging her to herself, her lips seeking out Anna Mae's lips, her tongue curling around her sister's tongue. Anna Mae whispered thickly, I love u Billie Jean, happy birthday. Billie Jean pulled her fingers through her sister's blonde hair. I love u too Anna Mae, I love u so much. Her hand cupped her sister's breast. They were both breathing hard. Anna Mae closed her eyes, her body heaved, God, I want u Billie, I want u. Billie sighed, pushing her sister away gently. I know, but there's no time now. Ma and Pappy r waiting on us. They made 8 o'clock reservations at the restaurant. We could not disappoint them by being late. It is real nice of them to b taking us out. This is a real special occasion for them. Anna Mae nodded. I know, and we have tonight. Her sister sighed, smiling. Slowly the twins began dressing.

They lived in a big white brick house, they had lived here all their lives. Pappy owned a real estate company. Texas was a growing state. He was a rich man, important in the community. Mama worked around the house, attended club meetings. She was junior league vice president and she collected antiques. Her girls were her first love, then came her antiques. The house was full of them. It was decorated in french provincial. Room after room of white and gold furniture, pink walls, except for Pappy's bedroom, all the rooms were pink. The girls slept in the same bedroom. It was the bedroom they slept in all their lives. Neither of them had ever slept anywhere else. Mama frowned on pajama parties. They lived at home during college. When they were younger, Pappy talked about adding a wing to the house so the girls could have separate rooms. Mama thought it was nonsense. The girls were twins. They shared everything. Besides, they were both afraid of the dark. So the girls remained in the same bedroom, a huge pink master bedroom with giant windows framed in organdy curtains and a queen size canopy bed. Years ago they shared the bed with dolls and stuffed animals. Now they did not need to fill the bed with other creatures. They had each other every night. They were satisfied. They had the best.

The girls walked into the livingroom side by side. Pappy and Mama were waiting. Pappy was reading the evening paper. Mama was working on her needle point. Their father stood up as they entered the room. Mama caught her breath at the sight of them. They were so pretty. They were her girls. It always amazed her. Mama Mae Bel was not a pretty woman. She was skinny with blotchy skin. Her hair was the color of straw. Her teeth lapped over. She wore big glasses. She knew the main reason why Gene had married her was for her money. She came from a rich family, so did Gene. It was a marriage of convenience, a society match. She had made it work. Gene was happy. She knew he philandered but he was quiet about it. Deep down inside her it was a relief to know she didn't have to endure his crude advances. She felt sorry for the other women. She and Gene were friends. She preferred it that way. They enjoyed each other's company. They played bridge, went riding. Her father had been in real estate. She had a head for it. They talked business. She advised him. She had her antiques. He had his work, and his other women to service him. It was a perfect marriage. It had yielded her daughters, Billie Jean and Anna Mae, her pride and joy. Well, Gene, don't u think your daughters look nice? Nice, why they are the most beautiful girls in all of El Paso. There's not one bachelor in town that wouldn't give his eye teeth just to steal a little kiss from these two young ladies. The twins blushed. Their father had a way of embarrassing them. They wanted to please him but they hated all the young bachelors. All the young men they dated all through high school and college. They were cheerleaders. They were never at a want for men. They were beautiful girls, round and creamy with long platinum curls that twisted like golden vines over their bosoms. Their bodies were ripe, white and full. Their noses turned up, their teeth were perfect, bright white. They were twenty-five. They looked like they stepped out of the pages of Seventeen magazine. They did not enjoy the dates with the young men. It was just the thing to do. The girls were brought up to conform. It was important to b socially accepted. It pleased their Pappy when they brought home football heroes. They wanted to please their Pappy. He was good to them. They hated the football heroes pawing their bodies, Anna Mae seated in the back seat, Billie Jean up front. It disgusted them to feel strange lips seeking out their own. The harshness of male skin rubbing against them. They never went out alone. They always double dated. It was safer. They never were separated. They couldn't do without each other. Male talk bored them. Most other people, except their mother, bored them. They never had any girlfriends. Other women were intruders. They had each other. They had all the same interests, fashion magazines, clothes, cake decorating, their stuffed animal collection, their charm bracelets, reading scary novels, watching old movies on TV together. They did everything together. It was easy to talk to each other. It was like talking to yourself. It was easy to touch each other. It was like masturbating. Nobody guessed about them. They were so beautiful, so sweet, people thought it was sure nice that two sisters could b so close. Strangers stared at them in wonder, like freaks in a carnival, two perfect mirror reflections. When they were younger they thought they might marry. They fantasized about their wedding gowns. Of course it was a double wedding to two brothers. Then they could live together in the same house. It would have been an acceptable life, having each other all day would have made it easier to endure their husbands at night, but it was just a fantasy. Times were changing. Women did not have to marry these days. They were twenty-five. Nobody seemed to mind that they were not married, that they were innocent virgins. Nobody wanted to take their purity from them. Their parents did not mind. They liked having them at home. Mae Bel often said that marriage was a dying concept. The girls had a good home. They were heiresses. They'd always have each other. What more could they want. Mama understood. Pappy did not care. For all his talk of young men, he did not care. They were still his baby girls. They always would b. He did not want to lose them. They had each other. Night after night they had each other for the last six years. They burned for each other, to look into eyes that were their own eyes, to feel themselves inside themselves. At first they were guilty. They did not know what was happening. Just the burning, but it was so sweet that it had to b right. They accepted it.

Mae Bel frowned, her jaw set against her husband. Nonsense, there is not one man in this whole city that could hold a candle to these girls. They are too good for all your young bachelors. The girls nodded silently in agreement. Gene gulped. Of course u r right dear, these little girls of ours r something special. U know since they've been working at the real estate office business has shot up. Anna Mae sighed. O Pappy, u know it's because of the new shopping center. Gene's mouth blew a raspberry. Shopping center, not in a pig's eye. Customers r coming in just to get a look at u two. Why u girls r the prettiest receptionists in town. The twins giggled. Their giggle was like swiss bells. O Pappy, Mae Bel interrupted, your Pappy is right; although I don't really approve of women working. U girls r doing a real fine job. Just the other day Mrs. Carson was telling me what a pleasure it was for her to walk into Pappy's business and b greeted by u two girls. Why, she said to me, Mae Bel, u know it was a joy and a pleasure to see those two girls. They r so fresh and pure, like a breath of spring, instead of some braless floozy shaking her butt as if she had fleas. Pappy laughed. Angela Carson said that? Mae Bel nodded, that woman has a fine sense of humor. The twins looked down at their patent leather shoes, demure and polite as they were brought up to b. Well, Mae Bel rose, I guess we should be going. Just a minute, Gene frowned, aren't u forgetting something my dear? Mae Bel nodded, O my yes, she tapped her foot, and a one, and a two, and a three, together they sang happy birthday to their daughters. Mae Bel pinned a corsage to Billie Jean's right shoulder. The corsage was tiny pink tea roses, the twins' favorite. Gene pinned the same corsage to Anna Mae's left shoulder. They were mirrors. Pappy helped the three women on with their coats, and into the car.

The restaurant was a popular steak house, full of little rooms and quiet atmosphere. Candles glowed on the tables. The maitre'd showed them to their table. Good evening Mr. Bronson, Mrs. Bronson, Anna Mae, Billie Jean, and happy birthday to u'all. The girls had gone to high school with the maitre'd. He was a poor boy. They never dated him. They nodded, thank u Hank.

They sat at a round table, Ma and Pa on one side. The girls hip to hip at the other. Anna Mae's ankle curled around Billie Jean's leg under the table. The waiter brought a bottle of champagne. Surprise, Gene's eyes twinkled. There's nothing too good for my girls on their birthday night. The girls smiled. Their eyes on the tablecloth. Thank u Pappy. Mae Bel smiled. Well now that is sure sweet of u Gene. They drank a toast, Mae Bel clearing her throat. This here's a toast to the two sweetest girls in the whole state of Texas, Happy Birthday darlings. She kissed their cheeks. The glasses clinked. The waiter took orders. Four tenderloin steaks. The girls excused themselves, walking off arm in arm to the restroom. Their parents' eyes followed them. We sure r lucky folks aren't we Mae Bel? They sure make a pretty sight. Mae Bel smiled, her face wrinkling up. They sure do, Gene continued, thoughtful, yup, we sure r lucky because they r good girls. U know I read about young people in the newspaper all the time. The way they behave, running around half naked, going wild, having sex orgies, taking drugs. It is disgusting, u know about Lavonne Davis' girl, got herself pregnant. Mae Bel frowned, her mouth ticked, a terrible thing. The Davises r such fine people. Lavonne's taking the girl down to Houston to have her fixed up. If u know what I mean? Gene nodded, yes. Mae Bel frowned, her face like a prune. That Davis girl is a wild one. U know it is not just her. Why I heard tell that little Peggy Raynolds is filing for a divorce. Gene's mouth pursed in pity. Is that so, and Jack Raynolds is such a hard working guy. Mae Bel nodded. He is very nice, and she with two little ones. Mrs. Carter said it's because he was fooling around. Well I just think a wife has to expect that. Men have different needs than women. It's a scientific fact. Gene blushed. He felt a twinge of guilt. U r absolutely right. We really r lucky Mae Bel, to have such good girls. U did a real good job with them. I feel so proud. Mae Bel smiled, taking her husband's hand, the father of her daughters.

The girls went into the same bathroom stall, locking the door behind them. Billie Jean watched Anna Mae pee. This sure is a nice place. Anna Mae nodded, sure is. It's nice being out with Mama and Pappy too. Billie Jean nodded, real nice. They switched positions. Anna Mae watched her sister. Do not sit on the seat. U could get germs. Billie nodded, smiling, don't worry I wouldn't dream of sitting on the seat in a public toilet. U never know who sat here last. Anna Mae nodded, that's for sure. Billie Jean stood up flushing the bowl. The stall was small. The girls stood face to face. Their bodies touching. Piped in music drowned out the sound of the pipes. Their lips met. Their arms encircled each other. Their fingers held each other's breasts. Anna Mae's hand slipped down to her sister's crotch. Her fingers curled under the panty hose rubbing the thick blonde hair. Billie Jean's hand slipped down to her sister's crotch pulling away the panty hose. Their thumbs plunged inside each other at the same time with the same movement in perfect rhythm. In and Out, In and Out. Hot liquid covered their thighs. Their thumbs moved faster and faster. Together, their bodies shuddered, coming together, as they did everything together. Their lips touched. They held each other kissing tenderly.

Anna Mae and Billie Jean sat in front of the bathroom mirror reapplying their lipstick. They smiled into the mirror at each other, contented. A woman came into the bathroom, Mary Peterson, a friend of their mother. They smiled at her, standing up politely. Hello Mrs. Peterson. How r u? It's so nice to see u, chorally, in two voices that were really one. They walked out of the bathroom smiling sweetly at the older woman. Mary Peterson went into the stall. Sitting, she smiled. What nice girls.

Jewelle Gomez

No Day Too Long

Gilda left the party, sure that the young girl, Effie, had been flirting with her. Although Gilda often went to the parties that the young women gave, she accepted that her life was separate from theirs. It had been too long since she had loved anyone.

While she sat at the piano, playing and singing, the girl stood across the room not moving or turning her eyes from Gilda. It did not matter how long she had been away from love, the look was unmistakable.

Gilda cherished singing for those enchanting women who were so full of energy. It fulfilled her in a different way from the nights on a bandstand singing to the clouds of smoke and noisy ice cubes. The checks from the clubs in the Village or casinos in New Jersey never enriched her as much as their tender hands on her back or the dazzling smiles they showered on her when she sat among them singing to them alone.

The heels of Gilda's boots were silent and swift as she descended the marble steps of the large old apartment building, and on the sidewalk outside. She sped quickly down Riverside Drive toward her apartment in Chelsea. The October air was brisk and fresh on her face. She glanced at the New Jersey skyline as she side-stepped the memory of Effie.

Gilda felt an almost imperceptible change in the air as the sun's rays began to push dawn into the sky. She looked to the east then hurried along, becoming invisible to the few who sat on parkside benches, anticipating the morning.

Once inside her apartment she bolted the doors and undressed for a shower. She looked around the small space that was so peculiarly hers. Her piano stood in one corner, its niche barely carved out of the mountain of books surrounding it. Bright cloth draped the ceiling and walls, hiding the fake wood panelling the realtor had mistakenly thought was a good selling point. Heavy blue velvet curtains covered the windows, whose panes were painted over with city scenes.

The Eiffel Tower adorned the top half of one, the market place in Accra enlivened another. Boston's Beacon Hill wound its way up the glass door which led to the back garden. She pulled the drapes around the rooms and dropped her clothes on the armchair.

219

She stood, not so tall without her boots, before the full-length mirror, while the steam from the shower filled the bathroom. She looked at her body, marvelling at its fineness. Her black skin shone like a polished stone. The rounded stomach and full legs were unchanged from those of her ancestors. Her teeth gleamed against soft lips and through the fog her dark eyes looked back at her as alive and sparkling as they had been when Gilda first saw herself in a looking glass 150 years before.

She washed her thoughts away from her as she lathered the rose scented soap over her body. She rinsed clean and turned her mind to sleep. She unlocked the small room where she would lie. The full platform bed was covered with satin sheets and a comforter that rested on warm Mississippi soil.

Gilda locked the door behind her and lay down, naked except for the juju bracelets that had adorned her arm since she was a young girl. She lay still on her back looking at the shadowless ceiling for a few minutes. Then she closed her eyes, resolved not to think of the girl, Effie. Locked in and safe, she slept the sleep of the dead.

Saturdays were too often the same. Saturday nights had to be special and this Saturday the women were coming. They had secured a van and journeyed to New Jersey to hear her sing.

In the cubicle the management called her dressing room, Gilda sipped red wine. The sound of the jazz trio on the bandstand was in the same room with her. Their music was sharp and sweet. It washed around her and relaxed her. The rhythms between her and other musicians created a family for her. Playing and singing had become the only constant joys in her long life. Now sharing this with the other women had raised the risk of discovery but still she held them to her. She refused to recall the number of times she had fled a city or friends, afraid they would demand too much of her.

Now whatever barrier she thrust between them dissolved when they laughed or called her name. They respected her whims or most obvious fabrication. Still when she arose at dusk and opened the mail there was always an invitation from one of them. They completed a circle of family that Gilda was desperate not to break.   •

She went to the side of the bandstand for the group's last number. She saw the women sitting there, attentive, but impatient for her to appear. There was Kaaren, the sleek, with her red nail polish and high heeled shoes. She sat next to her lover, Chris, whose serious face was softened by curls falling over her forehead. Ayeesha sat slightly apart. Her thick dreadlocks tied up in a richly colored piece of Kente cloth. When she opened her mouth in a smile the light played off of the tantalizing gap in her teeth. Cynthia, next to her, was tiny and brown, like an exquisite museum miniature of a Nigerian work of art. Lavern sat tall, her long legs apologetically sprawled into the narrow aisle between the tiny tables pushed together for them. She was surprised and pleased to see Alberta out with the group.

"Good for her," Gilda thought as she listened to the applause for the musicians. Her friends were a good audience. Most of them were clapping and stomping their feet. Marian applauded politely, reluctant to give a man anything. Her eyes darted around the room, looking for danger or an exit. Her face remained a mask. There was Effie! She applauded loudly, bouncing childishly in her seat and looking around at the same time.

Gilda heard the pianist introduce her before he left the bandstand. She blinked several times, drawing her face into the opened eyes smile that her fans expected from her. She stood on stage and looked down at her friends and sang a cappella, "I love you for sentimental reasons. I hope you do believe me. I've given you my heart."

For a moment they were hushed by the ringing quality of her voice alone, then they applauded wildly. When she sat at the piano it was only she and they again as it had been so often before. She looked out into the room unable to see them clearly over the lights which shone down on her.

"I want to sing a song I wrote that I haven't sung for anyone before tonight. It's dedicated to someone, of course, but I'm not sure who yet," she said wryly.

Her long fingers danced over the keys, gathering the rhythms and melodies of many ancient worlds. The notes cut through the smoky air silencing the random conversation. When she sang, her voice came out softly, caressing the air before slipping into the microphone.

> My love is the blood that enriches this ground
> The sun is a star denied you and me.
> But you are the life I've searched for and found
> And the moon is our half of the dream.
>
> No day is too long nor night too free
> Just come and be here with me.

The applause surrounded and engulfed her, a long awaited embrace. Each song brought her closer to them. Only in these moments did she feel at peace with the world. She kissed the air around her before she stepped down from the bandstand, exhausted. Even as she revelled in her success, she calculated how she would weaken the tide of their adoration. It was the only way she could go on luxuriating in the pleasure the singing gave her and still avoid the steady attention which would make her secret life came under suspicion. She must soon again become one of those many singers who blazed brilliantly then disappeared, a name no one quite remembered.

She put those thoughts off until later, now she joined her friends at their table. She signalled the bartender and he sent over the bottles of champagne she had ordered. The waiter poured freely and they all laughed and kissed each other, exultant at their discovery of this precious gem.

"Your new song is too good, girl. Why've you been keeping it to yourself?" Ayeesha said. Her penchant for organizing and promoting was barely hidden.

By the time the women had finally reached their boroughs, Gilda had been sitting in the back alley garden behind her apartment for over an hour. She looked up at the tenements rising around her and listened to the noises that lay in the air above her: babies sleeping in their cribs, Ismael Miranda singing through the speakers of a cheap stereo, and the low sounds of lovers.

She felt Effie trying to reach her through the night. Somewhere the girl lay alone in her bed, her body moving in rhythm with her quickened pulse and Gilda's name on her lips. Gilda withdrew from the night and returned to her room. She sat before her mirror bathed in candle light, watching her eyes for some resolve to her confusion.

The evening played before her. She pushed backward into her past, going far. There had been other friends, whose love she'd shared, whose graves she'd adorned with flowers. She looked into the history she knew and saw the angry words, secret looks, passion, jealousy, treachery and love. The machinations that make the world go around.

The light flickered around her memories as she sifted through them. Still, she found no counsel. She snuffed out the candle and crawled beneath the silken comforter, finding no comfort there. The ceiling remained a blank before her eyes. She could project no images except the face of the girl. She was young and hummed the tunes as if she knew them all.

Gilda turned over onto her side, unused to having rest elude her. More often it waited impatiently for her, eager to take her into its folds and protect her from harm. This morning she drew her knees up close to her chest and curled her toes, trying to recall what it had been like to be a child. Shortly before the first rays of morning sun began to tap unsuccessfully against her painted windows, she slept. This day she dreamed.

Before she dressed the following evening, Gilda sat at her piano in the corner nearest the window. She played the shadow game. The sun stole across the sky falling past the Hudson into the west. As it passed across an open alley opposite her rooms the fading yellow rays reflected through the opaque gold on her window panes. The painted Eiffel Tower turned into a beacon and refracted light cast shadows on the floor. She watched from the piano bench, poised like a cat, taut and confident, unseen by its prey. She tried to spin a world from that drop of light. She imagined it bathing the park and children sweating as they played beneath it. Before she could fix the picture in her mind the light was gone and evening had begun.

That night she sang in Queens, in a nightclub that embraced the small homeowners and winners from Belmont. The songs came easily but did not wipe the horrible memory from her mind. The blood she'd taken this evening had almost taken a life. She'd come upon a man, black and sure, smoking on a bench by the river. From his back she could see that he was strong, so she had no fear that he would miss the few ounces of life she drained from him.

She had slipped her arms around him, holding him immobile as she sprang over the bench and caught his gaze. The terror in his eyes was quelled by her tranquilizing stare. She sliced a small opening behind his ear and drank slowly. She held him to her breast so that anyone happening by would see them as lovers enraptured with each other. As his blood flowed into her she felt the spark that is all life rekindle inside of her. The blood was warm and soothing throughout her body. She closed her eyes and for a moment she was distracted by her thoughts. She took too much.

His fluttering lids over unseeing eyes startled her. She was angry at her indulgence and carelessness. There were others she knew who enjoyed the moment of death of their victims and revelled in satiation. Gilda did not need to kill, nor did she ever want to enjoy it. Unless it was her deliberate purpose.

When she lay him down on the bench, she measured his pulse and was relieved. She stepped away quickly and ran her tongue over her unpainted mouth clearing the last vestige of red and found her performance smile.

Her songs that night were sung savagely, filled with the anger she still felt. She spit them out at the smiling faces and somehow they took her pain as love. They applauded her anguish and congratulated her on her despair.

Through her second set she still could not clear the incident from her mind. She did not remember his face but the feel of his body filled her with revulsion. The unmistakable weight of death had made his body sag in her arms and she could not dispel the sensation. When the evening was over she hurried from the club, leaving through the back door. The rancid odor of garbage and decay filled the alleyway along with the sound of scurrying animals. Her footsteps were silent among them. She returned to the park and walked past the bench. He was gone.

She raced downtown, eager for the night to end. The Manhattan streets were alive with people returning home. The city was perfect for Gilda, living in the night was not unusual and her neighbors never noticed that she

was not about during the day. They too were locked into their own cof-
fins: offices, shops and factories, each one waiting for release into the freedom of night.

She turned the corner onto her empty street, relieved to be at home
again. She took the two steps that led down to her door. As she opened it
she heard a noise behind her and turned sharply.

"Gilda?" The girl, Effie, stood above her on the step.

She was startled by her abrupt appearance. Her mind ran in confusion
through the excuses she could use to send her away.

"I've been waiting for you to return. I hope you don't mind."

"No, I'm happy to see you." The words came honestly to Gilda.

"May I come in for a moment?"

Gilda noticed the slight trace of an accent she could not identify and
had not noticed before. Effie looked so tall standing on the steps and the
shadows hid her youthful face.

Gilda opened the door and stood aside to let Effie enter first. Gilda
turned on the lamp which glowed a dull red beside the one overstuffed
armchair.

"May I offer you something to drink, wine or a cup of tea?"

"No, thank you. I just wanted to talk to you."

Effie removed her short jacket and sat in the chair. Gilda paced the
room, uncomfortable. She washed her hands in the bathroom, trying to
think of conversation. When she finally sat down on the small trunk in
front of her, Effie spoke immediately.

"I know that you are avoiding me and that makes me very sad. I think
you know that . . .," the girl faltered a moment and her words trailed off
into the thick quiet. She glanced around the room seeking reassurance
from the shadows, then went on.

"You know what I feel for you but I had to face you with it. You must
say that you do not love me, then I will leave."

Gilda sat frozen on the trunk watching the girl's face. Her dark skin was
shining under the glow of the lamp and her lips were pressed firmly together holding back the tears that followed her burst of courage. Gilda's
fingers played mindlessly with the studs that lined the edge of the trunk.
Under its lid lay the few treasures that made up her inheritance: the dress
she'd worn in the fields before she had run away from the plantation, a
caning knife she'd stolen on the night she escaped. She'd used it only once,
to kill the white man who'd discovered her hidden in the tack house. Beside it lay the rusted metal cross her mother had made for her and a brown
leaf journal that had belonged to the woman in Louisiana who had found
her. She had taken Gilda to a fancy house and hidden her. She'd taken
Gilda's life and returned it to her, making Gilda a creature of the night like
herself.

"Old memories are so empty when they can not be shared," Effie said softly, watching Gilda's surprise.

"What do you mean?" Gilda asked as she rose from the trunk and walked over to the piano as if seeking its protection.

"Your coolness is a device to push me away, when I know it is not what you want. You are scampering around inside of your own thoughts when you should be joining with mine."

Gilda turned to face her. She looked directly into Effie's eyes for the first time. The lamplight swirled hypnotically and she felt herself being drawn inside. This girl, Effie, was a woman centuries older than she! In a brief moment Effie's history unfolded behind her eyes and Gilda saw a girl both young and old, who had lived longer than any other Gilda had ever met. There was no reason for Gilda to run away from her.

Gilda's heart pounded wildly and her body trembled. Effie was there holding Gilda in her arms too quickly for her movement to be seen. They stood in the dark room holding each other for a moment. The words to Gilda's song rang in their minds.

My love is the blood that enriches this ground
The sun is a star denied you and me.
But you are the life I've searched for and found
And the moon is our half of the dream.

No day is too long nor night too free
Just come and be here with me.

Gilda locked the doors behind them and the two women slipped under the comforter. They slept easily in each other's arms, the morning light kept safely at bay.

Elizabeth A. Lynn

The Woman Who Loved the Moon

They tell this story in the Middle Counties of Ryoka, and especially in the county of Issho, the home of the Talvela family. In Issho they know that the name of the woman who loved the Moon was Kai Talvela, one of the three warrior sisters of Issho. Though the trees round the Talvela house grow taller now than they did in Kai Talvela's time, her people have not forgotten her. But outside of Issho and in the cities they know her only as the Mirror Ghost.

Kai Talvela was the daughter of Roko Talvela, at a time when the domain of the Talvelai was smaller than it is now. Certainly it was smaller than Roko Talvela liked. He rode out often to skirmish at the borders of his land, and the men of the Talvelai went with him. The hills of Issho county resounded to their shouts. While he was gone the folk of the household went about their business, for the Talvela lands were famous then as they are now for their fine orchards and the fine dappled horses they breed. They were well protected, despite the dearth of soldiery, for Lia Talvela was a sorcerer, and Kai and her sisters Tei and Alin guarded the house. The sisters were a formidable enemy, for they had learned to ride and to fight. The Talvela armorer had fashioned for them fine light mail that glittered as if carved from gems. At dawn and dusk the three sisters rode across the estate. Alin wore a blue-dyed plume on her peaked helmet, and Tei wore a gold one on hers. Kai wore a feather dyed red as blood. In the dusk their armor gleamed, and when it caught the starlight it glittered like the rising Moon.

Kai was the oldest of the sisters; Alin the youngest. In looks and in affection the three were very close. They were—as Talvela women are even in our day—tall and slim, with coal-black hair. Tei was the proudest of the three, and Alin was the most laughing and gay. Kai, the oldest, was quietest, and while Tei frowned often and Alin laughed, Kai's look was grave, direct, and serene. They were all of an age to be wed, and Roko Talvela had tried to find husbands for them. But Kai, Tei, and Alin had agreed that they would take no lover and wed no man who could not match their skills in combat. Few men wished to meet the warrior sisters. Even the bravest found themselves oddly unnerved when they faced Tei's

226

long barbed spear and grim smile, or Alin's laughing eyes as she spun her oaken horn-tipped cudgel. It whirled like a live thing in her palms. And none desired to meet Kai's great curved blade. It sang when she swung it, a thin clear sound, purer than the note of the winter thrush. Because of that sound Kai named her blade *Song*. She kept it sharp, sharp as a shadow in the full Moon's light. She had a jeweled scabbard made to hold it, and to honor it, she caused a great ruby to be fixed in the hilt of the sword.

One day in the late afternoon the sisters rode, as was their custom, to inspect the fences and guardposts of the estate, making sure that the men Roko Talvela had left under their command were vigilant in their job. Their page went with them. He was a boy from Nakasé county, and like many of the folk of Nakasé he was a musician. He carried a horn which, when sounded, would summon the small company of guards, and his stringed lute from Ujo. He also carried a long-necked pipe, which he was just learning how to play. It was autumn. The leaves were rusty on the trees. In the dry sad air they rattled in the breeze as if they had been made of brass. A red sun sat on the horizon, and overhead swung the great silver face of the full Moon.

The page had been playing a children's song on the pipe. He took his lips from it and spoke. The storytellers of Ujo, in Nakasé county, when they tell this tale, insist that he was in love with one of the sisters, or perhaps with all three. There is no way to know, of course, if that is true. Certainly they had all, even proud Tei, been very kind to him. But he gazed upon the sisters in the rising moonlight, and his eyes worshipped. Stammering, he said, "O my ladies, each of you is beautiful, and together you rival even the Moon!"

Alin laughed, and swung her hair. Like water against diamond it brushed her armor. Even Tei smiled. But Kai was troubled. "Don't say that," she said gently. "It's not lucky, and it isn't true."

"But everyone says it, Lady," said the page.

Suddenly Tei exclaimed, "Look!" Kai and Alin wheeled their horses. A warrior was riding slowly toward them, across the blue hills. His steed was black, black as obsidian, black as a starless night, and the feather on his helmet was blacker than a raven's wing. His bridle and saddle and reins and his armor were silver as the mail of the Talvela women. He bore across his lap a blackthorn cudgel, tipped with ivory, and beside it lay a great barbed spear. At his side bobbed a black sheath and the protruding hilt of a silver sword. Silently he rode up the hill, and the darkness thickened at his back. The hooves of the black horse made no sound on the pebbly road.

As the rider came closer, he lifted his head and gazed at the Talvelai, and they could all see that the person they had thought a man was in fact a woman. Her hair was white as snow, and her eyes gray as ash. The page lifted the horn to his lips to sound a warning. But Alin caught his wrist with her warm strong fingers. "Wait," she said. "I think she is alone. Let us see what she wants." Behind the oncoming rider darkness thickened. A night bird called *Whooo?*

Tei said, "I did not know there was another woman warrior in the Middle Counties."

The warrior halted below the summit of the hill. Her voice was clear and cold as the winter wind blowing off the northern moors. "It is as they sing; you are indeed fair. Yet not so fair, I think, as the shining Moon."

Uneasily the women of Issho gazed at this enigmatic stranger. Finally Kai said, "You seem to know who we are. But we do not know you. Who are you, and from where do you come? Your armor bears no device. Are you from the Middle Counties?"

"No," said the stranger, "my home is far away." A smile like light flickered on her lips. "My name is—Sedi."

Kai's dark brows drew together, and Tei frowned, for Sedi's armor was unmarred by dirt or stain, and her horse looked fresh and unwearied. Kai thought, what if she is an illusion, sent by Roko Talvela's enemies? She said, "You are chary of your answers."

But Alin laughed. "O my sister, you are too suspicious," she said. She pointed to the staff across the stranger's knees. "Can you use that pretty stick?"

"In my land," Sedi said, "I am matchless." She ran her hand down the black cudgel's grain.

"Then I challenge you!" said Alin promptly. She smiled at her sisters. "Do not look so sour. It has been so long since there has been anyone who could fight with me!" Faced with her teasing smile, even Tei smiled in return, for neither of the two older sisters could refuse Alin anything.

"I accept," said Sedi sweetly. Kai thought, An illusion cannot fight. Surely this woman is real. Alin and Sedi dismounted their steeds. Sedi wore silks with silver and black markings beneath her shining mail. Kai looked at them and thought, I have seen those marks before. Yet as she stared at them she saw no discernible pattern. Under her armor Alin wore blue silk. She had woven it herself, and it was the color of a summer sky at dawn when the crickets are singing. She took her white cudgel in her hands, and made it spin in two great circles, so swiftly that it blurred in the air. Then she walked to the top of the hill, where the red sunlight and the pale moonlight lingered.

"Let us begin," she said.

Sedi moved opposite her. Her boots were black kid, and they made no sound as she stepped through the stubby grass. Kai felt a flower of fear wake in her heart. She almost turned to tell the page to wind his horn. But Alin set her staff to whirling, and it was too late. It spun and then with dizzying speed thrust toward Sedi's belly. Sedi parried the thrust, moving with flowing grace. Back and forth they struck and circled on the rise. Alin was laughing.

"This one is indeed a master, O my sisters," she called. "I have not been so tested in months!"

Suddenly the hard horn tip of Sedi's staff thrust toward Alin's face. She lifted her staff to deflect the blow. Quick as light, the black staff struck at her belly. Kai cried out. The head blow had been a feint. Alin gasped and fell, her arms folding over her stomach. Her lovely face was twisted with pain and white as moonlight on a lake. Blood bubbled from the corner of her mouth. Daintily, Sedi stepped away from her. Kai and Tei leaped from their horses. Kai unlaced her breastplate and lifted her helmet from her face.

"O," said Alin softly. "It hurts."

Tei whirled, reaching for her spear.

But Alin caught her arm with surprising strength. "No!" she said. "It was a fair fight, and I am fairly beaten."

Lightly Sedi mounted her horse. "Thy beauty is less than it was, women of Issho," she said. Noiselessly she guided her steed into the white mist coiling up the hill, and disappeared in its thick folds.

"Ride to the house," Kai said to the frightened page. "Bring aid and a litter. Hurry." She laid a palm on Alin's cheek. It was icy. Gently she began to chafe her sister's hands. The page raced away. Soon the men came from the house. They carried Alin Talvela to her bed, where her mother the sorcerer and healer waited to tend her.

But despite her mother's skills, Alin grew slowly more weak and wan. Lia Talvela said, "She bleeds within. I cannot stanch the wound." As Kai and Tei sat by the bed, Alin sank into a chill silence from which nothing, not even their loving touch, roused her. She died with the dawn. The folk of the household covered her with azure silk and laid her oaken staff at her hand. They coaxed Kai and Tei to their beds and gave them each a poppy potion, that they might sleep a dreamless sleep, undisturbed even by grief.

Word went to Roko Talvela to tell him of his daughter's death. Calling truce to his wars, he returned at once to Issho. All Issho county, and lords from the neighboring counties of Chuyo, Ippa, and Nakasé, came to the funeral. Kai and Tei Talvela rode at the head of the sad procession that brought the body of their sister to burial. The folk who lined the road pointed them out to each other, marvelling at their beauty. But the more discerning saw that their faces were cold as if they had been frost-touched, like flowers in spring caught by a sudden wayward chill.

Autumn passed to winter. Snow fell, covering the hills and valleys of Issho. Issho households put away their silks and linens and wrapped themselves in wool. Fires blazed in the manor of the Talvelai. The warrior sisters of Issho put aside their armor and busied themselves in women's work. And it seemed to all who knew them that Kai had grown more silent and serious, and that proud Tei had grown more grim. The page tried to cheer them with his music. He played war songs, and drinking songs, and bawdy songs. But none of these tunes pleased the sisters. One day in desperation he said, "O my ladies, what would you hear?"

Frowning, Tei shook her head. "Nothing," she said.

But Kai said, "Do you know 'The Riddle Song'?" naming a children's tune. The page nodded. "Play it." He played it. After it he played "Dancing Bear" and "The Happy Hunter" and all the songs of childhood he could think of. And it seemed to him that Tei's hard mouth softened as she listened.

In spring Roko Talvela returned to his wars. Kai and Tei re-donned their armor. At dawn and at dusk they rode the perimeter of the domain, keeping up their custom, accompanied by the page. Spring gave way to summer, and summer to autumn. The farmers burned leaves in the dusk, covering the hills with a blue haze.

And one soft afternoon a figure in silver on a coal-black horse came out of the haze.

The pale face of the full Moon gleamed at her back. "It's she!" cried the page. He reached for his horn.

Tei said, "Wait." Her voice was harsh with pain. She touched the long spear across her knees, and her eyes glittered.

"O my sister, let us not wait," said Kai softly. But Tei seemed not to hear. Sedi approached in silence. Kai lifted her voice. "Stay, traveler. There is no welcome for you in Issho."

The white-haired woman smiled a crooked smile. "I did not come for welcome, O daughters of the Talvelai."

"What brought you here, then?" said Kai.

The warrior woman made no answer. But her gray eyes beneath her pale brows looked at Kai with startling eloquence. They seemed to say, patience. You will see.

Tei said, "She comes to gloat, O my sister, that we are two, and lonely, who once were three."

"I do not think—" Kai began.

Tei interrupted her. "Evil woman," she said, with passion. "Alin was all that is trusting and fair, and you struck her without warning." Dismounting from her dappled mare, she took in hand her long barbed spear. "Come, Sedi. Come and fight *me*."

"As you will," said Sedi. She leaped from her horse, spear in hand, and strode to the spot where Tei waited for her, spear ready. They fought. They thrust and parried and lunged. Slowly the autumn chill settled over the countryside. The spears flashed in the moonlight. Kai sat her horse, fingering the worked setting of the ruby on her sword. Sometimes it seemed to her that Sedi was stronger was Tei, and at other times Tei seem-ed stronger than Sedi. The polish on their silver armor shone like flame in the darkness.

At last Tei tired. She breathed heavily, and her feet slipped in the nub-by grass.

Kai had been waiting for this moment. She drew *Song* from the sheath and made ready to step between them. "Cease this!" she called. Sedi glanced at her.

"No!" cried Tei. She lunged. The tip of her spear sliced Sedi's arm. "I shall win!" she said.

Sedi grimaced. A cloud passed across the Moon. In the dimness, Sedi lunged forward. Her thrust slid under Tei's guard. The black-haired woman crumpled into the grass. Kai sprang to her sister's side. Blood poured from Tei's breast. "Tei!" Kai cried. Tei's eyes closed. Kai groaned. She knew death when she saw it. Raging, she called to the page, "Sound the horn!"

The sweet sound echoed over the valley. In the distance came the an-swering calls from the Talvela men. Kai looked at Sedi, seated on her black steed. "Do you hear those horns, O murderous stranger? The Talvela sol-diers come. You will not escape."

Sedi smiled. "I am not caught so easily," she said. At that moment Tei shook in Kai's arms, and life passed from her. The ground thrummed with the passage of horses. "Do you wish me caught, you must come seek me, Kai Talvela." Light flashed on her armor. Then the night rang with voices shouting.

The captain of the guard bent over Kai. "O my lady, who has done this thing?"

Kai started to point to the white-haired warrior. But among the dappled horses there was no black steed, and no sign of Sedi.

In vain the men of the Talvelai searched for her. In great sadness they brought the body of Tei Talvela home, and readied her for burial. Once more a procession rode the highway to the burial ground of the Talvelai. All Issho mourned.

But Kai Talvela did not weep. After the burial she went to her mother's chambers, and knelt at the sorcerer's knee. "O my mother, listen to me." And she told her mother everything she could remember of her sisters' meetings with the warrior who called herself Sedi.

Lia Talvela stroked her daughter's fine black hair. She listened, and her face grew pale. At last Kai ended. She waited for her mother to speak. "O my daughter," Lia Talvela said sadly, "I wish you had come to me when this Sedi first appeared. I could have told you then that she was no ordi-nary warrior. *Sedi* in the enchanter's tongue means Moon, and the woman you describe is one of the shades of that Lady. Her armor is impervious as the moonlight, and Her steed is not a horse at all but Night itself taking animal shape. I fear that She heard the songs men sang praising the beauty of the women warriors of the Talvelai, and they made Her angry. She came to earth to punish you."

"It was cruel," said Kai. "Are we responsible for what fools say and sing?"

"The elementals are often cruel," said Lia Talvela.

That night, Kai Talvela lay in her bed, unable to rest. Her bed seemed cold and strange to her. She reached to the left and then to the right, feeling the depressions in the great quilts where Alin and Tei had been used to sleep. She pictured herself growing older and older until she was old, the warrior woman of Issho, alone and lonely until the day she died and they buried her beside her sisters. The Talvelai are a long-lived folk. And it seemed to her that she would have preferred her sisters' fate.

The following spring travelers on the highways of Ryoka were treated to a strange apparition—a black-haired woman on a dappled horse riding slowly east.

She wore silver armor and carried a great curved sword, fashioned in the manner of the smiths of the Middle Counties. She moved from town to town. At the inns she would ask, "Where is the home of the nearest witch or wizard?" And when shown the way to the appropriate cottage or house or hollow or cave, she would go that way.

Of the wisefolk she asked always the same thing: "I look for the Lady who is sometimes known as Sedi." And the great among them gravely shook their heads, while the small grew frightened, and shrank away without response. Courteously she thanked them and returned to the road. When she came to the border of the Middle Counties, she did not hesitate, but continued into the Eastern Counties, where folk carry straight, double-edged blades, and the language they speak is strange.

At last she came to the hills that rise on the eastern edge of Ryoka. She was very weary. Her armor was encrusted with the grime of her journey. She drew her horse up the slope of a hill. It was twilight. The darkness out of the east seemed to sap the dappled stallion's strength, so that it plodded like a plowhorse. She was discouraged as well as weary, for in all her months of traveling she had heard no word of Sedi. I shall go home, she thought, and live in the Talvela manor, and wither. She gained the summit of the hill. There she halted. She looked down across the land, bones and heart aching. Beyond the dark shadows lay a line of silver like a silken ribbon in the dusk. And she knew that she could go no farther. That silver line marked the edge of the world. She lifted her head and smelled the heavy salt scent of the open sea.

The silver sea grew brighter. Kai Talvela watched. Slowly the full Moon rose dripping out of the water.

So this is where the Moon lives, thought the woman warrior. She leaned on her horse. She was no fish, to chase the Moon into the ocean. But the thought of returning to Issho made her shiver. She raised her arms to the violet night. "O Moon, see me," she cried. "My armor is filth covered. My horse is worn to a skeleton. I am no longer beautiful. O jealous one, cease Your anger. Out of Your pity, let me join my sisters. Release me!"

She waited for an answer. None came. Suddenly she grew very sleepy. She turned the horse about and led it back down the slope to a hollow where she had seen the feathery shape of a willow silhouetted against the dusk, and heard the music of a stream. Taking off her armor, she wrapped herself in her red woolen cloak. Then she curled into the long soft grass and fell instantly asleep.

She woke to warmth and the smell of food. Rubbing her eyes, she lifted on an elbow. It was dawn. White-haired, cloaked in black, Sedi knelt beside a fire, turning a spit on which broiled three small fish. She looked across the wispy flames and smiled, eyes gray as ash. Her voice was clear and soft as the summer wind. "Come and eat."

It was chilly by the sea. Kai stretched her hands to the fire, rubbing her fingers. Sedi gave her the spit. She nibbled the fish. They were real, no shadow or illusion. Little bones crunched beneath her teeth. She sat up and ate all three fish. Sedi watched her and did not speak.

When she had done, Kai Talvela laid the spit in the fire. Kneeling by the stream, she drank and washed her face. She returned to the place where she had slept, and lifted from the sheath her great curved blade. She saluted Sedi. "O Moon," she said, "or shade of the Moon, or whatever you may be, long have I searched for you, by whose hand perished the two people most dear to me. Without them I no longer wish to live. Yet I am a daughter of the Talvelai, and a warrior, and I would die in battle. O Sedi, will you fight?"

"I will," said the white-haired woman. She drew her own sword from its sheath.

They circled and cut and parried and cut again, while light deepened in the eastern sky. Neither was wearing armor, and so each stroke was double-deadly. Sedi's face was serene as the lambent Moon as she cut and thrust, weaving the tip of her blade in a deadly tapestry. I have only to drop my guard, Kai Talvela thought, and she will kill me. Yet something held her back. Sweat rolled down her sides. The blood pounded in her temples. The salty wind kissed her cheeks. In the swaying willow a bird was singing. She heard the song over the clash of the meeting blades. It came to her that life was sweet. I do not want to die, she thought. I am Kai Talvela, the warrior woman of Issho. I am strong. I will live.

Aloud she panted, "Sedi, I will kill you." The white-haired woman's face did not change, but the speed of her attack increased. She is strong, Kai Talvela thought, but I am stronger. Her palms grew slippery with sweat. Her lungs ached. Still she did not weaken. It was Sedi who slowed, tiring. Kai Talvela shouted with triumph. She swept Sedi's blade to one side and thrust in.

Song's sharp tip came to rest a finger's breadth from Sedi's naked throat. Kai Talvela said, "Now, sister-killer, I have you."

Across the shining sword, Sedi smiled. Kai waited for her to beg for life. She said nothing, only smiled like flickering moonlight. Her hair shone like pearl, and her eyes seemed depthless as the sea. Kai's hands trembled. She let her sword fall. "You are too beautiful, O Sedi."

With cool, white fingers Sedi took *Song* from Kai's hands. She brought her to the fire, and gave her water to drink in her cupped palms. She stroked Kai's black hair and laid her cool lips on Kai's flushed cheek. Then she took Kai's hand in her own, and pointed at the hillside. The skin of the earth shivered, like a horse shaking off a fly. A great rent appeared in the hill. Straight as a shaft of moonlight, a path cut through earth to the water's smooth edge. Sedi said, "Come with me."

And so Kai Talvela followed the Moon to her cave beneath the ocean. Time is different there than it is beneath the light of the sun, and it seemed to her that no time passed at all. She slept by day, and rose at night to ride with the Moon across the dark sky's face, to race the wolves across the plains and watch the dolphins playing in the burnished sea. She drank cool water from beneath the earth. She did not seem to need to eat. Whenever she grew sad or thoughtful Sedi would laugh and shake her long bright hair, and say, "O my love, why so somber?" And the touch of her fingers drove all complaint from Kai's mind and lips.

But one sleep she dreamed of an old woman standing by a window, calling her name. There was something familiar and beloved in the crone's wrinkled face. Three times she dreamed that dream. The old voice woke in her a longing to see sunlight and shadow, green grass and the flowers on the trees. The longing grew strong. She thought, Something has happened to me.

Returning to the cave at dawn, she said to Sedi, "O my friend and lover, let us sit awhile on land. I would watch the sunrise." Sedi consented. They sat at the foot of an immense willow beside a broad stream. A bird sang in the willow. Kai watched the grass color with the sunrise, turning from gray to rose, and from rose to green. And her memories awoke.

She said, "O my love, dear to me is the time I have spent with you beneath the sea. Yet I yearn for the country of my birth, for the sound of familiar voices, for the taste of wine and the smell of bread and meat. Sedi, let me go to my place."

Sedi rose from the grass. She stretched out both hands. "Truly, do you wish to leave me?" she said. There were tears in her gray eyes. Kai trembled. She almost stepped forward to take the white-haired woman in her arms and kiss the tears away.

"I do."

The form of Sedi shuddered, and changed. It grew until it towered in silver majesty above Kai's head, terrible, draped in light, eyes dark as night, a blazing giantess. Soft and awful as death, the Moon said, "Dare you say so, child of earth?"

Kai swallowed. Her voice remained steady. "I do."

The giantess dissolved into the form of Sedi. She regarded Kai. Her eyes were both sad and amused. "I cannot keep you. For in compelling you to love me I have learned to love you. I can no more coerce you than I can myself. But you must know, Kai Talvela, that much human time has passed since you entered the cave of the Moon. Roko Talvela is dead. Your cousin, Edan, is chief of the Talvelai. Your mother is alive but very old. The very steed that brought you here has long since turned to dust."

"I will walk home," said Kai. And she knew that the old woman of her dream had been her mother, the sorcerer Lia.

Sedi sighed. "You do not have to do that. I love you so well that I will even help you leave me. Clothes I will give you, and armor, and a sword." She gestured. Silk and steel rose up from the earth and wrapped themselves about Kai's waist. The weight of a sword dragged at her belt. A horse trotted to her. It was black, and its eyes were pale. "This steed will bring you to Issho in less than a day."

Kai fingered the hilt of the sword, feeling there the faceted lump of a gem. She pulled it upward to look at it and saw a ruby embedded within it. She lifted off her helmet. A red plume nodded in the wind. She lifted her hands to the smooth skin of her face.

"You have not aged," said Sedi. "Do you wish to see?" A silver mirror appeared in her hands. Kai stared at the image of the warrior woman. She looked the same as the day she left Issho.

She looked at the Moon, feeling within her heart for the compulsion that had made her follow Sedi under the sea. She could not feel it. She held out her hands. "Sedi, I love you," she said. They embraced. Kai felt the Moon's cold tears on her cheek.

Sedi pressed the mirror into Kai's hands. "Take this. And on the nights when the Moon is full, do this." She whispered in Kai's ear.

Kai put the mirror between her breasts and mounted the black horse. "Farewell," she called. Sedi waved. The black horse bugled, and shook its ebony mane, and leaped. When Kai looked back she could not see the willow. She bowed her head. Her hair whipped her face. Beneath the silent hooves of Night the earth unrolled like a great brown mat. Kai sighed, remembering the laughter and the loving, and the nightly rides. Never would she race the wolves across the plains, or watch the dolphins playing in the moonlit sea.

The black horse traveled so fast that Kai had no chance to observe the ways in which the world beneath her had changed. But when it halted she stared in puzzlement at the place it had brought her. Surely this was not her home. The trees were different. The house was too big. Yet the token of the Talvelai family gleamed on the tall front gate.

Seeing this lone warrior, the Talvela guards came from the gatehouse. "Who are you?" they demanded. "What is your business here?"

"I am Kai Talvela," she said.

They scowled at her. "That is impossible. Kai Talvela disappeared fifty years ago!" And they barred her way to the house.

But she laughed at them; she who had fought and loved the Moon. She ripped her sword from its sheath, and it sang in the air with a deadly note. "I am Kai Talvela, and I want to see my mother. I would not suggest that any of you try to stop me." She dismounted. Patting the horse, she said, "Thank you, O swift one. Now return to Sedi." The horse blew in her ear and vanished like smoke. The soldiers of the Talvelai froze in fear.

Kai Talvela found her mother in her bedroom, sitting by the window. She was ancient, tiny, a white-haired wrinkled woman dressed in lavender silk. Kai crossed the room and knelt by her mother's chair. "Mother," she said.

An elderly man, standing at the foot of the bed, opened his mouth to gape. He held a polished wooden flute. "Lady!"

Lia Talvela caressed her daughter's unaged cheek. "I have missed you," she said. "I called and called. Strong was the spell that held you. Where have you been?"

"In the cave of the Moon," Kai Talvela said. She put off her helmet, sword, and mail. Curled like a child against her mother's knee, she told the sorcerer everything. The old flute player started to leave the room. A gesture of Lia Talvela's stopped him. When she finished, Kai Talvela lifted her mother's hands to her lips. "I will never leave Issho again," she said.

Lia Talvela stroked her child's hair and said no more. Her hands stilled. When Kai looked up, her mother's eyes had closed. She was dead.

It took a little time before the Talvelai believed that this strange woman was truly Kai Talvela, returned from her journey, no older than the day she left Issho. Edan Talvela was especially loth to believe it. Truthfully, he was somewhat nervous of this fierce young woman. He could not understand why she would not tell them all where she had been for fifty years. "Who is to say she is not enchanted?" he said. But the flute master, who had been the sisters' page, recognized her, and said so steadfastly. Edan Talvela grew less nervous when Kai told him that she had no quarrel with his lordship of the Talvelai. She wished merely to live at peace on the Issho estate. He had a house built for her behind the orchard, near the place of her sisters' and her mother's graves. During the day she sewed and spun, and walked through the orchard. It gave her great pleasure to be able to walk beneath the sun and smell the growing things of earth. In the evening she sat beside her doorway, watching night descend. Sometimes the old musician came to visit with her. He alone knew where she had been for fifty years. His knowledge did not trouble her, for she knew that her mother had trusted him. He played the songs that once she had asked him to play: "The Riddle Song" and other songs of childhood. He had grown to be both courtly and wise, and she liked to talk with him. She grew to be quite fond of him, and she blessed her mother's wisdom.

In the autumn after her return the old musician caught a cold, and died. The night after his funeral Kai Talvela wept into her pillow. She loved Issho. But now there was no one to talk to, no one who knew her. The other Talvelai avoided her, and their children scurried from her path as if she were a ghost. Her proper life had been taken away.

For the first time she thought, I should not have come home. I should have stayed with Sedi. The full moon shining through her window seemed to mock her pain.

Suddenly she recalled Sedi's hands cupped around a mirror, and her whispered instructions. Kai ran to her chest and dug beneath the silks. The mirror was still there. Holding it carefully, she took it to the window and positioned it till the moonlight filled its silver face. She said the words Sedi had told her to say. The mirror grew. The Moon swelled within it. It grew till it was tall as Kai. Then it trembled, like still water when a pebble strikes it. Out from the ripples of light stepped Sedi. The Moon smiled, and held out Her arms. "Have you missed me?" she said. They embraced.

That night Kai's bed was warm. But at dawn Sedi left. "Will you come back?" Kai said.

"I will come when you call me," promised the elemental. Every month on the night of the full Moon Kai held the mirror to the light, and said the words. And every month Sedi returned.

But elementals are fickle, and they are not human, though they may take human shape. One night Sedi did not come. Kai Talvela waited long hours by the window. Years had passed since her return to Issho. She was no longer the woman of twenty who had emerged like a butterfly from the Moon's cave. Yet she was still beautiful, and her spirit was strong as it had ever been. When at last the sunlight came, she rose from her chair. Picking up the mirror from its place, she broke it over her knee.

It seemed to the Talvelai then that she grew old swiftly, aging a year in the space of a day. But her back did not bend, nor did her hair whiten. It remained as black as it had been in her youth. The storytellers say that she never spoke to anyone of her journey. But she must have broken silence one time, or else we would not know this story. Perhaps she spoke as she lay dying. She died on the night of the full Moon, in spring. At dawn some of her vigor returned, and she insisted that her attendants carry her to the window, and dress her in red silk, and lay her sword across her lap. She wore around her neck a piece of broken mirror on a silver chain. And the tale goes on to say that as she died her face brightened to near youthful beauty, and she lifted her arms to the light and cried, "Sedi!"

They buried Kai Talvela beside her mother and her sisters, and then forgot her. Fickleness is also a human trait. But some years later there was war in Issho county. The soldiers of the Talvelai were outnumbered. Doggedly they struggled, as the orchards burned around them. Their enemies backed them as far as the manor gate. It was dusk. They were losing. Suddenly a horn blew, and a woman in bright armor rode from out of nowhere, her mount a black stallion. She swung a shining sword in one fist. "Talvela soldiers, follow me!" she called. At her indomitable manner, the enemy was struck with terror. They dropped their swords and fled into the night. Those soldiers who were closest to the apparition swore that the woman was tall and raven-haired, as the women of the Talvelai are still. They swore also that the sword, as it cut the air, hummed a note so pure that you could almost say it sang.

That was the first appearance of Kai Talvela's shade. Sometimes she comes unarmored, dressed in red silk, gliding through the halls of the Issho estate. When she comes in this guise, she wears a pendant: a broken mirror on a silver chain. When she appears she brings courage to the Talvelai, and fear to their enemies. In the farms and the cities they call her the Mirror Ghost, because of the mirror pendant and because of her brilliant armor. But the folk of the estate know her by name. She is Kai Talvela, the warrior woman of Issho, who loved and fought the Moon, and was loved by Her in return.

The daughters of the Talvelai never tire of the story. They ask for it again and again.

Sauda Jamal

A Mother
That Loves You

What's your name?

Deborah.

Deborah What?

Osgoode. Wit a "E." She sucked her teeth as best she could with her jaw resting in the palm of her hand.

Where d'ya live?

Queens.

Your address girl, look, don't gimme gas here, alright?!

The pudgy man reached into his vest pocket and pulled out a pack of cigarettes. Put the whole pack to his mouth and plucked one out with his teeth. Lit it.

Mista,

Wha? he squinted at her through smoke.

Can I git one of those?

Hell no!!

I'm old enough to smoke, I'm 14. Her voice dropped a bit—Shoot, I even know how to inhale.

You don't seem ta git the full gist of the situation here missy, I am not here to support your nicotine habit, I am here to protect Mr. Macy's property. You are a thief, a sneaking thief and you are going to jail. You will go straight to the Rock, you will not pass "Go" and you will not git two hundred bucks or a goddam stogey! He loved this part. Over the years he had worked this speech out til it was tight as the pink skin on his gut. They always got real quiet after he mentioned jail, this skinny black girl was no different. Runny nose. This one might go out and steal again but she sure wouldn't come back here, smartass. They made him sick these well dressed blacks from Queens. Always swiping quality stuff and crying the blues about how tough they had it. If they had it so bad why didn't they steal canned foods from the A&P insteada coming downtown to steal leather coats and silk shirts? Some goddamn nerve in her little pleated skirt and her knee socks, even had on a birthstone ring. Hell, he didn't get a birthstone ring til he started working and bought one for himself . . . She

239

straightened up in her chair and nervously twisted a thin braid with a finger as she gave him the information about her background. He gave her his authority.

Mista, I swear, this is my first time stealing. I was just trying the coat on then the next thing I know—maybe I'm crazy, a klep—

Hold it! Hold it right there. If you say kleptomaniac I swear I'll reach across this desk and snatch your kinky head off! Tears began to shimmer in the dark eyes.

Whataya think we got here, welfare or somethin', think you can just stroll outta here with a leather coat like Princess Caroline? Huh? Don't you think us decent working people would like leather coats too? You don't see us stealing. I'm sorry kiddo, you people gotta learn that the world don't owe you guys nothin'. The girl shrank into a knot. Sniff. Sniff.

So whataya got ta say now kiddo? Silence. Scared shitless no doubt. Some cold she has, all that sniffin'. He looked at his digital watch, 4:15. He'd hold her just long enough to teach her not to fool around with Macy's, then he'd send her home. He was hungry. A solitary tear dropped directly from her eye to the tip of her shirt. She was obviously not lying about her age—with little boobs like those she couldn't be a day over 14. She buried her small head with its myriad of braids in the crook of a thin arm and wept. Her bony shoulders heaved. He grinned to himself. The thought of going to jail at 14 must be a bitch, 'specially when you're used to having dessert every night and allowance every Saturday. This was no guttersnipe he had before him, he could tell by the way she was dressed, the way she talked and carried herself. He tossed her a box of tissues. She wiped her nose and her eyes. In that order. Damn.

Look kid, it's getting late—he checked his watch again, 4:45. If I call the precinct now I'll be stuck with paperwork til midnight, not to mention court appearances. You look like a decent kid so I'm gonna trust you this time and let you go, but I swear, if I ever see your shiny face in here again I will personally kick your butt and drag you to court—got that? She nodded her head. Eyes wide and solemn.

I mean, somewhere you have a mother that loves you, it shows. You got no business getting yourself into a jam like this. He pulled some mimeographed sheets from his drawer and slid them over to her. Fill out these release sheets while I go get the camera. I gotta get your mug for our little collection—he indicated a tattered row of color snapshots of shoplifters and pickpockets on the wall above the girl's head. She swiveled around and looked up at them. Noticed they were mostly women, mostly Black, said nothing. She stared at one of the women whose thick nappy hair was matted to her head. She had been wearing a wig before the picture was taken, the girl could see the mark its band made on the woman's forehead.

She could imagine this white man staring at the woman from across the room—'sat a wig? Yeah. Well, take it off. Jesus H. Christ! How do you people ever comb that stuff? The woman's face was bloated. The mouth turned down at the corners junkie style. The eyes were large and pretty, but empty. Like someone had turned her upside down and shook all the dreams out.

The man watched the girl as she stared at the photograph of the woman. He wondered what she was thinking, felt he had to say something profound, something she could take back to Queens with her to keep her out of trouble:

See her? Ugly right? Well, that's what you're gonna look like if you don't watch it kiddo, you'll be a shame to your race. You're lucky you got a decent home and good folks so don't fuck around. He left the room with an air of controlled divinity.

Outside his office a young woman sat at a desk near the cooler with a small radio at her elbow turned down low. The news was on. She was painting her long curved nails a putrid pink. Yolanda, I got a girl coming out soon as she finishes off some release forms. He pulled open the metal door on the cabinet and grabbed the camera and a film cartridge. When she's all finished send her home and lock up for me, okay hon? He returned to his office, slapping the cartridge into the camera. Yolanda looked up from her nails and rolled her huge eyes at his back. Hon indeed.

When he entered the office the girl threw her arms around his waist and sobbed into his chest. Thanks mista, I won't do it again, I swear. Sniff. Aw kid, you don't have to do that said the man. He unwrapped her arms so he could take her picture and go eat. As he fanned the print dry he told her to finish the remaining papers outside with the secretary. He pinned the snapshot to the bulletin board with the others (damn, she was so dark), then he closed his office door, locked it, winked at the young girl who sat across the room from Yolanda, dropped his keys on the latter's desk on his way out and disappeared for the day. Yolanda rolled her eyes goodnight at the door he had walked through, turned up the volume on the radio and continued to blow on her nails. From the radio a trumpet whined and a young man crooned Cuba, you know I love you, Salsa . . .

Miss, I'm finished.

So, go home. Puff. Puff.

But my coat is locked up in the office.

Yolanda rolled her eyes and tossed the keys in the girl's general direction, using the very tips of two fingers. The keys clattered rudely to the floor. The girl retrieved them and disappeared into the office she'd been detained in. She emerged shortly with her hooded grey coat folded neatly over her arm and locked the door behind her. She tossed the keys to Yolanda even though she had to pass her desk in order to get outside. She nearly tipped over the fingernail polish. Eyes.

Turn right after you get outside and use the employees' door.

Thanks. Miss.

More eyes.

Bones took the subway steps two at a time. When she reached the bottom she put on her grey coat and neatly folded the black leather one inside out, pausing for a moment to get a whiff of its newness. She ripped through a large black alligator wallet, got the money and discarded the Macy's security shield in a pile of trash as rush hour footsteps descended the stairs behind her. Her nose was runnin' bad. Gotta git home . . . As the No. 2 train rocked her away from 34th Street, she fingered the cool band of the man's Longine in her pocket. She was glad the day hadn't been a complete loss but she had hoped to go home with more. She fumbled around in her pockets looking for a tissue. She yawned, her eyes filled with tears involuntarily.

At 116th Street Bones ran up the stairs and crossed Lenox Avenue. The leather coat flapped at her side. A young man dressed in white on white leaned against the front of the barbershop with a hand resting absently on his crotch.

Hey Smack, if that thang's still down there you must be alive! The young man started, then laughed, easing the guilty hand into a pocket.

Where you going in them knee-socks skinny as yo legs is?

You know how it is man, I'm comin' from work.

As she continued up the street a familiar voice called out to her from Jack Daniel's bar:

Boney Baby, what chu got good?

A man's 'Gine ana woman's leather—size twelve.

Coat too small for Emma.

Serious watch Moses, gold digital.

Moses pulled up his sleeve to reveal two watches. He laughed—

Sorry youngblood, catch me next time, I need me a camera. Say hi to your mama for me.

Bones didn't answer him, she was in a hurry. Imagine a fool like that, wearin' two watches. Sho can tell a country boy that never had nothin' . . .

Two men and a woman were just leaving her building as she approached. They moved as one, leaning slightly forward. They looked first one way then the other. Coast was clear. When Bones said hey y'all they mumbled hey in unison, then scuttled on down the street.

Bones held her breath against the pissy cloud that lived in the hallway. When she got to the third floor where she lived she had to tilt her head back while fumbling around to open the door. Snot ran into her mouth anyway. Salty.

Is tha' my baby? Her mother's cracked voice reached her from the kitchen. It was cold and Bones could hear the oven going. She thought of how she had claimed to live in Queens. She shook her head. It hadn't been her first bust so she knew well that any Black girl that got caught boostin' from Macy's who gave an address like 240 W. 116th Street wasn't going nowhere but to jail. It made no difference to Bones where she lived, if she could only have some heat sometimes . . .

Bonita, is tha' you?

Yeah ma, I got something for you. Bones kicked off her shoes and walked into the kitchen. The naked lightbulb in the ceiling cast bold shadows on the bright yellow walls of the room. Gotta wash those dishes she thought as she stood across the table and looked down at her mother. Francis sat at the table nodding. It was a good nod too, a real chin-dropper. A huge jigsaw puzzle lay scattered on the table, she'd been working on it for months. As she nodded with one bloated hand suspended in mid-air a tiny piece seemed lost between two fingers. Bones checked the room for the stuff.

Ma, I'm sick. She sniffed extra loud to punctuate the statement. No answer. The woman continued on her silent journey with her chin on her chest and her bottom lip hanging. Bones circled the table and gently touched her arm. Ma? Always there was the fear that one day she would get no response, Francis would O. D. or run across some bad stuff, or maybe some dopefiend would come to buy stuff and decide to kill her and rob them—Francis had already been robbed twice. Once they beat her up bad. She kissed her mother on the shoulder and said into her ear:

Mommy, I'm sick. I got cramps. Sniff. The woman's head jerked up, the eyes barely opened.

Okay baby, mama got, mama got— She slipped off the curly wig and fumbled around in it before producing three small glassine bags of heroin. She pulled out another—an afterthought—but drifted off into another nod before she could hand them to Bones.

I got busted at Macy's today, but look what I got. I got us some pictures ma. She snatched the stuff from her mother's hand and replaced it with the two snapshots, her own and her mother's. Francis opened her eyes and looked at the picture of herself, sadly stroking her own matted hair and muttering something about getting a haircut. Bones placed the stolen watch on the table gently, solemnly. She folded the leather coat neatly over the back of a chair before removing her own. Francis smiled at her last surviving child. She was much smarter than all the other kids on the block and pretty to boot, all smooth black skin and pointy corners there in the snapshot. Looked much younger than sixteen, or was she seventeen?

Comon to mama, lemme hug you. You's a real hustler, won't have my baby bustin' huh ass from nine ta five or whorin' for no man. You can make money on your own, a real hustler . . . Bones could feel the cold floor through her skirt as she knelt there hugging her mother. She felt Francis grow heavy and knew she'd be out for a while so she gently loosened her grip.

As she emptied the dope into the Skippy top they always cooked up their stuff with, her stomach began to growl and her mouth filled with bit-ter-tasting saliva. Her hands shook as she filled the syringe. The oven hissed in its corner. She took the old brown leather belt from its hook by the re-frigerator and sat down on the floor near her mother. She tied up and held the belt tight with her teeth.

There on the floor that no longer felt cold Bones got off. She leaned back and rested her small head against Francis' legs. As she sank into the warmth of her own blood she saw once more her mother's face looking at her with empty eyes from the bulletin board at Macy's. Tears burned their way up the back of her throat and teetered on the brink of her eyes. Un-like the tears she had learned to shed to keep security guards feeling secure, these tears had substance, had been hidden rivers that barely rip-pled. These tears did not fall easily. The stuff was good, reeeal good, but she could not stop herself from thinking. Each thought a pebble falling from the top of her mind down through silence through darkness into chilled waters. Kerplunk, plunk ripples widening, widening into circles of pain. Tears. Salty. Hot.

Despair is a pale-eyed white man with icy fingers. He gripped the girl's heart and squeeeeezed it. Bone dry.

Hey Bones! Somewhere you have a mother that loves you/you live in Queens/you are warm Black&beautiful/pass go collect two hundred dol-lars/your mother is a shameshameshame to her race? Somewhere your mother has/you have a mother that loves you . . . . . . Mommy? Yes precious? What chu doin'? I'm tryin' to ease the pain baby, jus' tryin' to ease the pain . . . . Somewhere you have—

Many women in the life had left their children behind. Francis had brought her along. Wasn't that love? Wasn't it? The radiator pipes began to thump. They answered the nodding girl with the promise of heat.

Francine Krasno

Celia

The woman/I needed to call my mother/
was silenced before I was born.
  —Adrienne Rich, "Re-forming the Crystal"

Stories are told to you as a young child, some you remember, some stand out in your mind, and if I had heard them recently, there most likely was much more that had been told to me. But don't forget, as I said, grandpa's dead twenty-one years. You forget. It's frightening because these things when they're told to you, you feel—you want—it should go on and on, it should be remembered, and you don't. You have no one to talk to, family is gone, and you become involved in your own family, and you forget.

My mother and I are sitting in her living room, an uneasy distance between us; she sits at one end of the couch, I am at the other end, and between us is a tape recorder on a pillow of its own. "Just talk about grandma, how she came over here, where she lived; whatever you want. You'll forget about the tape recorder in five minutes." She begins eagerly. She does not have many friends to talk to. I am nervous because we do not talk easily to each other. It is a kind of miracle that we talk at all. There is the memory of her screaming at me two years ago, "You are not part of this family, you are *not* . . ." The tears, the old hatred flaring up, stunning me with its ferocity. But this time I told her I would not come home again. And she listened and apologized, saying over a long distance phone call that I "made everyone in the family tense." "But what about how you make me feel?" I asked. She didn't answer. Two months later she had a cancerous breast removed; I have been home twice to see her, but we have not talked about that phone call since.

I feel guilty extracting this family history from her. How can I explain—she has failed herself—and so I want to hear stories of my grandmother and greatgrandmother. I want to know what they have done so I will know what is possible for myself.

245

My greatest fear has been that I would grow to be like my mother: passive, discontented, confined. I want to know if there has been a time in her life when she was not all of these things. I want to find something to like in her. Which will be something to like in myself. Perhaps in my maternal history there is one story that is my own.

Let's first start with the story she used to tell about being in Europe. She tells of her father.

He came from a petit bourgeois family in Galicia, a province bordering Poland and Hungary. He was a musician by trade, but after immigrating to America in 1900, became a furrier on New York's East Side. He came himself; it was understood that he would send for his wife and children within the year.

Her mother. . . ? Her mother was a very strong and . . . a real matriarch, definitely. But what she did, I really don't know.

After a few months, his letters stopped coming. Nothing. It seemed that he had been swallowed up whole in America. My greatgrandmother wrote, waited, perhaps sent an ad to the "Gallery of Missing Husbands" in the *Jewish Daily Forward:*

> "Rachel Goodman is searching for her husband, 28 years old,
> slight build, medium height, blue eyes, black hair. Left me one
> year ago. I offer 25$ to anyone who will notify me of his
> whereabouts."

Nothing. When Rachel fears that he has deserted them, she resolves to come and find him. Buys tickets for herself and her two youngest, the infants. She leaves my grandmother, who is eleven, and the next oldest boy, who is deaf, with an aunt and uncle until she can send for them.

He has abandoned them; he has taken up with another woman; he wants nothing of his old life. Rachel's brother gives her some money, finds her a place to live. She may have applied to the United Hebrew Charities for relief. *What she did, I really don't know.* In some way, she survives. The story of her anguish is lost. But it is possible to imagine her shame, with what numbness she began a new life. Living with the babies in airless rooms; taking in boarders; learning "finishing" work from her brother who gives her an old sewing machine so she can work at home. She cooks and cleans. Ventures into the street to shop, learning to breathe the sunless air, learning to find the cheapest, fattest piece of meat. Numbness dissolving into a fierce determination to feed and clothe herself and the babies. The rhythmic clack of the treadle on the linoleum floor. Rachel sews, nurses a baby to quiet her, dishes out soup for a boarder, forgetting to eat herself, there is no time. She pedals away her anguish, her sexual longing for the one who has abandoned her, her youth. She will never remarry.

The story grandma tells is that three times she came to Ellis Island. Twice they were turned back. Part of it was that he was deaf. They wouldn't let him in, and there were also problems with their eyes.

Three times my grandmother, Bertha, came to Ellis Island. Rachel sent them tickets and instructions. Two children, traveling alone, across the German border to the major port, Hamburg, for embarkation. Inspection at the dock. Their baggage is taken from them. Bertha's brother, Saul, is separated from her. She is terrified she will lose him. People in white coats yelling, "Halt!" "Line up!" "Quick." He cannot hear. Where is he? They are undressed. Rubbed with disinfectant. Showered.

Two weeks' imprisonment in Hamburg in quarantine. Two children among hundreds of immigrants behind a brick wall. On the other side of the wall, the Atlantic. The sound of the vast water filling their dreams with blue pockets of terror.

Two children. There are one or two days after quarantine before embarking and she must find them a room in a hostel, keep her eye on their baggage, steer them past this man, who is a thief, past that one, who is a white slaver. To America. To Mama. Papa. Who has abandoned her.

On board. Packed into steerage. She has never known anything like this. The closeness, the stench, the sickness. The food is *treyf*, it makes her nauseous anyway, it is so bad. The sight of other children with their mothers makes her homesick. Galicia. America is nothing. Just Mama's face and body moving about in strange rooms. Saul is crying, he is thirsty; he cannot speak. She hugs him next to her, wrapping him in her coat; they sleep.

After eight days, there is a cry in the morning, "Ellis Island!" Magic words. Bodies move, sloughing off weariness. Get ready. Get our things together. She pushes him a little too roughly. Alert now, tense. Someone from the crew chalks letters and numbers on their coats. Come come quick!

Herded off the boat, almost running onto the Customs Wharf. She grips his hand, careful not to lose him, as they move slowly in a long line. There, up ahead of them, a doctor. What? She must let him go. All children over two years must walk alone. A doctor pulls a girl out of line, runs his hand down her spine, puts her behind a wire cage, writes something on her coat. She does not understand. Her stomach sinks. She cannot see him. There,

treyf (Yiddish)—unkosher, defiled.

someone in a white coat is talking to him. What is he asking? He cannot hear. He cannot hear. The inspector steers him into a cage. She has not counted on this. She pushes her way through the line to him, trying to talk to the inspector in her schoolgirl English. An interpreter from the Hebrew Immigrant Aid Society explains that they have picked her brother out because he is deaf. The Society can negotiate with the officials for some immigrants, but with deaf and dumb, it is hopeless.

She cries. It is not the cry of an eleven year old but sounds strangely like that of an old woman. Ageless grief. Her mother and uncle are found by Immigrant Aid and brought to her. There are hurried, tearful instructions from Rachel: she will go back to Galicia with him; there is nothing else to do. When she gets the money, she will send tickets, and they will try a second time.

The second ordeal in steerage. Back with the aunt and uncle, they wait. The third voyage. Again, the lines, quarantine, seasickness. She cannot bear the anguish of another rejection; she instructs her brother how to avoid the inspector's questions. She is terrified that they will remember his face. At Ellis Island, she pulls his cap low, keeps close to him. He is pulled aside. Impossible.

Back to Galicia. She does not know what will happen to them. Desperate letters to her mother. It is two years now since they have lived together. In that time, she has mothered herself and her brother. Now she wants her mother back. She waits. Then, instructions from America: leave him. Leave him? This is the greatest agony. She has no choice. At age thirteen, she makes her final voyage.

She had to leave him there with the aunt and uncle. He died young. She was notified of his death when our Uncle Dave was Bar Mitzvahed.

America. Nothing had prepared her for this ugliness. Sunless air; grey tenement brick; the din of busses, trollies, peddlers, drays, and refuse carts. The windowless bedroom. Mama sewing in the kitchen. The boarders in the parlor. She is ashamed of their poverty, but this is how everyone lives here. She at once determines to work her way out of this nightmare. She will not waste her years bent over a sewing machine like Mama. She will go to school, perfect her English, work in the summers, and save.

She does everything Rachel does: sews, cooks, feeds the babies, shops, learns her way among the pushcarts in the streets. And another thing Mama cannot do: translates English words into Yiddish for her uncle's family. She reads her schoolbooks aloud after supper, entertaining her sister and

Bar Mitzvah—the ceremony celebrating a boy beginning his thirteenth year, the age of religious duty and responsibility.

brother with stories about Canadian Indians and cowboys. She lapses into Yiddish to explain the complexities of public school; to marvel at an old peddler who collapsed on the street; to tell how it felt to ride a trolley for the first time. America. In the summer, she applies for working papers and gets a job as a feller in a glove factory. There are long hours in an unventilated room. The grimy walls and floors, the high temperature and bad light, make her sick. She gets another job the next summer as a finisher in a factory. At least this one is not filled with the stench from the water closet. The wage is a little better, 8$ a week. At the end of the day, she is exhausted. Once, walking home in the dark, a figure comes up behind her, grabs at her purse, whispers something obscene in her ear; from then on, she works the day shift.

She wants her privacy now. Her body is growing, developing, and she is ashamed around the male boarders. She escapes from the house with her friends to a lecture or a coffee parlor. But Mama warns her not to waste too much time playing. Mama doesn't know what fun is. Someday, she tells her, she'll have her own shop with her husband's name on the door. Uptown.

She works and dreams. On hot evenings, when the air is insufferably close, she goes up to the roof, standing in the great shadows thrown from the sheets on the lines; hundreds of sheets, clothes, hundreds of lines stretching from tenement to tenement. It is cool up here, the stench from the street is not so strong. She looks silently at this America, grey stone world. She has no dreams that are not of escape.

She always felt superior to grandpa.

He emigrated from Russia in 1906 to escape the pogroms. He was a tailor, like his father, and went to work in a garment factory in New York, boarding in different tenements, until he found the *Galitz* family. They were good people, a mother and her children, the place was clean, and there was Bertha. He married my grandmother when she was nineteen and he was twenty-one. They moved from the East Side to Brooklyn where their first child, my Aunt Ida, was born.

We had difficulty in his becoming a citizen because you had to be able to write your name in English, and grandma always felt how superior she was to him because she could read and write. He made the attempt. He was a very bright man, but found it difficult to—at that age—of course, he was much older because I was born already when he went to school to try to learn English. And he was able to write some and read some, but he did not have that education as a young boy. He had strong feelings of the union. He talked of the fights that would occur when they were trying to be unionized and all . . . Grandma was one who believed that one should have their own business and this was a sign of status. They didn't have the money for him to start. He was somewhat of a fearful person. To take a chance, he didn't want to, and—he worked for others. He would work in small shops. His work was very seasonal. You would work like three months, and three months you didn't. Three months you did, and three months you didn't . . . . He would go from one to the other. Towards the end, he had worked himself up into a factory that had a name— it was Carmel—and to work for them, that was quite an honor . . . . He was called a cloak operator. He was really quite a craftsman. I mean, you would see that when he would do work for us . . . He was a quiet person. When he got angry, he had a terrible temper, it was as though everything was in and then when he let it out it was ah . . . it all came out. But the relationship between grandma and grandpa . . . well, she felt that she was superior to him. And it was not so. As years went on, my feeling was one of resentment, because this was a man who was never really— she didn't give him credit for what he was.

But what happened to my grandmother's dream of owning a shop? To her determination when she could not go out and work for herself? In America, some wives simply did not work, and there were babies and the cooking and house to take care of. She pestered and badgered him to invest in a business. And when he failed her, turned to her son. He would be a teacher, equal in status to a shopowner. Terrible fights followed. He wanted to be a doctor. Grandpa was not set on an education; he wanted his son to go to work and learn a trade.

My mother and her sister were spared grandma's meddling—it was assumed that they would marry and take on the roles of wife and mother. But there were other problems, disappointments, failures. *My feeling was of resentment . . . she didn't give him credit for what he was.* For what *she* was: intelligent, sensitive, painfully shy. *A fearful person.* A frightened child. Forgotten by grandma in her ambition for her son, "the teacher." And my mother learns this lesson: how painful it is not to be seen. To be invisible, because of what one is, or is not.

In her mind, the most important thing was to be your own boss. She blamed grandpa the most because she didn't feel he was a strong enough character. Owning your own business. This was very important to her. And this she did not achieve in life.

My mother married the man my grandmother should have chosen, an ambitious student in medical school whose dream was to be looked up to as a professional. They moved from New York to a small town in Ohio, where he began his career as a doctor. She began her work as mother and housekeeper. She was shy and imprisoned with two babies. During the first year in the new house, she had fantasies of drowning her two children "like kittens." She grew lonely and bored.

My earliest memories are of her watching helplessly as my father spanked me for dancing around the kitchen table. She yelled at us during the day when he was gone, losing her temper easily, reducing us to tears. But there are other, happier memories. She liked to get us together on Friday nights to light the *shabes* candles. My father would rush in from work and take his *yarmulke* from the drawer; she gave us kleenex to cover our heads and put one on her own. She would light the two white candles and say the *brokhe*, moving her hands in fluid oval shapes over the flames.

Her hands were slender, with long fingers the color of the ivory keys on the piano she sometimes played.

I liked to say her name slowly. Celia. Rolling out the first syllable, letting my tongue effortlessly somersault around the "l," tickling the roof of my mouth, coming down neatly on the "a."

Celia.

In a photograph I have of her then, she is tall and thin, dressed in a stylish black dress. She is standing behind and a little to one side of grandma, smiling at the camera. Her arm is bent so that her hand is hidden behind grandma's hip, as if she were holding on to her in a tentative, childish way.

Two years after this photograph was taken, my grandfather died. Grandma came to live with us because my mother thought she would die of depression if she were left alone.

Her next five years were a gift. As the years went on she became younger rather than older . . .

She did what she had always planned to do with grandpa: traveled to Florida; mixed with people; joined Leisure Lounge, an organization for old women, and within two years she was elected president. The Council of Jewish Women chose her as the Outstanding Senior Citizen for that year. She flowered, and became younger.

The cancer was all over her body. It had spread to her brain.

There were times when she was quarrelsome and short-tempered, when she thought my mother might be stealing her clothes. Then she had her first seizure: rolling eyes, projectile vomiting, blackout.

shabes—the Sabbath.
yarmulke—skullcap.
brokhe—blessing.

Grandma doesn't feel well.

The doctor diagnoses stomach flu. Her food tastes bitter. Another doctor pronounces my grandmother is "depressed." My mother is a "meddling fool" because she is the only one who has seen the seizure and no one believes anything is seriously wrong. My mother begins to doubt her perception: it might not have been a real seizure; the doctors must know. Yet she is sure grandma's hearing is going. And it's clear, if you spend any time with her at all, that her thinking isn't right. She is paranoid, she is . . . no one sees it but my mother. Does she wish she were dying? But that is—impossible.

I had been pestering him constantly about—for the past year things had been getting from bad to worse and they were ignoring me . . . they didn't want to understand. This woman was not in her full mind. She didn't know what she was doing . . . She'd go into comas and you'd feel any day—and, of course, I felt a responsibility to Uncle Dave and Aunt Ida. You'd call them and—well, should they, shouldn't they come . . . I couldn't predict . . . They would come during those six months and visit me and say, "Oh, she's looking better," "she looks fine." And here she had just come out of a coma. The situation was so bad—I was made to feel guilty . . . I was looking upon her as she's dying and they were looking upon her as living . . . how dare I have such thoughts . . .

Grandma fell in the hospital and developed an aneurysm on her brain. When they operated, they found cancer all over her body. My parents took her home to die.

For the six months she was completely in a world—of her childhood, I guess. She looked upon me . . . it was as though you were—you know, things that you imagine in childhood, frightening things in childhood, these seem to have been the things that came out. The fact that her food was being poisoned. And this I will never forget: Aunt Ida coming to visit and listening, Grandma would tell her all these stories, and then she'd come out and say, "You know, it's very hard not to believe her." It was a horrible six months. It left me sick for ten years, really. It took me that long to get it all out of my system and, at times, it all comes back.

Thus began my mother's own long journey out of guilt and depression. I have a photograph of her taken a few years after grandma died. She is standing alone on the back porch, in a shirtwaist she has outgrown; her skin looks puffy and she is frowning at the camera. Lines of discontent and anger are set into her face.

My beautiful, slender, smiling mother had vanished.

I blamed myself for her unhappiness. I pretended to ignore her compulsive eating, the distant look she got in her eyes as she stuffed pieces of cake into her mouth, as if she were trying to ignore herself. She refused to clean the house, cooked for us grudgingly. Exploded in anger when my sister or I touched some hidden grievance. I remember meals when I choked on resentment, eating her misery. And it was always the same anger; there was no cleansing torrent of words. My monster mother. I longed for a perfect TV Donna Reed mother who handed her children bagged lunches as she kissed them good-bye and waved them out the door. My mother stormed out of the kitchen after supper and left my father to clean up and wash the dishes in silence.

It was impossible for me to love her then.

I was terrified that I had inherited her misery. She became very overweight, a near recluse. I was ashamed of her and rarely brought friends home from school.

As my body developed, I listened to her silences as if they were clearly spoken warnings. What do you suppose mothers tell their daughters? It is the words that are not spoken that we listen most closely to. My mother never told me, "When you have children, you'll see . . ." or, "When you're married you'll understand." I learned through her silence what was possible for myself.

When I left home to go to college, the list of activities forbidden by her grew longer: I was not to date gentile boys, I was not to go to political demonstrations, I was not to move off-campus, I was not . . . and yet, in some passive ways, she was *for* me. I was not happy in school. She tried to convince my father, who forbade me to drop out, that it might be good for me to work for awhile; but she gave in to his fear that "I would never go back." And another time, commiserating with me when I explained how shy and awkward I felt around other people, saying in intimate letters that yes, she too had felt shy and awkward at my age. She did not have any advice to give. I was old enough now to experience the pain for myself.

She was for me but could not help me. I turned away from her as I would hide an ugly photograph of myself.

I went to the political demonstrations; moved off-campus; made a new life, slowly, as an oyster would construct a pearl around a pin point of pain.

As I grew older and learned to love myself, I could let myself love her. A little.

She is talking to me now, my mother, as if we were old friends, bringing her story up to date, complaining about my father who has heart trouble and will not cut down on his work load. *She* has to do *his* worrying for him. He is like a sponge, taking, taking, taking. She is afraid he will drop dead and then who will she have to live out her years with? She should *do* something. What? Leave him? Who will support her? Trapped. And it is too late. I see that now.

It is depressing sitting with her in this room. This is the living room she has always wanted. We are surrounded by expensive furniture, an oriental rug, cut glass figures on polished wood. I look at her on the couch: she does not seem so much like a monster now. Her face is pale because she is on chemotherapy and cannot expose her skin to the sun. Her hair has fallen out but is growing back a beautiful snow white. She sits wigless in a cotton bathrobe, rubbing the sweat from her palms onto her robe.

"Well, do you have enough?" she asks, looking at the tape recorder.

"Yes, yes, thank you." But there is not one story that I can carry away with me like a favorite stone. There are long journeys and suffering, qualities of endurance and determination. An unbroken thread. Then there are the snags, the life stopped behind a sewing machine, smothered ambitions, hopeless complaints in a sterile ghost room. A mixed birthright.

"Lena," my mother says, "I just want to say one more thing." She pauses and looks away from me. "I don't want you to feel that you're going to get cancer. You know you have it on both sides of the family. I think—and some people might think this is crazy—I think you can make yourself sick. After grandma died, I was waiting for the day when I would get it. I was believing in it. This doesn't have to happen to you."

And I tell her that I understand.

Audre Lorde

The Beginning

Keystone Electronics was a relatively small factory as factories went in Stamford. It had a government contract to process and deliver quartz crystals used in radio and radar machinery. These small crystals were cut and processed from large quartz rocks which were shipped from Brazil, cut at the plant and then ground, refined, and classified, according to how heavy an electrical charge they held.

It was dirty work. The two floors of the plant rang with the whine of the huge cutting and refining machines. The mud used by the cutting crew covered everything, cemented by the heavy oil that the diamond-grit blades were mounted in. The mud saws, 32 of them, were always running. The air was heavy and acrid with the sickly fumes of the carbon tetra-chloride used to clean the crystals. Entering the plant after 8:00 in the morning was like entering Dante's Inferno. Offensive on every sense level possible, it was too cold an‹ too hot, gritty, noisy, ugly, sticky, stinking, and dangerous.

The guys ran the cutting machines. Most local men would not work under such conditions, so the cutting crew was composed of Puerto Ricans who were recruited in New York City and who commuted every morning up to Stamford on company-paid tickets. The women read the crystals on a variety of x-ray machines, or washed the thousands and thousands of crystals processed daily in huge vats of carbon tetrachloride.

All the help in the plant with the exception of the foreman and fore-women were black or Puerto Rican, and all the women were local, from the Stamford area.

Nobody mentioned that carbon tet destroys the liver and causes cancer of the kidneys. Nobody mentioned that the x-ray machines, when used un-shielded, delivered doses of constant low radiation far in excess of what was considered safe even in those days. Keystone Electronics hired black women and didn't fire them after three weeks. We even got to join the union.

I was hired to run one of the two x-ray machines that read the first cut-tings of raw quartz. This enabled the cutters to align their machines in such a way ‹s to maximize the charge from each rock. The electrical charge ran one way only, and differed from rock to rock. Two machines were therefore stationed directly outside of the cutting room, open to the noise and mud and grit flying from the stone-cutters. This was the least desirable job for women because of the unpleasant working conditions, and because there was no overtime or piecework bonuses to be made. The other machine was run by a young woman named Virginia, who everybody called Ginger. I met her the first morning in the luncheonette across the street from the plant where I stopped to get coffee and a roll to celebrate my first day on the new job.

We started work at 8:00 AM and quit at 4:30 PM. There was a 10 minute coffee break at 10:00 AM and at 2:30 PM, and a half-hour lunch break at noon.

The cutting 'boys' made the first cut through the thick grease and mud of the machines, and then brought those rough 2 inch slabs to Ginger or me to be read for an electrical charge. If the charge was too low, they altered the axis of their machines until the charge increased. I clipped the slab into a holder in the throat of my machine with my right hand and held it, while with my left hand, I turned the knob that altered the plane of the slab to reflect an electrical charge on the dial in the face of the machine. The reading was obtained by a small x-ray beam passed through the crystal. There was a hood to be flipped over that would cover my fingers and prevent the x-ray from touching, while the crystal was being read, but the second that it took to flip down the hood was often the difference between being yelled at for being too slow and a smooth working relationship with the cutters.

The rock was then sliced along the axis that had been marked with an oil pencil. We then read again, and it was sliced into slabs. Ginger and I read each of these slabs again, tossing them, thick with grime and mud, into the barrels next to our machines. Those slabs were then taken away, washed in carbon tetrachloride, and each slab cut into squares about 3/4 of an inch square. These finished crystals were then washed again and sent into the x-ray 'reading room,' a cleaner quieter place to work, where they were read on a finer x-ray machine and stacked according to degree charge.

The women in the x-ray reading room made piecework bonuses over a large base expectation output, and these jobs were considered desirable. By cutting corners and saving time and not flipping the hood, it was possible to make a small weekly bonus. It was not possible to cheat on readings, since the floorwoman spotchecked the readers' work.

How much x-ray we were exposed to was never mentioned, nor its effect.

After the first week I wondered if I could really stick it out. I thought that if I had to work under those conditions for the rest of my life I would slit my throat. Some mornings, I questioned how I could get through 8 hours of the stink and dirt and din and boredom. At 8:00 AM I would set my mind for two hours, saying to myself, you can last two hours, and then there will be a coffee break. I'd read my book brought from home for 10 minutes and then I'd set myself for another two hours, thinking, alright, you can last two hours until lunch. After lunch, when the machines behind us kicked over and began their roar and mudslinging, I would feel a little refreshed after my sardine sandwich, yet those two hours were the hardest of the day. It was a long time until the 2:30 break. But then I would tell myself, now, you can make it for two hours and then you'll be free.

Sometimes I stood waiting for the freight elevator in the early morning half-dark with the other workers, anxiously hoping the elevator wouldn't stall and the timeclock tick over into red, and I felt I could not possibly go through another day like the day before. But the elevator came, and I got on with the others.

There were women there who had worked at that plant for the ten years it had been open.

The coffee break for me meant a little time to get up from the high stool in front of the machine and walk around, or go to the bathroom. We were supposed to be allowed to go to the bathroom during working hours by the terms of the union contract, but Rose, my forewoman, didn't like it if we went too often. In my second week there, before I was taken into the union, she pulled me aside at lunchtime and with an archly significant smile told me that she thought I was a bright girl and could go places except I went to the bathroom too much.

I would not get paid for three weeks, and my meager hoard of NYC money was running dangerously low. It did not cover coffee breaks. Sometimes I would bring a book and stay at the machines and read. Ginger would bop off to the relative cleanliness of the "Reading Room" to talk with the other women. One day she clued me in.

"You better take your bottom off that chair in your breaks, girl, before you get glued to it. You can go crazy like that."

Those were my sentiments, exactly.

The cutters made piecework bonuses on their work although Ginger and I did not, and one day I had been hassled all morning by the men who said I was not giving them their readings fast enough, and was holding up their cuttings. At 10:00 they trooped downstairs for coffee, leaving their machines running, since it was only for 10 minutes. Under the cover of the noise, I dropped my head over the nape of the x-ray machine and burst into tears. At that point Ginger returned, having forgotten her change purse under the hamper of her machine. She punched me gently on the arm.

"See that? What'd I tell ya? You can go nuts with all that reading. What do ya take in your coffee? I'll buy ya a cup."

"No, thank you." I wiped my eyes, ruffled to be caught crying.

"No, thank you." Ginger giggled, mimicking my tone. "You sound just like a lady. C'mon, girl, please have some coffee. I can't handle these motherfuckers by myself for the rest of the day and they's out for blood this morning. Hurry up, what'll you have?"

"Very light with sugar." I smiled in gratitude.

"Atta girl," she said, with her usual jocular laugh, and rolled on off down the narrow aisle separating our machines from the cutting room din.

That's how Ginger and I became friends. That Thursday, she invited me to drive downtown with her mother and her to cash our checks. Thursday night was the big shopping night in Stamford.

It was my first paycheck in three weeks. It was customary for factories in Stamford to hold back your first week's pay until you left the job, as a deposit, so to speak, upon your space. By that time I was on pretty short rations. Thursday was payday in factories, and Stamford in those days was a factory town. On Thursday nights, the shops on Atlantic Avenue were lively and late, whereas on every other night the town rolled up the sidewalks at 5:30 PM. Everybody turned out to market and shop and cash checks and socialize downtown. People parked on the main streets and chatted with the passersby, no matter that tomorrow was Friday and work to contend with.

Ginger told me she had spotted me in town the first Thursday I was there, before I came to work at Keystone.

"That's right. Blue-jeans and sneakers on Atlantic Avenue on Thursday night! I said to myself, who's this slick kitty from the city?" I laughed at the idea that anyone could call me slick, and held my peace.

Ginger invited me home for dinner that Thursday night, and I realized as I had a third helping of mashed potatoes that I had almost forgotten what home-cooked food tasted like. I could see redheaded Ruth, Ginger's youngish brash mother, looking at me half in amusement, half in annoyance. Ginger had four younger brothers at home, and Ruth had a lot of young hungry mouths to feed. Ginger herself was twenty-five, and had returned home three years before after a bad marriage.

Sometimes Ginger would bring me a roll from home in the mornings, sometimes she would walk over to my house on Mill River Road in the evening after work and invite me out for a hamburger at the White Castle near the bridge, which was the only place in town open after 6:00.

Ginger had a battery-powered portable radio, a gift from her now divorced husband, and before the weather turned cold, we would go into the beautiful autumn evenings and sit out by the bankment of the Rippowam River that faced my house, and listen to Fats Domino on WJRZ. His "Blueberry Hill" was tops on the Hit Parade through most of that fall, and Ginger had a special place in her heart for him anyway, since they looked so much alike. She even walked like Fats, with a swing-bopping step.

Ginger talked, and I listened. I soon discovered that if you keep your mouth shut, people are apt to believe you know everything, and they begin to feel freer and freer to tell you everything, anxious to show that they know something, too.

"How'd you hear about the job at Keystone, anyway?"

"At the West Main Community Center."

"Good ole Crispus Attucks."

"What's that?" We turned the corner onto Main Street and headed for Grants.

"The Center, Stupid. It was just renamed in honor of a Negro, we shouldn't mind that they don't want us using the Center downtown."

"Yes, but who's it named for?"

"You mean you really don't know who he is?" Ginger screwed her face up, unbelieving. She cocked her head and wrinkled her brows at me.

"Well, I haven't been around here that long, you know," I countered, defensively.

"Well I'll be dipped. Slick kitty from the city! What kind of a school was that you all went to?" Her round incredulous eyes almost disappearing into the folds of her wrinkled-up face. "You never heard of Crispus Attucks? I thought everybody knew about him. The first cat to die in the Revolutionary War, in Concord, Massachusetts. A black man, name of Crispus Attucks. The shot heard round the world. Everybody knows that. They renamed our Center after him." Ginger squeezed my arm again as we entered the store. "And they got you the job at Keystone. I'm glad they've done something useful, after all."

But there was a sale on nylons, three pair for $1.25, or 50 cents a pair. The Korean War was already pushing prices back up, and this was a good buy. Ginger tried to decide if she wanted to spend that much for three pair, even at such a buy.

"Come on, girl, why don't you get a pair with me," she suggested, "they're real cheap, and your legs are going to get cold, even in pants."

"I don't wear them. I hate nylons. Besides, I can't stand the way they feel on my legs." What I didn't say was that I couldn't stand the bleached-out color they gave my legs, that so-called-neutral shade all cheap nylons were, the only ones I could afford. Ginger looked at me pleadingly, wanting me to help her decide. And I relented. It wasn't her fault really that I was feeling so out of sorts all of a sudden, so disjointed. Something had slipped out of place.

"Oh, buy them," I said. "You want them and you can always use them. 'Sides, your mother will never let them go to waste." I ran my fingers over the fine mesh of the display stockings, hung by their heels from a T rack on the counter. The dry slippery touch of nylon and silk always filled me with distrust and suspicion. The ease with which those materials passed through my fingers made me uneasy. They were illusive, confusing, not to be depended upon. Something about the uneven and resistant textures of cotton and wool seemed to me to allow for more honesty, a more straightforward connection through touch.

But most of all, I hated the pungent, unliving and ungiving smell of nylon, its adamant refusal to ever become human or evocative in its odor. Its harshness was never tempered by the scent of the wearer, no matter how long they wore the clothing, nor in what weather. A person dressed in nylon always approached my nose like a warrior approaching a tourney, clad all in chain-mail.

I fingered the nylon while my mind hammered elsewhere. Because Ginger was right. I prided myself on my collection of odds and ends of random information, more and less useful, gathered through my avid curiosity and endless reading. I stored these garnered tidbits on the back burner of my consciousness with attentive care, to be pulled forward on any appropriate occasion. I was used to being the one who knew some fact that everybody else in the conversation had not yet learned. It was not that I believed I knew EVERYTHING, just more than most other people around me.

Having made up her mind, Ginger handed the three pair of tissue-wrapped stockings to the woman behind the counter, and stood waiting for her change.

Crispus Attucks. How was that possible? I had spent four years in Hunter High School, supposedly the best public high school in New York City, with the most academically advanced, intellectually accurate, and historically informed education available for preparing bright, knowledgeable young women for college and career. I had been taught by some of the most highly considered historians in the country. Yet I had never once heard the name mentioned of the first man to fall in the American Revolution, nor ever been told the fact that he was Negro. What did that mean?

Ginger's voice was a cheerful, soothing murmur over my thoughts as she talked me partway up the hill back to my room in the house on Mill River Street.

"What's wrong with you, today? Cat got your tongue?"

Before long, I was totally dependent upon Ginger as my only human contact in Stamford, and her invitations to Sunday dinner represented the only real food I ever ate that winter. She built up an incredible mythology about me and what my life had been like in New York. I did nothing to dissuade her. All I ever told her was that I had left home when I was 17 and gotten my own apartment. She thought that was very daring. She had gotten married when she was 20 in order to get out of her mother's house.

Now she was back, divorced, but with a certain amount of autonomy, purchased by her weekly contributions to the family income. Her mother worked as a bench-press operator at American Cyanimid, and her father was diabetic and blind. Her mother's lover lived with them, and so did Ginger's four younger brothers.

Ginger was another one who thought I had everything taped. She saw me as a citified little baby butch, bright, knowledgeable and secure enough to be a good listener. I remained determinedly and blissfully oblivious to all of this for as long as possible. Ginger waited for me to make the first move, sure that I was an old and accomplished hand at the seduction of young divorcees. But her inviting glances and throaty chuckles were never enough, nor were the delicious tidbits she would sneak out of Ruth's kitchen and wrap up in handkerchiefs, persuading Charlie, her mother's lover, to drive her over to Mill River Street in his truck on his way to his night job. I determinedly refused to acknowledge what they were intended to tempt me toward. Perfumed and delectable, Ginger perched on my desk chair in the tiny 2nd floor room, watching incredulously as I sat cross-legged on my bed, wolfing down her mother's goodies.

One weekend Ginger stole a lobster claw for me. Charlie had bought the lobster as a make-up present for Ruth's dinner, and Ruth threatened to throw Ginger out of the house. Ginger decided this was all getting too costly, and she made her own move. Long goodnight kisses on the back porch were definitely not enough.

By the beginning of November, autumn was closing down. The trees were incredible colors, but the edge of winter was already in the air. The days were getting shorter and shorter, and my heart was not happy. There was very little time after work before sunset. If I went to the library it was dark by the time I walked back to Mill River Street. Keystone was a daily trial that did not seem to get better nor easier, despite Ginger's warmhearted attempts to cheer me up during our frightful days.

One Thursday after work, Ginger borrowed her brother Rayray's old, beat-up Ford and we went downtown to cash our checks alone, without Ruth or Charlie or any of the boys. It was still light when we were through, and I could tell Ginger had something on her mind. We drove around town for a while. "What's up?" I asked.

"C'mon," Ginger said, "Let's go up on the hill."

Ginger was not much of a nature lover, but she had taken me to see her favorite spot, a wooded hill on the west edge of town where, hidden from view by the overgrown bushes and trees, we could sit on two old tree stumps left from long ago, smoking and listening to Fats Domino and watching the sun go down.

I found ma' thrill-l-l-l-lll
On Blueberreeee Hill----lllll.

We left the car and climbed to the top of the hill. The air was chill as we sat on the stumps to catch our breaths.

"Cold?"

"No," I said, pulling my ragged suede jacket, inherited from Rayray, around me.

"I think you should get a warm coat or something, winters around here ain't like in New York."

"I have a coat, I just don't like to wear it, that's all."

Ginger sucked her teeth. "Yeah, I know. Who you think you kidding? If it's money I can lend you some till Christmas."

"Thank you, Ginger, but I don't need a coat."

Ginger walked back and forth, puffing nervously on her Lucky Strike.

I sat looking up at her. What was going on, and what did she want me to say? I didn't want a coat, because I did not mind the cold.

"You really think you're slick, huh?" Ginger turned to face me, regarding me with a slight smile and narrowed eyes, her head up and to one side like a pigeon. But her voice was high and nervous.

"You always say that, Ginger, and I keep telling you I'm not slick. What are you talking about?"

"Slick kitty from the city. Well, baby, you don't have to keep your mouth shut around me, because I know all about you, and your friends."

What was it that Ginger had discovered, or more likely, invented in her own mind about me that I would now have to pretend to fulfill? When I had told her I didn't drink, she didn't believe me. I promptly downed two straight vodkas to fulfill her image of hard-drinking New York Village girls. Whatever I had told her about my friends, and I talked about them more than about anything else, she had drawn the wrong conclusions.

"All about me and my friends?" I was starting to get the drift of her conversation, and I was beginning to get acutely uncomfortable. I didn't even know why.

Ginger butted her cigarette, took a deep breath, and moved a few steps closer.

"Look, it's no big thing. Are you gay or aren't you?" She took another deep breath.

I smiled up at her and said nothing. I certainly couldn't say I don't know. Actually, I was at a loss as to what to say. I could not bring myself to deny what I had just decided to embrace; besides, to say no would have been to admit being one of the squares. But to say yes might commit me to somehow proving it. And Ginger was a woman of the world, not one of my high school girl friends with whom kissing and cuddling and fantasizing sufficed, and I had never really made love to a woman before. Ginger, of course, by this time had made up her mind that I was a woman of the world and that I knew everything, having made love to all the women about whom I talked with such intensity.

I stood up, urgently feeling the need to have our eyes level with each other.

"C'mon, now, you can't just not answer me, girl. Are you or aren't you?" Ginger's voice was pleading as well as impatient. She was right; I couldn't not answer. I opened my mouth, not knowing what was going to come out.

"Yes," I said. Maybe it would all stop there.

Ginger's brown face broke into her wonderful full-cheeked half-smile, half-grin. Instinctively, I grinned back. And joining hands there on the top of the hill, with the sound of the car-radio drifting upward through the open door below, we stood grinning at each other while the sun went down.

I had known that Ginger was flirting with me, but had ignored it because I was at a loss as to how to handle the situation. As far as I knew, she was sweet and attractive and warm and lovable, and straight as a die.

Snapping little dark eyes, skin the color of well-buttered caramel, and a body like the Venus of Willendorf. Ginger was gorgeously fat, with an open knowledge about her body's movement that was delicate and precise. Her breasts were high and ample, and she had pads of firm fat upon her thighs, and round dimpled knees. Her swift, tapered hands and little feet were also deeply dimpled. Her high putchy cheeks and great mischievous smile were framed by wide bangs and a short pageboy that was sometimes straightened, sometimes left to wave tightly over her ears. Sometimes when Ginger had been to the beauty parlour she came back feather-bobbed and adorable but much less real. Shortly after we met at the plant, she began to resist her mother Ruth's nagging and stopped going to the hairdresser's altogether. Once I trimmed it for her, and the crinkly mass of hair hung down on either side of her face, standing out slightly as it fell, alive and wavy. With the straight bangs across her low forehead, Ginger looked like she was wearing an Egyptian headpiece.

"What's the matter? Cat got your tongue?" Ginger turned back to me; our hands, still joined, fell apart.

"It's getting late," I answered. I was very hungry.

Ginger's brow puckered and she sucked her teeth into the fading light. "Are you for real? What d'ya mean, it's getting late? Is that all you can think about?"

Oh. Obviously that was not what Ginger was expecting to hear.

What did she want me to say, I wondered. What am I supposed to do, now?

Ginger's round face was a hand's span away from my own. She spoke softly, with her usual cockiness. Her close voice and the smell of her face-powder made me at once both uneasy and excited. "Why don't you kiss me? I don't bite."

Her words were bold but beneath them I could feel her fear of rejection, belying their self-assurance.

Oh hell, I thought. What am I doing here, anyway, I should have known it wasn't going to stop there, I knew it I knew it and suppose she wants me to take her to . . . oh shit! What am I going to do now?

Afraid to lose some face I never had, obediently, I bent forward slightly. I started to kiss Ginger's cupid's-bow mouth, and her soft lips parted. My heart lurched and quickened, oddly. Down the hill, the car-radio was just finishing the news. I felt Ginger's quick breath upon my face, expectant and slightly tinged with coughdrops and cigarettes and coffee. It was warm and exciting in the chilly night air and I kissed her again thinking, this isn't a bad idea at all . . .

When Ginger and I got back to the house, Charlie had left for work with his Railroad Express supply truck. Ruth and the boys had already eaten dinner, and the two younger ones were ready for bed. As we came in the front door, Ruth was just coming downstairs with Teddy's dinner-tray. Ginger had explained to me that her father never left his room anymore except to go to the bathroom.

Ruth and Ray, her oldest son, had gone marketing for the week, and she was tired. Her henna-red curly hair was caught behind each ear with a baby-blue ribbon, and untidy bangs almost covered her heavily madeup eyes.

"We ate Chinese tonight to give me a break. And we didn't leave any for you girls because I didn't know if you were going to get something out. Ginger, don't forget to leave your house-money on the table."

There was only a hint of a triumphant reproach in Ruth's voice. Chinese food was a rare treat.

I usually spent the night at Ginger's house on the Thursdays we got paid. While Ginger put away the dishes her brothers had washed, and made the boys' lunches for school, I went upstairs to take a quick bath. The morning started early, at 5:00 AM, when Ruth rose to take care of Teddy before she went to her job.

"And don't leave that water running in the tub the way you like to, neither!" Ruth called out to me from the room she and Charlie shared as I passed by. "You're not in New York now and water costs money!"

I had grown up in apartments all my life. I was accustomed to thinking of hot water as an either/or commodity. Either you had it, or you didn't have it. If the water was hot, when it was hot, it was hot in inexhaustible amounts. This was not true of a 60 gallon tank serving 9 people.

When Ginger had returned to her parents' house after the end of her marriage, the small house on Walker Road was bursting with four growing boys, Ruth and Charlie the boarder, and diabetic, blind Teddy, Ginger's father.

Charlie and the boys glassed in the front sunporch and insulated it, and that became Ginger's room. Downstairs and at the front of the house with its own entrance, it was rather secluded from the rest of the house, once everyone had retired.

By the time Ginger finished taking her shower, I was already in bed. I lay with my eyes closed, wondering if I could pretend to be asleep, and, if not, what would be the sophisticated and dykely thing to do.

Ginger took much longer than usual preparing herself for bed. She sat at her little desk-table, creaming her legs and braiding her hair, humming softly snatches of songs under her breath as she buffed her nails.

"If I came home tonight, would you still be my . . . ."

"Come on-a my house, my house-a come on, come on . . . ."

"I saw the harbor lights, they only told me we were . . . ."

In between my anxieties about my anticipated performance, I began to feel the rising excitement of the hill returning. It challenged the knot of terror I felt at the thought of Ginger's unknown expectations, at the thought of sexual confrontation, at the thought of being tried and found wanting. I smelled little breezes of Cashmere Bouquet powder and Camay soap as Ginger moved her arm back and forth, buffing away. What was she doing?

It didn't occur to me that Ginger, despite her show of coolness and bravado, was almost as nervous as I. After all, this wasn't just playing around with some hometown kid at the plant. This was actually going to bed with a real live New York City Greenwich Village Bulldagger.

"Aren't you coming to bed," I asked, finally, a little surprised at the urgency of my own voice.

"Well, I thought you'd never ask." With an almost relieved chuckle, Ginger shed her robe, snapped off the dresser lamp, and bounced into bed beside me.

Until the very moment that our naked bodies touched in that old brass bed that creaked in the insulated sunporch on Walker Road, I had no idea of what I was doing there, nor of what I wanted to do there. I had no idea of what making love to another woman meant. I only knew, dimly, it was something I wanted to happen, and something that was different from anything I had ever done before.

I reached out and put an arm around Ginger, and through the scents of powder and soap and handcream I could smell the rising flush of her own spicy heat. I took her into my arms, and suddenly, Ginger became precious to me beyond compare. I kissed her upon her mouth, this time with no thought at all. My mouth moved to the little hollow beneath her ear.

Ginger's breath warmed my neck and started to quicken. My hands moved down over her round body, silky and fragrant, waiting to be opened and loved. Uncertainty and doubt rolled away from the mouth of my need like a great stone, and my unsureness dissolved in the directing heat of my own frank and finally open desire.

Our bodies found the movements we needed to fit each other. Ginger's flesh was sweet and moist and firm as a winter pear. I felt her and tasted her deeply, until my hands and my mouth and my whole body knew her rhythms. Her flesh opened to me like a peony and the richness and wonder of her woman's pleasure brought me back to her body over and over again throughout the night. The tender moist nook between her legs, veiled with her thick crispy dark hair, was a hidden harbour where I dove for treasure beyond naming, and surfaced dizzy and blessed with her rich taste and the sounds of completed loving.

Once, as she cradled my head between her breasts, Ginger whispered, "I could tell you knew how," and the pleasure and satisfaction in her voice started my tides flowing again and I moved down against her once more, my body upon hers, ringing like a bell.

I never questioned where my knowledge of her body and her need came from. Loving Ginger that night was like coming home to a joy I was meant for, and I only wondered, silently, how I had not always known that it would be so.

Ginger moved in love like she laughed, openly and easily, and I moved with her, against her, within her, like upon an ocean of brown warmth. Her sounds of delight and the deep shudders of relief that rolled through her body in the wake of my stroking fingers filled me with delight and a hunger for yet more of her. The wet sweetness of her body meeting filling my mouth my hands my whole physical self felt right and completing, as if I had been born to make love to this woman, and was remembering her body rather than learning it deeply for the first time.

In wonder but without surprise, I lay finally quiet with my arms around Ginger. So this was what I had been so afraid of not doing properly. How ridiculous and far away those fears seemed now, as if I thought it were some task outside of myself, rather than simply reaching out and letting my own desire guide me. It was all so simple. I felt so good I smiled into the darkness. Ginger cuddled closer: "We better get some sleep," she muttered, "Keystone tomorrow," and drifted off.

There was only an hour or so before the alarm went off and I lay awake, trying to fit everything together, trying to reassure myself that I was in control and did not need to be afraid. And what, I wondered, was my relationship now to this delicious woman who lay asleep on my arm? This Ginger by night seemed so different from the Ginger I knew by day. It was as if some beautiful and mythic creature created by my own need had suddenly taken the place of my jovial and matter-of-fact buddy.

Once, earlier, Ginger had reached out to touch the wet warmth of my woman's place and I had turned her hand aside without thinking and without knowing why. But I knew that I was still hungry for her cries of joy and the soaring wonder of her body moving beneath mine, guided by a power that flowed through me from the charged core between my legs.

Ginger was my friend, the only friend I had made in this strange town, and I loved her, but with caution. We had slept together. Did that mean we were lovers?

A few months after Gennie had died, I was walking down Broadway late one spring Saturday afternoon. I had just had another argument with my mother, and I was going to the A&P to get milk. I dawdled along the avenue looking into shop windows, not wanting to return to the tensions and misunderstandings waiting for me at home.

I paused in front of Stolz's Jewelers, admiring their new display. In particular, I marked a pair of hanging earrings of black opals, set into worked silver. "Gennie will love those," I thought, "I must remember to tell her . . ." and then it hit me again that Gennie was dead, and that meant that she would never be there ever again. It meant that I could not ever tell her anything more. It meant that whether I loved her or was angry at her or wanted her to see a new pair of earrings, none of that mattered or would ever matter to her again. I could share nothing at all with her anymore because she was gone.

And even after all the past weeks of secret mourning, Gennie's death became real to me in a different way.

I turned away from the Jewelry Store window. And right then and there in the middle of Broadway and 151st Street on a Saturday afternoon at the beginning of the summer of my 16th year, I decided that I would never love anybody else again for the rest of my life. Gennie had been the first person in my life I was conscious of loving. And she had died. Loving hurt too much. My mother had turned into a demon intent on destroying me. You loved people and you came to depend on their being there. But people died or changed or went away and it hurt too much. The only way

to avoid that pain was not to love anyone, and not to let anyone get too
close or too important. The secret to not being hurt like this again, I de-
cided, was never depending on anyone's being there, never needing, never
loving. It was the last dream of children, to be forever untouched.

I wiped my eyes on the shoulder of my shirt and got to the A&P just
before it closed.

I heard the oil-burner in the basement at Walker Road kick over at
5:30 AM, and Ginger shifted and sighed softly in her sleep. I started to
kiss her awake and stopped, as the smells of our loving and the moist top
of her sleepy head engulfed me in a sudden wave of tenderness so strong
that I pulled back.

"You better watch out," I said to myself soundlessly in the dark.

The alarm went off, and Ginger and I, galvanized by the hectic morning
routine of the house, grabbed our robes and raced upstairs to the bathroom.

One minute more and we would have to stand in line with the boys,
and maybe miss our ride with Charlie, who would soon be returning from
work. There was just time for a hurried hug and a kiss over the washbowl,
as Ginger brushed out the tangles in her hair that had become unbraided
during the night.

Charlie dropped us off on the other side of the railroad tracks, a block
away from the plant. Ginger stopped in and bought buttered rolls and
coffee for us in the luncheonette across the street from Keystone.

"We gonna need something to keep up awake today after last night,"
she grunted, nudging me under-cover of pushing through the mob at the
entrance to the plant building. We winked like conspirators at each other
as we waited in the crowd for the freight elevator to take us up into hell.

All day I watched Ginger carefully for a lead as to how we were going
to treat the extraordinary events of the night before.

Ginger refused to believe that I had never made love to a woman before, and I did not press the point. A piece of me, also, was invested in
her image of me as the gay young blade, the seasoned and accomplished
lover from the big city.

I enjoyed paying court to Ginger, and being treated, in private, like a
swain. It gave me a sense of power and privilege that was heady, if illusory,
since I knew on one level it was all play-acting.

On that level, it was play-acting for Ginger because she could not really
regard a relationship between two women as anything other than a lark.
She could not consider it important, even as she sought it and cherished
it. On that level, it was play-acting for me because I knew I wasn't the assured and experienced bulldyke Ginger fantasized me as being. At the
same time, on a true and deeper level, Ginger and I met as two young

black women in need of each other's warmth and blood-assurance, able
to share the passions within our bodies, and no amount of pretending that
we were pretending could change that.

But we were both very much invested in the denial of our importance
to each other. For different reasons, we both needed to pretend we didn't
care.

Each of us was very busy being cool, and totally ignoring and misnam-
ing the passionate intensity with which we came together wherever possible, usually on that old brass bed in the insulated sunporch, that drafty
haven on Walker Road which we turned tropical with the heat of our wild
bodies.

As long as I convinced myself that I wasn't really involved emotionally
with Ginger, I could delight in this new experience. After all, wasn't her
favorite expression, "Be cool, girl!"?

I congratulated myself on how cool I was. It didn't bother me, I main-
tained, that Ginger went out on dates which Ruth arranged.

With her typical aplomb, Ruth welcomed my increased presence around
the house with the rough familiarity and browbeating humor due another
one of her daughters. If she recognized the sounds emanating from the
sunporch on the nights I slept over, or our haggard eyes the next day, she
ignored them. But she made it very clear that she expected Ginger to get
married again.

"Friends are nice but marriage is marriage," she said to me one night as
she helped me make a skirt on her machine, and I wondered why Ginger
had asked me over and then gone to the movies with a friend of Ruth's
from American Cyanimid. "And when she gets home don't be thumping
that bed all night, neither, because it's late already and you girls have
work tomorrow."

But I thought about little else now at work besides the night pleasures
of Ginger's body, and how I could arrange to get her over to Mill River
Street for an hour or so after work. It was a little more private than Walker
Road, except that my old bed creaked so badly too that we always had to
put the mattress on the floor.

I gave up my room on Mill River Street with its creaky bed, and moved
my belongings into the sunporch on Walker Road. The $10 a week room
and board was less than what I was spending for both before. Ruth said,
the extra cash was a help to her already strained budget, and besides, I
was eating her out of house and home anyway. With the exception of my
father, I had never lived around men before. Ginger's family, Ruth, her
four adolescent brothers and her father and Uncle Charlie, was a revelation
to me. Ginger's mother, Ruth, for all her independent ways and sharp
tongue, served others before herself, always. Ginger and Ruth's tacit assumption that women deferred to all men, even 14 year old man-samples,

shocked and infuriated me. In my mind, this was one of the oddities of the Thurman household.

Later, Ginger told me that it was my questioning her on Ruth's making the boys school-lunch every morning before work that made Ruth conclude, "She's gotta be a bulldagger." But on the whole, Ginger's brothers were inoffensive boys, and to me, the most annoying sign of their presence was finding a drop or two on the edge of the toilet bowl, or having to check always to see that the toilet seat was down before I perched in the middle of the night.

Ginger told me that a new girl, Ada, had been hired to run my machine at the plant. Since I was a member of the union, I was given another job. I was moved on to an x-ray machine in the Reading Room, where the finished electronic crystals were fine-read according to strength of charge, then racked for packing.

Although this job paid the same $1.10 an hour, all the jobs in the RR were preferable and sought after. The room was enclosed by glass panels which set it off in the middle of the floor from the rest of the factory, and the fierce sensory assaults of the rest of the plant were somewhat muted.

We sat at our machines in a circle, facing outward, our backs to each other to discourage talking. There were 6 commercial x-ray machines and a desk in the middle for Rose, our forewoman. We were never long away from her watchful eye.

But working in the RR meant there was a chance to make piece-work bonus.

Each reader obtained her crystals from the washing cage in boxes of 200. Taking them back to our machines, one by one we inserted the tiny, 3/4 inch squares of wafer-thin rock into the throat of the x-ray machine, twirled the dial until the needle jumped to its highest point, powered by the tiny x-ray beam flashed across the crystal, snatched it off the mount, racked it in the proper slot, and then shot another crystal into the machine. With concentration and dexterity, the average amount one could read in a day was 1000 crystals.

By not taking the time to flip down the protective shield that kept the x-ray from hitting our fingers, we could increase that number to about 1100. Any crystals over 1200 read in one day were paid for as piece-work, at the rate of $5.00 a 100. Some of the women who had been at Keystone for years had perfected the motions and moved so swiftly that they were able to make from $5.00 to $10.00 some weeks in bonus. For most of them, the tips of their fingers were permanently darkened from exposure to x-ray. Before I finally left Keystone Electronics, there were dark marks on my fingers also, that only gradually faded.

After each crystal was read, it was flipped out of the machine and rapidly slipped into one of five slots in a rack that sat to the side of each of our machines. From these racks, periodically, a runner from the packing department would collect the crystals of whatever category was needed for the packers. Since it was not possible to keep track of the crystals after they were read, a tally was kept at the washing cage of how many boxes of crystals were taken daily by each reader. It was upon this count that our bonuses were based.

Throughout the day, Rose came by each machine regularly and spot-checked crystals from each of our racks, checking to make sure that no one racked unread crystals, or rushed through crystals with incorrect readings in order to raise our counts and make bonus.

The first two weeks I worked in the RR I talked to no one, raced my readings every day, never flipped the shield, and made three dollars in bonus. I decided I would have to reassess the situation. Ginger and I talked about it one night.

"You'd better slow down a little at work. The word's going out you're an eager-beaver, brown-nosing Rose."

I was offended. "I'm not ass-kissing, I'm trying to make some money. There's nothing wrong with that, is there?"

"Don't you know those rates are set so high that nobody can beat them? If you break your ass to read so many, you're going to show up the other girls and before you know it, they're going to raise the day rate again, figuring if you can do it so can everybody. And that just makes everybody look bad. They're never going to let you make any money in that place, don't you know that yet? All the books you read and you don't know that yet?" Ginger rolled over and tapped the book I was reading on my pillow.

But I was determined. I knew I could not take Keystone Electronics for much longer, and I knew I needed some money put aside before I left. Where would I go when I got back to New York? Where would I live until I got a job? And how long would I have to look for work? And on the horizon like a dim star, was my hope of going to Mexico. I had to make some money.

Ginger and Ada went to the movies more and more often now that I was living at the Thurman's, and I was determined not to care. But my sixth sense told me I had to get away, and soon.

My daily rate of crystals began to increase steadily. Rose came by more and more often to my machine, but could find nothing wrong with my crystals nor their slotting. She even went so far as to ask me to turn out my jeans pockets, one evening as we were leaving at 4:30. I was outraged, but complied. By the next pay day, I had made an additional $30.00 in bonus money for one week. That was almost as much as my weekly wages. It became the talk of the RR women.

"How does she manage to do all those?"

"Just wait and see. She's going to burn her fingers off before she's through." The women lowered their voices as I came back from the cage with a fresh box of crystals. But Ada, Ginger's new workmate who had stopped by for a brief chat, did not care whether or not I heard her parting words.

"I don't know what she's doing with them crystals, but I bet she's not reading them!"

She was right. I could not even tell Ginger how I was managing to pull down such high bonuses; although she often asked. I knew she was hurt by my silence, and by what she saw as my disloyalty to the other RR women. I was angered by the feeling of persistent guilt that her words aroused in me, but I could say nothing. I could also say nothing about the increasing time she and Ada spent together.

I longed for a chance to be alone, to enjoy the privacy that was not possible once I started to share the sunporch on Walker Road. I hated the amount of time I spent thinking about Ginger and Ada. I began to feel more and more desperate to get out of Stamford, and my bonuses at the plant went up.

I made bonus by slipping crystals into my socks every time I went to the bathroom. Once inside the toilet stall, I chewed them up with my strong teeth and flushed the little shards of rock down the commode. I could take care of between 50 and 100 crystals a day in that manner.

One day in the beginning of March, I saw Rose talking to Bernie, the plant's efficiency expert, and looking after me speculatively as I came out of the john. I knew my days at Keystone were numbered. That week I made $40 in bonuses.

On Friday Rose told me that the plant was cutting back readers and they were going to have to let me go. Since I was a member of the union, they gave me two weeks severance pay so I would leave immediately and not make a fuss. Even though it was what I wanted to happen, I still cried a little on the way home. "Nobody likes to be fired," Ginger said, and held my hand.

Ruth was sorry to lose the extra income. Ginger said she'd miss me, but was also secretly relieved. I made plans to return to New York City.

Lesbian Short Fiction in the Classroom

Contributors' Biographies

Work by Contributors

Elly Bulkin

Lesbian Short Fiction in the Classroom

I.

Nothing in my formal education prepared me to teach lesbian short fiction—or, for that matter, any lesbian literature. I had learned, of course, about the history of the short story in the United States and the proper things to say about narrative form, character development, and point of view. I had been assigned a number of short stories written by women who were described in our classes and texts as "single," "spinsters," or "living with their widowed mothers." But about how to teach literature that was clearly *by* lesbian writers, much less literature that was *about* lesbian characters, I learned nothing at all.

The articles that have appeared in the past few years about teaching lesbian material have all been written by women who are lesbians, and, for the most part, have been directed at other lesbian teachers.[1] Nothing, as far as I know, has yet been published by a non-lesbian teacher about how to approach the related subjects of lesbianism and homophobia in the classroom. The silence is, I think, reflective of what is going on—or, perhaps more accurately, not going on—in far too many women's studies classrooms.[2]

Women not already known as lesbians have some understandably good reasons for being nervous about teaching lesbian material. Some are connected to the fear of being identified as a lesbian, accurately or not, and of the attendant dangers of loss of job security, future work options, or the respect and affection of non-lesbian students and colleagues. On most campuses, the existence alone of a women's studies program or women's center raises the specter of a lesbian presence: writing about "Lesbians in Academia," Peg Cruikshank says: "I had been on campus less than a week when a woman professor said to me, 'Now, Peg, don't let those lesbians take over the women's center.' Curious, I went to the center to ask what it offered for lesbians. Nothing. 'We haven't been able to get any lesbians to come here,' said the person in charge. So much for lesbian takeover."[3] Assumptions like these, which threaten the funding of a women's program, contribute to the overall pressure not to speak out as a lesbian or, regardless of sexual/affectional preference, not to be identified as a woman who takes strong anti-heterosexist positions—using lesbian material in her own courses in an organic way, raising issues of homophobia consistently in classes and departmental meetings.

The non-lesbian teacher also has to contend with her fear of saying the "wrong" thing, of making the comment that clearly signals her own homophobia. The fear can stem, I think, from some combination of her own conscientious commitment and her own feelings about coping with the anger of lesbian women. Too often, the temptation is to wait to speak about lesbianism in the classroom until some point at which homophobia has been totally eradicated, along with even the faintest possibility that one's own bias might be publicly revealed. In many ways, the dynamic of the non-lesbian woman teaching lesbian material parallels that of the white woman teaching work by women of color. As Nancy Hoffman has said in "White Woman, Black Women: Inventing an Adequate Pedagogy":

> There are two principles for white women who would teach about black women. First, do your research and class preparation more thoroughly than you would for teaching about your own female tradition or the majority white male Anglo-American one. You must be able to generalize about black women's culture when appropriate, and you will probably feel ill at ease when doing so. Second, be prepared to play dual and conflicting roles; only sometimes will your own anti-racism and your solidarity with other women protect you from representing the group oppressing black women.[4]

These comments have particular relevance for the teacher of lesbian literature, lesbian and non-lesbian, who does not share class, race, or other identities with a given writer.[5] As a white, middle-class lesbian, for example, I have a far easier time teaching the work of lesbians of my own race and class, than the work of poor, working-class and/or Third World lesbians. While some non-lesbian women might consider me simply "a lesbian"—just as some people might consider me simply "a woman"—I need to be clear in my teaching about the complexities of my multiple identities.

Both teaching and preparing to teach lesbian fiction—or other lesbian writing—involve exploring the implications of these differences in personal/political *as well as* intellectual terms. For the non-lesbian teacher, exploring her homophobia and then confronting it consistently in herself and in her teaching involve values totally alien to the prevailing academic reverence for abstraction, intellect, and "objectivity," and the dismissal of experience, feeling, and subjective awareness. Making such a commitment means considering the issues raised by Cherríe Moraga:

> But it is not really difference the oppressor fears so much
> as similarity. He fears he will discover in himself the same
> aches, the same longings as those of the people he has shitted
> on. He fears the immobilization threatened by his own incipi-
> ent guilt. He fears he will have to change his life once he has
> seen himself in the bodies of the people he has called different.
> He fears the hatred, anger, and vengeance of those he has hurt.
>   This is the oppressor's nightmare, but it is not exclusive to
> him. We women have a similar nightmare, for each of us in
> some way has been both oppressed and the oppressor. We are
> afraid to look at how we have failed each other. We are afraid
> to see how we have taken the values of our oppressor into our
> hearts and turned them against ourselves and one another. We
> are afraid to admit how deeply "the man's" words have been
> ingrained in us. [6]

The failure to explore this fear, to make connections between feelings
and actions in the classroom, necessarily impedes the non-lesbian teacher
from dealing as effectively as she might with lesbian literature and related
issues. For teacher and student alike, written information *alone* is extremely limited in changing the homophobia that stands between the non-lesbian
woman and the lesbian literature. Even when the *knowledge* of lesbian
existence and oppression is present, some level of unexplored homophobia
can remain as a barrier.[7]

Crucial to my analysis is my own assumption that we have all—lesbian
and non-lesbian—been socialized to be homophobic; in this society, it is not
possible to have avoided it. If we have chosen (or discovered) our own lesbian sexual/affectional preference, we have had to overcome our own
homophobia to have done so—and each of us continues to deal periodically with its remnants. In this, as in other areas where we have learned a bias
and can serve, however unintentionally, as oppressors, the responsibility is
not for what we have been taught, but for our willingness to confront and
change what we have internalized, and then to make our words and actions
reflect that change.

In terms of homophobia, the non-lesbian woman needs to see herself
working not out of an abstract concept of what is "good" or "politically
correct," but out of her recognition that her failure to take positive steps
to overcome bias in herself and others has a direct, tangible effect on real
women, herself included. A serious barrier to taking such steps is the persistent belief that the sole beneficiaries are external. As long as heterosexism remains pressing only for lesbians, each non-lesbian woman remains

isolated from women whose lives contain some significant difference from hers, whose experiences and words have the potential to enrich her own. Within this context, each non-lesbian woman suffers a significant deprivation—loss of knowledge, fear of change, separation from all but an illusory sense of connection with lesbian women, "all the ways," as Audre Lorde has written, "in which we rob ourselves and each other."[8]

The mandate to confront homophobia is particularly compelling because of the teacher's role as a *model* in any classroom interaction. If she indicates that a writer's lesbianism is unimportant, barely worth mentioning, she encourages non-lesbian students to take the easier, more comfortable path of denying lesbianism as a serious aspect of women's lives and totally distancing it from their own. If she leaves its discussion entirely to a guest lecturer, to lesbian students, or to a lesbian co-teacher, she teaches that non-lesbian women can only remain too fearful and too ignorant to engage in such dialogue. If she allows lesbianism to be "covered" in a single unit or class session, she implies that it has little or nothing to do with everything else that is discussed in the course. If she shows obvious signs of discomfort with the subject while insisting that she has "no difficulty at all" with it, she discourages non-lesbian students from exploring and hopefully, transcending their homophobia sufficiently for them to hear clearly and positively the words of lesbian women. If she speaks about "women" when she actually means "heterosexual or non-lesbian women," she verbally moves lesbians to some outer border of true womanhood and reinforces the concept of lesbianism as "deviance from the norm." If she assumes that all of her students are heterosexual simply because none has come out either to her privately or to the class as a whole, she performs just one more great disservice to her students, lesbian and non-lesbian. If, however, she admits her lack of knowledge as well as her active attempts to learn more through reading and hearing the words of lesbian women, if she admits her discomfort, present or past, as well as ways she has worked/is working to overcome it, she teaches her non-lesbian students that their future attitudes can be different from their past and present ones, and she teaches her lesbian students that she regards their history and current lives with serious respect.

Although I think that lesbian material can be most adequately discussed by a woman who is a lesbian, the non-lesbian teacher needs to be able to handle lesbian material on her own in any women's literature, introductory women's studies, or other course whose focus is not lesbian women. A guest lecturer might teach a class or two, and it's always tremendously beneficial to have students who feel able to speak as open lesbians. However, the regular (non-lesbian) teacher needs to be able not only to teach lesbian material but to incorporate it into every facet of the course.

II.

When I teach lesbian short fiction, I make two basic assumptions: 1) the author's lesbianism is an essential fact that must be considered; and 2) discussion must focus not only on our literary and political *ideas*, but on the *feelings* that influence our words and actions. I also strive toward the concept of feminism that Barbara Smith has defined as:

> ... the political theory and practice that struggles to free *all* women: women of color, working-class women, poor women, disabled women, lesbians, old women, as well as white, economically privileged heterosexual women. Anything less than this vision of total freedom is not feminism, but merely female self-aggrandizement.[9]

When I teach lesbian short fiction, as with writing by other groups of women, I intentionally assign stories that reflect a diversity of perspectives and experiences, work that illustrates the extent to which "categories" o women actually overlap. I think this is especially important in terms of lesbian material, given the pervasiveness of the stereotypes held by non-lesbian students and the Establishment media image of lesbians as all white, young, able-bodied, middle-class or wealthy, and free from family responsibilities.

In a course that takes an historical perspective, I can assign lesbian short fiction chronologically to show its development in relation to lesbian history, the lesbian novel, and lesbian poetry, as well as to the history and literature of non-lesbian women. I can also assign it within an overall course design that focuses on literature by women who are in some way "outsiders" as a consequence of some factor other than their femaleness. Or I can assign lesbian short stories on the basis of theme: growing up, sexuality, mothers and daughters, violence, relationships, creativity, aging, work.

In one introductory women's studies class where I had chosen this last organizational approach, I was reminded forcefully of the power of homophobia when I—rather foolishly, in retrospect—assigned Flying Clouds' "Another Place to Begin" at the very beginning of the semester, two classes before we were scheduled to talk about lesbianism as an issue. The discussion of class and work that I had anticipated got totally sidetracked with the opening comment of a heterosexual woman that, "Of course, the protagonist is like that because she was raped." For me the reference to the rape was a passing one, not at all central to the story. But to this woman, who could not imagine lesbians as doing anything but responding negatively to their (bad) experiences with men, the issue of causality loomed large. The ensuing discussion, which I should have initiated *before* we had begun to talk about the story, helped confront some of the stereotypes that made an open reading of the fiction quite impossible for the non-lesbian women in the class. Only after the discussion, which did not deal at all with *fiction*, could we talk concretely about the story itself.

Unfortunately, at that point in the semester, I was the only lesbian in the class who was out. I therefore had to be especially careful to stress that my views and experiences were both individual and reflections of my own particular background. As a white, middle-class, able-bodied, Jewish lesbian in her mid-thirties, a lesbian-feminist who came out in the early seventies, the mother of a pre-adolescent girl, I could certainly not speak for the many lesbians who differed in some significant way from me. When I had spoken in classes as a guest lecturer, students felt quite free to ask personal questions designed to fill in the gaps in their knowledge: about my coming out, my daughter, lesbian sexuality and relationships, my parents' reactions to my lesbianism, the relationship between lesbianism and feminism. But in my own class, where I was not only going to show up every day but give out grades at the end, the non-lesbian students were understandably more reticent. Fortunately I was helped by the supportive comments and bits of information offered rather obliquely by two of the three lesbians who only later came out to the class (one Black, one Puerto Rican, one white, including one woman who was then married), and by another woman, the non-lesbian mother of four children whose own mother was a lesbian (an experience shared, it turned out, by one of the lesbians).

Once we returned to reading the short stories, some students questioned the relevance of identifying the lesbian writers *as lesbians*. I argued in terms of the historic need for the visibility of oppressed people and the specific need for recognition in an area where lesbians are, in fact, making considerable contributions to women's writing as a whole. Why, I asked, were they questioning the label "lesbian" when they accepted without a second thought the labeling of other writing as "women's" or "Black" or "Jewish"? Weren't they also criticizing me because I had assigned more than a token lesbian short story and therefore we were spending "too much" time on lesbian writing?

We discussed the stereotypes that the lesbian label conjured up, particularly the one of the lesbians as madly sexual twenty-four hours a day. A friend of mine had been asked, quite seriously, in one class: "What do lesbians *do* during the day?" and she had had, once again, to confront the assumption that our lives encompass only bars and beds. When I had spoken at a Psychology Club panel attended by well over a hundred students at a large urban university, the school paper headed their article, "It's Not All Bed-Hopping" and I had had to thumb through the paper several times before recognizing that particular article as the coverage of my panel.

Where lesbian sexuality was explicit or implied in the assigned stories, few non-lesbian students responded positively. In some cases, their homophobia emerged as a form of denial. Some students thought that "nothing happened" in Maureen Brady's "Grinning Underneath" because they refused to recognize the sexual tension in the story. I spoke of my own history of denial: how I had needed to be told, for example, in 1971 by a friend of eleven years' standing that she and the woman she lived with were lovers, that they did not use their second bedroom for anything but guests.

For some students, the discomfort with lesbian sexuality had more to do with their own sexual awkwardness: they did not feel very comfortable with the explicit heterosexual love poetry we read either. For many, it had to do with their discomfort with the whole idea of two women making love: they could cope with women being "lesbians" a whole lot better if they didn't then have to think about the fact that such women might actually go to bed together. We discussed both the writing and the reading of explicit descriptions of lesbian sexuality within the general context of writing by women, the problems of reclaiming language that doesn't reflect some aspect of sexual politics.

In some instances, student prejudices against lesbian sexuality intersected with other biases. For instance, Audre Lorde describes Ginger in "The Beginning":

> Snapping little dark eyes, skin the color of well-buttered caramel, and a body like the Venus of Willendorf. Ginger was gorgeously fat, with an open knowledge about her body's movement that was delicate and precise. Her breasts were high and ample, and she had pads of firm fat upon her thighs, and round dimpled knees. Her swift, tapered hands and feet were also deeply dimpled. Her high putchy cheeks and great mischievous smile were framed by wide bangs and a short pageboy that was sometimes straightened, sometimes left to wave tightly over her ears.

How did the students feel about this erotic description of a "gorgeously fat" woman? How did they feel about this description of a Black woman? And how did they feel about the sexual relationship between the two disabled women in Lynn Michaels' "Oxblood Shawls"? How did they feel about the sexual relationship in Jane Rule's "In the Attic of the House" between Alice and Harriet, who allowed Alice to make love to her only when she feigned sleep and "was no longer officially aware of what was happening"? How did they feel about the ongoing sexual needs of a woman who is past sixty-five?

The assigned lesbian stories had been aimed at including lesbian sexuality as an important aspect of lesbian lives, but not the totality. "The Beginning," for instance, is partly concerned with being a Black woman worker in a small-town factory. The selection we read from Jan Clausen's "Today Is the First Day of the Rest of Your Life" deals with the relationship between a white lesbian mother and her pre-adolescent daughter, the mother's thoughts about racism, her daughter's friendship with a Black girl, and politics in general.[10] Judith McDaniel's "Present Danger" is about a lesbian who, alone in the Adirondack Mountains, is first gang-raped and then left in the wilderness with a single blanket. We discussed how the societal tendency to see lesbians only in sexual terms denies the reality of lesbian lives and intensifies the alienation that some of the non-lesbian women were expressing; we drew parallels with other stereotypes—the idea, for example, that women of color write only about racial issues or that Jewish women write only about Jewish identity and anti-semitism.

The very limited exposure of many of the students to the writing of women who were significantly different from themselves encouraged the sense that the little that they had read could stand as representative of an entire group. Students who had read little or no lesbian fiction tended to read the stories as if each were *the* statement about lesbian experience. I mentioned the experience of Julie Blackwomon, who had written about a friend of hers who "read 'Kippy' [and] suggested that it did not relate to the experience of some black lesbians because Kippy and her mother once lived in a collective and some black lesbians are into roles and have no problem with being referred to as bulldaggers."[11] And because, in much of our discussion, the issue of feelings/attitudes toward lesbianism intersected with some of the student attitudes toward fiction, the stories were seen not only as representative, but were given the weight of a political statement far more appropriate to an essay than to fiction.

Consistently, as with work we discussed by non-lesbian students, the subjective nature of our reading experience was central. How did each of us respond to writing by women who were very like us? Did our identification interfere in any way with our reading of the story that the *writer* was telling? How did we each respond to writing by women who differed from us in one or more critical ways? How did the non-lesbian women feel as they read about the harassment of the small-town lesbian couple Miss Katheryn and Miss Renita in Pat Suncircle's "A Day's Growth"? Why did one white woman manage to "overlook" the distress of Leslie's aunt in that story because she found Leslie in her room with a girl who was *white*, even though fifteen-year-old Leslie clearly states that in her Black family, "the only thing worse than bringing home a white boy was to bring home a white girl"? In one class meeting on violence against women, we talked about the feelings of a number of middle-class students that the mother in Barbara Sheen's "Maria," a Mexican prostitute living with her toddler daughter, was irresponsible because she took her child with her on a date with a blonde male American doctor she had been seeing who then mutilated her in front of the child and threw her body overboard.[12] Here, in a story written about a heterosexual woman by a lesbian, issues of class became pre-eminent; one woman who had been on welfare and knew that it wasn't necessarily financially possible to get a babysitter, felt so outraged by this student response that she temporarily left the room.

Repeatedly, we found that the voices of the women we read had been traditionally absent from the literature that had been accessible to us, in some cases because these writers were lesbians, in others because they were outsiders in other ways. As a means of understanding both the absence of certain voices from fiction and the steps that have been taken to reclaim them, we read both Toni Morrison's *Sula* and Barbara Smith's "Toward a Black Feminist Criticism," which offers a lesbian reading of Morrison's novel.[13] The assignment enabled us to discuss from another perspective what made some students uncomfortable with the use of the word "lesbian" to describe the relationship between Sula and Nel: were they uncomfortable, I asked, with applying the label "heterosexual" to an intense, central relationship between a woman and a man that was not explicitly sexual?

Reading Smith's article helped us make connections between women who shared some oppressions but not others. While lesbian writers are certainly influenced by other *lesbian* writers, they are influenced too—sometimes even inspired—by the fiction of non-lesbian women. Often the discovery of work by a non-lesbian writer who shares some other central aspect of a lesbian writer's identity can be particularly important.

As with other assignments, the combined emphasis on difference *and* similarity in terms of the lesbian short fiction shattered the expectations of many of the students that we were going to get together to discuss "women" as some sort of unified group. Instead they discovered that learning about women's lives was not just a question of seeing "how we are all oppressed," that learning about lesbian lives was not just a question of seeing how lesbians are oppressed *as lesbians*. While there was, I think, some initial anxiety that exploring differences would lead to ongoing tension and overall fragmentation within the class, students seemed to find that their acknowledgment and exploration led instead to bridges, however fragile, across lines of difference. It also led to a far greater understanding of the individual biases that interfered with the reading of assigned fiction and enabled non-lesbians to make connections with the lesbian short stories that would have been far less likely had serious attention not been given to the personal/political barriers between student and story.

III.

Even as I put forth an approach to teaching lesbian short fiction that involves the teacher in modeling the kind of openness and directness that she would like her students to adopt, I am well aware of the increasing obstacles, not only to the specific approach, but to the inclusion of lesbian material in the classroom at all. As the "Moral Majority" has more and more books removed from library shelves; as teachers at every level fall under increasing scrutiny by those who claim to support "the family"; as the likelihood grows that other states besides Oklahoma will pass bills prohibiting *anyone* who assumes its essential validity from discussing lesbianism and male homosexuality in the classroom; as Congress considers the Family Protection Act that, if passed, would prohibit federal funding to an organization "for the purpose of advocating, promoting, or suggesting homosexuality, male or female, as a lifestyle," the pressures against teaching lesbian short fiction and of being—and being identified as—a lesbian are increasingly severe.

One temptation, "especially," as Judith Stitzel has written, for those "buffered by relative privilege," is to "lower consciousness," to "cope with fear, frustration and fatigue by retreating from awareness, from action, from both."[14] For a teacher, such a retreat can be reflected in her decision *not* to teach lesbian short fiction (or other lesbian material), or to teach it with minimal discussion of its characters, its themes, and its history. For someone who is also a member of a women's studies program, it can also be reflected in her decision *not* to insist that her colleagues deal forthrightly with lesbian material.

The alternative is to accept the risk consistent with a radical, feminist theory and practice that "struggles to free *all* women," and to move that vision as concretely and consistently as possible into the classroom. The non-lesbian teacher and all of us who possess some type of "relative privilege" must ask ourselves: which women are we willing to leave out of our theory, our practice, and our classrooms for the sake of our own personal comfort and/or academic expediency? And, if we make such exclusions, for how long can we honestly believe that we retain the right to call what we are doing "feminist"? As Audre Lorde has written:

> Those of us who stand outside the circle of this society's definition of acceptable women; those of us who have been forged in the crucibles of difference; those of us who are poor, who are lesbians, who are black, who are older, know that *survival is not an academic skill*. It is learning how to stand alone, unpopular and sometimes reviled, and how to make common cause with those identified as outside the structures, in order

to define and seek a world in which we can all flourish. It is learning how to take our differences and make them strengths. *For the master's tools will never dismantle the master's house.* They may allow us temporarily to beat him at his own game, but they will never enable us to bring about genuine change.[15]

Notes

[1] See, for example, Bonnie Zimmerman, "Lesbianism 101," *Radical Teacher 17* (1980), pp. 20-24, and Bulkin, " 'Kissing/Against the Light': Teaching Lesbian Poetry," originally published in *Radical Teacher 10* (1978), pp. 7-17; available in an expanded version from the Lesbian-Feminist Study Clearinghouse and in *Lesbian Poetry: An Anthology*, eds. Bulkin and Joan Larkin (Watertown, MA: Persephone Press, 1981).

[2] Bulkin, "Heterosexism and Women's Studies," *Radical Teacher 17* (1980), pp. 25-31; Bulkin, "A Response to Annette Kolodny's 'Dancing Through the Minefield: Some Observations on the Theory, Practice and Politics of a Feminist Literary Criticism'," *Feminist Studies* (Spring, 1982); Marilyn Frye, "Lesbian Perspectives on Women's Studies," *Sinister Wisdom 14* (1980), pp. 3-7; Judith McDaniel, "Is There Room for Me in the Closet or My Life as the Only Lesbian Professor," *Heresies No. 7*, Vol. 2, No. 3 (Spring, 1979), 36-39.

[3] Peg Cruikshank, "Lesbians in Academia," *Our Right to Love: A Lesbian Resource Book*, ed. Ginny Vida, produced in cooperation with the women of the National Gay Task Force (Englewood Cliffs, NJ: Prentice-Hall, 1978), p. 164.

[4] Hoffman, *Women's Studies Newsletter*, 5 (Spring, 1977), p. 22.

[5] Rena Grasso Patterson discusses classism in "A Response to Annette Kolodny's 'Dancing Through the Minefield: Some Observations on the Theory, Practice and Politics of a Feminist Literary Criticism'," *Feminist Studies* (Spring, 1982). See also Margaret Strobel, "Fighting Two Colonialisms: Thoughts of a White Feminist Teaching about Third World Women," *Radical Teacher 6* (December, 1977), pp. 20-23; *This Bridge Called My Back: Writings by Radical Women of Color*, eds. Cherríe Moraga and Gloria Anzaldúa (Watertown, MA: Persephone Press, 1981); Bulkin, "Racism and Writing: Some Implications for White Lesbian Critics," *Sinister Wisdom 13* (Spring, 1980), pp. 3-22, available from the Lesbian-Feminist Study Clearinghouse; Adrienne Rich, "Disloyal to Civilization: Feminism, Racism, Gynephobia," *On Lies, Secrets, and Silence: Selected Prose, 1966-1978* (New York: Norton, 1979), pp. 275-310; Minnie Bruce Pratt, "Rebellion," *Feminary*, Vol. XI, Nos. 1 and 2 (1980), 6-20; *Top Ranking: A Collection of Essays on Racism and Classism in the Lesbian Community*, ed. Sara Bennett and Joan Gibbs (Brooklyn: February 3rd Press, 1980), available for $3.50 from Bennett/Gibbs, 306 Lafayette Ave., Brooklyn, NY 11238.

6 Moraga, "La Güera," *This Bridge Called My Back*, p. 32.

7 "Heterosexism and Women's Studies" includes consciousness-raising guidelines for non-lesbian women and critical guidelines designed to help non-lesbian teachers formulate an anti-heterosexist approach to teaching.

8 Lorde, "The Transformation of Silence into Language and Action," *Sinister Wisdom 6* (Summer, 1978), p. 14; reprinted in Lorde's *The Cancer Journals* (Argyle, NY: Spinsters, Ink, 1980), p. 23.

9 Smith, "Racism and Women's Studies," *Frontiers* (Spring, 1980), p. 48.

10 Clausen, *Mother, Sister, Daughter, Lover* (Trumansburg, NY: The Crossing Press, 1980), pp. 60-101.

11 Blackwomon, questionnaire response, Winter, 1981.

12 Sheen, *Shedevils* (Chicago: Metis Press, 1978), pp. 57-64.

13 Smith, *Conditions: Two* (Fall, 1977), pp. 25-44, available from the Lesbian-Feminist Study Clearinghouse.

14 Stitzel, "Can Consciousness Be Lowered?" *Women's Studies Quarterly*, Vol. IX, No. 2 (Summer, 1981), 23.

15 Lorde, "The Master's Tools Will Never Dismantle the Master's House," *This Bridge Called My Back*, p. 99.

Contributors' Biographies

Dorothy Allison, *b. 1949, Greenville, South Carolina.* Dorothy Allison is a working-class expatriate southerner now living in New York City and thoroughly enjoying her life. She hopes to complete the manuscript of *A Bastard Out of Carolina* this year, and thereby become more notorious. She can be recognized by her "wicked, evil, mean and nasty" T-shirt, her femme style and her butch attitude.

Julie Blackwomon, *b. 1943, Saluda, Virginia.* Raised in Saluda and Philadelphia. Julie Blackwomon, a.k.a. Julie Carter, is a black working-class lesbian feminist writer who supports herself and her teenage daughter at a hardhat job in a Philadelphia refinery. Julie has read widely in the Philadelphia area and has been published in *Sinister Wisdom, Pennsylvania English, Azalea, Dyke Magazine, Lesbian Poetry,* and others.

Sandy Boucher, *b. 1936, Columbus, Ohio.* Of working-class parents, forty-five years old, six feet tall. Have lived in the Bay Area of California for twenty years. I've been writing since I was eleven or twelve years old, have published many stories and articles in many publications. Book of stories: *Assaults and Rituals.* Nonfiction book on women in the Midwest: *Heartwomen* (to be out late 1981 or early 1982).

Maureen Brady, *b. 1943, Mt. Vernon, New York.* Grew up: rural upstate New York (Laurens) and in Dunedin, Florida. Maureen Brady is a writer who has published short fiction in *Conditions, Sinister Wisdom, Feminary, So's Your Old Lady, Southern Exposure.* She has also published articles, reviews, and a one-act play in feminist periodicals and is a co-founder of Spinsters, Ink. Her work is concerned with understanding the forces of racism, classism and other forms of ranking operational in the culture, and writing in the strength and courage of those the patriarchy attempts to erase.

Jo Carrillo, *b. 1959, New Mexico.* Spent early childhood in Portugal and the rest in Washington and New Mexico. I was born in Las Vegas, New Mexico and have spent most of my life in that land. My work is in the tradition of the storytellers. It is said that without the storytellers we would lose our way and not be able to continue; without the storytellers we would lose our past. As it turns out, we are all storytellers—if we want to be. That's what I've heard.

Jan Clausen, b. *1950, North Bend, Oregon.* Poet and fiction writer. Raised in the Pacific Northwest; moved to New York in 1973. An editor of *Conditions* magazine; activist, most recently with the Women's Pentagon Action. She has self-published two books of poetry. Her story collection is *Mother, Sister, Daughter, Lover* (Crossing Press, 1980); her novel *Sinking, Stealing* will be published by Persephone Press.

Flying Clouds, b. *1946, Shawnee, Oklahoma.* Grew up: Oklahoma and Texas, in the country usually, sometimes in small towns. I am living in Oklahoma. Stories are important to me. There is a great deal of freedom in telling stories and freedom in listening to them. This is a good freedom for me, like I imagine the birds flying. And if we were to have lots and lots of them from Indian women there would be not only that much freedom and beauty but also a *pride*, the feeling that comes from watching the stream of blackbirds traveling in the fall, unable to see the beginning or the ending, just many, many passing overhead, hearing their voices.

Jewelle Gomez, b. *1948, Boston.* My background is black and native american. I was raised by my great-grandmother. My M.S. is from Columbia in Journalism and my B.A. from Northeastern in Sociology. I've worked in public commercial television and theater production. I'm the author of a collection of poetry, *The Lipstick Papers.*

Judy Grahn, b. *1940, Chicago.* Judy Grahn is presently embroiled in historical research. She has a book tracing Gay history and culture (Persephone Press, Inc., Spring, 1981) and is working on essays and a novel (*The Motherlords*) as well as new history poems, *A Chronicle of Queens.* Her poetry is collected in *The Work of A Common Woman* (St. Martin's Press, NY) and is recorded on an album, "Where Would I Be Without You" (Olivia Records, with Pat Parker). She has edited stories of women's lives, *True to Life Adventure Stories* (The Crossing Press, Trumansburg, NY).

Sauda Jamal, b. *1951, New York City.* A New York City poet and photographer. Working on a novel and a collection of short stories about Black women.

Irena Klepfisz, b. *1941, Warsaw, Poland* Came to New York City in 1949. Grew up in the Bronx. I write out of a strong Jewish identification. My Jewishness was the first "fact" abou. myself that I realized had severe consequences in the world. Other "facts" came later: economic status, feminism, lesbianism. I hope my writing reflects them all. I consider myself primarily a poet, *Periods of Stress* (Piecework Press); "The Journal" represents my first published fiction.

Francine Krasno, *b. 1951, Philadelphia.* Grew up: Wilkes-Barre, Pennsylvania. Francine Krasno is a writer and teacher with special interests in the social history of women and radical Jewish politics. She is associate editor of *The Correspondence of Lydia Maria Child* (University of Massachusetts Press). Her fiction, reviews, and essays have appeared in *Conditions, The Chicago Daily News,* and other publications.

Audre Lorde, *b. 1934, New York City.* Black, feminist, mother. Professor at Hunter College. Latest book is *The Cancer Journals,* published by Spinsters, Ink.

Elizabeth A. Lynn, *b. 1946, New York City.* Elizabeth A. Lynn lives in San Francisco and writes fiction. Her novels include *A Different Light, Watchtower* (for which she won the 1980 World Fantasy Award), *The Dancers of Arun,* and *The Northern Girl.* She teaches a feminist science fiction course at San Francisco State University. She has two cats, one dog, a first degree black belt in aikido, mild arthritis, and a teen-age foster daughter.

Judith McDaniel, *b. 1943, San Antonio, Texas.* Born on an Air Force base; grew up in most of the U. S., Europe and Mideast. Judith McDaniel is a writer and teacher who lives in an old farmhouse in very rural upstate New York. With Maureen Brady, she operates the feminist publishing company Spinsters, Ink. Her poems and reviews have appeared in *Conditions, Sinister Wisdom,* and other lesbian and feminist journals.

Lynn Michaels, *b. 1939, New York City.* Grew up: Florida and New Rochelle, New York. Lynn Michaels is Jewish and disabled. For a year during World War II, and for a year during her later girlhood, she lived in the South. She began writing seriously during college, has been active in the women's movement, both teaching women's studies courses at various colleges and contributing to anthologies of women's writing. She has had fiction published in *The Ladder* and in the Diana Press anthology of *Ladder* short stories. She is interested in feminist literary criticism, the novels of Elizabeth Bowen, Kay Boyle, Enid Bagnold, and enjoys reading and motoring about the countryside.

Barbara Noda, *b. 1953, California.* Barbara Noda is a writer of Japanese ancestry. She grew up in the Salinas Valley in California. Her first book of poetry, *Strawberries,* is published by Shameless Hussy Press. She has written a play titled *Aw Shucks (Shikata Ga Nai)* and is currently working on a novel.

Diana Rivers, *b. 1931, New York City.* Grew up in New Jersey. Am living in rural Arkansas, on woman's land, in a small cabin I built myself. Have been writing stories about 9 years, taking them seriously for about 4, and am now working on a full-length Lesbian fantasy, wanting to give voice and form to our visions.

Jane Rule, *b. 1931, Plainfield, New Jersey.* Jane Rule grew up in the midwest and in California, graduated from Mills College in 1952. In 1956, she moved to Vancouver, Canada, where she and Helen Sonthoff lived, teaching and writing for twenty years. Canadian citizens for some years, they now live on Galiano Island, active in the writers', women's and gay communities.

Aleida Rodríguez, *b. 1953, Güines, Havana, Cuba.* Lived in the U.S. (Illinois, California) since the age of nine. I am a 28-year-old Latina lesbian living in Los Angeles with my lover, Jacqueline, and no cats now, but a parrot and canaries. Writing "Sequences" moved the muscle that let me begin work in Spanish, reclaiming my Cuban childhood. My work has appeared most recently in *De Colores, Bachy, Beyond Baroque 802,* and will be forthcoming in a Latina poets anthology by Capra Press.

Barbara Sheen, *b. 1949, New York City.* Barbara Sheen resides in New Mexico. *Shedevils,* a collection of her stories, is available from Metis Press. She is also the author of a series of children's bilingual textbooks. Her first novel, *The Pirate Queen,* based on the real life of the pirate Anne Bonney, is in search of a publisher. She is currently working on a children's book and a book on women, macho and life in Colombia.

Ann Allen Shockley, *b. 1927, Louisville, Kentucky.* A southern academic librarian, who writes whenever possible. A new novel is scheduled next year by Avon.

Katherine Sturtevant, *b. 1950, Oakland.* Grew up: Santa Clara Valley. Katherine Sturtevant received her B.A. in creative writing from San Francisco State in 1976. Her work has appeared in *Calyx, Sinister Wisdom,* and the *Deepest Valley Review.* She has been awarded fellowships to artists' colonies in Taos, New Mexico, and in Virginia, where she spent the spring of 1981 working on a novel titled *Privacy.* She is a resident of Portland, Oregon.

Pat Suncircle, *b. 1949, Brownsville, Tennessee.* Went to high school in Chicago. I am a black woman writer living in Oakland, California. In the past I have concentrated on short stories and plays. At present I am working on my first novel; it is about women and rock n roll.

Kitty Tsui, *b. 1952, Hong Kong.* Grew up: England and Hong Kong. Kitty Tsui was born in the City of Nine Dragons in the year of the dragon.

She is a feminist writer, artist and actor; a member of Unbound Feet Three, a San Francisco-based writing/performing collective and the co-founder and co-director of Kiwi Productions with her lover, Willyce Kim. In America the first publication Tsui appeared in was *Third World Women*, an anthology of writings and graphics that she co-edited in 1972. She has written a play entitled "A Grain of Rice" and is currently at work on the biography of her grandmother, the late Kwan Ying Lin, a renowned Chinese opera singer.

t

Work by Contributors

The following is a list of currently available short story collections, novels, and other individual publications by contributors, anthologies they have compiled, feminist journals they edit, and recordings of their work. Addresses are included for all lesbian, feminist, and other "small" presses; if a press has published the work of more than one contributor, the address is included under a separate heading at the end of this listing. Most of this work is available in feminist bookstores; all of it can be ordered directly from the presses or distributors. All books are paperbacks unless otherwise indicated.

The price information that follows each entry does not include a charge for postage and handling; while these rates differ slightly from press to press, most costs would be met by your including 85 cents postage/handling for each book (or record) you order. If you live in the same state as the press from which you are ordering, you should also include any applicable state sales tax. While large commercial presses have the resources to bill you, women's presses do not—so help them out by prepaying (in U.S. currency).

SHORT STORY COLLECTIONS

Sandy Boucher, *Assaults & Rituals* (Mama's Press; distributed The Crossing Press), 1975, 49 pp., $2.50.

Jan Clausen, *Mother, Sister, Daughter, Lover* (The Crossing Press), 1980, 136 pp., $4.95.

Elizabeth A. Lynn, *The Woman Who Loved the Moon and Other Stories* (Berkley), 1981, 208 pp., $2.25.

Jane Rule, *Outlander*, short stories and essays (Naiad Press), 1981, 207 pp., $6.95. *Theme for Diverse Instruments* (Talonbooks), 1975, 185 pp., $5.95.

Barbara Sheen, *Shedevils* (Metis Press, P.O. Box 25187, Chicago, IL 60625), 1978, 74 pp., $3.50.

Ann Allen Shockley, *The Black and White of It* (Naiad Press), 1980, 103 pp., $5.95.

NOVELS

Maureen Brady, *Give Me Your Good Ear* (Spinsters, Ink), 1979, 134 pp., $4.50.

Elizabeth A. Lynn, *The Northern Girl* (Berkley Publishing Co.), 1980, 415 pp., $2.50. *The Dancers of Arun* (Berkley), 1980, 275 pp., $1.95. *Watchtower* (Berkley), 1980, 226 pp., $1.95. *A Different Light* (Berkley), 1980, 183 pp., $2.25.

Jane Rule, *Contract with the World* (Harcourt Brace Jovanovich), 1980, 339 pp., $12.95 (hardcover). *The Young in One Another's Arms* (Totembooks, 100 Lesmill Road, Don Mills, Ontario, Canada), 1977, 204 pp., $2.25. *This Is Not for You* (McCall; reprinted Naiad Press), 1970, 296 pp., $6.95. *Desert of the Heart* (Talonbooks), 1964, 251 pp., $3.95.

Ann Allen Shockley, *Loving Her* (Avon), 1974, 205 pp., $1.75.

OTHER WRITINGS

Elly Bulkin, *Racism and Writing: Some Implications for White Lesbian Critics,* reprinted from *Sinister Wisdom 13* (Lesbian-Feminist Study Clearinghouse), 1980, 11 pp., $.90. *An Interview with Adrienne Rich,* reprinted from *Conditions: One* and *Two* (Lesbian-Feminist Study Clearinghouse), 1977, 30 pp., $1.30. " 'Kissing/Against the Light': A Look at Lesbian Poetry" (Lesbian-Feminist Study Clearinghouse), 1978, $1.00.

Jan Clausen, *Waking at the Bottom of the Dark,* poetry (Long Haul Press, Box 592, Brooklyn, NY 11215; also distributed The Crossing Press), 1979, 78 pp., $3.00. *After Touch,* poetry (Out & Out Books; distributed Long Haul Press and The Crossing Press), 1975, 80 pp., $2.00.

Jewelle Gomez, *The Lipstick Papers,* poetry (Grace Publications, 310 W. 93 St., No. 6E, New York, NY 10025), 1980, 44 pp., $4.00.

Judy Grahn, *The Work of a Common Woman: The Collected Poetry of Judy Grahn, 1964-1977* (Diana Press—out of print; reprinted St. Martin's Press), 1978, 158 pp., $8.95 (hardcover). *She Who,* poetry (Diana Press; distributed The Crossing Press), 1977, 89 pp., $6.00. *A Woman Is Talking to Death,* poetry (Women's Press Collective; distributed The Crossing Press), 1974, 19 pp., $2.50. *Edward the Dyke and Other Poems* (Women's Press Collective; distributed The Crossing Press), 1971, 66 pp., $2.50.

Irena Klepfisz, *periods of stress,* poetry (Piecework Press, P.O. Box 2422, Brooklyn, NY 11202), 1975, 64 pp., $2.00.

Audre Lorde, *The Cancer Journals* (Spinsters, Ink), 1980, 79 pp., $4.00. *Age, Race, Class and Sexuality: Women Re-Defining Difference* (Lesbian-Feminist Study Clearinghouse), 1980, 17 pp., $1.35. *Man Child: A Black Lesbian Feminist's Response,* reprinted from *Conditions: Four* (Lesbian-Feminist Study Clearinghouse), 1979, 4 pp., $.35. *The Black Unicorn,* poetry (Norton), 1978, 122 pp., $3.95.

Uses of the Erotic: The Erotic as Power, reprinted from *Chrysalis No. 9* (Out & Out Books; distributed by The Crossing Press), 1978, $1.00. *Scratching the Surface: Some Notes on Barriers to Women and Loving*, reprinted from *The Black Scholar* (Lesbian-Feminist Study Clearinghouse), 1978, 5 pp., $.40. *Coal*, poetry (Norton), 1976, 70 pp., $2.95. *New York Head Shop and Museum*, poetry (Broadside Press, 12651 Old Mill Place, Detroit, MI 48238), 1974, 68 pp., $3.50.

Judith McDaniel, *Reconstituting the World: The Poetry and Vision of Adrienne Rich* (Spinsters, Ink), 1979, 24 pp., $1.50.

Barbara Noda, Kitty Tsui [and Z. Wong], *Coming Out: We Are Here in the Asian Community: A Dialogue with Three Asian Women*, reprinted from *Bridge: An Asian American Perspective* (Lesbian-Feminist Study Clearinghouse), 1979, 3 pp., $.25.

Jane Rule, *Lesbian Images* (Doubleday), 1975, 246 pp., $8.95 (hardcover).

Ann Allen Shockley, *The Black Lesbian in American Literature: An Overview*, reprinted from *Conditions: Five* (Lesbian-Feminist Study Clearinghouse), 1979, 6 pp., $.50. *A Handbook of Black Librarianship* [and E. J. Josey] (Libraries Unlimited, Littleton, CO), 1977, 392 pp., $17.50 (hardcover).

ANTHOLOGIES EDITED

Elly Bulkin [and Joan Larkin], *Lesbian Poetry: An Anthology* (Persephone Press, P.O. Box 7222, Watertown, MA 02172), 1981, 336 pp., $10.95. Free to women in prison and elderly women in nursing homes. Available also from Womyn's Braille Press, P.O. Box 8475, Minneapolis, MN 55408.

Judy Grahn, *True to Life Adventure Stories, Vol. II* (published The Crossing Press and Diana Press; distributed The Crossing Press), 1981, 224 pp., $5.95. *True to Life Adventure Stories, Vol. I* (Diana Press; distributed The Crossing Press), 1978, 224 pp., $5.00.

FEMINIST JOURNALS EDITED

Conditions, A Magazine of Writing by Women with an Emphasis on Writing by Lesbians. P.O. Box 56, Van Brunt Station, Brooklyn, NY 11215. $11/3 issues; $6 "hardship" subscription/3 issues. $22/institutional subscriptions. $4.50/single issue; $8/single issue to institutions. Free to women in prisons and mental institutions. Elly Bulkin and Jan Clausen, members of editorial collective; Irena Klepfisz, founding editor (1976-1980).

rara avis. 1400 Macbeth St., Los Angeles, CA 90026. $6/3 issues; $12/institutional subscriptions. $2.00/single issue. Aleida Rodríguez, co-editor.

RECORDINGS

A Sign/ I Was Not Alone: A Poetry Reading, Joan Larkin, Audre Lorde, Honor Moore, Adrienne Rich (Out & Out Books; distributed The Crossing Press), 1978, $6.00.

Where Would I Be Without You: The Poetry of Pat Parker and Judy Grahn (Olivia Records, P.O. Box 70237, Los Angeles, CA 90070), 1976, $5.50.

PRESS ADDRESSES

The Crossing Press, Trumansburg, NY 14886.

Lesbian-Feminist Study Clearinghouse, Women's Studies Program, 1012 CL, University of Pittsburgh, Pittsburgh, PA 15260 (minimum order: $3.00)

Naiad Press, P.O. Box 10543, Tallahassee, FL 32302.

Spinsters, Ink, RD 1, Argyle, NY 12809.

Talonbooks, 201/1019 East Cordova, Vancouver, B.C., Canada V6A 1M8